HELL ON EARTH

HELL ON EARTH SERIES, BOOK 1

BRENDA K DAVIES

BRENDA K. DAVIES

ALSO FROM THE AUTHOR

Books written under the pen name
Brenda K. Davies

The Alliance Series
Eternally Bound (Book 1)
Bound By Vengeance (Book 2)
(Coming Winter 2018)

Hell on Earth Series
Hell on Earth (Book 1)
Into The Abyss (Book 2)
(Coming 2018)

The Road to Hell Series
Good Intentions (Book 1)
Carved (Book 2)
The Road (Book 3)
Into Hell (Book 4)

The Vampire Awakenings Series
Awakened (Book 1)
Destined (Book 2)
Untamed (Book 3)

Enraptured (Book 4)

Undone (Book 5)

Fractured (Book 6)

Ravaged (Book 7)

(Coming Fall 2017)

Historical Romance

A Stolen Heart

Books written under the pen name

Erica Stevens

The Captive Series

Captured (Book 1)

Renegade (Book 2)

Refugee (Book 3)

Salvation (Book 4)

Redemption (Book 5)

Broken (The Captive Series Prequel)

Vengeance (Book 6)

Unbound (Book 7)

The Fire & Ice Series

Frost Burn (Book 1)

Arctic Fire (Book 2)

Scorched Ice (Book 3)

The Kindred Series

This book is dedicated to all the demons out there.

GLOSSARY OF TERMS:

- **Adhene demon** <Ad-heen> - Mischievous elf-like demon. Corson is the last of his kind.
- **Akalia Vine** <Ah-kal-ya> - Purple black flowers, orange berries. Draws in victims & drains their blood slowly. Red leaves. Sharp, needle-like suckers under leaves. Behind the 6th seal.
- **Barta demons** <Bartə> - They were locked behind the 55th seal. Animal of Hell. Now part of Lucifer's guard.
- **Calamut Trees** <Cal-ah-mut> - Live in the Forest of Prurience.
- **Canagh demon** <Kan-agh> - Male Incubus, Female Succubus. Power thrives on sex but feed on souls on a less regular basis than the other demons. Their kiss enslaves another.
- **Ciguapa** (see-GWAH-pah) - Female demon with backward feet.
- **Craetons** <Cray-tons> - Lucifer's followers.
- **Drakón** <Drak-un> - 101st seal. Skeletal, fire breathing dragons.
- **Fires of Creation** - Where the varcolac is born.

- **Forest of Prurience** <Proo r-ee-uh nce> - Where the tree nymphs reside. Was also the original home of the canaghs and wood nymphs.
- **The Gates** - Varcolac demon has always been the ruler of the guardians of the gates that were used to travel to earth before Lucifer entered Hell.
- **Ghosts** - Souls can balk against entering Heaven, they have no choice when it comes to Hell.
- **Gobalinus** (goblins) <Gab-ah-leen-us> - Lower level demons, feed on flesh as well as souls. 79th seal.
- **Hellhounds** - The first pair of Hellhounds also born of the Fires of Creation, with the first varcolac who rose. They share a kindred spirit and are controlled by the varcolac.
- **Jinn** - 90th seal. Can grant wishes.
- **Lanavour demon** <Lan-oh-vor> -The 3rd seal. Can speak telepathically and know people's inner most secrets and fears.
- **Macharah** - 103rd seal. Creature with 30 plus tentacles at the bottom.
- **Manticore** - 46th seal. Body of a red lion, human/demon head.
- **Ouroboros** - 82nd seal. Massive, green serpent.
- **Palitons** <Pal-ah-tons> - Kobal's followers.
- **Púca** <Poo-ka> - 80th seal. Shape changers which can take on animal or human form. Could also be the source of vampires as they drain their victim's blood.
- **Skelleins** <Skel-eens> - Guardians of the Gates.
- **Tree Nymphs** - Live in the Forest of Prurience. Men and women. Striking and very free sexually. Smaller than wood nymphs and live in the trees.
- **The Wall** - Blocks off all of Washington, Oregon, California, Arizona, New Mexico, Texas, Louisiana, Mississippi, Alabama, Georgia, Florida, South Carolina,

North Carolina, Virginia, Maryland, Delaware, New Jersey, Connecticut, Rhode Island, Massachusetts, Vermont, New Hampshire, and Maine. Blocks parts of Nevada, New York, Pennsylvania, and Arkansas. Similar wall blocks off parts of Europe.

- **Wraith** - A twisted and malevolent spirit that the demons feed from. On earth they only come out at night.
- **Varcolac demon** <Var-ko-lack>- Born from the fires of Hell. Only one can exist at a time. When that one dies another rises from the Fires of Creation. Fastest and most brutal of all the demons. They are the only kind that can create and open natural gateways within Hell as well as close them. They control the hellhounds.

Demon Words

Mah lahala 'Mɑ: <la-hall-a> - My Love.

CHAPTER ONE

Corson

Seizing the lower-level demon by its alligator-like tail, my talons slipped free from the backs of my hands to pierce its scaly, gray flesh. The demon grunted, but it was the only sound it made before I lifted it, spun it around, and smashed it against a tree trunk. His back broke with an audible crack, and the demon released a gurgled cry as its stubby arms flailed at the air.

Before the demon could begin to heal, I released the tail and sliced my talons across its neck. Purple blood spilled forth; clawed hands flew to its throat to try stifling the flow. Turning, the demon swung out its tail to knock me back, but I leapt over the tail and lashed out to slice its head the rest of the way from its shoulders.

I grinned down at the decapitated head when it hit the ground with a thud. I'd needed a good kill to distract me from the reason I'd taken this watch to begin with, and this demon had provided me with it, even if it had been a brief, rather boring fight.

Bending, I heaved the scaled body over my shoulder before lifting its head. I stalked deeper into the forest, away from the camp the human Wilders and my fellow demons were working to establish.

I discarded the body far enough away from the camp that it wouldn't attract the attention of other scavengers to our location.

With the body disposed of, I turned to head back toward the camp to resume my watch. I kept my senses honed to the world around me, searching for more enemies, as trees whipped by me in a blur. When I reached the tree I'd used to batter the lower-level demon against, I grabbed its trunk and propelled myself up it. Settling onto a branch, I kicked my feet back and forth as I surveyed the forest.

The tree I sat in towered over the ones surrounding it, but most of the other trees were about twenty feet high now. Some had grown taller, while a few others struggled to keep up.

Most of the trees that once grew here had been destroyed by the explosive force of the gateway into Hell opening, or the bombs the panicked humans released in the area afterward.

Like me and the other paliton demons who fought for Kobal, the rightful king of Hell against Lucifer, this tree was a survivor. It had somehow managed to remain alive in an area that became inhospitable to it in an instant, much like the humans who had survived here since the gateway opened. Wilders, those people termed themselves.

When it had been decided to send groups into the Wilds to eradicate what remained of Lucifer's followers, Kobal had appointed Bale and me to lead the mission traveling the deepest into the Wilds in search of them, the craetons. Bale and I were the two demons who had worked with Kobal the longest, the two he trusted most, and we would not fail him.

Recently, Bale and I had discussed dividing our group but decided against it. Smaller groups moved faster and were less likely to attract attention. However, the larger group had numbers on its side and offered more protection to everyone in it. Both choices offered benefits and drawbacks, but all of us working together was the deadlier combination.

For the most part, I liked the Wilders. It was difficult not to like humans who spent their days plotting, hunting, and killing. I could relate to that way of thinking, it was how I'd spent most of my thirteen hundred years. There were a few who were assholes, but many would say that about me too. Most of them were friendly and accepted working with us with more ease than I'd anticipated from people who had spent the past fourteen years killing demons.

After the gateway opened, the Wilders chose to remain in these savage lands and away from the demons and humans residing at the wall. The Wilders deemed the people living at the wall, or on the other side of it, a civvy. It didn't matter if those humans were trained soldiers or not; the Wilders thought they were all weak.

Ever since the gateway to Hell was closed two months ago, we'd been working with the Wilders. During that time, a few of them admitted to me that the chance to take a break from running, and the constant fear they lived with in the Wilds, was worth putting aside their animosity toward demons and civvies. No matter if they believed most civvies were just fodder for the demons in the Wilds, and the best kind of demon was a dead one, they agreed helping us was the best way to gain a better life for themselves.

Over the months, their distrust of us lessened and as word spread through the Wilders that they would be safe at the wall, more groups of them arrived to offer their help. Members of those groups found their way into civvy and demon beds, started to share their food with the civvies, and were teaching us some of their tricks. They kept some of their secrets carefully guarded, but as long as they didn't hurt any of our group, or put us in unnecessary danger, they could keep their secrets.

If they got someone hurt or killed, I'd make them pay dearly for it before killing them.

Then there was Wren. The enigmatic woman who had led the first group of Wilders to the wall to speak with Kobal and strike a deal to help us, if we helped them. Despite the fact Kobal placed Bale and me in charge of this mission, Wren mostly refused to acknowledge my existence, which was unfortunate, because as much as I irritated her, she intrigued me.

I had no idea what it was about the woman, but I hadn't been able to get her out of my head since first meeting her. However, flirting with her only made her retreat further from me. I'd never had to try with a woman before, or ever wanted to try, so I had no idea how to get her to warm up to me.

I'd taken this watch to get away from her after I'd found myself focused on her while she draped a small piece of canvas over two branches as she established her sleeping spot for later. The unusual jerkiness to her movements as she worked, confused me. She was normally all grace, but she'd been off somehow, and there was a sadness in her eyes that I'd never seen before. When I found myself contemplating pulling her into my arms to comfort her, I'd decided it was time to get away from her and clear my head.

She'd stab me if I tried to touch her, and I was not in the mood for holes in my body today.

Breaking a twig off the branch above me, I searched for any hint of an enemy within the shifting shadows of the forest while I absently chewed on the twig. To distract myself from thoughts of Wren, I tried to identify the different tree species around me.

When I'd lived in Hell, Earth and its people had fascinated me. I'd spent more time watching them than most demons did. I'd found their species annoying, but I also admired their resilience. Now that I lived on the human plane, I was determined to learn as much about it as I could. My human friend Erin had been teaching me the different plant and animal life, but without their leaves, I had a difficult time identifying the trees.

When my ass went numb from sitting, I pulled the twig from my mouth, tossed it aside, and shifted on the branch to find a more comfortable position. Rough bark broke away beneath me and landed with a soft clatter on the debris below. I kept my hearing, my most well-developed sense, attuned for any new noise as I broke another twig off and popped it in my mouth.

I should go back to the camp; I'd been out here longer than necessary for a watch. It was time for me to switch off with someone else, but I remained where I was. I'd had enough of people and demons for the day. And going back meant watching Wren avoid me.

A small step on the forest floor turned my head to the left, and the subtle crackle of a leaf caused my ears to twitch. The prickling of my skin told me who was nearby before I spotted Wren slipping through the trees.

She moved with the stealth of a wraith through the woods. Her normal grace had returned to replace her awkward movements from earlier. I'd come to learn that many of the Wilders were as at home in these woods as a squirrel, and Wren was no exception. Her time in the Wilds had honed her into a killing machine more lethal than many of the demons and coyotes who also resided in the forest.

Since leaving the wall behind to travel deeper into the Wilds, I'd watched Wren unleash her ability to destroy on more than a few unsuspecting demons and Hell creatures. I had to admit, though she relished killing my kind, I admired the way she did so and the precision with which she did it.

Crouched down, Wren crept through the woods inch by inch. I followed the direction of her gaze to a deer. She was so focused on the animal that she'd failed to notice me. I hadn't believed this little mortal capable of missing anything, until now.

The deer kept its head down while it munched on foliage. Rising slightly, Wren lifted her bow as she moved. Without a sound, she reached over her back and pulled an arrow from her quiver. Like my talons, the bow and arrow seemed an extension of her as she nocked the arrow and pulled back the string.

The concentration on her face fascinated me as the sun spilling through the trees illuminated her striking features. Her brown pants hugged her long legs, rounded hips, and firm ass. Most Wilders were slim and honed from their lack of food and constant physical activity. Wren was no exception, but she also possessed curves, and her breasts would fit perfectly in my hands.

The deer still hadn't noticed her, or me, as it continued to eat. Lifting my feet, I perched them both on the limb I sat on, propped my elbows on my knees, and planted my chin in my palms to watch as Wren closed in on the animal. She was only thirty feet away from it, and the deer still had no idea she was there. Some demons, with their superior reflexes and strength, didn't hunt as well as she did.

Wren released her arrow. The twang of the bowstring and the thud of the arrow hitting flesh spooked birds from the trees. The still shaking branches marked where the birds had perched as they took to the sky with a shrill protest. The deer hit the ground with a thump. From here, I could see the crimson stain of blood seeping across its pale, brown coat, but the blood flow stopped almost immediately as the arrow had pierced straight through its heart.

"Nice shot," I called down to her.

In one fluid motion, Wren spun, pulled another arrow free, and lifted her bow to aim at my chest.

CHAPTER TWO

CORSON

Her crystalline, sky blue eyes narrowed when she spotted me. Her pale blonde hair dangled in a braid over her shoulder to one of her breasts. Anger flashed across her face, but I had a feeling the anger was more at herself than me. She hadn't noticed me, and I'd been watching her the entire time. That had to piss her off.

She would take my head off with the same glee she'd sliced off so many others, but I couldn't tear my gaze away from her. My hand went to my empty right ear as I recalled the first time I'd met her. At one time, an earring from a woman would have dangled from the tip of one of my ears, or both, and possibly from my earlobes too. When I first encountered Wren, I'd been wearing three different earrings from the three women I'd been with the night before, but none had pierced my ears since that day.

At first, my wearing of the earrings had been a joke. The first human I slept with had tried to hook one of her earrings around the tip of my ear. She'd laughed and blushed prettily as she sought to balance it there. Taking the thing from her, I'd pushed it through the point of my ear to let it dangle there.

"Now, you'll always have something to remember me by," she'd said with a giggle.

The only thing I remembered about her was the flower earring she'd given me. It had been a rose that I'd lost soon after. The next day, we'd traveled to a different section of the wall, and I moved on to my next human. That woman hadn't wanted to be undone by the other one, so I'd stuck her earring through my other ear.

Over time, wearing the assorted earrings became a thing for me —a thing Kobal *hated*, and as much as I respected my king, I couldn't deny I enjoyed annoying him by wearing the jewelry. Plus, the human women liked it. For some reason, they found me more approachable and fun once I started wearing their decorations. It didn't take me long to realize that having something dangling from my ears equaled more women warming my bed.

Most demon women didn't wear earrings, but the human jewelry hadn't deterred them from my bed either. However, demon women were like me and simply easing the needs of their body before moving onto another partner. Human women made me laugh more than demons did and were often more enthusiastic in bed. Because of that, I'd started to spend more time with human females than demon ones over the years.

I'd laughed in Hell, but not like I had since coming to the human realm. Things were easier here, for demons at least. People had taken a beating since the gateway opened, but many of them still found laughter in things.

Not Wren. I'd never heard her laugh, and I was determined to make her do so one of these days. She never wore any jewelry either, but I wouldn't be surprised if one day she created a necklace from the teeth of the demons she'd killed.

"Spying on me, demon?" Wren demanded.

"Not likely, human," I replied and dropped my feet down to swing them back and forth again. "I was on guard duty so I could have some time away from you mortals, but you interrupted my break."

"Unlike you, and the rest of your *brethren*"—she spat the word brethren like it was something foul—"I don't get a break, and we mortals require actual *food* to live. I don't expect you to understand; this isn't your world."

"That, my dear Wren, is where you're wrong. Some of your fellow humans made this my world when they fucked up and tore open a gateway into Hell. Even with said gateway now closed, there is no going back to the way things were. We're a part of your world now."

Her jaw clenched, and her eyes burned, but she didn't reply as she swung her bow onto her back and turned away from me. I would far prefer her beneath me, her nails raking my back as she screamed in ecstasy, but I couldn't stop myself from smiling. At least she'd spoken to me; she often avoided doing that much.

Maybe things would be different between us if I hadn't tried to flirt with her the first time we met. During that brief encounter, I'd inquired if she wore earrings, told her I'd be willing to go without them for her, and that demons were capable of fucking all night.

Many women would have blushed, laughed, flirted back, or told me to screw off. Wren tried to punch me. She slaughtered demons and Hell creatures without blinking an eye, but my flirting was something she didn't seem to know how to handle and I suspected that infuriated her.

My first impression had been the completely wrong one with her. I didn't know how to fix it, so I continued to exasperate her, and she continued to despise me. Humans were prickly creatures sometimes, and Wren was the sharpest of them all.

I'd always been confident in my ability to get a woman; Wren had proven I didn't know females as well as I believed I did. I'd never chased a woman in my lifetime, never expected I would, but I found myself strangely infatuated with this one.

Does she fascinate me because I can't have her?

I didn't think that was it either. I'd had women tell me no over the years, not many, but it had happened. I'd shrugged them off and moved onto the next one. That wasn't working now.

Wren knelt next to the deer to examine it. Her fingers hesitated on its forehead before she bent her head and brushed back its fur in what looked like an apology. My eyebrow rose at this exchange. I'd never seen her look regretful after killing something, but she did now.

She rested her fingers against the deer's chest and murmured something I couldn't hear. Then, she gripped the deer by its legs and pulled it toward her.

"Are you going to carry that back to camp by yourself?" I asked.

"Yep," she replied.

Shifting the deer, she somehow managed to lift it onto her back. Turning back to me, she gave me a smug smile as she stuck out a hip. My gaze drifted to where the weight of the deer pulled her shirt back to emphasize her breasts. Bark broke off beneath my hands as images of cupping those breasts flashed through my mind. They'd fill my hand as I bent to lick her nipples until they stood out from her body. Then, I'd run my tongue across the hardened buds before scraping my teeth over them.

I tore my attention away from her breasts and back to her face. Her cheekbones were high, her mouth full and a soft pink color. Her chin had a small point to it, giving her a stubborn look that matched her personality.

I wanted to run my hands over every inch of her—while she would prefer to shoot me with her arrow. She wouldn't brush the hair back from my forehead after shooting me through the heart. No, she'd cut my head from my body to make sure she'd completed the job.

"It will make an excellent meal," I told her.

"It will," she replied.

The deer hadn't bled much, but I detected the coppery tang of its blood on the air when the breeze shifted.

"Are you sure you wouldn't like a hand with it?" I inquired.

"Not from you, demon," she retorted.

"I do have a name."

"I know," she replied with her usual aplomb. "I don't care to use it."

"I see." Releasing the branch, I dropped thirty feet and landed noiselessly on the ground. "If we're working together now, you should call me by my name. You call the others who came with me by their names."

Wariness flashed across her features when I stepped toward her. I'd never seen her fear anything before, not even Kobal.

"Don't take offense, demon; I don't use the names of the new Wilders who join us either. They may have survived this long out here, but I never know how long they'll last with us. If they make it more than three months, then I stop calling them 'new guy' or 'new girl.'"

"So next month you'll start using my name?"

"Probably not."

"And why is that?"

"Because I don't like you."

"Liar," I teased.

She shifted her weight and adjusted the deer on her shoulders. "I think lying is a demon's specialty, not mine."

"I can assure you that demons are not liars. Most of us are brutally honest."

"Is that so?"

"It is," I confirmed.

"Good for you. Would you like a treat for your honesty?"

I grinned at her. "Only if you're the treat."

A muscle in her jaw twitched. She'd most likely try to kill me in my sleep one of these days, but for some reason, I couldn't stop myself from teasing her.

CHAPTER THREE

CORSON

The talons, which were a part of my skeletal structure, slid silently from the backs of my hands as I released them from my body. At nearly a foot long, they almost touched the ground while I walked toward her. Wren showed no response to them. She'd seen me use them multiple times since we'd started our journey into the Wilds, but no matter what she thought of me, she knew I wouldn't use them on her. I wouldn't have released them if I'd believed they would upset her.

"I could gut and skin that deer for you without a problem," I offered, hoping to distract her from our conversation by helping her. I lifted one hand and held my hand before my face. The white talons shone in the sunlight filtering through the trees. "These will make quick work of it for you."

"I don't require help, demon," she replied

"Corson," I said. "You could call me by it."

I itched to trace my finger over the tip of her chin when it rose more stubbornly into the air. "I'd prefer not to. You may be immortal, and it may take a decapitation to off you, but you're still more likely to die out here than I am."

"Is that so?" I drawled.

"Yep."

"Are you afraid you'll get attached me if you use my name and then something will happen to me?"

"Of course not," she scoffed.

The sun setting over her shoulder made her pale hair shimmer with oranges and golds as I strolled closer to her. Eyeing the string tied around the end of her braid, I contemplated pulling it free to undo the braid and run my fingers through her hair. *Does it feel as silken as it looks?*

"You think I'm incapable of surviving the Wilds when I survived Hell?" I inquired.

Stopping before her, I searched her eyes for the small flecks of sea green I'd noticed the first time I'd seen her. Every time I got close to her, I looked for that green. The color was such a striking contrast to the blue of her eyes, but so small it was barely noticeable.

"I think you knew Hell and that, once you were free, you knew the safety and protection of the wall, but you don't know the Wilds."

"And you don't know what the fallen angels that recently escaped Hell are like," I reminded her. "You also don't know what the creatures who lived behind the seals in Hell are like."

"You don't know what those creatures are like either," she retorted.

"True," I agreed.

I'd lived with Hell creatures, demons, and fallen angels, and I'd dealt with some of the things locked behind the seals while in Hell, but not all of them. Now, the seals that once kept the worst of Hell locked away to keep demons and other Hell creatures safe, had been destroyed and the occupants were free. Not all the things imprisoned behind the seals had managed to escape Hell, but *none* of the seals existed anymore. Many of those seal creatures were determined to slaughter everything in their way and were incapable of any reasoning.

Unless a new gateway opened into Hell, one Kobal didn't control, a lot of the creatures that escaped the seals would remain trapped within Hell, but enough had broken free to wreak havoc on this plane.

I may not give a shit about most of mankind, but there were a few people I'd come to consider friends. Plus, the existence of demons and angels hinged on the survival of mankind. Out of the three species, humans were the only ones with a soul and the only ones capable of creating new souls. If humans became extinct, without the souls of their dead to feed us, angels and demons would perish too.

That was why we'd left the wall, built to separate these wildlands from the civilian population, to travel into the Wilds. Most of the old occupants of the seals, and the angels, avoided going near the wall. Not only was Kobal at the wall, but so was a human military presence and a fair number of paliton demons.

Until recently, most of the civilians on the other side of the wall hadn't known about the existence of Hell and demons. When the gateway opened, they were told that a war with a foreign government had torn their country apart and left the central states decimated. The people who resided on the other side of the world had been told the same thing about the countries affected there. After the gateway opened and Hell spilled free, the human governments built the wall in an attempt to keep their citizens safe.

When the seals fell and Hell came to Earth, the wall and all those defending it were incapable of keeping the outpouring of monsters back. The tidal wave of Hell creatures going over the wall had eased since the initial rush, but the truth could no longer be hidden from the civvies.

Most of the escapees from the seals remained in the Wilds of this country and Europe. The fallen angels hadn't been seen much since Lucifer's demise, but I didn't doubt they were trying to gather a new army to fight Kobal, and I would do everything I could to stop the bastards.

Until then, I had Wren to contend with, and she was probably more hostile than most of the seal creatures.

"One day I'll hear you say my name, Wren," I said.

"I doubt that, demon," she snorted. "Where are your earrings?"

Hostility flashed through her eyes. Did I crave her so badly that I'd imagined the tinge of jealousy in her words? She'd only ever seen me wearing earrings once, but I knew the others talked and that she was aware of what those earrings meant.

My neck warmed as the flecks of green in her eyes deepened in hue and her steady gaze held mine. I wasn't embarrassed or ashamed. I'd never be ashamed of pursuing the things I wanted. It was the way of demons after all, but I found myself not liking the fact Wren knew so much, yet so little about me. She'd judged me and found me lacking.

Normally that wouldn't have bothered me, but it did with her.

I rubbed my thumb and index finger together as I resisted running them over the high arch of her cheekbone. "I've decided to try something new," I replied with an indifference I didn't feel.

"Hmm," she said by way of reply.

She turned and stalked into the woods with far less caution than she typically exhibited. I stared after her for a moment as I debated following her. Wind howled through the branches, causing them to click loudly together. A shiver ran up my spine as the chilly air cut through my clothes. The Wilders had revealed to us that when the gateway into Hell opened, this area became warmer. They said the closing of the gateway hadn't changed that, but it was nowhere near as hot as Hell was, and I hated the chilly November air.

It didn't surprise me the gateway shutting hadn't put the temperature back to what it was supposed to be. The closing of the gateway had done little to repair the damage its opening had wrought on Earth. That's why demons could now retain their immortality on this plane, when before we would have been forced to return to Hell.

Earth was far different from Hell, mostly in a good way, and I had adapted to it during the fourteen years I'd lived here. The only thing I missed about Hell was the constant heat. I found snow worse than a barta demon on a rampage, and I despised the bear-like barta demons now roaming Earth as well as Hell, but I enjoyed the changing seasons and the sunrises and sunsets that marked the days.

All my days in Hell had blended one into another with no way to mark their passing. I found myself stopping to watch every sunrise and sunset with an awe that hadn't dissipated over my years here.

Unlike humans, I felt no dread over a sense of time slipping away from me when each of those days ended. While in Hell, I'd watched some people complain about their gray hairs and aching joints. Since coming to Earth, I hadn't heard anyone complain about aging. Probably because many of them knew they might never get the chance to grow old and those who did were fortunate to have made it so long.

I was aware my time on Earth had changed me. It had changed most demons in some way and it had also changed the humans. Every species adapted or died. Many demons had become a little more caring, like humans, while many people had become more vicious with their need to survive and more able to endure adversity, like demons.

Wren was one of those who had adapted exceptionally well, I decided as I watched her walk away. Knowing that it was time for me to return to camp, I started after her.

CHAPTER FOUR

WREN

The weight of the deer dragged on my shoulders and compressed my spine, but I refused to let Corson help me with it. I wouldn't have let anyone help me with it, except for maybe Randy, and there was a very distinct possibility Randy was dead.

The deer could crush my spine before I ever allowed that highly annoying, if not somewhat attractive, demon who insisted on flirting with *me* to carry it.

I despised demons. Okay, well, not despised, at least not anymore. For many years, I hadn't known the truth of what happened with the gateway opening, and I'd blamed demons for everything.

Living in the Wilds, I'd known more than the civvies about what had happened to this land, but I still hadn't known everything. I knew the truth of it now.

The demons didn't somehow find a way to break free of Hell on their own and invade Earth with the sole intention of striking down everything in their way. No, imbecilic human governments had been messing with things they shouldn't have. In doing so, they accidentally opened a gateway into Hell and allowed its hideous occupants to spill free.

Before encountering Kobal a few months ago, I'd only ever seen demons as monsters, and I'd gleefully slaughtered any I came across before they could kill me. I hadn't known Kobal was the king of Hell when I tried to ambush him or I would have stayed far away.

I still shuddered when I thought about what could have happened to my fellow Wilders if Kobal hadn't spared us that day. Losing my life was one thing, but losing theirs was something else entirely. Randy had appointed me in charge when he left; the lives of the Wilders following me rested on my shoulders, and I felt the weight of that more than the weight of the deer draped around me.

At the time, it had seemed like such a simple attack against Kobal. Disable them, kill the demons, get the stuff, and get out fast. We'd done it countless times before, but Kobal had somehow known we were there and come up behind us with some of his friends while we'd been waiting for them. We could have been killed that day and all because I'd made a bad decision.

Now, I could only hope that I'd made the right decision in approaching the demons to keep the Wilders safe.

But after Kobal let us live, it was a risk I was willing to take. Granted, Kobal left us tied up in the woods and vulnerable to anything lurking nearby, but he'd still given us a chance to survive. It was more than any other demon had given us before. Intrigued by the fact he hadn't torn our heads off, my curiosity got the best of me, and I'd followed him to the gateway.

After witnessing numerous monsters pouring out of Hell when the seals fell, I decided to put aside my hatred of demons and work with those following the king and queen. It was the only way humans and demons would survive what had fled the gateway. I'd seen everything from a drakón —massive, skeletal, dragon-looking things —to tiny gobalinus—hideous, two-foot-tall goblins—escape the gateway, along with countless other things that should belong only in nightmares.

Corson's steps sounded behind me, but I didn't look back. I didn't know what it was about him that unnerved me far more than any of the other demons. Maybe it was because his eyes, the startling color of citrine, were more than a little intriguing. Or maybe it was because he had this way of flirting with me that made me actually feel like a woman.

Not many men had done that. Not many men were brave enough to flirt with me in the first place. But Corson did, and he seemed to *enjoy* it. He also looked at me in a way…

I broke the thought off and gave myself a mental shake. *I will not be attracted to a demon!* Abso-fucking-lutely *not*. It would never happen. My hands tightened on the legs of the deer as I kept repeating this to myself, but I couldn't stop my gaze from going to him.

He sauntered through the woods as if he belonged in this world— which, no matter how they'd arrived here, demons were not *meant* to be here. However, the opening of the gateway had caused Hell and Earth to become intertwined so completely that there would never be any undoing it.

This was our joined world now.

Being around Corson had been easier when we'd all been at the wall. I'd mostly stayed in the houses by the wall and with people, while he'd resided in one of the tents on the hill with the other demons. He'd also left for a couple of weeks to travel through Hell and over to the other side of the world with Kobal. I hadn't thought of Corson at all while he'd been gone. Nope, not once had it crossed my mind to wonder if he still lived.

With a sigh, I had to admit that even I wasn't buying the shit I was trying to shovel to myself. He had crossed my mind a time or two, but only because I'd been curious to know if the king still lived or if he'd died when he'd returned to Hell with the others. That was the only reason Corson had entered my mind once he left.

Liar. Ugh, sometimes I hated my stupid little inner voice. It never let me lie to myself.

But most of my thoughts of Corson had consisted of eviscerating his earring-wearing, smug ass. There had been *zero* dreams of skin touching skin, lips brushing against lips, of my fingers sliding through the thick black hair falling in curls around his pointed ears— hair that was so black it appeared blue in some lights.

Corson smiled when he met my gaze, and his eyes sparkled. With him standing about nine inches taller than my five-seven height, I found my chin lifting to hold his stare. My hands twitched on the deer's legs as I was hit with the impulse to trace the tip of one of his pointed ears.

And the first time I'd seen those ears, they'd been decorated with three different kinds of earrings from *three* different women.

I turned away as that reminder lodged firmly into place. It hadn't taken much time to learn what Corson's earrings meant. The civvies at the wall were eager to gossip about the demons residing in their midst, except for the queen, River. Few knew much about the queen of Hell, and those who did remained silent about what she was and what she could do. I'd heard rumors that she was Lucifer's daughter, one where she was an angel, and some whispered she was a witch, but no one confirmed any of those rumors. I suspected the demons enjoyed the numerous tales floating around and that they'd probably started some of them.

The civvies spilled every juicy detail they had on the demons. I'd also learned the civvies didn't call us Wilders but had different names for us. Some considered us lunatics, others called us savages, and some believed we were stupid to remain in the Wilds instead of retreating to civilization or evacuating when the government commanded it.

However, after everything we saw on the day the gateway opened, Randy didn't trust the government enough to come forward when, a year later, they swept through near where we were in search of survivors. When the Wilders learned the government and demons had teamed up to work together, it only confirmed that the government couldn't be trusted. Other Wilders had never encountered the rescue parties and had chosen not to travel to the wall.

Talking with the civvies, I'd quickly realized that Corson had made his way through a fair amount of the women, and this was only one small area of the wall. The king and his closest advisors moved around the extensive wall often, and they'd traveled the wall on the other side of the world too. Corson had probably likely worn earrings from the women he'd met while traveling too, which would have been a *lot* of women.

Stretching all the way around the United States, the immense wall blocked the outer states from the central states. Those outer states hadn't been as severely affected by the gateway opening, the release of demons, and the nuclear bombing that followed.

Thankfully, Hell absorbed the nuclear fallout before it could spread across the land. Otherwise, I might be sporting a tail or third eye, or some other radiation deformity. The only concerns I had about fashion were if the clothes fit me, did they blend in with the trees, and were they warm? But even I wouldn't have appreciated having to cut holes into my pants to slip my tail through.

Or I could have been killed outright and ended up like so many others I once knew. I'd lived in Kansas, close to the gateway when it all started. It was *my* home, my *family*, my town that was devastated.

I was only eight when everything I knew changed, but I stopped being a child that day. I barely recalled the good of my childhood, and I rarely thought about the people I'd lost or the things taken from me. It was easier not to remember.

The child I'd been never would have survived in this world. On the day the gateway opened, her existence was burned away as surely as if the bombs had fallen on her home.

I shifted the deer on my shoulders and hurried faster through the woods to get away from Corson. Unlike at the wall, there was nowhere for me to hide from him anymore, nowhere to lose myself as we camped together these last couple of weeks while moving deeper into the Wilds.

We'd abandoned the two vehicles we left the wall with on the fifth day of travel. It was much easier to go undetected on foot in the woods than in a truck on the pitted roads. Finding gas was also difficult, if not impossible out here. Travel may be slower on foot, but it was safer, and my feet were used to walking.

We were about ten miles from the gateway now, if the markings I'd seen along the way and my calculations were correct, and they almost always were. I hadn't lived this long by not learning how to navigate. I could thank Randy for that too, but then I could thank Randy for almost everything that made me who I was now.

But even without the markings and my ability to navigate, I would know where we were. I walked faster as the memory of what we'd traveled past yesterday shoved to the forefront of my mind. I'd never forget what I'd seen there, but I would spend the rest of my life trying. Unfortunately, no matter how fast I walked, the memory stalked me.

CHAPTER FIVE

WREN

"You might want to slow down. We haven't explored this area much," Corson said from behind me.

I glanced back at him, my gaze running over his narrow face and lean body. He moved with the grace inherent to all demons, including the giant, lumbering ones. With Corson, it seemed more natural as his body moved like water rippling over rocks, effortless in its fluidity.

"I don't recall asking for your insights, demon," I retorted, but I was irritated with myself for being reckless in my need to escape him and my memories. The last time I was in this area, it had been safe, but even before the seal creatures escaped Hell, places were always changing in the Wilds. What was once safe, might not be safe an hour later.

I'd never been reckless before Corson strolled into my life, not in these kinds of situations. I wouldn't be alive if I wasn't cautious. I'd watched countless others die because of their stupidity or irresponsibility, and I would *not* be one of them because of some demon.

Easing my pace, I focused on my surroundings as I decided

firmly against looking at him or acknowledging him again. I searched the shadows and inhaled the familiar aroma of rotting leaves, dirt, and animals. I'd lived in the Wilds for enough years to pick out the various scents in the different areas.

We were more north than I normally would have been at this time of the year. It was the custom to head south when the leaves started to turn. The humans surviving in the Wilds had become like birds over the years. Not only did we start migrating and flying away when an enemy approached, but if cornered, we also turned on them and pecked out their eyes until they died. I'd always preferred going for the eyes rather than flying away, but I also knew when to retreat.

Going south was going to have to wait a bit for us this year though. After some discussion between the demons and Wilders, we'd determined to return to the gateway before moving south and deeper inland. The gateway was closed now, but the king believed many of the things that escaped it might go back to it. It was a place they knew, and the remnants of the power of Hell may draw them back.

As we traveled, we'd remarked and remapped the land while hunting our enemies. Besides our group, there were other factions of demons, Wilders, and civvies working around the country to map out different areas and destroy any enemy residing there.

The Wilders were used to the constant moving and mapping of terrain. The various groups of Wilders knew much of this area. When those groups encountered each other, they openly shared their knowledge, but things had changed now that more enemies wandered our country.

Areas we'd once believed relatively safe weren't anymore. The Wilders had become nomads over the years, but the demons who settled into the Wilds after the gateway first opened had mostly stayed in certain areas. Those demons sometimes roamed, and there were always rogues to watch out for, but we'd mostly had an idea of where they were… we no longer did.

Out of all the groups sent out from the wall, we were the only one that would travel deeper and deeper into areas of the Wilds even *I* didn't know in search of the remaining fallen angels. The other groups would establish a perimeter between us and the wall that would hopefully offer more protection for the civvies.

Having more than one team moving inland had been a hot debate while we'd still been at the wall, but in the end, it was determined that too many teams pushing inland could attract the attention of the things we hunted. It would also put more lives at risk for a mission that might turn up nothing. The angels could be anywhere in the world.

Our group was also the only one with a demon who could communicate with the other groups telepathically. Malorick kept in touch with the other groups, letting them know our position and if it was safe for them to travel through certain areas.

The crunch of a stick drew my gaze to the right. I searched the shadows as the breeze caused the tendrils of hair that had worked free of my braid to tickle my face. I didn't hear Corson move, but I felt the warmth of him against my elbow when he stepped closer.

I buried the thrill going through me at having him so near. My hand went to the gun at my side; I rested my palm on the handle as I listened to the scratch of a squirrel's claws against the oak tree to my right. The branches shook when the animal flew from one limb to another and scampered down the next tree trunk. My hand fell away from my gun. The squirrel wouldn't be moving with such reckless abandon if a predator was nearby.

I gripped the deer's legs again and stepped forward. The second my foot hit the ground, the dirt collapsed beneath it. Rocks clattered and banged as they spiraled into the pit opening before me. Cold air rushed out of the blackness as more dirt gave way to reveal an ever-growing hole in the ground. The stale scent of Earth and something feral rose to greet me.

Death. It's death below.

Time froze for a second as my foot hung suspended over open air, and then I felt myself tilting forward. I tried to yank my foot back, tried to regain my balance, but my angle caused the deer to shift on my shoulders, and its weight toppled me forward before I could shove the carcass off me. There was nothing I could do to stop myself from tumbling into the abyss with the deer still draped around my shoulders.

Corson's hand enveloped my wrist. He jerked one of my arms up and away from the deer as he caught me. Swinging back, I slammed against the dirt wall, and my breath burst from my lungs with a loud, *oomph.*

I gasped for air as my feet dangled over nothing. I waited for some hideous monster to surge up and close its mouth over me, to snatch me away with so much force that Corson was left holding only the stump of my arm. I resisted the urge to kick my feet as if I could somehow run out of the hole.

Is there a bottom to this thing? Is this another gateway into Hell? But then I heard the last of the falling rocks clatter against a distant bottom. The pit did have an end, but it was a long way down.

"Are you okay?" Corson demanded.

Lifting my head, I spotted him above me. His face was strained with worry as his eyes searched mine. "I think I shaved a few seconds off my life, but I'm fine."

"I'm going to pull you up."

"That would be appreciated."

His mouth quirked in a smile as he looped his other hand under my armpit. Cool dirt fell down my shirt; my back was scoured by the wall as he began to lift me from the hole. Holding my breath, I stared at my dangling feet and tried not to think about what had created this.

Corson almost had me to the top when more dirt gave way beneath him. A scream lodged in my throat when I dropped a couple of feet back into the hole. Corson fell into the hole up to his waist before stopping himself. His hands tightened on my arms as the rest of the ground collapsed beneath him and we fell.

The deer dragged me down so fast I couldn't claw at the sides of the tunnel to ease my plunge. Corson released his hold under my arm, and a scraping sound filled the air. The rate of descent lessened, and I realized Corson was using his talons to keep us from plummeting straight to the bottom.

My other arm remained lifted awkwardly above me from Corson's hold on my wrist. In the hopes of slowing our descent, I tried to maneuver the deer off my shoulders the best I could, without breaking his grip. Hooves kicked me in the head, and one caught the corner of my eye. I could feel it swelling already, but I'd deserved it; I had shot the animal through the heart, a few bumps and bruises were nothing in comparison.

The weight of the deer sliding to my left, caused my shoulders to pull further down. My neck and back screamed in protest; I feared my shoulder might pop out of its socket as I was pulled in two directions like a puppet on a string. Somehow, I managed to maneuver enough to grab the deer's front legs and pull it the rest of the way off.

I breathed a sigh of relief as its weight eased from me and its body tumbled away. The rate of our descent eased a little more. Craning my head back, I watched Corson tear at the wall in an attempt to halt our plunge. Sparks flew off the tips of his talons as they struck rocks. The muscles in his forearms bulged, but he couldn't get any traction on the wall.

He'd be able to stop himself if he had both his hands free, but the earth was too loose for him to get only one hand into it. He had to know that if he sacrificed me, he could save himself.

He's going to throw me aside, and I won't blame him if he does. Survival of the fittest and all.

Even as I thought it, his hand clenched on my wrist, and our plunge continued.

CHAPTER SIX

WREN

"Help!" I screamed and leapt at the wall.

Dirt embedded beneath my fingernails and abraded my palms as I scrambled for purchase. Stepping back, I panted for air while I gazed at the distant circle of light overhead. At least five hundred feet above me, that daylight seemed about as achievable as Heaven right now.

"He—aggghh," my scream for help cut off when a hand slid over my mouth.

Pulled back against Corson's solid chest, his breath sounded in my ear when he pinned me firmly to him. Too stunned to move for a second, I leaned against him as his lips brushed my ear. "Quiet!" he hissed.

Lifting my hands, I tugged at his wrist as I twisted to break free of his hold. Releasing me, he strolled away, his boots crunching the debris we'd toppled into the pit. His casual demeanor seemed entirely out of place considering where we now stood. I didn't have to see the creature to know we'd fallen into the trap of something awful. Seeing it would probably only make it worse.

I strained to follow Corson as he disappeared and reemerged from the shifting shadows while circling the pit. He stopped before another tunnel and rested a hand against the dirt wall. Leaning forward, his head turned back and forth as he inspected the opening.

I strained to hear anything coming from that tunnel as I reached over my back. My heart sank when I realized a familiar weight was missing even as my hand connected with my shirt instead of my quiver and bow. Glancing around, I spotted my bow half hidden in the dark.

Striding over, I bent and drew it toward me. When I lifted it into the air, the bottom half of the bow clattered onto the ground while the snapped string floated in the air before me. "It took me a week to find the perfect branch, whittle it, and smooth it to get this where I wanted it," I muttered. "I've had it for five years, and one *stupid* misstep snatched it away from me."

"We will find you another," Corson murmured.

I sighed and set the bow aside. "Better the bow than us." It still stung though, especially since it had been *my* misstep that landed us here.

You're still alive.

But for how long? I wondered as I glanced at the distant light overhead before focusing on the cavern once more.

I spotted the edge of my quiver peeking out from under the deer. Walking over, I lifted the back of the deer as much as I could with one hand. After some maneuvering, jerking, sweating, and unspoken swears, I managed to tug the quiver out from under the animal. I lifted the crumpled remains and turned it over to empty it out. The broken pieces bounced across the ground and scattered around my feet.

Bending over, I placed my hands on my knees and took a second to steady myself before looking to Corson again. "Can you climb out of here?"

He didn't look back at me as he replied, "By the time we made it to the top, it would be too late."

I liked the sound of that about as much as I liked the idea of having my fingernails pulled out. "What does *that* mean?"

"It means our fall and your yelling will have woken the beast. It will be looking for its dinner."

"And we're its dinner?"

"Yes."

I wiped my sweaty palms on my pants and straightened. He wouldn't know the apprehension his words roused in me. "And what is the beast we woke?"

"The ouroboros."

"What is that?"

"A giant serpent. It devours its own tails when it's starving. When it has a food supply..."

"It eats the supply," I whispered when his voice trailed off, and he gave me a pointed look.

"Yes."

"A giant snake, fantastic."

I turned back to the wall and tried to ignore the galloping beat of my heart as my mind spun. There was always a plan, always an action to take; I just had to calm down enough to think of one. *Deep breaths. There are options.*

"What about Malorick?" I blurted as I recalled the telepathic demon. "Can't you reach out and tell him where we are?"

"It doesn't work that way," Corson replied. "He can reach out to communicate with me, when and if the others realize we're missing, but I can't talk with him until he opens the pathway into my mind."

I gazed at the distant, unattainable circle of light as I ran through more options. "If we call for help, maybe the angels will hear us and come."

I wasn't overly fond of either of the angels. Not Raphael with all his golden beauty, or Caim with the black wings the fallen angels possessed. Both of them had proven to be loyal to the king and queen, but Raphael was often an asshole, and Caim...

Well, I actually kind of liked Caim's blunt, sort of crazy ways, but he'd been on Lucifer's side until a few months ago, so I didn't trust him. Fighting for us now or not, Caim had proven he was willing to change sides.

"Never trust a traitor," Randy's words from years ago whispered across my mind.

They were words I'd followed ever since, just as I'd followed most of Randy's advice. The only reason I was still alive was him. Many had perished, but Randy had made sure I survived, and over the years, I'd come to love him as much as he loved me. I didn't know what I would do if he were dead, couldn't imagine the world without him in it, smiling at me and guiding me, but somehow I would survive that too.

However, traitor or not, I preferred riding Caim's shoulders out of here over being the stomach contents of a self-eating, behemoth snake any day.

"Yes, by all means, keep shouting. I'm sure the angels will hear you all the way down here and arrive before the ouroboros does. At least the appetizer you present will keep the ouro occupied while I'm hauling ass out of here," Corson drawled.

I shot him a ferocious look as my hand fell to my gun. His gaze followed the movement. He widened his stance and seemed to dare me with his eyes to do it. My bullets wouldn't kill him, but it would feel good to shoot one into his arrogant face.

I never would though. This demon irritated me more than any other, but I'd agreed to work with the demons, and I wouldn't do anything to jeopardize our agreement with them.

Never trust someone who doesn't keep their word. Randy advised in my mind. I had no idea what he would think about my agreeing to work with the demons. He'd broken his group of followers in half, entrusting me to lead half of them while he took the other half with him. If he were dead, he'd probably rolled over in his grave half a dozen times by now over my course of action. If he was still alive, then he might consider *me* a traitor now.

The idea of Randy being dead tore at my heart until I found

myself struggling to breathe. The possibility of Randy turning on me unnerved me more than the giant snake probably making its way toward us right now. I wouldn't be able to handle it if he came to despise me, but I'd done what I believed was best to keep the Wilders alive, and if there was one thing Randy understood, it was keeping his people alive and being loyal to those who were loyal to him.

I never would have extended the offer to work with the demons if the other Wilders hadn't agreed to it beforehand. After witnessing what escaped the gateway, and with what we'd come to learn of the demons, we decided that working with them was our best, and maybe only, chance for continued survival.

No, not survival, our best chance for *hope*. We'd spent the past fourteen years doing everything we could to live until the next minute. Working with the demons offered us the first promise of a future that we'd had in years—a promise none of us had dared to hope for before.

Even now, trapped in this hole with *Corson*, and with the possibility that I might end up being snake shit by the end of the day, I still wouldn't have changed anything. The Wilders above had a chance at a better life because we were working with the demons. My death was worth *one* of them having an opportunity to age enough to wrinkle and go gray.

But I wasn't dead yet, and I didn't plan to go down easy if my end was coming soon.

"How do you intend to get out of here?" I asked Corson.

Lifting his hand, Corson pointed down the tunnel he'd been inspecting. My gaze followed his talons to the nothingness beyond him. I resisted gulping. The tunnel was twenty-plus feet in diameter. I did *not* want to be anywhere near the thing capable of creating *that*.

"Are you nuts?" I asked.

"I've been told it's a possibility."

"We'll be walking straight into that thing's *home*. It opened its door for us"—I waved a hand at the hole above us—"but I don't think it's going to offer us coffee and cake."

Corson grinned at me. *Yep, he's nuts,* I decided.

"Probably not coffee, but maybe it has some snake cake," he replied with a wink, and I glared at him. "There are going to be more side tunnels in there. The ouro wouldn't have only one way in and out. We have to make it into one of those side tunnels and soon. This is a trap, and the ouro most likely sensed when it sprang."

"What if it's in one of those side tunnels?"

"Then we have to face it," Corson replied.

"Wouldn't it make more sense to wait here, in this bigger room to kill it?"

"It has more space to maneuver in here, which will make it a lot harder to kill."

My hands fisted as I realized he was right. Why was I so stupid right now, while he was calmly pointing out all the facts I should have seen on my own? Was it just that I was standing in the pit of a gigantic snake, or because I was stuck here with *him*? When I thought about it, the idea of being alone with Corson scared me more than the ouro did.

I resolved *not* to think about it.

Taking a deep breath, I gazed longingly at the faint source of light over my head. Once we moved away from it, there would be nothing to guide us, no proof the world existed beyond this underground cavern.

"We have to go," Corson urged. "Now."

I tore my eyes away from the distant hole and back to the most infuriating demon in existence. Long ago, I'd resolved not to let others know how I was really feeling. There were those who would use any fear or hesitance they saw in me against me. I didn't think Corson would, but years of ingrained habit rushed to the forefront now.

With a confidence I didn't feel, I thrust my shoulders back and grinned at him. "Well, all right then. Let's go do some snake hunting. I've always wanted a pair of snakeskin boots."

The look Corson gave me said he wasn't buying it, but he refrained from commenting before he started into the hole. I stepped away from the wall and followed him into the ouro's den. I only made it three feet into the ouro's tunnel before it became so dark I couldn't see Corson's back in front of me.

There was nothing like blindly winding deeper into the home of a giant, self-eating snake.

CHAPTER SEVEN

CORSON

With no light piercing this deep into the bowels of the earth, it was impossible to see what lay before me, even with my enhanced demon senses. I kept my right hand raised; my talons extended straight ahead as we wound deeper and deeper into the labyrinth the ouro had created.

My left hand ran over the cool dirt wall. The ouro had traveled through here enough times that the earth and stone beneath my fingers had been smoothed by its passing. I kept my hearing attuned to any hint of danger as my hand fell into the open air of another tunnel.

We'd already slipped into two different passageways since leaving the main pit behind. I had no doubt the ouro was coming for us, but if we kept taking turns, there was a chance we might be able to avoid it. A *tiny* chance.

Fifteen minutes ago, a vibration beneath my feet alerted me the ouro was traveling toward the trap it had created and we'd fallen into, but I hadn't felt any vibrations since then. If I'd been Shax, I would have been able to detect the faintest movement of earth, would have known the ouro was coming long before it arrived, but Shax remained above with the others.

I strained to hear the faintest hint of sound, but Wren's breaths were all I detected, and she kept those so quiet I knew no one beyond us would hear them. I'd seen the flash of fear in her eyes earlier before she'd declared she wanted to do some snake hunting, but she didn't display any unease now.

When Wren had been at the wall for a bit, River had told me she believed Wren might be a little insane, and maybe River was right, but I didn't think so. I thought Wren was more scared of the things residing in her world than she'd ever let on to others, especially demons, and she hid behind a bravado some would find off-putting. Wren would probably shoot me if I ever told her that though.

Instead of dirt, rocks began to increasingly scratch my palm as we traversed a gradually sloping descent. Wren's arm grazed mine while I followed the dips and hollows of the ground. The heat of her body warmed my skin, and her natural scent of leaves and pine filled my nostrils. She lived and breathed the Wilds, and it radiated from her pores as she stepped so close to me that her breasts brushed against my back.

Gritting my teeth, I flexed my right hand as my cock stirred. Now was not the time to be thinking about taking her, but my body wasn't accustomed to being denied sex for as long as it had been and I'd never been this close to her before. She'd affected me without ever touching me in the past. In these tight confines, she was likely to drive me mad. Her hands fell briefly on my waist when I came to an abrupt stop.

Images of her naked and straddling me burst through my head, making it difficult to think about anything else.

My breath hissed in through my teeth as I struggled to regain control of myself. As soon as we were out of this place, I'd find another woman and slake my lust with her. A night of screwing would purge Wren from my system. My head would be on straight once I had sex again, but if I didn't get it on straight right now, I'd be dead.

And so would Wren.

For some reason, the thought of Wren's death was more of a wake-up call than the possibility of my own. It doused the lust she so easily roused in me. I would *not* allow anything to happen to her.

"Why did you stop?" she whispered.

"To listen."

Her hands fell away from me. The end of her braid tickled my arm when she tilted her head to the side. My hands flexed as I focused my attention away from her and onto the tunnel.

The absence of noise in this place made it feel as if I'd gone deaf as well as blind. We were so deep below the earth now that I couldn't detect so much as a worm moving through the soil. Anything capable of living at this depth had either fled the ouro or been devoured by it.

The only time I'd ever seen the ouroboros was when the seal caging it fell. That glimpse had been more than enough to sear the one-hundred-foot-long and twenty-foot-wide, green serpent into my memory. The ouro possessed two hooked fangs and a hood that unfurled from the sides of its diamond-shaped head. Its black and red, forked tongue flickered in the air when it hunted its prey.

"Do you hear anything?" Wren asked.

The beat of her heart drifted to me as it increased. She would never admit it, but she was scared. Placing my palm against the tunnel, my fingers dug into the rocky wall, and I took a steadying breath to ease the unexpected rage growing within me. I should have protected her from this. She shouldn't be here. She was in jeopardy because I'd enjoyed baiting her and watching the sway of her hips as she stalked away from me.

"I'll get you out of here," I promised.

She stiffened against me. "I don't need anyone to rescue me."

I turned my head to try to see *something* of her. She was inches away from me, but black encompassed my vision. "I didn't say you did, and no, you're all I hear."

"Then maybe we should keep going."

"Demanding woman," I murmured as I continued forward with her following closely.

"Can this giant snake do anything special, like is it poisonous too?" Wren inquired.

"Its venom can kill, and it eats everything in its way. If it requires more room in its stomach to kill, it throws up so it can eat more. From its back, snake tails curl out every fifteen feet, and each of those tails has a rattle at the end. If it doesn't have any other food, it will eat those tails and wait for them to regenerate before eating them again."

"So it surpasses most expectations of horrific Hell creature."

"Yes."

"Good to know."

My left hand fell into open air again. I paused to inhale the rich aroma of dirt and the more mineral-like tang of the rocks. Unlike the tunnel we were in now, a rancid breeze stirred the air from within this new branch.

It smells like rotting corpses, but it could be a way out. As the possibility entered my mind, some instinct within me shouted it wasn't a breeze I detected, but a breath.

Leaping back, I wrapped my arms around Wren and spun her to the side at the same time something hit my arm and knocked me back. I pressed Wren against the wall, my body melding over hers as the smooth ripple of scales ran across my flesh. The suppleness of the scales was surprising given the rigidity and thickness of the body beneath them.

Then a smaller tail hit me. The rattle bashed my cheek as it vibrated in the air. The distant echo of more rattles resonated down the tunnel and bounced off the walls.

Wren gasped as another tail lashed out with a whistle. Throwing my hand up, I honed in on the sound the tail created and sliced it away before it could hit her. The appendage thudded against the ground, its flopping movements hitting my calf as the pitch of the rattles became higher, and a loud hiss filled the air. I didn't need my vision to know the ouro's head had swung toward us. I felt the shift in the air currents when its tongue flicked out, and the stench of death washed over me.

Lifting Wren, I pinned her to my chest. I much preferred to stay and attack, to slice the ouro to shreds and end it, but I couldn't risk her getting hurt while I battled the beast.

Wren's hands shoved against my shoulders, and her feet kicked my shins as I turned and fled down the tunnel with her. "Put me down," she ordered. "I can run; I can fight."

Rocks and dirt clattered behind us, the rattles reverberated against the walls as the ouro came after us. Where the silence had been deafening, this cacophony beat against my ears until it became my entire world. Wren went still in my arms before she wrapped her legs around my waist and clung to me while I ran.

CHAPTER EIGHT

WREN

My mouth went dry, and my fingers dug into Corson's shoulders as he raced across the ground. That hiss seemed to come from only feet away, but the constricting walls and the blackness threw all sounds off. The ouro could be only inches behind us or fifty feet away. The not knowing was worse than the ouro's foul breath, which smelled like it had fifty dead skunks trapped in its fangs.

I should tell Corson to put me down again. I shouldn't be relying on a demon to save me, but I couldn't run as fast as he could, and I definitely couldn't outrun the snake breathing down our necks. I didn't have so much pride I would put it ahead of my life. Mine may not be the greatest of lives—it was often difficult, terrifying, and bloody—but I far preferred it to the alternative of *not* having it.

The part of me clinging to my pride was muzzled by the far larger part of me trying not to slap Corson's shoulders and yell at him to go faster.

When the ouro hissed again, its breath blew the loose strands of my hair back from my face and nearly set my gag reflex off. Then, something slithered against my face. I yelped before I could bite my lip to suppress it. Bile rushed up my throat when the ouro's hideous, wet tongue stroked my cheek again. Then, the tongue either retracted or Corson sped beyond its reach.

"Faster," I breathed, and Corson grunted a reply.

For all I knew, we were running into a dead end, but I was willing to take that chance. Corson's arms tightened around my waist as he spun suddenly to the side. Unprepared for the movement, my head snapped sideways, and my neck screamed in protest.

I lowered my head and rested my chin on his shoulder as he ran down what I assumed was another tunnel. His lean muscles flexed against me; his arms held me as if he would never let go while his long legs effortlessly ate away the ground. Air whipped around me and whistled past my ears as he ran deeper and deeper into the earth. I'd been trying to keep track of our steps and turns, but that was all lost now as I held Corson tighter.

A monstrous Hell creature was on our asses, and somehow I felt inexplicably safe clutched in his arms. He wouldn't let anything happen to me. I didn't know how I knew that, but once it rooted in my mind, it wouldn't let go. Releasing me to save himself would be the smart thing to do, the thing most likely to keep him alive. I would have done it to him, but Corson would keep me safe.

Would I have done it to him?

I'd done some pretty shitty things to ensure I'd lived this long. I'd killed other humans—they had deserved to die, but their blood still stained my hands—but I'd never left an ally behind or abandoned them to save myself. I'd been tempted to leave a few behind over the years because they were weak or assholes, yet I'd always stayed by their side. I'd nearly died a time or two because of it.

Now I realized that, demon or not, I wouldn't have left Corson behind either. It was one thing to save my skin; it was another to have to live with the knowledge that I'd sacrificed another to live. I never could have lived with that knowledge.

A loud crash sounded from behind us. The walls quaked, and the debris falling from above clattered against the ground at a faster rate.

I threw my arms up to protect Corson and me from the rubble raining down on us. I'd prefer being buried alive to being devoured by an ouro-what's-it-called, but they were two of the worst possible ways I could think of to go.

I turned my face into Corson's neck as more rocks pelted off my arms. The musky scent of him filled my nose; beneath that I smelled the faint hint of fire. I realized that Hell was forever stamped upon his skin, branding him as the demon he was. Before, such a reminder would have caused loathing to coil within me. Now I felt relief that *this* demon was carrying me away from our enemy.

When the debris stopped falling, I lowered my arms and gripped his shoulders once more. I was no lightweight, but he showed no signs of tiring. One of his arms remained locked around my waist as his other hand slid up to grip my neck.

The possessive hold made me acutely aware of how close we were to each other. The increased scent of him battered my senses as his lean muscles flexed against me and I felt the power flowing through him. For the first time in my life, I found myself experiencing an intense sexual attraction to someone, and it was a *demon.*

I'd hit my head when we fell into the ouro's trap, or I'd completely lost the last bit of my sanity.

Now was not the time for this, yet I found myself fighting the impulse to turn my mouth into his neck. To run my tongue over his skin and taste his fire-scented flesh as I pressed my breasts more firmly against his chest.

You're an idiot!

Yes, I was, but my hands had a mind of their own as they flattened against his back. I full-on deserved to be eaten for my stupidity right now, but I still slid my hands a little lower to run them over his shoulder blades. The rapid beat of my heart was no longer just from the creature pursuing us.

Corson skidded to a halt, pebbles kicked away from him and clattered against something solid. I felt like I'd jumped into a lake in the middle of January as all my desire turned to icy dread.

A wall! There is a wall before us! Dead end. In more ways than one! I almost laughed bitterly at my own bad joke, but I couldn't get enough saliva into my mouth to make a sound.

Sweat beaded my palms as I held Corson and gazed into the blackness before me. The rattling had ceased, and no vibrations shook the tunnel. Lying inside a coffin couldn't be worse than the awful hush that encompassed the tunnel. Then, I felt the smallest stirring of air to my right.

Corson pushed me off him like I was on fire. Unprepared for the abrupt movement, my legs couldn't catch me in time, and I hit the ground with a thud. My tailbone shrieked in protest, and the air burst out of my lungs.

Scuffling sounded, that awful hiss filled the air, then more rattles went off as I struggled to inhale air into my non-working lungs. Corson grunted; something solid thwacked against something else. Feeling my way across the stone lining the cold ground, I crept back, or at least I assumed I was edging away from the noises. The dark had robbed me of all sense of direction.

I would have given anything for a match, for a chance to see *something* if only for the briefest of seconds. *What is happening? Where is Corson?*

Another hiss followed a wet thwacking noise. All at once, numerous rattles went off. I resisted clapping my hands over my ears to dampen the deafening sound while the rattles reverberated all around me. More dirt and rocks fell from the ceiling; they pelted my shoulders and legs as I continued to crab crawl toward... something.

My back hit a wall, and I slid up it as I finally succeeded in inhaling completely again. My hand fell to the gun hanging at my waist. My fingers closed around the handle and froze. I didn't dare pull it free and start firing when I had no idea where Corson was. I couldn't take the risk of injuring him. The bullets wouldn't kill him, but they would slow him down when he needed his speed most. However, I couldn't stand here and do *nothing*.

Flesh split open with a wet tearing sound I'd heard more than a few times in my life. Demons had a way of ripping people to shreds before tossing them aside as if they were no more than the dolls I'd flung aside as a child. The coppery tang of blood permeated the air. Something or someone had been sliced open. I wanted to scream, not with fear, but with frustration as numerous rattles went off.

Is Corson okay?

My blood thundered through my ears at the possibility it was his blood I smelled and that the ouro could be gulping down bits and pieces of him right now. I opened my mouth to call out to him, but I didn't dare risk distracting him or revealing my location to the ouro. The snake didn't seem to have as much of a problem navigating this dark underworld as we did, but right now I didn't think it knew where I was. That small element of surprise was all Corson and I had going for us right now.

Don't snakes hunt by heat sensors or something? I didn't remember where I'd heard that before, probably from Randy, but it would make sense if this thing had pursued us with such ease. That also meant there would be no surprise and this thing already knew where I stood.

The rattles abruptly stopped, and then a loud crash echoed through the tunnel. The ground heaved; the wall behind my back quaked. My stomach dropped when rocks and dirt plummeted from the ceiling at a far faster rate. The weight of the debris bore down on my toes as it crept toward my ankles.

I'm about to be buried alive!

All the hair on my arms rose as I waited for the battle to continue or for something more than the rubble to keep piling up around me. "Corson?" I dared to whisper when the debris reached my ankles.

I nearly shrieked when a hand fell on my shoulder. "It's okay," he murmured. "We have to get out of here."

"No shit," I retorted and immediately regretted being bitchy when he'd saved my life.

He chuckled, and his hand squeezed my shoulder. Before I could try to pull myself free from the rubble rising up my calves, he rested his hands on my hips to lift me. The dirt clutched at me, refusing to let go as Corson tugged at me.

The unsettling thought that it wasn't only the rising debris keeping me in place, but a hand had risen from the grave to drag me into Hell, hit me. I imagined the dead, gray skin of the hand flaking away as it tugged at me with inhuman strength, refusing to release me. The dead coming to life, and hands rising from graves wasn't impossible after everything else I'd seen and experienced over the years.

With a sucking noise, Corson finally succeeded in wrenching me from death's grip. He carried me through the hailstorm of rubble cascading over us and into what I assumed was another tunnel. This one was blessedly clear of a collapsing ceiling.

He set me down, and I stepped away from him to wipe the dirt from my hair and clothes. When I was done with that, I took a minute to stabilize my shaking hands. Slowly, above the muted noise of the collapsing tunnel, a dripping sound pierced my ringing ears.

"What happened?" I whispered when I felt stable enough to speak again.

"To escape me, the ouro punched a new hole into the ceiling of the tunnel."

I realized he'd moved and that I was facing away from him when he spoke. I turned toward his voice as his words settled in. That thing had fled *him*? I'd seen Corson kill, witnessed his ruthlessness, but now I knew I'd only glimpsed what he was truly capable of doing.

"Are you hurt?" I asked.

He'd moved closer so that his breath warmed my ear. My heartbeat escalated in response to his nearness. The memory of being held close to him earlier rippled across my mind. *What would it be like if he turned his head, so his lips touched my skin?*

"Nothing serious," he murmured. "Are you okay?"

I edged away to put some distance between us again. He was a demon, and sexual attraction or not, nothing could *ever* happen between us.

"Fine. What is that dripping noise?" I inquired when I heard a plop again.

"Ouroboros blood," Corson replied. "I'm pretty sure I eviscerated it while it was fleeing."

Sexy. I wasn't sure if the thought was as sarcastic as I'd meant it to be though, or if I did find it sexy. Corson was a warrior, and there was something unbelievably sexy about that, but eviscerated snakes weren't exactly a turn-on.

Then why am I still wondering what it would be like to feel his lips on me? Because my brain had bounced off my skull more than a few times when we'd tumbled into the ouro's trap, I decided. That *had* to be the reason.

"We should go," Corson said. "The ouro will take some time to heal, but it will come back for us, and it will be more vengeful when it does."

"Where are we?"

"I have no idea anymore."

CHAPTER NINE

CORSON

I assumed I'd be relieved to see light again. Instead, my steps slowed and my hand went out to stop Wren when she strode forward as if she were going to stalk straight into the light and announce her presence. She shot me an irritated look and went to shove my arm down. Leaning over her, I sank my talons into the wall on the other side of her to plant my arm before her.

The green flecks in her eyes shot fire at me. I didn't doubt she'd happily slice my arm off if she could have. Her breasts rose and fell with her breaths, bringing them into contact with my forearm. Despite her torn, soiled shirt and the dirt streaking her cheeks and forehead, she was still undeniably enticing.

My eyes fell briefly to her pursed lips before rising to meet her gaze again. "We have no idea what is up there."

"I know that, demon."

My teeth ground together. "My name is Corson," I grated. "And I suggest using it since I just saved your fucking life."

Her mouth dropped. Before she could reply, I tore my talons from the wall and stepped away from her. I didn't look back as I proceeded cautiously down the widening tunnel toward the orange glow ahead. I had no idea what was causing the light, or why it would be in the convoluted maze the ouro had burrowed through the dirt.

Ten feet away from the end of the passageway, I crouched until my ass brushed against the heels of my boots. I studied the glow illuminating the earthen walls of what appeared to be a large cavern before us. Craning my head, I couldn't see past the tunnel enough to discover the top or bottom of the cavern. When I sniffed at the air, I inhaled the damp odor of the earth, the woodsy scent of Wren, and the musky aroma of sex.

My brow furrowed at the final scent. I rested my fingers on the ground, as the distant sounds of flesh slapping against flesh reached me. I had no idea what was going on, but though sex was usually harmless enough, my instincts disagreed.

Wren knelt at my side as a laugh floated up from below and someone released an erotic moan. Neither things sounded menacing, but whatever lay ahead was intimidating enough to keep the ouro away, which meant it was something Wren shouldn't be anywhere near. She was stronger and more lethal than many humans, but whatever lay down there would destroy her.

I couldn't retreat from here without knowing what it was though.

"Stay here," I whispered to her.

She opened her mouth to protest before closing it again. I took that as a sign she would remain, but I doubted it. I'd have to get up there, see what lay below, and return to her before she could move any closer to it.

Creeping forward, I stayed low as I approached the end of the tunnel. I settled before the edge, rested my hand on the wall, and leaned forward to peer into the cavern below. My brow furrowed when I caught sight of the creatures gathered there.

At first, I didn't recognize what they were as I'd only seen them once before. At the time, they'd been floating by me while I ran out of Hell. Then, their striking faces were tilted back as they gazed toward the surface. Now, they lay on thick red pillows, laughing as they watched a young couple having sex on top of one of those pillows.

A female jinn prowled around the couple, smiling as she ran her hand between her breasts before cupping one of them. Color rose in her cheeks; ecstasy flooded her face as she slid her other hand between her legs. While the jinn pleasured herself in rhythm to the couple, tears streaked the woman's cheeks and the man's flushed face twisted in agony.

Sweat dripped from the man's forehead and onto the woman's breast. Blood soaked his back from where the woman's nails repeatedly raked his flesh. Then, the man threw his head back and cried out as if he were climaxing, but his hips kept plunging forward, and the woman kept clutching at him.

I didn't know what the couple had wished for, but I doubted it was anything close to this macabre act the jinn had twisted it into becoming. I suspected these two unfortunate humans would be screwing until they died.

Wren arrived at my side as I set my foot back to return to her. Any annoyance I felt over her taking a risk by coming closer vanished when her hand flew to her mouth. The fires the jinn had created with their powers danced over the cavern walls. The flames illuminated her sun-kissed skin and the revulsion in her blue eyes. She shouldn't be anywhere near this.

Grabbing her hand, I held it firmly in mine as I gave it a small tug and tiptoed back. Instead of trying to tear free of me, or telling me not to touch her, she held on as I maneuvered her away from the jinn.

"What was that?" she whispered when we were far enough away that her voice wouldn't carry back to them.

"Jinn, or genies as they're better known to humans," I explained.

She looked like I'd just socked her in the stomach as she glanced over her shoulder at the cavern. "Do they grant wishes?"

"Yes. The jinn usually aren't fighters, but they're manipulative, and the wishes they grant often turn into nightmares. They have a way of getting others to make wishes without realizing they're making them."

"Is that what's happening with the couple?" she inquired. "Is it a wish gone wrong?"

"Most likely."

"We have to help those people."

"They made their bed, and they're lying it in—in more ways than one. The two of us cannot take on a cavern full of jinn. Whatever you do, don't wish for *any*thing while we're in here. I have no experience dealing with the jinn, but I do know they aren't brought forth by rubbing a lamp."

Wren's breath sucked in, and whether she realized it or not, she moved closer to me. "Are you saying if we *think* a wish, they could come to us?"

"I don't know, but I'm not willing to take the chance."

"Neither am I," she murmured and glanced over her shoulder again.

I pulled her back, flattening her against the wall and pinning her there with my body as something shifted in the shadows before me. Wren's fingers rested on my arm; she leaned to the side to peer around me as the ouro emerged from a side tunnel fifty feet in front of us. The serpent cut across the chamber we stood in before entering another tunnel.

Wren stopped breathing when the ouro continued to slither endlessly onward. Its smaller tails rose to stand out from its sides and back, but they bent down again before they slid into the other tunnel. The extra tails seemed to help propel the ouro as it sped onward.

When none of the rattles went off, I realized the ouro didn't know we were here, or it didn't want to attract the attention of the jinn. Wren's hand tightened around my arm before going to the gun at her side.

I rested my hand on hers before she could pull it free. Not only would her gun not kill the ouro, but it would attract the jinn and alert the ouro to our presence if it didn't already know about it.

Wren glanced at me before her hand fell away. Looking over her shoulder, her eyes went between the ouro blocking our way and the jinn behind us. Then, the ouro's massive rattle at the end of its tail came into view before slipping away. The cloud of dust settling into place afterward was the only thing marking the ouro's passing.

"We have to go," I whispered and stepped away from Wren.

She followed me as we continued down the channel the ouro had crossed. All ability to see vanished once more as I turned into another tunnel. The serpent had bisected this tunnel and gone a different way, but it was only a matter of time before it tracked us down again.

CHAPTER TEN

WREN

Exhaustion was something I'd experienced hours ago. Now, I had no words to describe the bone-deep weariness encompassing me. Every step felt like I was wading through a swamp. Keeping my eyes open had become a losing battle, and I was certain I'd fallen asleep while walking a few times.

Once, the rumbling of my stomach had woken me, but I'd adjusted to my hunger pangs and the dryness of my throat. Food and drink were two things I was used to going without. I could go another day, possibly two if it remained cool in here, before dehydration really started to affect me.

I kept my hand on Corson's back, so I would know if something gulped him down. My other hand rested on the butt of my gun, but it slid off every time my head drooped forward. Stopping was death, but I'd love to be able to sit for a minute. I didn't dare wish for it. The idea of drawing the jinn to us was almost as frightening as the serpent stalking us through its lair.

The rancid stench of something worse than the ouro's breath hit me. I was slapped awake by the smell burning my nose. It caused my eyes to water and nearly sent me reeling away to vomit. The possibility of retching on Corson's boots was the only thing that kept me from throwing up.

"What is that?" I choked out as I pinched my nose in a useless attempt to block the odor.

"I think we've found where the ouro is stashing its regurgitated meals for later feeding."

I gulped as bile surged up my throat and my hunger vanished. "Is it ahead of us?" Or worse… "Are we standing in its saved food?"

The possibility had me gulping again and afraid to take another step. I'd seen countless atrocities over my life, but I'd never had the misfortune of standing in snake vomit.

"No. It's coming from a side tunnel. Come," Corson said and briefly touched my arm.

I fell into step behind him again, unwilling to release my nose until I believed it was safe to do so. My nerves had gone beyond the point of frayed, and I couldn't stop imagining we would simply walk into the ouro's mouth. If that happened, I'd slice the ouro's tongue off and fire holes into its throat as it gulped us down, but that wouldn't stop it from swallowing us like the whale swallowed Jonah.

Even with that horrible prospect in mind, my energy deflated again, and I found myself shuffling behind Corson instead of lifting my feet off the ground. I didn't know how far we'd traveled before my chin hit my chest and my head jerked up.

Blinking, I realized there was still nothing but darkness surrounding us. The firelight by the jinn had been so warm and inviting; those pillows a little bit of Heaven, but what looked so pleasurable at first glance, revealed itself as a nightmare upon closer inspection.

The suffering etched onto the woman's face was something I'd never forget, or the blood seeping down the man's back. My experience with sex had been far from earth-shattering, but it had been more pleasurable than *that*.

Sometimes I wondered if the circumstances of my life had left me frigid and unable to enjoy sex. A lot of the women Wilders gushed about sex, especially my friend Jolie, but I could take it or leave it.

I'd never revealed those thoughts to anyone. I knew it wasn't normal to feel that way, knew I'd be met with shocked expressions if I did tell someone that. Jolie would probably be determined to fix me and shove me at the first guy who walked by. She'd insist I try again, as if it were like learning to shoot and the more I did it, the better I'd get at it. Maybe that was true, but I had no interest in trying again.

Well, maybe I had some interest in trying again, I realized. Corson made me feel not so frigid, and whereas I'd decided sex wasn't necessary in my life, I found myself *craving* him as my hand slipped down his back.

When I realized I was licking my lips, I jerked my hand away from him and rubbed my eyes with my knuckles. Exhaustion and a concussion, that was what was wrong with me and why I had these bizarre imaginings about being with a demon.

My thoughts turned back to the jinn and the poor couple. Guilt tugged at me over leaving them behind, but dying to save two strangers who might not deserve saving was pure stupidity. I hadn't lived this long by being stupid.

"Why would they do that?"

"Do what?" Corson whispered, and I realized I'd spoken the question out loud.

I shook my head, then felt like an idiot when I realized he couldn't see me. "The jinn, to those people, why would they do that to them?"

"Like other demons, the jinn survive by feeding on suffering."

A shiver ran down my spine at the stark reminder of what he was and how he survived.

"The jinn feed on it more than others," Corson continued. "Most demons survive solely by feeding on wraiths, but other demons like the jinn and canagh require more."

"I see."

I smacked into his back before I realized he'd stopped before me. A tingle of awareness slid over my nerve endings when my hand brushed over his before I stepped away from him.

Does he infuriate me so much because I am so aware of him? I wondered. I'd noticed other men over the years, but none of them had riveted or unsettled me as much as Corson did.

"It is necessary for demons to feed on wraiths," he whispered. "It's part of the circle of life. Without it, *all* life would cease to exist."

"Really?" I asked, hating that I found myself intrigued.

Corson's sigh caused his breath to caress my cheek. There was a smoky hint to his breath that I found surprisingly pleasant. "For someone with so much hatred toward demons, you know nothing of us. Our existence is necessary for your survival."

"And humans are necessary for yours," I retorted. "Maybe I don't know all there is to know about demons, but I know that much. The demons who follow the king, such as you, wouldn't be fighting to preserve the human race if you didn't need us for your survival."

Demons may not be as atrocious as I'd believed all these years, but they weren't warm or loving either. They'd let us die without blinking an eye if they didn't need us for something. Some of them were friendly to humans, but most were completely indifferent, and others couldn't hide they found us as useless as a rudder on a duck's ass and as annoying as gnats.

Corson was probably the most social of all the demons, except for maybe the skelleins. And the odd little skellein demons were as happy drinking the beer they brewed as they were chopping off an enemy's head. Sometimes I believed they'd be as happy chopping off *any*one's head, enemy or not.

"Yes, humans are necessary for our survival," Corson replied. "And the demons who follow the king are known as palitons. Those who stand against him, the ones who followed Lucifer and are now either scrambling to find a new leader or already have found one, are known as craetons."

"Oh."

The softest footstep was the only sign I had that he'd started walking again. I hurried to catch up with him.

"Demons took everything from me." I crashed into his back when he stopped walking again. "Stop doing that!" I snapped as I stumbled away.

"*Humans* took everything away from you," he growled. "Your species was playing with things they never should have played with. Because of that, they opened a gateway into Hell, into *our* world. Their ignorance tore apart the intricate balance between Hell, Heaven, and Earth. A balance that took millions of years to form, yet they ruined it in an instant.

"What happened after Hell opened was a result of the human's actions. We worked hard to make everything right again by closing the gateway, but it was too late. There is no undoing what was done. I don't think we ever could have fixed the destruction the humans wrought, not even if we closed the gateway seconds after it opened."

He was right; I knew that now, but... "It was *demons* who tore my mom limb from limb while I watched," I spat at him. "Not humans."

When he rested his hand on my arm, I moved it away from him. I couldn't deal with any sympathy from anyone while the familiar rage and sorrow over that memory swelled in my chest. Screams resonated in my head, and tears burned my eyes as the lump in my throat choked me. For the first time in years, the memory of her face, her fervent words to me on that day, and her love for me broke free to swirl through my mind.

Afraid the grief would bury me, I shoved the memories aside and focused on the now.

"Yes, humans screwed up big time," I whispered, "but they weren't the ones laughing as they poured my mother's blood all over them and down their throats."

"I'm sorry, Wren. You shouldn't have had to experience that. No one should."

I was glad I couldn't see his face, because if I'd seen pity in his eyes, I would have punched him in the nose. I didn't know why I'd told him about that day in the first place. What did he care what had happened to my mother, or anything about my life? Why had I revealed to him something I'd only ever told Randy before?

I certainly didn't trust him as much as I trusted Randy. I also loved Randy; I barely tolerated Corson.

Liar! There was that stupid little inner voice again, and I hated it!

It's the dark and the possible concussion, I decided. *That's why I revealed that to him.*

I couldn't see him; he almost wasn't real if I couldn't see him. Plus, these could be the last moments of our lives. Of course, I was thinking about my mother more now when I'd spent years trying to forget her and that day. I'd watched her die, and my death could be unfolding in these tunnels. For all I knew, my next breath might be my last.

And after what I'd seen yesterday—or at least I thought it was yesterday, I had no idea how much time had passed since we'd fallen into the ouro's trap—it only made sense the memories of my past would be closer to the surface than they'd been in years.

CHAPTER ELEVEN

WREN

Corson pulled me from my reverie when he stepped so close his chest brushed against my arm. "Not all demons are like that. Some—"

"We should probably stop talking now." I couldn't stand to hear him making excuses for the monsters who had brutalized my mother. "That *thing* will hear us."

"We're not all like that," he said again. His warmth against my side vanished when he turned away from me.

And what are you *like*? I almost asked him, but I clamped my mouth shut against the question. I didn't want to know what he was like, or anything more about him than necessary. So why did I suddenly feel so alone? Why did his lack of warmth leave me feeling like that eight-year-old child watching her mother die all over again?

This time I heard his footfalls stop before I walked into him. I didn't hear him turn, but his hands fell onto my arms and then slid up to my shoulders. I tried to shrug him off, but the gesture came out feeble, and even I recognized it as half-hearted.

"How old were you when your mother died?" he asked in a raspy voice.

"What difference does that make?" This time my attempt to shrug him off was stronger, but he still didn't let go.

"I'm trying to get to know you better."

"Why?" I asked distrustfully. I would give anything to see his eyes, to try to read what he was thinking, but the dark wouldn't yield its secrets.

His thumb stroking my cheek caused a strange flutter in my belly. Was this what people meant when they said they had butterflies in their stomach? It had to be, and these weren't small butterflies; no, these were behemoths flapping against my insides. My mind screamed at me to get away from him, but my head turned until his thumb brushed over my lips.

My heart beat so fast I believed it might explode out of my chest. Corson moved closer until I could feel him standing over me as he touched me with a reverence I wouldn't have expected from him. With tender hands, he lifted my face, and his thumb stilled on my lips.

I felt the increase of his breathing against my chest, and I realized my breath had fallen into rhythm with his. He pulled my lip down a little, and before I could register the thought, my traitorous tongue slid out to lick his thumb.

I quickly regained control of my insanity and stopped, but the salty taste of his flesh lingered on my tongue, and I wanted more of it. *Why does he have to taste so good?* I wondered as my head spun and a sound of pleasure rumbled from him.

Step away! But I remained unmoving as his thumb caressed my lips again.

It's only because of the dark, only because this could be the end that you're allowing this!

My mind screamed this at me, but I knew it was more. Corson had intrigued me since we'd first met. The dark and possibly impending death made me more willing to let some of my curiosity be satisfied, but they were not the only reasons why I was allowing this to continue.

Would he kiss me?

If he tried to kiss me, I'd knee his nuts into his stomach.

Liar!

Damn inner voice! But it was right, and I found myself unable to breathe as I waited to see what he would do next.

He drew me closer until his breath tickled my mouth. I barely felt the feathery touch of his lips as they moved over mine, but they sent prickles of awareness throughout my body. He was barely kissing me, yet I felt it all the way to the tips of my toes, and I wanted more.

Then, he stopped. The fullness of his bottom lip and the stiffness of his upper one pressed against mine as he remained unmoving.

I almost mewled a protest over this unbearable teasing, but I managed to keep it back so I could at least maintain some semblance of dignity. Was he playing with me? Why was he not—

I never had a chance to finish that question before Corson spun away from me. His arm swung up against my chest, and a hiss sounded. The hair on my nape rose as I realized what the dark hid. Something splattered over the rocks, but whether it was ouro blood or Corson's, I didn't know. The weight of Corson's body was ripped away from me. Something thudded, and Corson grunted as rocks clattered against each other.

Pulling my gun free of its holster, I aimed it before me. Corson wasn't directly in front of me anymore, that was all I knew as I fired and prayed I didn't hit him with any of the bullets. The deafening reverberations caused my ears to ring as I kept pulling the trigger.

We'd brought a lot of ammunition with us when we'd left the wall, but after years of skimping on bullets, it felt reckless to fire so many now when I had no idea if I would hit anything, but shoot them I did. Most Wilders knew how to make bullets, but wasting necessities wasn't something we ever did.

I'd do whatever it took to help Corson though and put an end to this monstrosity stalking us. Flashes lit the tunnel every time I pulled the trigger, and I found myself preferring the dark as each shot briefly illuminated the ouro I'd seen by the jinn.

Dirt and rocks crunched under my boots as I shuffled rapidly from side to side. I kept firing so the creature wouldn't know for sure where I was, though it wouldn't be difficult to locate me in this tunnel.

Each flash from the gun revealed something new about the snake. All the numerous tails curving out of the ouro were bent over and pointing toward me when their rattles went off. Its forked tongue flicked in the air, missing my hands by only centimeters as a bullet embedded in its flesh. Black, beady eyes met mine in the next flash. There was no soul behind those eyes; there was nothing but insatiable hunger.

On the next flash, Corson leapt from the shadows.

Flash.... Corson clung to the monstrous creature.

Flash.... His talons were buried straight through the snake's head.

Flash.... Pulling backward, Corson tore a line down the center of the ouro.

My stomach turned. My gun clicked as I continued to squeeze the trigger a few more times before registering that the weapon was empty. I shoved it back into my holster and pulled my knife free from where it hung on my hip. No matter what happened, I'd make the ouro regret swallowing me every inch of my way down its vast throat.

I gripped the knife, holding it steady in preparation for an attack. I no longer experienced nervousness or doubt when it came to fighting. There was no room for either, and I'd taken on so many demons over the years that fighting was as normal to me as eating. Once, years ago, I'd questioned what that said about me and who I was becoming, but those questions had long since ceased.

I barely remembered the girl I'd been before the gateway opened, and it often felt like she was an entirely different person. I knew she'd enjoyed apples and baking cakes, pies, and cookies. She'd loved dolls and dresses. Her favorite dress had been black with a fluffy skirt and red apples all over it. She'd twirled in it for her parents, who had laughed and clapped over her antics.

I wouldn't be caught dead in a dress now, I had zero use for dolls, and the extent of my baking was sticking an animal on a spit to roast it. That girl wouldn't have survived a week in the Wilds. I had survived fourteen years.

I strained to hear anything over the incessant ringing in my ears. Something screeched against the rocks, Corson grunted again, and the creature released a hissing scream that caused my ear ringing to ratchet up a notch. I tried to follow the sounds of the fight while I hunted the ouro with my knife at the ready.

Then something hit me with the weight of a door bashing against my whole body. Flung back, my breath exploded out of me when I smashed into a wall. Rocks and dirt fell around me; my teeth knocked together so violently I was certain they'd shattered, but I managed to keep my knife.

Revulsion swept me when one of the rattles on a smaller tail ran over my face. Another tail slithered up and down my arm while the tip of another ran over my outer thigh. I thrust my knife into the ouro. The blade caught in the thick snakeskin before giving way beneath the weight of my body.

The skin felt a foot thick, too thick for my blade to get too far into the ouro, but it had to have hurt the serpent as one of the tails started thumping the side of my face. A rattle beat on my head and another one hit my arm with enough force to bruise the bone.

"Son of a bitch!" I gasped and tore my knife free.

I swung the knife at one of the tails and embedded it in the bottom of it. As I sawed back and forth, more rattles went off and beat me. I didn't stop, not until I succeeded in severing the tail.

Hot liquid gushed over my face. I recoiled from the blood pumping forth as another tail bashed into my arm and the ouro thrashed to the side. I didn't know if I was the one causing the ouro to writhe in pain, if it was Corson, or if it was a combination of the two of us. Either way, I wasn't about to stop slicing it apart.

My palms slipped on the handle of the knife as I gripped it in both hands, lifted it over my head, and drove it down. The snake hissed, and another tail pummeled my head.

CHAPTER TWELVE

CORSON

My talons slid over the back of the ouro as I felt it throw its head up. Something crashed and I guessed the sound was that of the ouro driving its nose into the ceiling when debris rained down on me. Stones pelted my skin with so much force that some of them broke in half before tumbling away. I held onto the creature, refusing to let it flee from me again. It would only continue to stalk us if it escaped now, waiting for us to become too exhausted to fight.

The hoods on the sides of the ouroboros's head opened with a swish before they battered back against my chest. Not being able to see the thing was infuriating, but I felt my way over it as I worked to destroy it.

Wren's gun fired in brief flashes that revealed where she was as she dashed around the tunnel. The bullets hit the ouro with a thud; the creature hissed and lunged forward as I dug deeper into it. I sliced it from the top of its head, down its neck.

Wren's shots ceased. The ouro flung up the back half of its body, bashing it off the ceiling. My head bounced off the rocks above me, and a chunk of my hair tore out as the ouro tried to batter me off it. I ducked before the serpent could smash my brains out and slid to the side.

My talons sliced across the ouro's neck and throat as I swung down. The ouro reared back; more debris fell when it rose again to attempt burrowing its way out of there. When it failed to knock me free, its head twisted in such a way that I knew it was trying to sink its poisonous fangs into me.

Wren groaned, and rock shattered. Renewed fury surged through me. I'd tear this thing apart piece by piece; I'd make it pay in the most excruciating ways possible for harming her. The scent of the ouro's blood filled my nostrils, fueling my bloodlust.

I pulled my other hand back and drove my talons into its throat. The ouro released a choking sound that did nothing to ease my wrath over whatever it had done to Wren. As I worked to destroy the ouro, I strained to hear anything from Wren, but I didn't perceive any sounds from her.

She has to be alive; she has to be!

I bared my teeth at the possibility she wasn't and pulled my hand back again. I swung my fist forward to batter the ouro with my talons. I was determined to end this so I could get to her. I *had* to touch her again and know she was okay.

I pummeled the ouro until I tore away enough flesh to maneuver into its throat and grasp its tongue. When I yanked the ouro's tongue backward, the snake recoiled as I tore its tongue out and sliced it off. The ouro released a strange screaming hiss before its body exploded with movement and it reared upward again.

The deafening cacophony of rattles bounced off the tunnel walls. The ouro tried to thrash me off but only succeeded in raining down more rubble on us. I scrambled up the side of the snake, my talons digging through scales and corded muscle as I worked myself around its back and down to its throat. It continued to twist in attempt to sink its fangs into me or knock me off as it rose up, but it couldn't shake me off.

Sliding back down the other side of it, I worked around in a circle that cut deeper and deeper into the ouro. I clung to the snake as it surged upward again. The ouro hit the ceiling with a hard thud. More debris rained down as the ouro made another attempt to break further through the earth overhead, but beneath me its movements had become sluggish as I continued to slice at it.

Its flesh gave way with a wet tearing sound before its head tipped forward at an unnatural angle. I scrambled to get out of the way before it could pin me against its chest when its head drooped forward, and all the rattles ceased. I hacked my way through the remaining sinew of the ouro's neck until its head hit the ground with a thump.

Still holding onto its headless neck, I felt the body hurl upward once more before becoming rigid against me. The ouro's neck remained in the air for a second then it went limp. I rode the ouro to the ground where it flopped up once more before going still. Kneeling on the ouro, I strained to hear anything from Wren, but the tunnel had become quiet once more.

"Wren?" I demanded, my heart thudding as I waited for a reply.

My shoulders heaved as I retracted my talons to run a hand through my blood-soaked hair before leaping to my feet. Blood adhered my shirt to my chest and dripped down my flesh as it fell from my hands. I had no idea what I would do if she didn't respond to me, but I did know anything that got in my way after this would regret it.

"Wren!" I whispered. "Where are you?"

Silence met my question.

WREN

The small tails beating against my arms stood up straight against my sides. All the rattles went off at once before ceasing abruptly and going limp as the snake sagged. The heavy weight of the ouro pinned me to the wall.

I didn't know what had happened, but I remained unmoving as I waited for the tails to renew their attack on me.

"Wren!" I heard a note of panic in Corson's voice from somewhere in the tunnel.

Panicked for me? I refused to acknowledge the little thrill of happiness that came with the question.

"Wren, where are you?" he demanded.

"He…"

I spit away the ouro blood I hadn't realized was on my lips. Lifting my arm, I ran it across my mouth to wipe the blood away. I only succeeded in smearing more of it over my face as ouro goo also splattered my forearm. Fine, whatever, snake blood in the mouth was not the worst thing to ever happen to me.

"Here," I said and cringed at the acrid taste filling my mouth.

"Are you okay?" His voice was closer than it had been.

"Peachy keen," I muttered and shoved uselessly against the dead weight holding me prisoner.

My hands stilled on the snake. That phrase had been something my mother used to say to me. Never before had I uttered those words, but they'd just fallen from my lips with ease.

No, my mother hadn't said that. She'd said something different, or something *more*. My mind spun as I tried to recall what that more had been. Past and present lurched together disconcertingly. I never delved into the past, never tried to remember, but now I felt memories sliding forth to take over my mind. The scent of baking cookies rose up to replace the stench of ouro death.

Peachy keen, jellybean! That's what she'd said to me!

The words floating across my mind held the faintest hint of her Scottish accent. She'd come to the U.S. as a child, and had lost most of her accent over the years, but occasionally Scottish undertones would slip back into her speech. She'd always been laughing as she'd uttered that saying to me, and I could hear her laughter once more. It had been so long since I'd recalled those words and her laugh, but now they reverberated in my head.

My mother hadn't just laughed; she'd *embraced* the laugh. I'd never heard anyone laugh like her. Whenever she laughed, people smiled, and I had smiled too. It used to make me happy just to be in the presence of someone who embraced life with the open abandon my mother had.

I tried to shut the door on the memory, but it remained stubbornly open to let more memories spill free.

No! The word blasted angrily across my mind. I didn't have the time to deal with the past while this snake trapped me! I pushed against the unbudging ouro. I tried to pry my feet from under it, but they remained stuck.

No matter how I struggled to rid myself of the snake and my mother's laugh, they both refused to let me go. I'd barely spared my mom more than a second's thought in years, but now it was as if her death had occurred only yesterday. The scabs on my heart peeled away, leaving me raw.

It took another minute, but I finally succeeded in tucking my mother right back into the box I kept her in, and I pried my feet out from under the ouroboros. Propping one hand against the wall and the other on the ouro's supple scales, I lifted myself up. My shaking arms gave way, and I slumped against the wall with my legs sprawled out across the snake.

I couldn't stop myself from smiling when I realized I finally had a chance to sit.

A crunch sounded in front of me. I lashed out with my foot and came up against something solid.

"Dammit, Wren," Corson hissed, and I realized I'd kicked him in the shin.

"Sorry," I muttered. "Next time warn a person."

"Yes, let me do that and give away my location."

"Do you think there's still something in here with us?" I frantically looked around at nothing.

"I'm not taking any chances, and the jinn most likely heard your gunfire. We have to get away from here. Are you injured?"

"No. Are you?"

"My wounds are already healing."

"Oh, yeah."

Not only were demons stronger, faster, and immortal, with enhanced senses, they could also regenerate their body parts, heal with incredible speed, and didn't get diseases or even catch a cold. The only thing that killed them was decapitation. It hadn't taken us long to figure that out in the Wilds, and we'd adapted to aim for the head on all our enemies.

"Is it really dead?" I asked.

"Yes."

"Are you sure?"

"We can carry its head out as a trophy if you'd like?"

"I don't have a wall to hang it on, so I'm perfectly fine with leaving it behind."

He chuckled, and his hand touched my arm. "That's what I figured. Let me help you up."

"I don't need help."

His hand fell away. "Of course you don't."

Was that a note of sadness in his voice? That couldn't be possible. He enjoyed flirting with me, and he would take me to his bed if I agreed to it, but he didn't care about anything else when it came to me. Then I recalled his lips against mine, the brief taste of his skin on my tongue. The remembrance of it was sharp enough to shove aside the sour taste of ouro blood lingering in my mouth.

I pulled my hand away when I realized I'd lifted it to my lips. Yes, we'd kind of kissed, but what difference did that make? He'd probably kissed thousands of women in however many years he'd been alive, and I'd kissed men before. But none of those men made my heart race, my palms sweat, and my stomach flutter like Corson did.

Ugh, it didn't matter. All that mattered was leaving before any more crappy things could arrive to try killing us. Bracing my hand against the wall, I pushed myself up. "How do we get out of here?" I whispered.

"I have no idea," Corson replied.

My heart sank. "We're lost?"

"Unless you can recall how to get out?"

I shook my head and then almost stomped my foot in frustration when I recalled he couldn't see me.

"No, I can't." I hated that the words came out as a croak, but as bad as being hunted by the ouro was, realizing we had no idea how to get out of this maze it created was worse. "Are there any more of these things?"

"No."

"Being lost in here is at the top of my shit list, but at least we can check one seal creature off the list."

"That we can," Corson agreed. "Now let's go before the jinn arrive."

This time I did stomp my foot on the snake when I nodded my agreement instead of speaking it. "Yeah, let's go." I shuffled down the curve of the ouro's body and into the tunnels once more.

CHAPTER THIRTEEN

CORSON

Wren and I didn't speak as we traveled deeper into the labyrinth. I didn't know if we were going in a new direction, heading back the way we'd come, or wandering in endless circles. Without light, there was no way to mark where we'd been or to detect any significant difference from one tunnel to the next.

When the rockier walls became mostly dirt once more, I thought we were making our way back up and possibly out, but the soil had given way to rock again after a hundred or so feet. The air felt and smelled the same no matter where we went, stale and earthy. Some tunnels had a breeze in them, and those were the ones I turned into with the hope an exit had created the breeze, but they never offered a way out.

Now we were in what I assumed was a small cave system due to the solid stone walls and the trickle of water drawing me onward. I ran my hand over the walls until my fingertips dipped into cool water. Wren's arm brushed mine as her fingers fumbled over the wall too.

"Here," I said and took her hand to guide it into the water. "Drink some."

"I don't dare," she whispered. "Not when we don't know the source, and I can't boil it."

"You have to be thirsty."

"And I can remain thirsty for another day or two. That water could kill me before then. I've gone longer without water before, believe me, and at least it's cool in here, so I'm not sweating. I do want to wash some snake gunk off me though."

I listened to water splashing as she tried to clean herself in the thin stream while I struggled to control my impulse to grab her and hug her against me. She was so frail, so mortal. This water was something so simple, something I had no concern for at all, yet it was life to her, and there was nothing I could do to give her what she needed.

"You next," she whispered and I heard her step away from the wall.

I cupped my hands and let the water fill them before splashing it over my face and hair. I washed myself the best I could before moving away. "I'll get you out of here," I promised her.

"Not if we keep standing here," she retorted, but her tone held none of her usual defensiveness against me, and I heard the exhaustion in her voice.

I touched her arm, drawing her after me as I turned to wind my way through the maze once more. I wanted to return to the ouro and tear it apart some more for trapping us in this place, but I'd never be able to find my way back to it.

Wren stumbled behind me, and her hand hit me in the back. I turned and caught her before she fell to the ground. Drawing her closer, I closed my eyes as I recalled my lips brushing over hers. She'd been about to let me kiss her, something I'd never thought she would allow, but she hadn't pulled away.

I'd been so close to tasting more of her when I'd sensed the ouro slithering toward us. If my instincts hadn't alerted me in time, we'd both be dead right now. She was a giant distraction in this place, but I found myself wondering if she would let me taste her again now.

Then, her legs wobbled with exhaustion. Protective instincts I hadn't known I possessed rushed to the forefront. She'd never admit it, but she needed to rest.

"We'll stop here for a bit," I said.

"We have to…" I heard her gulp. "We have to get out of here."

"We're not going to escape if you can't walk."

"I can walk!" Though I couldn't see it, I knew her chin had shot up.

"You are an obstinate creature."

"I'm not a creature; I'm a human being. You're a creature."

I would have laughed if her stubbornness hadn't been so infuriating. "I'm an adhene demon. Not a creature."

I was waiting for her wise-ass reply when she pulled herself out of my arms. "What is an adhene demon?"

"To the human world, the closest equivalent might be your elves. Adhenes aren't magical or anything like that, but your elf legends are probably based on us. Adhenes are fast, powerful, and known to be mischievous."

I almost jumped away from her when her fingers brushed over the tip of my right ear. At first, I half-expected her to cut it off until she caressed it. Unable to stop it from happening, I hardened instantly against my zipper. If she had any idea how sensitive my ears were to stimulation and what she was doing to me, she would pull away.

Unable to resist, I stepped closer until her chest pressed against mine, but I was careful to keep my waist away from her. Her breasts were the perfect size to fill my hands. I should know, I'd often fantasized about touching and tasting them since meeting her.

"Adhene demons are rare," I murmured as I tilted my head into her stroking fingers and closed my eyes. "I've been the last purebred adhene in existence since my parents died, but the few demons who also possessed adhene blood were killed during the final battle with Lucifer."

"I see," she said, and her hand fell away from my ear. "It must be lonely for you."

I restrained myself from seizing her hand and returning it to me. For the first time, I was grateful for the dark so she couldn't see when I adjusted my erection. "I've become used to it," I told her, though I didn't like to dwell on the knowledge I was the last of my kind and that *no* other purebred adhenes would exist after me.

"So you believe the elf legend to be based on you because of your ears, and I'm assuming your build. I remember elves are supposed to be tall and lean," she said.

"Yes."

"I don't remember any elves with talons sprouting from the backs of their hands."

"It's not like humans saw everything through the veils once separating our worlds, and most of what they did see they jumbled up, or the passing of years twisted their tales into something entirely different."

"What are the veils?" she asked.

"Some humans were able to glimpse into Hell and Heaven through the veils separating our worlds. It's how many human myths were born and how some people knew about the existence of demons and angels. Some people glimpsed things in Hell and Heaven and revealed what they saw to other people. Other humans encountered demons and angels when they were allowed to walk the Earth. From werewolves to vampires to leprechauns, many demons are the basis of your legends. I am the closest thing to an elf you will find in the demon world."

"What about Magnus? I could also see him as an elf, especially since he does have magic of a sort."

I thought of Magnus, the last demon of illusions, and his ability to weave things out of thin air. I didn't like the idea of humans twisting Magnus and me into the same legend, but with his magical abilities, lean build, and ice-blond hair, I couldn't deny that it might be true.

"He has horns instead of pointed ears, but yes, Magnus or one of his ancestors could also fit into the elf legends," I agreed.

"Interesting," she murmured.

"Didn't you learn anything about us at the wall?" I asked her.

"I never thought to ask about these kind of things," she admitted.

"Why not?"

"Because I knew most of what I needed to know about demons."

"How to kill us," I said flatly.

"Yes."

I didn't know why her confirmation aggravated me; I knew what Wren was and that she'd only agreed to work with us to save the other Wilders. "With the way you think about demons, you must be expecting me to leave you here to die."

"No, I'm not. You would have let me fall into the ouro's hole by myself if you'd planned to let me die."

At least she gave me that much credit.

"Besides, worse things than you have tried to kill me and failed," she stated.

"And one day they might succeed." I had to work to keep my talons restrained over the idea of her dying.

"Most likely," she replied with a yawn. "But I never expected to live this long to begin with."

"This long? How old are you, twenty-five?"

"Twenty-two, but some days I feel like I'm a hundred. How old are you?"

"A great deal older. I'm thirteen hundred years old."

She snorted before coughing. "Did you say *thirteen hundred*?"

"I did."

"Impressive. I didn't think I'd make it to thirteen. I sure didn't expect to turn twenty, and I doubt I'll see thirty, but *thirteen hundred!* I can't imagine living so many years. Most days, I can barely imagine the next hour, never mind tomorrow."

Her words stirred sympathy within me, something I didn't have much of, and I rarely had it for humans. When it came to Wren though, I only wanted her to be safe and know peace. However, I wasn't sure Wren could ever know peace, not in these Wilds and not when she would do everything she could to keep the Wilders with her safe.

I didn't know what she'd endured in her lifetime or what she'd done to survive it. In many ways, her life had been as brutal as mine, maybe more so, and it had probably been more brutal than most if not all of the civvies. Even now, with escapees from Hell roaming more freely across the planet than they ever had before, the wall and towns beyond it, were still safer than the Wilds.

Wren yawned again.

"This is a good place to rest. Get some sleep, and I'll keep watch," I told her.

"There's nothing to watch and what about the jinn? Are we far enough away from them?"

"I don't know, but I'll stay awake and alert for anything coming."

"Okay."

I heard the scratch of something sliding down the rocks. When Wren spoke again, her voice came from lower than before.

"Corson?" she murmured.

She was so tired that she'd said my name. I didn't point that out to her as I slid down the wall to sit beside her; it would only shut her down if I did. "Yes?"

"How many seals were there?"

"Two hundred three."

"Shit," she whispered. "And there was something different behind each of them?"

"Yes. The jinn were behind the ninetieth seal and the ouroboros behind the eighty-second."

"And you're sure *all* the seals fell?"

"I am, but not everything behind the seals broke free of Hell.

Some were killed before they could reach Earth, and others were trapped in Hell when the gateway closed again."

"At least there's a bright side," she murmured.

"There is."

Her soft breaths filled the air, and I realized she'd fallen asleep sitting up. After a few minutes, she slumped toward me and her head dropped to my shoulder. A strange sense of tranquility settled over me as her body warmed mine while I listened for something stalking us through the tunnels. I'd cut them to pieces before they got anywhere near her.

CHAPTER FOURTEEN

WREN

"Here you go, my bonnie girl."

I clasped the silver spoon my mother extended to me. Some of the batter was sliding to the side and threatening to fall off, but I licked it away before any of the precious dough could plop onto the floor. My feet thudded against the cabinet under me as I swung them back and forth while sitting on the counter.

Twisting the spoon, I rotated it to get more batter as some slipped down to settle on my fingers. I'd save that for after I cleaned off the spoon. My mother scooped out little balls of dough from the glass bowl before her and plopped them onto the cookie sheet.

Three years ago, we'd started the tradition of baking cookies once a week when my dad had started working Saturdays in the summer. We'd decided it would be our special way to make his weekend better.

When my dad came home from work, he'd kick off his shoes and inhale whatever new concoction my mom and I had whipped up for him. He would then call for his lasses. His Scottish accent had faded over his years in the States, but it was still noticeable. It was most noticeable when he said lass, which always made me giggle.

When I heard him arrive, I'd leap off the counter and run eagerly into his open arms, while my mom patiently waited her turn to kiss him. Tugging on my father's red beard was the way I greeted him every time we were reunited, and he would swing me around until both of us became dizzy and couldn't breathe from laughing. I couldn't wait for him to come home today as we were baking his favorite cookies.

Though both my parents had come from Scotland as children, they hadn't met each other until they were in their twenties. Both of them had gone to the same college in Kansas and happened to meet at a coffee shop. My mother had accidentally dumped her ice coffee in my father's lap.

My mom once confided in me that it hadn't been an accident. When she'd heard him talking with his friends, her curiosity was piqued, and she'd been determined to talk to him. Due to her shyness, she hadn't known how to approach him and had thought her ice coffee would be a good way to break the ice. My father later confided in me that it hadn't been an accident and he'd been so intrigued by her that he'd accidentally tripped her. Cold, wet clothes had been a small price to pay for love, he'd declared.

The way they told it, they'd been inseparable ever since, and I often asked them to tell me their story while they were tucking me into bed at night.

I licked the spoon again as, through the open window behind me, the birds' songs floated on the hot July air. Usually, we made the cookies earlier in the day before it became this hot out, but we'd had to go to the store for more ingredients before baking today. The heat of the oven would make the kitchen unbearable soon, but it was worth it for my dad to have his oatmeal cookies.

I was almost done licking the spoon when a strange *whoosh* went through the air. I had no idea what had caused it, but it blew the hair back from my face and silenced the day. My tongue froze on the spoon; I didn't move as I tried to figure out if what I'd experienced was real. It had looked like the whoosh created a blast of air across the room like ripples spreading out from a stone tossed into a lake.

Maybe I'd imagined the ripple of air, but my hair *had* blown back. I glanced behind me at the open window. I hadn't felt a breeze coming through it before, and I didn't feel one now. Plus, the rush of air had blown my hair *back* not forward.

My tongue remained stuck to the spoon as I turned toward my mom. She'd frozen with her finger in the middle of scooping cookie dough onto the sheet. Gravity took over, and the ball fell with a wet plop onto the sheet. The sudden intrusion of sound caused me to jump.

My tongue returned to my mouth, and I slowly lowered the spoon as my mom lifted her head and her eyes met mine. Was that fear I saw there? My mom wasn't afraid of anything!

I was struck with the overwhelming urge to cry as I gazed at her blue eyes, so similar in hue to mine. However, I'd turned eight last month, which meant I didn't cry anymore. I certainly didn't cry because I'd imagined seeing a ripple of air and it had suddenly become very quiet outside. That was something seven-year-olds did, and only because they were babies.

I resolved not to cry, but I squeaked when a bunch of car alarms went off at the same time and the high-pitched noise pierced the air. The spoon clattered onto the counter when I dropped it to clap my hands over my ears. My mother wiped her hands on her apron before gathering me into her arms.

I was small for my age, but I'd stopped letting her carry me two years ago. Now, I was happy to let her lift me off the counter as car horns and alarms continued to blare. I lowered my hands from my ears and hugged her. When the neighborhood dogs all released an eerie howl, my arms tightened around her neck.

"It's okay, my bonnie girl," she whispered, but her voice trembled before she kissed my temple.

Leaving the kitchen behind, she walked into the living room and toward the front door. Shifting her hold on me, she gripped the knob, twisted it, and stepped onto the porch. It was my porch with its peeling white paint, familiar red door, and drooping potted plants hanging from the beams. However, I felt as if we'd stepped into another world as dogs howled, horns honked, and people shouted to be heard over the cacophony.

My eyes went to the sky and the hundreds of birds rising from the trees. Their multicolored feathers would have been beautiful if there were a couple dozen of them, but now their colors blended until it became a rainbow of death spreading over us to block out the sky as they soared higher. Shade spread across the ground as the sun vanished behind their bodies, and it seemed as if it were closer to dusk than early afternoon.

The birds didn't caw or shriek; they simply flew higher and higher. I couldn't rid myself of the feeling that they knew something was coming and were fleeing from it. I wished for wings to take my mom and me away too, but that wish went unanswered as we remained standing on our sagging porch. Despite the summer day, a shiver ran down my spine and the hair on my arms rose. My mom choked when I hugged her tighter.

"Easy," she said and tugged at my arms until I loosened my grasp.

My gaze scanned the nearby homes as people emerged to see what was happening. Most of them appeared as confused as I felt. Some of them had their keys pointed at their cars, and some of the alarms shut off. The noise lessened, but my ears still throbbed.

A lot of the adults had gone to work for the day, but most of those who remained had children standing by their sides. As I watched, a pack of teenagers slid from the woods across the street and crept closer to my neighbor's porch.

Then, all the blaring car alarms abruptly ceased. The sudden hush of the world frightened me more than all the noise had. Tears welled in my eyes. I had no idea why I was crying, but they spilled out of my eyes and soaked my cheeks before I could stop them.

"Mommy," I whispered as a few more people emerged from their homes.

"It's okay," she murmured as she rubbed my back. "A small earthquake probably set off the alarms and stirred up the birds."

I'd never experienced an earthquake like it before, and I'd *never* seen the birds act so crazy, but I didn't argue with her. I wanted her to be right too much to argue. I almost stuck my thumb in my mouth, something I hadn't done in years, but I'd have to let her go, and I refused to do so.

You're a baby. Sniffling, I stifled my sobs.

My mom shifted her hold on me, her arms drooped and I knew she was going to set me down before she did. When my feet hit the porch, I stepped into her side and pressed as close as I could.

"What happened?" the elderly neighbor across the way called out. He leaned heavily on his cane as the teens stopped at the corner of his porch.

"Earthquake!" another neighbor called out.

"Sure didn't feel like an earthquake!" Mrs. Campbell called out.

Mrs. Campbell's son Chuck had his arms around her waist as he leaned against her side. I didn't feel like such a baby now as Chuck was my age and my friend. If it hadn't been cookie day, Chuck and I would have been in his backyard hunting for salamanders or playing king of the castle. I had planned to head over there as soon as the cookies were cooling.

Lifting my hand, I gave a small wave to Chuck. He slid one of his arms away from his mom and waved back at me.

"What else could it have been?" another woman demanded.

What else could it have been? I wondered as I gazed up and down the street. The sun had baked the asphalt until a haze wafted into the air and the scent of tar permeated the day. It was such a warm, summer thing to see and smell, yet my chill sank deeper into my bones, as did the certainty something was coming.

Some of our neighbors descended their stairs and jogged toward their cars. The dogs all released a shrill yapping before beginning to howl and bark. I slapped my hands over my ears again as fresh tears streamed down my cheeks. My mom wrapped her hand around my head and pulled me close. She cradled me against her stomach when some of the dogs yelped in pain before their cries no longer blended with those of the others. My heart ached for those animals before they abruptly went silent.

As one unit, the birds all swooped away from my neighborhood as fast as they could. Their disappearance caused a burst of sunlight to stream down. I blinked rapidly as my eyes adjusted. All the neighbors stopped where they were, and their heads slowly turned back and forth as they searched the street.

I held my breath until my lungs burned and I gasped in air. My fingers curled into my mom's belly as that impending sense of something looming closer grew stronger with every passing second.

And then I saw a shadow creeping through the side yard toward the teenagers. I didn't know what the shadow was until a creature emerged. The creature resembled a man, but it had two black horns curving out of its head and the legs of a goat. It jumped on one of the teen boys. The teen girls shrieked and fled across the street toward our house and the neighborhood beyond. The other two boys tried to pry the weird-looking man off the teen. When they were unsuccessful in freeing their friend, they turned and fled too.

I felt as if I were viewing one of those horror movies I wasn't supposed to see, but that Chuck and I had snuck out of his parents' collection and watched in my basement. The man-looking creature couldn't be real and neither could the teen's screams as that thing tore into his belly. Those vivid red intestines spilling across the ground certainly couldn't be real. It was all make-believe, but those were the most genuine and pain-filled screams I'd ever heard.

Some of our neighbors fled into their homes and doors slammed. Others raced toward their cars, and new shadows slid forth to reveal more hideous creatures. The creatures all had human-like qualities to them, but they were also deformed in some animalistic way.

A scream lodged in my throat as more of my neighbors were

pounced on and torn to pieces. My mom turned and ran into the house with me against her side. I didn't realize I was sobbing loudly until the door closed behind us. The thick wood door shut out some of the shrieks of the panicked and dying, but they still drifted through the open windows. The screams grew louder when more of them filled the air, and I had the unsettling feeling I was listening to all my neighbors dying.

And we would be next.

"It's okay. It's okay," my mom breathed over and over again as she turned the locks on the door. "We'll just... we'll..." She never finished what she was going to say. Propelling me forward, she snatched the phone from where it sat on the table by the couch. She frantically hit buttons before holding the phone to her ear. She pulled it away, hit more buttons, listened to it again, and flung it aside. "Shit!"

I started to cry harder. My mother never swore in front of me. I found it more unsettling and real than seeing the teen boy being torn apart by some human-animal mix.

"It's okay; it's okay," she said again as she rubbed at my arms. "You have to stop crying. You have to be a big girl now, and big girls don't cry, right?"

I nodded, but I found I couldn't speak as terror pulsed in my veins. I blinked away my tears and wiped off the snot pouring from my nose with the back of my hand.

"Good girl," my mom said as she crept over to one of the windows and leaned over to peer out it. She jerked back. She tried to hide it, but I felt the tremor running through her.

"Daddy," I whispered when she edged me away from the window.

"He's fine," she said. "You're going to have to hide now."

Something smashed against the front door, glass rattled, and a jagged crack raced up one of the windowpanes. My mother's hand covered my mouth before I could cry out. She ran with me into the kitchen and flung open the cabinet doors under the kitchen sink.

With one swipe of her arm, she shoved all the cleaning products to the side.

"Get in!" she ordered as another bang shook the windows of the house.

I crawled inside, avoiding the white, curving pipe beneath the sink and drawing my legs against my chest. I huddled as far back as I could to make room for her to fit inside with me. "Come on, Mommy," I whispered and held my hand out to her.

"This is just for you, my bonnie girl." Her beautiful face filled the gloomy interior as she leaned forward to kiss me. Her blonde hair, only a shade darker than mine, tickled my face. "No matter what happens, stay in here and don't make a noise. Promise me, promise me you'll stay here and remain silent. *No matter what.*"

She clutched my hand, bringing it to her mouth and kissing the back of it. "Promise me," she pleaded, and for the first time, I saw tears shimmering in her eyes.

"I promise," I whispered as wood splintered.

"Be brave, always be brave. And always know how much I love you."

I didn't get a chance to reply before she closed the cabinet doors. *I love you too, Mommy*, I opened my mouth to say, but I'd promised to remain silent, so I didn't speak the words out loud.

Caught on the dishtowel hanging from it, the left cabinet door didn't close all the way. I pressed my eye to the small sliver as my mom ran behind the kitchen table and toward the back door. The sand-colored tile floor gleamed in the sun spilling through the windows. The scents of lemon and cookie dough mingled together to become the welcoming aroma my mom's kitchen always possessed.

The wooden kitchen table shone from a fresh polishing and a vase of sunflowers sat in the middle of it. I'd spent countless hours at that table eating meals, grumbling over homework, and playing games on family night. Over my mom's shoulder, I saw the gray sign she'd proudly hung on the wall last month. It read, *Kitchens bring families together.* She believed those words, and this kitchen had always been a place of love and laughter for my family.

The two creatures who burst into the room did *not* belong here. Fresh tears streamed down my face; I shoved my fist into my mouth to keep my promise to stay quiet as I watched the monsters tear my mother to pieces. She tried not to scream, but it was impossible for her not to when they pulled her arms off. I closed my eyes to shut it all out, but opened them again when the screams and darkness frightened me more than the seeing.

After they were done pouring my mother's blood over them, the creatures ripped the back door from its hinges and fled into the day.

I curled into a ball against the back of the cabinet as my mother's blood seeped across the tile toward me. *It's no longer spotless,* I realized as a part of me died, and the world became eerily silent.

CHAPTER FIFTEEN

WREN

"Wren, Wren, wake up."

The hand shaking my shoulder dragged me from the nightmare clinging to me. The dream had haunted me for years after my mother died, but at least five years had passed since I'd last experienced it. Wetness streaked my cheeks, and I lifted a hand to wipe it away. I was appalled to discover *tears*.

I couldn't recall the last time I'd cried, probably while I'd been under that sink. Tears had no place in this world; they were a weakness, and weaknesses got a person killed.

I blinked away the wetness as I tried to take in my surroundings, but blackness engulfed me. For a second, I had the disconcerting notion my tears had caused me to go blind. I almost bolted to my feet before I recalled what had happened and where I was.

I'm exhausted, and I should have avoided that street, that house. That's why the nightmare has returned now, why my mother is on my mind so much.

Exhaustion had allowed the memory to slip back in, and going by my old house yesterday, or whenever it was, hadn't helped. I should have made an excuse to take another route to the gateway, they all would have believed me and followed me, but my old road was the most direct way to get to where we needed to go.

Plus, if I made an excuse to avoid my old house and something happened and someone was hurt or injured because of it, I would never forgive myself. Determined not to be weak and refusing to hide from what couldn't be changed, I'd sworn to myself that seeing my old house wouldn't affect me, but it had.

Now I was paying for it.

However, I couldn't have known I would see what I'd seen there. I couldn't have expected that years wouldn't have erased some of the horror of what occurred there. I still wouldn't have taken a different route if I'd known, but I would have prepared myself better and I wouldn't have *looked*.

I jerked my shoulder away from Corson's touch as fresh tears welled in my eyes. *No crying!*

"Are you okay?" he inquired.

It's okay; it's okay, my mother's frantic voice whispered through my mind again. But it hadn't been okay; nothing had been okay since that day.

"No," I whispered before realizing I'd spoken the word instead of thinking it. "Yes!" I blurted. "I mean yes. I'm fine."

I realized I'd slumped down when I'd fallen asleep against the wall. I pushed myself into a seated position. Now that I'd stopped moving, the cold earth of the wall felt far cooler as it leeched the warmth from my body. I leaned away from it and drawing my legs against my chest, I wrapped my arms around them.

"You were having a nightmare," he stated.

"We humans do dream, so it happens," I replied more casually than I felt.

"We may not require as much sleep as you, but demons dream too."

"Interesting." I pushed back the strands of hair sticking to my damp face. "I'll take watch now."

"What was the nightmare about?"

"That's none of your business, demon."

I didn't have to see him to feel his anger over me calling him demon again, but I had to keep my distance from him. It was because of him my mother was dead.

No, not him, I reminded myself, but things *like* him. The ones who had ripped my mom to shreds had the snouts of dobermans and crocodile tails. They'd looked nothing like Corson or the other demons I'd come to know, but they'd all originated in Hell.

I lowered my head into my hands as I tried to regain control of myself. The nightmare had torn apart my restraint over my memories, and now I couldn't hold onto one thought or emotion. Part of me wanted to climb into Corson's arms and sob out my grief in a way I never had before. The other part wanted to kill him for what he was. It was irrational, I knew it hadn't been his fault, but I felt anything but rational right now.

I knew demons weren't all bloodthirsty monsters, but I still shouldn't be yearning to touch one as badly as I did Corson. It was a betrayal to my mom, my dad, and all the other people slaughtered that day and over the many following days. It was a betrayal to the Wilders Randy had ordered to follow me, and it was a bigger betrayal to *Randy*.

I released a choked sob. Corson rested his hand on my shoulder again. When I didn't push him away, because I simply didn't have the energy to, he slid his arm around my shoulders and drew me against his side. The warmth of his body enveloping me made me feel secure in a way I hadn't felt in years.

His fingers wiped away the lingering wetness of my tears. "What was the nightmare about?" he asked again.

I opened my mouth to tell him it was none of his business again. Instead, words tumbled out so fast I barely processed what I said. I told him every detail about cookie day, my mom's laughter, and later her screams. Told him about my dad's boisterous shout for his lasses and his bear hugs.

I revealed how my mom died, what they'd done to her, and how cramped my legs became beneath the sink. How I'd shook when I heard the whistling sound of the bombs plummeting from the sky. I'd never seen the bombs, but somehow I knew what they were before I heard their explosions. I'd held my breath and waited to burn alive or blow up, but that never came. I told him how the sun set and rose all with me under the sink, too scared to move.

I shamefully admitted I'd had more than a few accidents under that sink when my bladder couldn't contain its contents anymore. Revealed how I became so hungry my stomach knotted and it became so hot that my sweat pooled around me. Then, how I'd vomited the meager contents of my stomach when the stench of my waste and my mother's decomposing body permeated the air, and all the while, I remained under the sink.

"At sunset on the second day, thirst drove me out from my hiding spot. When I nudged open the door and slid free, I couldn't avoid my mother's blood. It had spread forward to coat the area before the cabinets. I tried to touch as little of it as possible, but I was unable to get my cramped legs to hold me, and I slipped and fell into her blood," I whispered.

"I lay there for a while, crying, before recalling I was supposed to be brave too. I forced myself to get up. Starving, I fell on the cookie batter and ate it all; then I threw it up. Some of it must have stayed down as after eating it and drinking some water, I felt stronger, but I still couldn't get up the energy to go anywhere.

"So I sat there, staring at my mom's body and listening to the nothingness my world had become. The screams had been endless in the beginning, and over the following two days, an occasional one still pierced the air, but hours had passed since I'd heard anything beyond the tick of the kitchen clock.

"The screams had been awful, and there had been *so* many of them, but the silence was worse. At least I'd known I wasn't alone when I could hear the screams. Without them, I became convinced I was the last person on Earth and I'd never felt so alone. He found me the next day," I said.

"Who found you?" Corson asked when I stopped speaking.

My fingers curled into my pants when they fisted on my thighs. "Randy did. He was going through houses scrounging for supplies. There were two other survivors with him. Both of them were disgusted when they found me sitting next to the sink, covered in blood, vomit, and waste. I'd have been disgusted too, but not Randy. He lifted me up, carried me into the bathroom, and set me in the tub clothes and all. He turned on the water and hosed me off the best he could before finding fresh clothes and telling me to put them on. While he waited outside, I did as he'd instructed and struggled to put the clean clothes on.

"He made me get up, made me continue, and refused to let me die when I would have been fine with that. There was no arguing with him; he wouldn't allow it. But it was a long time before I argued with anyone as I didn't speak again until months after that day. I'm not sure if I forgot how to talk, or if my voice became trapped beneath the screams I never issued while those demons slaughtered my mom."

I couldn't believe I was telling him these things. Later I could blame it on the dark and our circumstances. The ouro may be dead, but we were far from free of danger while in these tunnels. Everyone tried to unburden themselves before they died, right?

"Randy packed a bag for me and took me from my house. I never looked back," I said.

"Did you know Randy before then?"

"No. He lived a couple of neighborhoods over from mine. He could have left me there, and most would have understood if he had. Few others would have dragged a traumatized eight-year-old around with them when the world was literally going to Hell, but he did, and he was only twenty-one at the time. It would have been much easier for him to leave me, but he kept me safe. He taught me how to survive and became like a father to me."

"Where is Randy now?"

I leaned closer to the heat he emitted. *Slightly warmer than a human,* I realized. It didn't make me pull away from him like it would have yesterday.

"I don't know where he is," I murmured. "He left to travel beyond the Rockies and explore more of the Wilds. We've never gone into or over the mountains before, and he decided it was time to check out some uncharted territory."

"Why?"

"Because Randy still holds out hope there is a safer place for us in the Wilds, a place where we can stop moving and settle down. He's determined to find it."

"And you don't believe there is such a place?"

"I don't know," I admitted. "Anything is possible, right? It's part of the reason why I decided to reach out to Kobal. None of us want to live at the wall, but I think Randy would have sought Kobal out too, if he'd experienced what I had with the king. Despite everything that's happened, Randy remains a dreamer who is determined to give me, his wife, and the rest of his followers a better life."

Randy may have gone to speak with Kobal, but he definitely wouldn't have cuddled up with a demon like I was right now. I didn't want to know what he or the rest of the Wilders would think if they ever learned about this.

While at the wall, some of the Wilders had gone to the tents where the demons resided on the hill. I knew some of them had had sex with the demons, but I was their leader right now. I was supposed to keep an eye out for the Wilders and keep my distance from the demons who might turn on us. I'd led them to the wall, and yes they were adults, but if something went wrong with the demons, it would be my fault.

"Randy divided his followers before he left so we weren't all put in danger. He placed me in charge of the ones who remained. The Wilders agreed to my lead while he was gone, even though many of them are older than me, because he's their leader and he raised me.

In the beginning, I demanded to go with him, but he refused to take me. He insisted it was necessary for me to be in charge here, but there were others who could have done it. I think he left me behind to keep me safe."

"Probably," Corson said.

"We were supposed to meet up again in May, but that was before the seals broke. Now, I have no idea what will happen or if Randy is even still alive. We may also be traveling into the mountains to hunt for the angels before he has the chance to return."

His palm ran over my hair, soothing me as much as the heat of him did. My hands unfurled from my clothes and edged toward him, one settled on his thigh while the other rested against his back. His head turned toward me, and his lips brushed my temple.

"You said you were making the cookies for your father," Corson said. "Did you ever find him?"

Closing my eyes, I lifted my hand from his thigh to rub my forehead as the world lurched precariously. "His body was on the porch when Randy led me outside. My dad made it all the way home only to be brought down by a demon at our front door. The blood soaking him turned his red hair and beard a scarlet color. There's no red anymore. Now he's all white," I murmured as older memories gave way to newer ones.

"What do you mean?" Corson inquired.

I removed my other hand from him and folded them both in my lap. I clasped them so forcefully together that the bones in them grated. "We traveled past my house on our way to the gateway. It was the fastest way to get to where we're camped now." He stiffened beside me. "We made camp about a quarter mile away from my old home."

"You should have led us a different way."

"We all have painful memories. I did what was necessary."

"Wren—"

"I did what was necessary," I insisted. "I just wasn't...." My voice trailed off as I twisted my hands. "I wasn't expecting his body to still be there. Parts of him were missing, probably taken away by animals, but most of his bones remained."

I swallowed the lump in my throat as I recalled the skeleton lying on the front porch. My father's bony fingers remained extended toward the door, forever reaching for the family he would never see again. There was no more garish blood covering him, only the stark white of his bones.

Maybe seeing my old house again wouldn't have been so bad if the red door hadn't been faded and chipped, but the red color evident all the same. It hadn't helped that one of my mom's potted plants remained hanging from a hook. Nothing remained of the flowers, but the plastic pot had swayed in the breeze as we walked by. The porch sagged with age, most of the windows were broken, yet the house remained standing when many others didn't.

For one split second, as I'd stood there gazing at my old home, the laughter and smells once filling it came back to me, and I'd been a child all over again. Not a frightened, waste-covered child, but a happy one with dreams and laughter.

Then, the past faded away and I was a woman staring at her father's bones. A woman who hadn't laughed in years, who no longer dreamed of the future, and who was well aware her time could come as suddenly as her dad's had. I was certain my mother's bones were still in the kitchen, but I would never climb those stairs again to see them.

That house and those bones were the reason the nightmare had returned and why I'd felt like an unsettled mess since seeing them. *I will get myself under control again. I have to.*

"We see bones everywhere we go," I murmured. "There is no avoiding that, especially so close to the gateway."

"You should have taken us a different way."

"No. I shouldn't have. The past is the past. It's done. When I was a child, I tried to stop on that porch and sit next to my dad's body. I think I would have stayed there with him to die, but Randy twisted his hand into the collar of my shirt, lifted me, and carried me away. This time, I carried myself away from it."

"Where did Randy take you after you left your house?"

"Into the Wilds. I became a part of the woods, and I found a new family amongst the Wilders. There was no other choice for me but to accept my new life."

"When the government evacuated the Wilds, you could have gone with the refugees to the wall. It wasn't completed at that time, and some sections of the wall still aren't entirely secure or sturdy, but you would have been safer there. You could have helped with the building of it."

"You mean I would have been a safe *prisoner* there. The government didn't allow the evacuees from the Wilds to travel beyond the wall. Most became the first soldiers on the wall and were kept away from the civvies who were fed the government's lies. Those who knew the truth of what happened that day weren't permitted to mingle with the civvies or to live their lives freely. I'd felt like a prisoner under that sink, and I would *not* become one again."

"Demons and the human governments worked together to keep the threat from Hell contained and away from the outer areas," Corson said. "The people on the other side of the wall were told those things to keep them from panicking."

"They didn't panic when the truth finally came out," I retorted.

"No, but they'd also had fourteen years to adjust to their new lives by then. Lives that lacked most of the luxuries and stable food supply they'd once taken for granted. When the truth came out, they had no choice but to accept it and Kobal's rule as the demons escaping the seals were spreading beyond the wall at that point, so were Lucifer and the fallen angels. What remained of the still-ruling human governments collapsed at a rapid rate, although some continue now.

"Kobal had established a leadership role with the human rulers before the truth became public knowledge, so it was easier for him to take control of the chaos. Demons have also become better at dealing with people over the years and are able to interact better with the civvies now."

"Were we so difficult to deal with?" I asked.

"We weren't exactly welcomed with open arms in the beginning. Many government officials distrusted us, and we didn't establish a functional relationship with them until a year after the gateway opened. We had no say in the lies the governments initially created to keep their citizens safe. We also never planned to remain in this realm, so we didn't care what lies they fed the humans, but things always have a way of changing."

"I see. When the gateway closed, if things had gone back to the way they were before, would you have gone back to Hell?" I asked as I leaned into the warmth of him once more.

CHAPTER SIXTEEN

CORSON

"I wouldn't have wanted to return," I admitted. "During my time here, I came to enjoy Earth, but if my king had chosen to go back to Hell, I would have followed him."

"Will you follow Kobal anywhere?" she asked.

"Yes. I have been on Kobal's side since I was born. My parents fought for him before me, and once I was old enough to fight too, I did. I will continue to do so without fail. As the varcolac, Kobal is the rightful king of Hell, but Lucifer stripped the throne from the ruling varcolac when he entered Hell six thousand years ago. Lucifer tried to rule there, but he was never meant to be the king, and there were many in Hell that denied Lucifer, including myself and numerous other demons."

"What is so special about the varcolac?" she inquired.

"The varcolac is the only demon born from the fires of Hell themselves. Only one of them can exist at a time, and when the varcolac dies, a new one rises. The rest of us upper-level demons are all born as humans are, from a mother and a father. Our abilities develop with us as we mature from babies to adults, but the varcolac rises in adult form and with their powers fully developed. The fires that forged Kobal did so with the intent of making him strong enough to rule all of us and to defeat Lucifer."

"Yet some demons chose to fight on Lucifer's side," she murmured and stifled a yawn.

"Some demons *still* fight with the fallen angels," I replied. "There will always be those who seek only to destroy. That's one of the reasons why the varcolacs before Kobal locked so many creatures behind the seals. They needed to be contained before they destroyed Hell. Now the seals are gone, and those trying to destroy Earth will be hunted down and killed."

"What if some of the things from the seals decide not to work with the angels or against Kobal?"

"We're all starting over again in this world—demons, Hell-creatures, and humans alike. Those who don't seek only to destroy will be allowed to live, even if they once resided behind the seals. There are some things, like the ouro, that have no purpose other than to kill and must be put down."

"What of the jinn and what they were doing with those people?" Renewed energy filled her voice, and she sat up against me.

"What little I know of the jinn, they're manipulative and cruel, but those people made a choice to partake in what the jinn offered. No one gets something for nothing."

"Some people have no idea what they're getting into or what some demons are capable of doing."

"No, but some people have no idea what humans themselves are capable of doing. I've seen some awful things from your species over my many years too."

"So have I," she whispered.

I drew her closer when I heard the sorrow in her voice. "Has anyone hurt you?" The question came out amazingly calm considering the fury slithering through me at the possibility of some human having done something to her.

"I can handle myself," she replied.

"Wren—"

"I took care of anyone who tried anything with me."

The steel in her voice cautioned me away from pursuing this questioning. This was the most she'd ever opened up to me; I wouldn't be surprised to learn it was the most she'd ever opened up to anyone. Why she'd chosen me and this place, I didn't know. I wouldn't ask her either; she would only shut me out again if I did.

She remained silent for long enough that I believed she would stop speaking, but then she continued. "You said you were born, that all demons are. How?"

"Well, when two demons love each other, they get together to create a child. I've heard you humans refer to it as the birds and the bees. I have no idea why, since I don't think either of those things penetrates their mates, but what do I know? However, I can assure you there are *no* storks involved," I couldn't help but tease and smiled when I sensed her scowling at me.

"That's not what I meant."

"I know." I brushed my hand over her hair to soothe her as I inhaled her pine scent. "Do you know how the different realms of Hell, Earth, and Heaven were formed?"

Her chin lifted against my chest in her stubborn way. "No," she finally admitted, her curiosity winning out over her obstinacy.

"The planet was created by a colossal force of energy; I guess you could call it the Big Bang. That colossal force was also powerful enough to create what many call God, but over the years it's been named many things, including numerous gods and goddesses. Demons and angels simply call it the Being because as far as we know, it has no true name.

"At first, Hell, Heaven, and Earth were all one thing, but they separated millions of years ago when humans and demons were the tiniest of evolving specks. When they were still together, the three realms battled one another to thrive. However, as time moved on and the massive energy that created the planet expanded, the dimensions of each realm became more clearly divided.

"Hell was the first to break away. The loss of Hell's severe heat made Earth more inhabitable for the life starting to grow within its waters. The newfound life that had thrived on heat broke away with the waters of Hell. The life in those waters managed to evolve until it became demons and other Hell creatures."

"Hell has water?" she inquired.

"Yes. Its red currents are different than the waters on Earth and, from what Caim has said, the water in Heaven, but the red waters sustain life."

"Interesting," she murmured. "So what happened after that?"

"Heaven broke off after to leave the air on Earth more breathable for the burgeoning life there. Humans and demons evolved in a nearly parallel manner, as did the other beasts on Earth and in Hell. When Hell first broke away, the Being, or God, or whatever you prefer to call it—"

"God," she stated. "I gave up having faith in a higher power while I huddled under a sink fourteen years ago, but I was once a believer."

My teeth ground together at the reminder of what she'd endured. If not for her mother, Wren would be dead. Those demons would have torn into her with little consideration for the fact she was only a child.

"We were all confused and disoriented when Hell was suddenly opened by humans who had never been able to open a gateway into it before," I said. "The initial blast of the gateway opening threw me and Kobal into the lower levels of Hell. The demons who immediately fled onto Earth struck out at anything they deemed a threat to them."

"Are you trying to defend what they did to my mom and countless others?" she grated.

"No. I am telling you what happened. From the way you described them, lower-level demons are the ones who killed your mother, but there were also upper-level demons, ones who fight on our side, that burst out of Hell and slaughtered anything in their way.

The humans releasing their bombs only escalated the situation. It was a while before everything settled down enough for us to learn what had happened and that it had all been a giant fuck up."

"I know," she murmured.

Yes, she would know. She'd been in the thick of it, and it would have taken the Wilders some time to grasp the situation too.

"I didn't race out to kill everything in sight like others. However, I've done my fair share of killing to those who deserve it, and I'll continue to do so," I told her.

"So will I," she murmured and eased against me once more. "It seems I should have been praying all this time. There really *is* a greater power."

"That greater power isn't on this planet anymore," I said.

"Where did it go?"

"No one knows, but Raphael is convinced it will return."

"If anyone should be convinced of that it's an angel," she said. "Raphael told me he chose to leave Heaven, unlike Caim."

"He did," I confirmed, "but like Caim, he can't return."

"So he said," she murmured. "So what happened when Hell broke away?"

It took me a few seconds to recall what we'd been talking about. "When Hell first broke away, the power—"

"God," she corrected.

"God resided in Hell until Heaven broke away. When that happened, God left Hell and went to Heaven. With its inhospitable air, life doesn't evolve in Heaven, so to sustain the cycle of life beginning to flow between the dimensions, God forged the angels in the image of man. Over time, the three planes became a symbiotic network of different species. Humans are the only ones with a soul and the only ones who can create a new soul. When a person perishes, their soul goes to Heaven or Hell, though some remain on Earth and serve their time in Purgatory as ghosts. Where they end up in death all depends on a human's deeds while they're alive."

"I've met some of the ghosts at the wall. Some of them are assholes, but a few are nice."

"Most are selfish, one-way pricks, but at least many of them are trying to help us now."

"I guess you don't like ghosts."

"No, but they also serve their purpose. They do nothing for us though as both angels and demons feed on the souls who travel to our realms until they are ready to be reincarnated. Demons create pain for the souls as punishment until they become twisted wraiths. Angels give them pleasure as a reward for their deeds. When a soul's time is up in either dimension, it is reborn on Earth. Just because a soul makes it to Heaven once doesn't mean they won't make it to Hell a time or two also. Without this life cycle, no one knows what would happen, but we do know all our species rely on each other to survive."

"What about demons and angels when they die? Do they reincarnate too?"

"No," I said. "That is where our death and rebirth cycle differs from humans. When an immortal dies, that is the end for them. We experience no afterlife, but that is the price we pay for immortality."

"Oh." Wren remained still against me as she tried to process everything I'd revealed. "Where do Lucifer and the fallen angels come into all this?"

"There was a time when angels and demons walked the Earth. They didn't do so freely, but they did move amongst people. The varcolac can open a gateway between Hell and Earth. The demons who passed back and forth were carefully monitored and had to pass tests to travel to the mortal plane.

"Then, six thousand years ago, the asshole angels above had a fight, and they solved it by tossing their trash onto Earth."

"And that trash was Lucifer and the other fallen."

"Yes. All angels can leave Heaven, but only the archangel Michael is capable of opening a gateway from Earth and into

Heaven. When they threw Lucifer and his followers out, they did so with the belief they would die on Earth."

"Why did they think they would die if the angels are immortal too?" she asked.

"All immortal creatures used to become mortal while on Earth. The only way an angel or demon on Earth could retain their immortality was to return to Heaven or Hell. When humans opened the unnatural gateway into Hell, it changed everything. Our worlds became so intricately entwined that immortals are now capable of remaining undying while on Earth."

"Oh," she breathed, "and Michael never planned to let the fallen angels return to Heaven."

"Exactly. The fallen should have perished on Earth, but once here, they sheared off their wings in the hopes of becoming more human. It didn't work, and it only caused most of their wings to grow back twisted and black. The fallen angels started to become more demonic while on Earth, and during that time, Lucifer figured out how to open a gateway into Hell. Once the angels entered Hell, they retained their immortality, became far more demonic, and wreaked havoc. They were able to do all this because the golden angels couldn't take care of their fucking mess."

"I take it you don't like the angels much," she said.

"Those self-righteous pricks started this whole thing, and only Raphael has done anything to try to help fix it. I don't trust him or Caim, but out of the two of them, I trust Caim more. I never believed I'd say that about one of the fallen, but Caim is more open, whereas I think Raphael may still be hiding things from us. They've both sacrificed to help us though, so I'll work with them unless they give me a reason to kill them. Then, I won't hesitate."

She shifted against me as if to pull out of my arms, but then her head fell onto my chest. I froze, uncertain of what to do. With any other woman, I would have known what to do, but dealing with Wren was like walking on thin ice. I never knew when she might crack and try to kill me.

"Your feelings for the angels are much like my feelings toward demons," she said.

"Yes."

"Where are your mother and father?"

I held her closer before realizing what I was doing and easing my grip on her. After all these years, I still hated recalling the end of my parents' lives. "Dead. I watched them both die."

CHAPTER SEVENTEEN

WREN

"I'm sorry," I said, sensing the pain beneath his words.

Demons *grieved*?

Months ago, I would have said that was impossible. That demons didn't care about anything other than destruction, but then I'd seen the king with his queen and the bonds of friendship between Corson and some of the other demons. Between Corson and some of the *humans*. I saw the way he cared for and protected his friends Erin and Vargas who were as mortal as me.

"They died a long time ago," he replied.

I considered asking him what had happened to them, but his tone remained more distant than I'd ever heard it before.

"It was a long time ago," he said again. "And when a demon says a long time, then you know it was a *long* time. The years are not the same for us as they are for people. For you, a decade may seem long. For me, it's but a day."

"You still miss your parents though," I guessed.

"You might find this difficult to believe, but demons care greatly for their young. It is rare for us to have offspring. When we do, demons love their children as much, if not more so than a human loves their child. My parents were no exception to this, and I loved them too."

The hard muscles of his chest rippled beneath my hand when my finger stroked his shirt. I found myself momentarily distracted from his words as the beat of his heart increased beneath my ears. My hearing and sense of touch seemed stronger in this world of darkness, or perhaps it was simply Corson who made me more aware of my body and his.

I swallowed as I forced my attention away from my growing awareness of him and back to our conversation. "I don't find that difficult to believe," I finally said. "I may not like most demons, but I've seen the way some of you are with those you care about. That a demon would love their children or their parents isn't hard to believe. What happened to yours?"

I hadn't intended to ask, but I wanted to learn more about *him*.

"My father was slain during a battle with Lucifer when I was twenty years old," Corson stated as if he were reciting memorized lines. "I tried to reach him, but I was still young, not fully matured, and unable to save him. If I'd been at my full strength, I might have gotten to him in time, but it was another seven years before I matured into my immortality and my abilities. So, instead, I watched him die. Afterward, my mother, unable to face spending an eternity without her Chosen, threw herself into the fires of Hell."

I bit my lip to keep from crying out in sorrow over his loss. I tried to think of a reply as I processed his words, but I didn't know what to say.

"I'm sorry," I finally said, but I knew how inadequate those words were. They never did justice to the hole the loss of a loved one left behind.

If his mother had loved him so much, how could she have preferred to die rather than stay with her son? That was a question I would *not* voice. It wasn't my place, and I refused to inflict more anguish on him.

"For a demon to lose their Chosen is an agony I can't imagine. I have experienced what it is like to suffer, but not like that. I understand my mother's decision," he said as if he'd read my mind. "I've seen others endure the loss of their Chosen. Witnessed how broken it left them. Many demons decide not to carry on once their Chosen is gone. The ones who do become like walking dead."

"How..." I tried to think of the right word, but all I could come up with was, "sad. What is a Chosen?"

"Some demons have a Chosen one. Perhaps all demons do and they aren't born yet, or we haven't discovered them, or they perish before we find them. No one knows how it all works. Some of the demons who went to Earth before the angels entered Hell found their Chosen amid humans. The demons who found their Chosen there never returned to Hell and perished on Earth with their mates."

"Oh," I breathed, as this whole new aspect of demons opened up to me. "That is such a..."

"Sacrifice," he said when my voice trailed off.

"Yes, but also romantic in a sort of insane way." I couldn't imagine loving someone so much I would give up everything I'd ever known for them.

Corson chuckled as he ran his hand over my hair again. I snuggled closer to the gentle touch while I tried to recall the last time someone had held me so tenderly.

"Demons can be more than a little insane sometimes," he replied. "And a demon will do *anything* for their Chosen as it is an eternal bond. They also can only breed with their Chosen. Males and females will often know, or at least suspect another is their Chosen before they have sex, but that is the way to confirm it. Demons also only bite another during sex if it is their Chosen. If for some reason, their bite marks should fade, other demons will always know when another has been claimed and stay away from them."

"A bite and sex are what decides a Chosen?" I asked incredulously.

He rested his chin on my head. "No, there is *far* more involved in the bond than that. Male demons don't produce sperm until they find their Chosen and the females don't produce eggs. Call it a form of immortal birth control, if you will. Even if they find a Chosen, females only produce an egg every ten to fifteen years, and it's still rare for a female demon to conceive when they do enter their fertile time. A male can always scent when his Chosen is fertile, and the couple usually locks themselves away for the month it occurs. I've also been told sex is more pleasurable with a Chosen, and I've witnessed that the Chosen bond makes a demon stronger."

"Amazing." I couldn't deny I was fascinated by this insight of love and monogamy from a species I'd mostly considered heartless monsters. "So how many women have been your Chosen?" I joked, though the idea of him with all his numerous women set my teeth on edge.

His hands tightened on my arms. "*None*. Once a Chosen is found, there is *never* another for a demon."

"Oh," I said dully. "What about past girlfriends?"

"Demons don't have girlfriends. We know our Chosen is the only one who will matter, so romantic bonds with others aren't forged. Besides, the only feeling involved for a demon when it comes to sex is getting off. It may sound cold to humans, but that is simply the way of things for us, outside of the Chosen bond."

"Does it get tiring to constantly be moving on like that?"

"Maybe, but that is the way things are and will continue to be unless I meet my Chosen."

"Do you want to meet her?"

"I've thought about it more since Kobal and River met, but it might never happen for me. I am content with going about my life the way I always have."

"But somewhere out there is the demon or human you're meant to be with?" I asked.

"Perhaps. Maybe she isn't alive yet, maybe she is already dead, maybe she is something else, or maybe I am never meant to find my Chosen."

"What else could she possibly be?"

"Angels and demons left offspring behind when they were here all those years ago. Some of those descendants still walk this Earth. My Chosen could be one of them."

"I see." And then a thought occurred to me. "Is that what the queen is? Is River one of those angel or demon children?"

"River is many things," Corson replied.

"But—"

"I will not discuss it."

That was all I would get from him on the subject. River was another one of those he cared about, and with his loyalty to Kobal, Corson wouldn't reveal anything River and Kobal didn't make public knowledge.

"What happens if two demons meet and only one of them feels the Chosen bond?" I asked.

"That has never occurred," he replied. "Not between two demons anyway. There is a connection between them both, no matter what type of demon they are. Many demons are a mix of breeds because of that. Bale is a cross between a fire and visionary demon. She has visions, which are often sporadic, and can withstand fire, but she is unable to use fire as a weapon like other fire demons."

"I see," I murmured. "What about a demon with a human? Would a human feel the Chosen connection?"

"No."

"So if your Chosen is a human, you would have to make her fall in love with you?" For some reason, this idea almost made me laugh. I couldn't picture Corson trying to romance anyone.

"I guess," he muttered, sounding less than thrilled about the prospect.

"It wouldn't be that horrible. Well, maybe it would be for the woman."

"Oh no, Wren, it would be extremely enjoyable for the woman."

My breath caught at his purred words and the promise behind them. For a minute, I allowed myself to imagine how pleasurable

Corson could make it. Would I like sex more if it was with him? Demon or not, I felt the answer to that was a resounding yes.

"Humans are mortal," I managed to get out when I found my voice again.

"Are they now?" he drawled. "I'd never heard such a thing before."

"That's not where I was going," I replied with more snippiness than I'd intended.

I hated that he always had me on such a roller coaster ride of emotion. Hated that he had me wondering what would happen if I slid my hand between the buttons of his shirt and pressed my palm against his flesh. Or what he would do if I slipped my hand between his legs. I gulped at the idea and my skin tingled with excitement.

"I meant that a demon would have to watch their Chosen grow old and die if it was a human," I finally said. "They wouldn't be able to become mortal by staying on Earth and dying with their Chosen anymore."

"Perhaps," he replied. "Or maybe the human could become like Hawk."

I considered Hawk, the handsome soldier camped with us. I didn't know all the details of what had happened to him, but from what I'd seen of his healing ability, speed, and the fact that I'd seen him emerge from Hell with River, I knew something had changed him from mortal to immortal. No normal mortal could have survived that long in Hell.

"However, not all humans survive the change, and many cannot handle the consequences of it or their newfound powers. Hawk is a rarity," Corson continued.

"Hmm." Resting my hand against my mouth, I stifled another yawn.

"You should rest some more," he said gruffly.

I nodded, but after that nightmare, I doubted I would get any sleep tonight or today or whatever time it was. Reluctantly, I detached myself from his arms and lay on the ground. I instantly missed the heat of him, but I would never let him know that. I curled into a ball and rested my hands beneath my head.

Dirt and rock scraped when he shifted. Then he was lying beside me and wrapping his arms around me. "What are you doing?" I demanded, even as my body sank into his.

Damn, traitorous body!

"You can't be so stubborn as to deny you're freezing." His breath stirred my hair against my ear, but he released me.

I couldn't deny it. However, it was one thing to take comfort from him, but to snuggle up next to him while I slept? *You've done it with countless others to keep from freezing to death.*

The only difference was he was a demon, yet I liked some of the demons. Bale was about as welcoming as a rabid dog most of the time, but I admired her ferociousness and dedication to her king. The skelleins were amusing. Shax was friendly enough, so was Hawk. And Magnus, though smug, protected those he cared about.

I also liked Corson, a little. So why was I always so snippy and jumpy around him? Why did he always make me feel like I teetered on the edge and if I leaned too far over I'd plummet to my death?

Okay, maybe not my death, but I'd plunge into something I couldn't handle, and I had to keep control at all times. Allowing my control to slip even a little could spell my death and the death of others.

But sometimes, I would give anything to loosen my hold on my restraint, especially now when I was aching for his arms again.

"Is it okay if I hold you?" he inquired.

"Yes," I forced out.

When his arms slid around me again and my chill eased, I realized I could no longer deny that I liked him a lot more than a little.

CHAPTER EIGHTEEN

Corson

I tried to ignore my throbbing erection as Wren slept soundly in my arms, but the woman had draped herself across me and burrowed her head beneath my chin. Her breasts were pressed firmly against my chest. One of her hands rested an inch above the head of my cock, while the other was beneath my neck.

The infuriating woman knew how to drive me mad even in her sleep.

When she murmured and shifted, her mouth ended up in the hollow of my throat. My dick became impossibly harder as her breath whispered over my skin on each of her exhalations. She may be a form of torture, but I didn't dare move and chance waking her.

It was a first for me to put someone else's needs ahead of my own. The only one I'd ever put ahead of myself was my king and later River when she became my queen, but not a bedmate. When morning came, I parted ways from my partner and rarely returned to the same woman again. I didn't hold them after sex, but I found my arms drawing Wren closer.

I would return to her. I didn't know where the knowledge came from, but it blazed across my mind and lodged inside me.

My heart beat faster than it ever had with a woman, and I couldn't begin to count the number of women I'd been with over the years. I didn't recall most of them, but I did know none had affected me as much as this prickly bird in my arms did. I frowned as I pondered why she affected me as much as she did.

Before I could delve too deeply into it, she murmured something before going rigid against me. I didn't have to feel the flutter of her lashes against my skin to know she'd woken. I expected her to bolt away from me, but she remained unmoving in my arms.

Afraid she might jerk away from me, I leisurely rubbed my hands up and down the cloth covering her arms. She didn't move an inch when I caressed her sleeves before sliding a hand up to clasp her nape. I lifted my head and placed a kiss on her forehead.

When she still didn't pull away from me, I slid my lips lower over her cheek. Her heartbeat thundered in my ears, and she stopped breathing when my mouth found hers. I ran my tongue over her lips, tasting them as she remained still against me and the warmth of her soft mouth branded mine.

Then her lips parted enough to allow my tongue to slide into her mouth. I flicked my tongue over hers as her body stretched out on top of me and her tongue hesitatingly entwined with mine before becoming more assured with her thrusts.

My hand rose from her nape to cup the back of her head and draw her closer. Her fingers dug into my shoulders. Her other hand dropped down and brushed over my dick. She stiffened when she discovered how hard I was, but when I nipped at her lower lip before sucking lightly on it, she relaxed against me once more.

She moved her hand to grip my waist, and then her hips shifted and her legs opened to let my shaft slip between the junction of her thighs. For a moment, she froze, and I became convinced she would stop this, but then she rose before sliding down the length of my erection.

Running my hand along the side of her slender body, I traced the lithe muscles of her abdomen before clasping one of her breasts through her shirt. The hardened bud of her nipple burned my palm through her shirt and bra. When I ran my thumb around her nipple, she moaned and pressed closer to me.

My excitement rising, I released her head and grabbed her hips to guide her faster against the length of my erection. The sensation of her body riding mine caused me to growl as she rotated her hips in such a way that she was fucking me without ever pulling my cock from my pants.

Her fingers dug deeper into my flesh; her breath came in small pants as she eagerly met my movements. For the first time in my life, I knew I was going to come before entering a woman, and I welcomed the release.

WREN

Not real. Not real. The dark makes all of this not real.

But it felt too good not to be real. Everything about Corson felt *so* amazingly good. From the heat of his lips on mine to the smoky taste of him. He wove a spell over me as every time I considered returning to reality, his hands pulled me back under his magic once more.

And he wasn't even touching my skin!

What would it feel like if he placed his hands on my flesh? I desperately wanted to know even as I tried to pull myself from the drugged stupor he wove over me.

This is wrong; I shouldn't, we shouldn't.... Every time a new protest rose in my mind, it died away.

Am I dreaming?

The question was answered when he pushed the evidence of his erection against me. I became wetter with need as I instinctively met the rhythm he set.

It had been a couple of years since I'd been with a man, but horniness was no excuse for making out with a demon. While my brain shot out this reminder, my body decided my brain could deal with it later. My body was in charge now, and it demanded more of Corson.

My nipples ached, and my breasts became heavier as he kneaded one before turning his attention to the other. His tongue moved in ways I'd never known one could move. He drew me deeper and deeper into his kiss until the mineral scent of the tunnel and the wintry air ceased to exist.

There was only Corson and the tension building between my legs and coiling higher into my belly. I thrust against him and rotated my hips until he was rubbing my clit just right. He nipped at my lip again before lifting his hips off the ground.

He likes that.

The realization brought a rush of power with it. He was as lost in this moment as I was. This was already more intense than anything I'd ever experienced with someone before, yet I found myself wondering what he would feel like inside me.

Amazing, he would feel amazing within me.

My pulse beat faster in my ears as I contemplated pulling his dick out and sliding myself onto it. I could feel the thick length of him through both our pants, and I knew he would stretch and fill me completely when he slipped inside me. He would demand nothing less than a complete loss of control from me, and for the first time in my life, I *craved* that.

I was too far gone in this moment to take the time to stop though and when I circled my hips against him once more, something within me fractured. I cried out as the orgasm rushing through my body caused my back to bow. Corson drove my hips harder against him before groaning. The sound he emitted was almost as erotic as his hands, and it had me on the verge of riding him again.

In the end, exhaustion won out, and I slumped on top of him. My head fell to his chest as his hand ran leisurely over my hair. I inhaled his scent and relished the lingering thrills of pleasure coursing through my body.

Closing my eyes, I took a minute to pretend we weren't in this place. That he wasn't a demon and I wasn't a Wilder. That so many hadn't been lost, and Hell and Heaven were still abstract concepts everyone only speculated about.

But I could only keep reality at bay for a few minutes. Then, ice slid over my skin, and the dank scent of the tunnel filled my nose once more. When I shivered, his arms enveloped me. He drew me closer to nuzzle my forehead with his lips. How many other women had he held like this? And what did it matter? He was a demon. I shouldn't be allowing him to cradle me at all.

But God help me, no matter how wrong it was, I wanted *more* of this demon.

What would the other Wilders think if they learned what I'd done in this tunnel? They accepted working with the demons, and some Wilders had done more than just work with them, but I was supposed to remain distant, and I definitely was *not* supposed to be crawling into the arms of one.

Worse than what my fellow Wilders would think of me was what would Randy think?

Dread coiled through me at the possibility of seeing revulsion in Randy's eyes, or of him turning against me. There had always been the possibility he wouldn't agree with my decision to work with the demons, but he wouldn't have hated me for making the choice. However, he might *loathe* me if he learned of this. He'd lost a lot to demons too.

Reality was like a bucket of cold water dumped over my head. I was enfolded securely in the arms of a demon, but not just *any* demon. *Corson.* The one demon I'd vowed never to give in to. Well, I'd vowed never to give in to *any* of them, but especially not this one! Not the one who proudly displayed the jewelry of all his conquests and would happily add me to that list, if he could remember my name for long enough to add it.

What was wrong with me? A day or two trapped in his presence had made me like the other numerous women who had fallen into his bed. Maybe we hadn't had sex, but it had been close, and I'd gotten off on it. If I wore earrings, he'd be smugly parading them around for everyone to see. Now, he'd give me that knowing look and I'd hate myself and him for it.

But worst of all was the knowledge that I didn't want to be one of the many, not to him. With horror, I realized that I might actually be coming to care for him. If I wasn't careful, he'd break my heart and have no idea what he'd done.

Distance. I need distance from him and all of this. Unfortunately, there was little distance to be found in this maze, but I didn't have to stay in his arms.

I pulled out of his embrace and rolled away from him. He grunted when I accidentally sank my elbow into his stomach before launching to my feet. I miscalculated his position on the ground and tripped over his foot. I almost sprawled onto my ass in an incredibly inelegant move, but he moved with the speed of... well, a demon as he shot to his feet beside me and grabbed my elbow to steady me.

"Wren—"

"This never happened." He stiffened against me before I ripped my arm free of his grasp. "This *never* happened!" I didn't know if I was trying to convince him of that or myself. It had to be him as I couldn't deny the wetness between my legs. "It was a mistake."

"Is that so?" he inquired in a tone of voice I'd never heard from him before. Something about it reminded me of a snake coiled to strike.

Except I knew Corson would never strike me, never hurt me, at least not physically. I didn't kid myself into believing he was humane, but he was fair, and he didn't harm those who didn't deserve it.

Is that so? My mind spun with his question as I tried to figure it all out. But how could I figure this out when I was freezing, yet my palms were sweating, and my body still had little bolts of pleasure running through it from him? This demon made me melt, but there could never be anything more between us than a stolen moment in this awful place.

"Yes. It won't happen again," I said crisply. I was glad I couldn't see him and that he couldn't see me. I was afraid he would see the longing on my face as I uttered those words. "It's time to get out of here."

Without waiting to hear what he would say, I turned on my heel and started down the tunnel. "You're going the wrong way," he said from behind me.

I stopped and craned my head up and down the tunnel, but I had no way of knowing if he was right or not. Still, I reluctantly headed back toward his voice.

CHAPTER NINETEEN

CORSON

Beside me, Wren threw her arm up to shield her eyes from the sun. She blinked rapidly against the influx of light. Turning, I gazed into the tunnel until my eyes adjusted to the day. Unlike the trap we'd fallen into, this tunnel entrance didn't drop into the earth but had a gradual ascent until it became a twenty-foot hole that was even with the ground.

When my eyes stopped burning, I faced forward again. I stared at the small trees before us while I tried to get my bearings, but I had no idea how far we'd traveled from the others or where we were now.

Wren pulled her knife from its holster and crept into the forest. I stayed close to her side, listening and searching for any hint of an enemy as she circled some of the trees in an ever-widening pattern. She hadn't spoken to me since telling me that what happened between us was a mistake. She may believe that, but I still wouldn't allow anything to happen to her, and I was determined to prove to her it hadn't been a mistake.

Her eyes searched the barren canopy of tree branches overhead before looking to the trunks. She ran her fingers over a couple of them, her brow furrowing as she studied the woods. In the short time we'd been in the Wilds with them, I'd come to realize that the Wilders had their own way of marking and learning the land.

She walked over to a boulder and circled behind it. I couldn't tear my gaze away from the concentration etched onto her face or the grace with which her lithe body moved. It felt like it had been weeks since I'd last seen her, instead of however much time had passed below ground. This woman had no idea how pretty she was.

"Do you recognize this area?" I asked.

"Not sure."

She glanced at me before hastily looking away again. Pink color tinged her cheeks as she strode over to a boulder that stood a good two feet over her head. She circled behind it, but when she didn't reemerge, I stalked around to find her kneeling on the other side. Her left hand rested against the stone, she looked from it to the trees and back again. She adjusted her hold on her knife to trace something on the rock with her fingers.

Stepping closer, I stared at the jagged lines on the surface of the stone. The lines looked as if they'd been etched there by weather and time, but they fascinated Wren. Her fingers stilled on the second line, it was more jagged than the others and had a lightning bolt appearance to it. Wren glanced around the trees again before focusing on the boulder once more.

Her fingers traced the third line then moved five feet over to dip into a thumb-sized hole there. Her mouth pursed as if she'd tasted something bad. Then, her hand fell away and she rose.

"I know where we are," she murmured, and her haunted eyes finally met mine. "We emerged about ten miles from where we left the others."

"How do you know that, from those lines?" I asked with a wave of my hand at the stone.

"The Wilders have a way of marking things. Before you ask, no, I'm not going to reveal it to you."

"I see," I replied.

My eyes fell to her mouth when her tongue licked her lips. She caught the direction of my gaze and stepped away from me. "I know where we are," she said again, "but we have to be careful. The last time anyone was in this area, there was a threat here."

I glanced at the wavy lines and small hole on the stone. *What kind of strange secret language do these Wilders have?*

If Wren had her way, she would take that knowledge to her grave.

Unreasonable anger surged through me at the possibility of Wren's demise. The tips of my talons prodded against my flesh. They sought to break free to destroy any threat to her, but I kept them restrained. The only risk to her now was her mortality, and I couldn't fight that. Her death was inevitable.

My teeth grated together as I inhaled a steadying breath before speaking again. "What kind of a threat?"

"Not the ouro or jinn. This threat was before either of those creatures came to Earth. Most likely it was demons."

I stared at the markings as if I could somehow figure out her words from those three lines and the indent.

"Probably lower-level," I said as I lifted my head to survey the woods again.

The wind lashing through the trees caused branches to click together and created a howl that rivaled the hell hounds when they were on the hunt. The air smelled of rotting leaves, but I didn't scent other demons on it.

"What makes you say that?" she whispered.

"Lucifer kept a leash on the upper-level demons following him. Few of them came to Earth until Lucifer himself did. It was the same for many of the lower-level demons, but they're not always the brightest, and they're more intent on murder and mayhem than the upper-level demons such as me.

"Some of the lower-level demons who broke free when the gateway first opened probably chose to remain on Earth rather than return to Hell. I'm sure some upper levels also opted to stay instead of returning to be ruled by Lucifer. However, they probably would have preferred to reside wherever Kobal wasn't."

"And Kobal wasn't in Hell," she said.

"Not often. We stayed mostly on Earth to protect the humans after the gateway opened."

"What is the difference between an upper and lower-level demon?"

"Upper-level demons are born of two other demons. Lower-level demons are created by those souls who are so malignant they are never allowed to leave Hell to be reborn on Earth again. Lower-level demons feed off the remains of the wraiths when the higher-level demons finish with them. Or at least they used to get our leftovers. On Earth, they'll be able to feed off whatever wraith they find instead of having to wait for us to finish with them. Lower-level demons are strong, but they have no other abilities beyond their strength. They have animalistic features, and I don't mean just horns and a tail."

Her eyes went to something beyond me as she replied. "I've seen the difference between upper and lower. Those twisted monstrosities came into my house."

I fisted my hands to keep from reaching out to comfort her. She would only turn me away or shut me out again if I tried.

"Yes, they did," I agreed. "There are more lower-level demons than upper because of how we reproduce, and all of the lowers were on Lucifer's side."

"And now they're scattered like the rest of the things from Hell," she said.

"Or they've regrouped under new leadership. Most likely under one of the other fallen angels."

"Whether the threat was upper or lower demons in this area, we'd still better get out of here."

Her eyes briefly met mine before darting away again. I resisted grabbing her shoulders and *making* her look at me. I stepped closer to draw her eyes. Instead, she turned away to inspect the trees.

"In the beginning, the demons would attack a place and move on after destroying everyone they came in contact with," she said. "After a while, they started settling into areas that we learned to avoid. We could be near one of those areas now, but I don't know. I haven't been in this section of the Wilds in years, and whoever left these markings didn't leave a date. They were probably in a rush."

"With the entrance to the ouro's den so close, I doubt many demons are around here anymore," I told her. "The ouro didn't care who or what it ate, or which side its prey fought on. It only cared that its prey screamed while it died."

"Delightful."

She pushed back the loose strands of hair that had come free of her braid. Her nose wrinkled when dry ouro blood flaked off her hair and she glanced down at her blood-splattered clothes.

"If there is anything nearby, it will smell us," she murmured.

"There's no preventing that unless you plan to walk around naked."

She frowned as if she were considering it. Then, she glanced around the trees again. "It's too cold for that, and we'll be slower if we're freezing. Plus frostbite and hypothermia could become an issue, for me at least." She worried her bottom lip between her teeth as she contemplated this. "No, we're better off staying dressed."

I now had another reason to hate the colder weather in this area of the world. I'd expected her to flat out refuse my suggestion; I knew how unreasonably attached some humans were to their clothes. Apparently not Wren, but I should have expected her response. She hadn't survived out here by clinging to misguided modesty.

"Do you run around naked often?" I'd meant the question to come out as teasing, but instead, it had been a near growl. The idea of others seeing her exposed in such a way irritated me far more than I'd expected.

She glanced at me from under her thick fringe of blonde eyelashes. "Only when necessary. Do you?" she retorted.

"In Hell, some demons wore clothing, but I preferred not to be encumbered by it. Most of us started wearing clothes on Earth so we could fit in better with the humans. Our nudity was odder to many of them than our looks."

"I can see that," she murmured.

"Can you?"

"Yes. Even if it makes no sense, many people stick to what they know. Most still expect others not to run around naked in front of them. Sometimes, it can't be helped."

"No, it can't," I agreed.

She wiped her hands down the front of her shirt to brush away more of the blood. When she was done, she bent and scooped up handfuls of dirt. It must have rained while we were in the ouro's nest as a thin wet sheen glistened on the leaves covering the ground. The dirt she pulled from the earth oozed from between her fingers as she smeared it over her shirt.

Before the yellow blood of the ouro had streaked her, the shirt she wore had been a pale brown; now it was swiftly becoming the deeper color of mud. She rubbed more of it across her cheeks and over her forehead until it covered her face.

"Normally, I wouldn't care if you walked around with a giant sign over your head, alerting every carnivore within a hundred-mile radius that you'd make a tasty treat. However, I'm going to be walking with you, so..." Her words trailed off as she scooped up more mud. She gestured toward my hands, and when I held them out, she plopped the mud into my palms. "Dirty up."

I smiled at her as the mud squished between my fingers.

"What are you smiling about?" she demanded.

"You think I'd be tasty," I replied with a wink.

The scowl she gave me only made me smile more. "I hope something eats you," she stated.

"We both know you don't mean that."

She didn't respond, only slid her arms into her shirt and spun it around so she could coat more dirt onto the back of it. Through the brown caking her face, I saw the blush creeping over her cheeks.

I had to resist running my hands over her cheeks to brush away the dirt so I could expose more of her enticing blush. Instead, I focused on rubbing mud over me as she smeared some over her ass and down the backs of her thighs. I didn't think she knew how close she was to playing with fire as she worked, but my gaze fastened ravenously on her hands while they traveled over her body.

After a minute or two passed, she looked up at me and froze. Then, she wiped off her hands on the boulder, pulled her knife free and turned dismissively away from me. I didn't have a chance to finish with the dirt before she disappeared into the trees.

"What's the rush?" I asked when I caught up with her.

"The less time I spend with you, the better," she retorted.

"You weren't complaining about my company in the tunnels. In fact, I think you rather enjoyed it when you were riding me."

A muscle in her jaw twitched, but she still refused to look at me. "It's been a while for me, and one dick is as good as another in the dark," she replied flippantly.

My talons unleashed as unexpected rage burst through my chest. Wren's head shot toward me when I growled. Her eyes widened on my hands before sliding up to my face.

"Is that so?" I inquired of her, unable to keep the fury from my voice.

She edged away from me and shifted her hold on her knife. The last thing I wanted was to scare her, but I couldn't regain control of myself as my blood pumped hotly through my veins. I knew Wren was brazen, knew the only thing she feared was her desire for me, but her words had pushed a button in me that I'd never known existed. I didn't care how many other partners the women I'd fucked had. Didn't care if they left my bed and climbed into another's an hour later.

But Wren was different. I hadn't even fantasized about another woman since meeting her, yet she'd just lumped me in with all her other men—men I'd gladly kill before letting them take her again.

She was *mine*.

Something niggled at the back of my mind, something important, but I didn't stop to think about what my possessiveness meant as I prowled toward her. It didn't matter what it meant; it only mattered that it was true. She stopped backing away from me, planted her feet, and lifted her chin as she gazed at me.

"I will stab you if you don't back off," she vowed.

"No, you won't. You'll try, I have no doubt, but you will *not* succeed."

"You underestimate me, demon. You have no—"

Her words cut off when I moved to stand before her in the space of one second to the next. Gasping, she swung her knife up, but I caught her wrist and pinned it to her side before she could sink the blade into my heart. Turning to the side, she stomped on my foot and drove her elbow into my ribs. I bit back a grunt and grabbed her other arm when she tried to slam her palm into my nose.

The second I seized her hand, she swung her head back and smashed it off my face. Blood burst from my nose as it broke with an audible crack. She was gearing up to headbutt me again when I retracted my talons and spun her around. Wrapping her within my embrace, I pinned her arms to her sides and lifted her off the ground.

"Enough, Wren!" I commanded when she thrashed in my arms. "I'm not going to hurt you. I would *never* hurt you."

She threw her head back in response. I managed to dodge the blow that would have taken out some of my teeth, but before I could completely recover, she swung her foot back. The flexible maneuver had me questioning if she was part ciguapa demon with their back-ward feet, when her heel connected with my balls.

My breath exploded from me as fire lanced from my groin to the rest of my body. Gritting my teeth, I turned her to face me. She yanked one of her arms free and swung her hand at me. Throwing my arm up, I knocked the knife from her grasp and pulled her down to the ground. Straddling her waist, I pinned her hands above her head while she squirmed beneath me. Despite her human status, she was a hellion who was determined to castrate me.

She bared her teeth at me and planted her feet on the ground to thrust her hips up. The abrupt movement knocked me forward a little, but I quickly righted myself.

"Enough! I am not your enemy, Wren!"

She went still beneath me, her chest rose and fell with her rapid inhalations as she gave me a look that made my heart sink.

"Are you going to rape me now like I've seen so many others of your kind do, demon?" she spat.

Those words made me feel like she'd broken my nose and kicked me in the balls all over again, and I finally realized that I'd been going at Wren completely wrong. She didn't flirt, didn't appreciate being admired by a man—never mind a demon—and she wanted nothing to do with being teased.

I'd assumed she would warm to my ways, but I knew now that if I continued to push at her, I would only succeed in pushing her away.

She wasn't like the demons of Hell who saw sex as a recreational pastime. She wasn't like the humans at the wall who had seen a lot in their lifetimes, but most not as much as Wren. Most of those people hadn't seen the worst of what demons and humans could throw at them; Wren had.

The people at the wall had bedded demons out of curiosity; most had come back because they enjoyed it. I'd watched some of the Wilders come to the tents of my friends too. Those Wilders had seen some of the worst of what Hell could throw at them, but they'd still been curious. Wren's curiosity was outweighed by the fear she would be hurt, and that I would be the one to do it.

I didn't want her to be like any of the others I'd been with, not my Wren, but I didn't know how to convince her that she could trust me. Though she would never admit it, the vicious sides of humans and demons frightened her. This woman who had tried to kill Kobal, followed us back to the wall, and remorselessly broken my nose was far more vulnerable than I'd ever realized.

She couldn't deny the attraction between us. Actually, she could and often *did* deny it, but deep down she knew the truth, even if she would never admit it. However, she didn't need someone flirting with her; she needed someone to hold her and assure her that the atrocious things she'd witnessed over her lifetime wouldn't happen to her. Wren's biggest nightmare was my kind and all the things they could do. Her abrasive, self-assured demeanor had hidden her insecurity from me, until now.

Releasing her, I leapt up and landed three feet away from her. She lay on the ground, blinking at the sky before rolling to her side and rising. Her eyes were wary when they met mine, but she braced her legs apart in preparation of fighting again.

"You will never have to fear me, Wren," I promised her. "I will never harm you. I desire you, I will not deny it, but I'll *never* push you into something you're not ready for."

"Since the day we met, all you've done is push me!" she retorted.

"And for that, I am sorry."

She gawked at me before clamping her lips together and giving me a sideways glance as she edged toward her knife. "What is your game now, demon?"

My teeth ground together as she called me demon in that disgusted way she had of spitting the word out. "No game," I assured her. "Reclaim your knife, Wren. I will not take it from you again."

She hesitated before striding over to pick up her blade. She never took her eyes off me as she slid the knife into its holster. "Lead the way," I told her and wiped the dried blood away from my upper lip. My nose had already set back into place, but it still throbbed.

She glanced at the flakes of blood on my hand. "I don't want you behind me."

"It was a good blow," I told her, "but my nose is healing, and I don't hold grudges."

She rested her hand on her knife. "So you say."

I couldn't help but smile at her. "So I say. I will walk beside you if you prefer."

"In front of me."

I didn't say a word as I walked past her and into the woods. I didn't look back, but I heard the crunch of footsteps as she fell in behind me. My senses remained focused on her, the increased beat of her heart and scent. I offered no threat to her right now, yet her trepidation didn't ease. Eventually, she would learn to trust me.

CHAPTER TWENTY

WREN

I'd been determined to kill Corson earlier, but the harder I tried not to look, the more I found my gaze running over his lithe body. The pants he wore hugged his firm ass as he walked with his shoulders back. He didn't speak, didn't ask me if I enjoyed my view in some sarcastic way. I did enjoy the view, but I'd never admit it to him.

I didn't know what had come over me earlier. Corson unsettled me; he brought out the better-forgotten memories of what had happened to some of my fellow Wilders. He stoked fears I didn't know I had. I'd seen demons rape and kill men and women before, but in my heart, I *knew* Corson wouldn't do that to me. I felt he would keep me safe no matter what.

So why had I said that to him? If I felt so safe with him, then why would I ask him if he was going to rape me? I bit my lip as I pondered this question and tried to figure out the answer.

Because he scares me more than the demons who rape and kill, I realized. I knew what those demons were after, but with Corson, I had no idea what he wanted from me, and my convoluted feelings for him petrified me. Sex was one thing, but when it came to Corson, there would also be feelings involved, *my* feelings.

I couldn't stand to have my heart stomped on, and I didn't know how to tell him that.

Didn't know how to tell him that the memories I'd worked hard to bury for so long were spilling forth all the time now and at a more rapid rate. Each new memory left me feeling as if it had stripped my skin away to expose my raw nerve endings. I couldn't try to figure out what Corson wanted from me, or defend myself against him when I couldn't stop the flow of anguish cascading through me.

The scent of my mother's perfume had returned to me in the tunnel. The lavender aroma of it had been so intense that for ten steps it had been more real to me than the mineral odor of the rocks. I'd nearly been driven to my knees when I recalled the way my father slapped his knee when he released a good belly laugh. Tears had burned my eyes when I remembered how I would often find them embracing each other as they danced in the kitchen.

There had been so much I'd succeeded in forgetting, but now it was all pouring forth like lava from a volcano. No matter how I tried to shut them down, the memories kept coming until I felt as battered as a ship in a hurricane.

There's nothing left of me to give.

Forcing my eyes away from Corson, I searched the woods around us and tuned all my senses to our surroundings. Over the years, I'd learned how to detect the subtle differences in separate areas of the Wilds. Unlike at the wall, and from what others had told me of the towns beyond it, the wild animals here weren't so brazen in their movements. Like the people who lived in the Wilds, the animals had become more cautious.

At the wall, the squirrels running through the trees and the singing of the birds had been much louder. The birds, squirrels, foxes, deer, and numerous other animals in the Wilds were far more subdued than they'd been when I was a child.

I'd barely noticed their actions as a kid. Unless it was something exceptionally cute, they were the background noise and sights of my life. Then the gateway opened, and I didn't see a bird again for almost a week.

After a while, they'd started re-emerging and singing once more, but it was never the same. As if they somehow sensed the melancholy hanging over the wilds, a sad hesitance had found its way into their songs.

"Where are we going?" Corson asked, pulling my mind away from the animals.

"There's a town a few miles ahead. If we keep following the sun, we'll be there soon."

To my right, a squirrel ran halfway down the trunk of an oak tree and froze. At first, I assumed our presence had caused it to hesitate, but its head turned toward the woods ahead of us. Its nose twitched, and its black eyes bulged as it lifted its tail over its back and gave it a shake. Soundlessly, the squirrel spun and fled up the tree.

My hand shot out. Gripping Corson's arm, I pulled him to a stop. He glanced at my hand before his eyes met mine. His eyebrows drew tightly together over the bridge of his nose as I placed a finger against my lips. Releasing his arm, my hand slid to my knife and I pulled it free.

Then, to my left, a stick cracked and a footstep sank into the leaves. Corson's head shot in that direction. He stepped forward to stand slightly before me as a lower-level demon emerged from the shadows of the trees.

The demon resembled what some had imagined the devil to look like. He had two, foot-long black horns curving toward the center of his head, a broad chest, red skin, and the legs of a goat. The penis hanging between his legs was impossible to miss and would have made a horse jealous. Its cloven hooves dented the ground when it stepped closer.

"Corson," it greeted in a guttural voice slurred by his snake nostrils and lack of lips.

"I'm at a disadvantage here," Corson said with a smile that would have made any sane living thing tuck tail and run. The demon didn't move. "You know my name, but I have no idea who you are. However, I have to admit I don't care what it is, and you probably won't live long enough to tell me."

The demon's yellow eyes narrowed on him before sliding to me. My hand tightened on Corson's arm when a forked tongue slid out to lick over the demon's grotesque face. "Lovely," he hissed.

$\sim$

CORSON

My talons slid free as the lower-level demon's gaze raked Wren from head to toe again. I watched his eyes as I determined to tear those out of his head first for looking at her in that way. I knew exactly what he would do to her if he got the chance, and for that, I would make him pay. If Wren wasn't with me, I would have been on him by now, but I couldn't take the risk of him somehow getting by me to her.

Wren's head tilted to the side as she mimicked the lower-level demon's perusal of her. "And you're an ugly…" her voice trailed off when her eyes landed pointedly on his cock, "bitch, I'm guessing."

I couldn't stop myself from smiling at her as the demon stomped one of his cloven hooves. I knew well how Wren could bait someone into action. She knew exactly how to get this demon to react with reckless abandon.

"When I shove it in you, you'll know," he snarled.

"Shove what in me, honey?" Wren taunted.

The lower-level grabbed himself and wagged his dick in the air. "This," he declared as if it could be missed.

"Oh, that little thing, I've seen bigger dipsticks on the wild dogs roaming through here," Wren replied with a dismissive wave of her hand, and the lower-level stomped his feet again. Any demon with half a brain would know she was trying to goad them into doing something stupid, but most lower-level demons didn't possess a quarter of a brain, never mind half of one.

"It will tear you in two, bitch!"

"This guy is original," Wren said to me. "Do they have someone who teaches them all the same lines?"

"Those are the only ones they can remember," I replied.

"Makes sense."

The demon's eyes bounced back and forth between us before he stormed toward us. He bent forward to lead with his shoulders as he sought to barrel us over. When he was within arm's reach, Wren spun out of the way. The lower-level roared as I leapt into the air and swung my fist forward. He dropped his head to ram me with his horns, but I'd anticipated the action and lowered my hand to pierce straight through his eyes.

A grim smile curved my mouth as the lower-level opened his mouth to roar again. Before it could release a sound, Wren sank her knife through his neck until the blade burst out of the demon's throat, effectively silencing him. The demon's hands flew to his throat as Wren placed her foot in his back and tore her knife free.

I would like nothing more than to cut this thing into tiny pieces for what he'd said and anticipated doing to Wren, but she couldn't witness me doing that. She'd seen and experienced too much violence in her life already, and I wouldn't expose her to any more than what was necessary. With a swing of my other hand, I sliced the demon's head from his shoulders.

Wren's eyes met mine over the demon's back as I pulled his head away. The body remained standing for a minute before slumping to the ground. When I retracted my talons from the demon's eyes, the head thumped onto the ground. Wren bent, wiped her blade on the ground, and slid it into her holster.

"It's a good thing most of them are so predictable," she murmured.

"That they are. We make a good team."

"Yes," she said, and I hid my surprise over her agreement as she rose. "We should go."

CHAPTER TWENTY-ONE

WREN

Hanging low over the trees before us, the sun touched the horizon as the first remains of a house came into view. Thick vines encircled the sagging roof and walls of the home like a snake choking the life from its prey.

All that remained of this town were the fragments of homes and the ghostly memories of those who had resided here. These streets had once been filled with neighbors like mine, who had baked pies, held cookouts, and kissed the skinned knees of their crying children. Now, they held nothing but bones.

There were so many of these abandoned towns in the Wilds that it was impossible to differentiate one from another if they weren't marked somewhere by those who had already traveled through here.

I hoped someone had come through this town recently and left some indicator that it was a safe place to stay. I knew where we were in relation to where we'd left the others, but they could have moved on already, and even if they remained in the same place, we'd never reach them before nightfall.

We had to be somewhere safe before sunset. Demons didn't

strictly travel and hunt at night, but they moved around more once the sun set. With only the two of us, it wouldn't be safe to camp out in the open.

The browning grass surrounding the homes brushed my knees as I walked through it. The further out of the forest we walked, the more broken pieces of wood stood up from the crumpled remains of collapsed and burnt-out houses. In between the remains were the few structures that had managed to withstand bombs, fires, fighting, and time.

Sunset streaked the sky with vibrant pinks, yellows, and oranges, but when I glanced back, I spotted black clouds creeping across the sky. A subtle shifting in the air and the growing ozone scent forewarned of a coming storm.

Stepping out of the thick grass and onto the pitted road, Corson strode boldly down the street while my eyes darted around it. The further we traveled the road, the more homes remained standing, though most looked like I could push them over. The gravel crunching beneath our boots was the only sound in the growing twilight.

"We're going to have to find somewhere to bed down for the night soon," Corson said.

"We will."

I halted to examine a stop sign. Signs were a favorite place for fellow Wilders to leave messages as few signs remained, and those that did drew the attention of others. The rusting sign post slanted precariously to the side, and in the center of the O in "stop" were two rectangles. Beneath the word stop and inside one of the rectangles was the number five. Within the other rectangle, someone had written #2-25.

The rectangles specified brick houses, but there were numerous brick homes on this stretch of road. However, when I counted five down from the sign in both directions, there was only one made of bricks while the other was a wooden duplex.

I didn't look for the second house indicated by the #2; I'd be able to find it if it became necessary for us to retreat there. However, if the first house remained safe, there was no reason for Corson to know there were two safe houses in this town. We were all working together now, but some secrets had to be kept just in case.

"This way," I said to Corson and walked toward the brick house.

Throughout the Wilds, there were at least fifty different Wilder groups spread across the land. In the beginning, there had been distrust between the groups, raids, and murders. Quickly, many Wilders realized that if they continued to fight each other, they would never survive the demons. Representatives from each of their groups met to write and sign a pact to work with each other. The agreement set down laws and punishments for the way rule breakers would be handled. Since then, the Wilders had become a symbiotic network throughout the Wilds, though a few factions kept mostly to themselves as they preferred to remain as hidden as possible.

After I first approached Kobal, word had been sent out with messengers to let the other groups know I'd agreed to work with the demons and that they would be safe if they also came forward. Most of them decided to work with the demons once they realized they wouldn't be slaughtered and that they needed help to survive what had escaped Hell this time.

Randy's group had always been one of the largest and strongest, but Wilders regularly rotated in and out of the various groups to travel to different areas or for other reasons. Over the years, and with all the various movement between groups, the Wilders had adopted a universal marking system no one would notice or understand unless they knew what it meant. The system was kept as simple as possible so people could remember it and so those who couldn't read would still be able to understand it.

Turning onto the broken walkway leading toward the brick house, I picked my way over the chunks of rubble to avoid twisting an ankle. I clambered up the sagging steps of the porch.

"What are you doing?" Corson inquired from behind me.

"Eventually, I'll be going inside," I replied.

"Let me go first."

I gave him a hard stare. "I don't need you to protect me."

"I never said you did; I know you don't. But you can count on me to help you."

"Is that so?"

"Yes."

The certainty with which he'd stated it left me speechless. He turned away before I could respond and stalked over to one of the windows. Cupping his hands against the sides of his face, he bent to peer inside but I knew he wouldn't be able to see in. I stared at the chipped, white front door before turning to search the porch.

A terracotta plant holder sat beside a broken bench. Walking over, I lifted the pot of dry soil and gazed at the numbers on the wood beneath. Some numbers were carved into the wood; others had been written on it.

The last date, scrawled in black marker, revealed someone had been here three months ago. The earliest date was only five months after the gateway opened. This house had been used as a refuge often by Wilders over the years, but that was before the seals fell. There was no telling if it remained safe now.

I didn't hear Corson move, but I felt his body against mine as he peered over my shoulder. "So it was safe here in August," he stated.

Setting the pot down, I covered the numbers. If I wasn't careful, he'd figure our language out. Unlike the lower-level demons, he was far from stupid, and it wasn't exactly a complicated way of communicating.

His citrine eyes were a honey brown hue when they met mine. I found myself gazing into them for longer than I should have. Turning my head away, I pushed past him to return to the front door.

I gripped the handle and gave it a small turn, but the wood, sagging on its rusting hinges, groaned and held firm. I leaned my shoulder against it and was about to shove it when something leapt through the shadows next to the house.

Jumping away from the door, I pulled my knife free, but whatever moved there slipped into the dark. Adrenaline pulsed through my system as I prepared to attack.

"That won't work against them," Corson said and gestured at my knife.

"What are they?" I whispered.

"Hell shadows. They must have also escaped Hell, and now they're spreading out. They can't hurt you, but unlike your shadows on Earth, they can move on their own."

"Delightful," I muttered. "Shifting shadows won't make trying to locate an enemy more difficult for us at all."

Corson's mouth quirked at my sarcasm. Walking over to the front door, he grabbed the knob and pushed his shoulder into it. The door groaned as it swung open. He didn't look back at me when he stepped into the house. A shadow slid forth to dance over the porch banister before retreating again. I returned my knife to its holster, threw the shadows a disgusted look, and entered the house.

CHAPTER TWENTY-TWO

CORSON

The flickering candle flame played over Wren's face as she used her fingers to scoop out the last of the food from the glass jar she held. Her eyes closed as she shoved the food into her mouth. It was clearly empty, but she dipped her fingers back into the jar and ran them over the cleaned glass. She stared morosely into it for a minute before setting it aside.

Walking over to the cabinet she'd retrieved it from, I removed another jar of food from the dozen or so stocked on the shelves. Wren was shaking her head at me before I could return to her with the jar.

"You're still hungry," I stated.

"Yes, but if we take from a safe house, then we have to leave something behind. I've already taken something without being able to replace it. I can't take more. I have nothing of use, except for my knife, and I can't leave my only working weapon behind right now. Leaving a gun without bullets is pointless and could get someone killed if they don't check it first. But I guess if they don't check it first, then they deserve to die."

She didn't know how demon of a thing that was for her to say, but I refrained from pointing it out to her. She was talking to me, and my balls still ached from her kick.

"They do," I agreed. I stared at her and then the jar in my hand. "It's ridiculous for you not to eat when there is food."

"We have to count on each other in the Wilds. If everyone took and didn't give, there would be a lot less Wilders."

I walked over and handed the jar to her when her stomach growled. I wouldn't allow her to go hungry when there was food. "I'll return here with something after we meet up with the others again. You need your strength."

She hesitated before taking the jar of yellow stuff from my hands. She unscrewed the lid and dipped her fingers into it. I returned to the cabinets to close the door on the remaining jars and a handful of water bottles stacked neatly inside. The hinges creaked as the door swung shut.

I'd entered a few other houses in the Wilds before, but unlike those long-abandoned homes, this one didn't have leaves and dirt covering the scuffed, white flooring. Earlier, Wren and I had pumped water from the well out back and brought it in the house. The water was cold, but when Wren was done, I'd stood in the upstairs tub and used it to clean the ouro blood and mud from me.

Like most demons, I bathed often and despised being filthy. Cold or not, I could have spent hours washing myself. However, concern for Wren had driven me quickly from the bathroom. She may refuse my protection, and I would try to give her the space she needed, but I would make sure she stayed safe.

Before going into the bathroom, Wren had shown me where to find a stash of clothing, and I'd donned some of them afterward. The bottom of the pants only fell to my ankles, while the sleeves of the shirt ended at mid forearm, but at least they were clean.

Wren had rolled her shirt sleeves up, but as she ate, one of them worked its way free to fall over her wrist and down to her hand. She didn't bother to shove it back up. Her pants were also rolled and tucked above her ankles. The overly large clothing and her enthusiasm for her dinner made her look far younger. This was a rare glimpse of her with her guard down that I never got to see. Sensing my attention, she glanced at me before digging into her food again.

"Are there many of these... ah, what do you call these houses?" I asked.

She paused with her hand in the jar and lifted her head to look at me. A suspicious look crossed her face. *She's won't even tell me this.*

Then, she shrugged and scooped more mushy food out of the jar. "We call them safe houses, and they're numerous."

"And every one is set up the same?"

"Why do you ask?"

"Just curious."

"No, they're not." Her brisk tone indicated she wouldn't discuss it any further.

Lifting a candle holder away from the others on the counter, the small flame flickered as I walked over to stand in the doorway of the living room. We'd searched this entire place to make sure it was safe before settling in for the night. However, as I stared into the small room, I realized something was off in this house. It wasn't menacing and there was nothing here that could attack us, yet something was wrong.

I gazed at the bare, dingy walls and dust-coated furniture as I tried to figure out what was different about this house. Now that I pondered it, I realized there had been something unusual about the upstairs too.

Then, my gaze settled on a darker spot of paint on the wall and it hit me. "Where are all the pictures?"

All the homes I'd been in before, including the abandoned ones, always had some photos left behind. Humans were oddly obsessed with documenting their time here as it progressed toward the inevitable end.

"Probably stashed somewhere," she replied.

"Did the owners of this house put them away?"

"Doubtful."

"Then who did?"

"Why does it matter?" she demanded.

I glanced over my shoulder at her. Resentment had tinted her words, but the look on her face was defensive. Her knuckles turned white on the jar as she held it between her crossed legs.

"It doesn't," I replied.

"Good." She returned to scooping food out of the jar, but the hunched-over position of her shoulders made it seem as if she were waiting for a blow.

I turned my attention back to the bare walls. There was nothing personal in this house; unless I included the furniture, which I didn't. Where had it all gone and *why* had it gone?

"Whoever established this safe house probably removed the pictures," she said after a few minutes passed. "If not them, then someone else who stayed here put them away, along with any other things."

I didn't look at her or ask why; she would stop talking if I did. I suspected the other things were any personal items the original occupants had left behind when they fled their home or were killed.

"It's easier that way," she muttered.

Easier not to see the reminders of the people who had lived here and the lives they'd led. Lives similar to the ones the Wilders had once led, I realized.

"I see," I said when she stopped speaking.

"I'm glad you do because I don't. Not anymore." She set the empty jar next to the first one.

"What do you mean?" I waited for the wall to slam down and Wren to stop speaking with me, but she continued.

"We take their things away because we don't like seeing the reminders of a past lost to us all, but..."—her gaze traveled to me before flicking away—"we never really forget the past. No matter how much we try, it's still there. Even when we think we've forgotten, pictures or not, the past and the dead come back to haunt us."

She lifted her hand to rub her forehead, and I understood that Wren seeing her father's remains again had affected her more than I'd known. The shadows under her eyes and the lines framing her mouth weren't only from lack of sleep, but also sorrow. Seeing her house and her father again had done more than trigger an old nightmare into returning, it had torn her open and propelled her back into a past she'd buried for fourteen years.

She looked young and vulnerable now because in many ways she'd become that child watching her mother die all over again. Right then, I'd never wanted to hold someone as much as her, but I remained where I was. She had to work through this in her own way.

Her hand fell away, and she blinked at the kitchen as if she were seeing it for the first time. "I don't know what I'm saying. In reality, the dead should only matter to demons, angels, and ghosts. Not to the living, not anymore. We can't do anything for them. We bury them where they fall, if we're able to take the time to bury them, and move on as if they never existed to begin with."

"The dead should always matter to those they matter to," I said. "If you prefer to remember them, then do so. If it's easier to forget, then forget."

"Thanks for your permission!" she retorted before heaving a sigh. "Sorry. I'm not usually so bitchy. Well, at least I'm not usually this *consistently* bitchy."

She stared at the back door as she ran her fingers through her still-damp hair. It was the first time I'd seen her hair free of its braid, and I was unable to resist following her fingers as she worked the tangles from the pale blonde tresses free.

"I must bring out the best in you," I teased.

She gave me a small smile. "I think I'm starting to realize that it's not easier to forget."

"No, it's not," I agreed.

Rising to her feet, she wiped her ass off before bending to lift the jars and placing them in the sink. She stared into the flames of one of the three candles on the counter as she spoke. "When every safe house is established, one of the first things the Wilders do is put all the personal items away. This might sound a little crazy, but sometimes I leave something behind when I stay in one of them. Not something from the family who lived there, but something of *mine*. Usually, it's a rock I found somewhere or a tree branch. Once I cut off a piece of my hair and left it under a couch cushion."

The metal candle holder scoured the counter when she started twisting it. "I know it's an odd thing to do, but I still do it. When I'm gone, all my useful things will be divided between the Wilders, as they should be. Anything personal of mine will be left behind. Though, I have nothing personal.

"Like the families who originally lived in the safe houses, I'll be forgotten too, which is okay. I understand that, but by leaving small things behind, I know something of me will remain somewhere on this planet. Even if it's something no one else will ever know about or recognize as mine, *I* know it's there."

She stopped turning the candle and hunched her shoulders up to her ears. "Why am I telling you this?" she murmured.

Lifting the candle, she turned to face me. Vulnerability shone in her eyes, but so did anger at herself, at me, and at the world, I was certain.

"I watched the human race more than most other demons while we were in Hell. Most never cared to see what was happening on Earth, but I did. I watched Charlemagne fight, the progression of what was later called the Middle Ages, the plague, the Crusades, the settlement of the new world, and the numerous wars and deaths over religions you humans had wrong. I followed the rise and fall of kings and queens, presidents, buildings, and time.

"Technology fascinated me. People made so many achievements in such a short period. Things that once wiped out entire cities and towns stopped being threats. Views changed, people changed, the clothing became less, the advances more, and then one day it all ended. Most of human civilization fell, most of what I'd seen ceased to exist in an instant, and I no longer had to watch from afar, but I was here."

"Why did you watch us so much?" she inquired.

"I'm not sure," I admitted. "For some reason, humans fascinated me. Maybe it was because, by the time I was born, demons weren't allowed to cross back and forth between Hell and Earth. I think I would have ventured to Earth often, if the skelleins, the hellhounds, and the varcolac deemed me worthy of being able to do so."

"What say would they have in it?"

"Kobal is the only one who can open a gateway between Hell and Earth, but when demons were allowed to travel to Earth, the varcolac, hounds, and skelleins worked together to guard the gates and the demons who passed through them. They also decided who they thought was worthy of passing through."

"I didn't know that." She set the candle down again. "Did you watch the humans while they were naked and stuff?"

"I'm not that perverted," I assured her with a laugh. "Besides, the oracle never revealed anything that specific."

"What is the oracle?"

"It's a lake of fire, deep in the bowels of Hell where demons could look on the human realm. Unlike some of the humans who glimpsed between the veils separating Hell and Earth, I didn't see between those veils so I had to travel to the oracle. Few other demons made the journey as the oracle was also the central focus of heat in Hell."

"Oh."

"I am a little perverted though," I teased and mentally kicked myself in the ass as soon as the words were out of my mouth. *Not with Wren*, I reminded myself, but to my surprise, she smiled.

"Not you, demon," she teased back, and for the first time, she didn't say the word demon as if it were something distasteful. Then her smile slid away and she reclaimed her candle. "Do you want the first watch or should I take it?"

"I'll keep watch while you sleep."

"Wake me in two hours."

"I will," I assured her and stepped aside to let her pass into the living room, but I wouldn't wake her. She needed her sleep.

She walked over to the couch, set the candle down on the table, and glanced at the window. All the shades and curtains had been pulled over the windows before we'd entered the house. I assumed they always stayed that way so no one walking by would notice if something about the windows changed from one hour to the next.

I sat in the armchair across from Wren as she settled onto the couch. She pulled her knife free and placed it under a cushion before laying her head on it. Curling up on her side, she tucked her hands beneath her head.

She may tell herself she distrusted me, but she was asleep in minutes. Her breathing slowed, and her lips parted. My hands dug into the armchair as I drank in every detail of her until I couldn't take it anymore. Rising, I stalked over to the window, before pacing back to gaze at her again. I had no idea what it was about this woman, but there were sirens with less pull over men than what she had over me.

That niggling feeling started at the back of my mind again. There had been no women since meeting her, and I had no desire for any others. The protectiveness I felt for her wasn't something I'd ever experienced with a woman before, and I'd been infuriated when she'd compared me to her other partners. These were all things that were not *me*. Jealousy was not an emotion I'd ever experienced before, but Wren evoked it from me in an instant.

I ran a finger over one of my empty ears. I recalled thinking about finding another woman to rid myself of my lust for Wren, but the idea of bedding another repulsed me. Unless Wren started wearing jewelry, there would be no earrings for me in the future. Maybe there never would be again.

My hand fell away from my ear as I continued to stare at her and that niggling feeling became more incessant until it started to take a firmer hold over me.

She couldn't be what I was beginning to suspect. Yes, she enchanted me, but she was human. *Demons have found their Chosen with a human before.*

And humans died far too easily.

CHAPTER TWENTY-THREE

WREN

A burst of noise jerked me awake. My hand slid down to grip the handle of my knife as I listened for something that would reveal what had woken me. Then, a low rumbling built until it became a crescendo of noise.

Releasing the knife, I pulled my hand away and looked at the chair where I'd last seen Corson. He wasn't there. Turning my head, I spotted him standing by the window, his hands raised over his head as he gripped the frame. His shirt sleeves had fallen back to reveal the corded muscles of his forearm.

My breath caught, and my heart hammered as a series of lightning bursts illuminated his lean body and the chiseled planes of his angular face. Not gorgeous like Magnus, Shax, or the angels, but there was something entirely fascinating about Corson.

This demon could make someone scream in pleasure as easily as he could in pain. I thought that should make my dislike for him return, but it didn't. Instead, I found myself imagining what it would be like to feel his hands moving over me again, but this time they would be on my flesh as he slid deep inside me and took possession of my body.

I hadn't found much enjoyment in sex those few times with Todd. However, I hadn't been overly attracted to Todd either. He'd been cute and nice, but I hadn't screwed him out of any real desire or feelings for him. I'd done it to ease my curiosity about sex, and because I lived with the constant knowledge that I could die in the next heartbeat.

I'd seen people die that fast before too. There had been one time when a man had been walking and talking beside me, the next second he'd been pounced on by a demon. I was alive only because the demon had chosen that man instead of me. I could die at any time, and I'd refused to be a virgin when it happened, so when Todd came around, I decided he was a good option.

But then sex with him hadn't been all that wow-inspiring, and now I found myself still speculating what people talked about. With Todd, there had been discomfort; I'd expected that, but I hadn't expected the constant worry that something might eat one of us or how fast it would all happen.

Deciding the first time was practice, I'd practiced a few more times with him before realizing practice was not making it any better. I'd finally given up on sex, and him, altogether. I hadn't liked him much to begin with and hadn't cried when I'd learned he died.

What did that say about me? Was I so cold, so broken by everything that I couldn't feel sad over the death of my one lover?

I supposed someone didn't watch their mother get slaughtered and turn out normal. The world going to shit hadn't helped with the whole "being normal" aspect either.

Unlike with Todd, when I watched Corson, I felt desire.

I hadn't gushed about Todd and sex, like Jolie and some of the other women did. After Todd, I'd assumed they were exaggerating what it was like to want a man and be with him… until Corson. Now I better understood what they were talking about, but Corson wasn't simply a man; he was also a demon.

Why couldn't he be human?

Looking at him, I realized I didn't want him to be anything other than what he was.

Another crash of thunder rattled the windows and shook the house. The next flash of lightning illuminated Corson and the curtains as rain began to tick loudly off the windows. Seeming to sense my attention on him, Corson's head turned toward me.

There was something primitive about him as he gazed at me, something I'd never seen in him before. The glow of the candle reflected in his eyes as he studied me with a predatory hunger. My heart hammered when I realized I was the prey trapped in the hunter's stare.

I didn't know what to do. Part of me contemplated bolting from the room, but the far larger part wanted to open my arms to him. Corson could make me forget, if only for a bit, all the death lurking around every corner.

I dealt with people all the time, but I'd never dealt with anything like him. With Todd, things had been almost mechanical between us. He'd initiated things by kissing me while we were searching for food, and I didn't stop it when it progressed further. Quick and efficient, that had been Todd. If I remembered correctly, we'd both left our socks on every time, and he'd still had his boots on too.

There'd been no flirting, no searing looks making my toes curl, but then there was no way Todd had the experience Corson did with his millennia worth of women.

Three different earrings, I reminded myself. *He was wearing* three *different earrings the first time you met.*

That helped to brace me against him again, but not much. Why did I care who he'd been with before? I shouldn't, yet the thought of him with so many women made jealousy churn in my stomach.

Corson was all hunting grace when he stalked toward me. I tilted my head back to stare at him as he stopped before me. When his hand cupped my cheek, I didn't push it away as I should have. I craved his touch against my skin. His thumb traced the arch of my cheekbone before sliding down to caress my lips. My breath caught and I waited to see what he would do next.

"You're exquisite," he whispered.

Shock rolled through me. I'd seen myself in enough mirrors to know I wasn't ugly, but no one had ever said anything like that to me before and I didn't know how to respond. "No, I'm—"

I stopped speaking when his eyes shot up to mine and his lips thinned out. "Yes, you are. I do not lie."

"You spout pretty tales to get women into your bed though," I retorted, hating myself for saying it, yet unable to stop myself from doing so. What was it about him that drove me so crazy in every single way and turned me into a catty bitch?

"No," he said. "I don't spout anything to get a woman into my bed. I have no reason to. Women come to my bed because they want to be there, not because I talked them into being there. Every woman I've been with has known there would never be anything more than sex between us. Some of those women I took to bed again, most I didn't."

"I see," I said. "And now I know it too."

"Are you coming into my bed then, Wren?"

"No." *Yes!* My body screamed at me. I felt as taut as a bowstring right then, and I wanted him to be the one to release me.

"If it makes any difference, I don't want you to know it."

I frowned at him. "What do you mean?"

He shook his head as if confused by his words and pulled his hand away from my face. "What of you, Wren? What have you told the men you took to your bed?" he asked. "Did they believe it was something more with you?"

"I didn't tell *him* anything."

Something dark flared within his eyes. It was something I'd never seen from him before. Was it possessive? Angry?

"Him?" he asked, his voice hoarser than normal.

I threw my shoulders back and lifted my chin as I stared defiantly at him. "Yes, *him*. I was curious; Todd was there. It happened a few times. I didn't see the big deal about sex and ended it with him. Now he's dead, as are so many others."

He went to grip my chin, but I leaned away from his touch. "Wren…" His hand fell. A lost look flashed over his face before he bowed his head and stepped back from me.

I *despised* that lost look on his face.

"I'm curious about you too," I admitted on a whisper.

CORSON

I wasn't sure I'd heard her right, and then her words sank in. My eyes fell to her mouth, and it took everything I had not to pounce on her. I'd scare her if I did, so I remained where I was, barely.

"And what are you curious about?" I inquired in a hoarse whisper.

Her soulful blue eyes held mine as she responded. "If it would be as mechanical with you as it was with Todd."

"Mechanical?" What had that man been doing with her if she considered sex mechanical?

"Yes." A line appeared across the bridge of her nose as she pursed her lips. "Maybe there's something wrong with me. Maybe, after everything, I've become broken or frigid or something."

"You're not frigid or broken," I assured her.

"And how do you know that?" she demanded.

"Because there was nothing frigid about you in the tunnel."

A blush crept into her cheeks. "Maybe it's different if I'm actually *having* sex and it would be mechanical with all the men I slept with, human or demon," she continued. "But I'd have to experience it with someone else to know."

My teeth scraped together at the thought of her with *any* other man. If Todd had been standing before me, I would have slaughtered him. If she tried to turn to another… The skin on the backs of my hands tingled as the tips of my talons prodded against it.

The more I considered it, the more certain I became she was not just any other woman to me. Whether she was my Chosen or not, I couldn't say for sure unless we had sex, but she was special to me, and there wasn't anything I wouldn't do for her.

"And so you're considering experimenting with me?" I asked her.

I couldn't tell if that idea pleased me or pissed me off more. She might be curious enough to have sex with me, but I didn't want to be an experiment she would move on from afterward.

"No, I didn't say I intended to experiment with you. I said I was curious. That's all," she replied, breaking into my thoughts.

"I am more than willing to ease your curiosity, Wren, and I can guarantee there will be nothing *mechanical* about it."

"You don't know that," she muttered.

I stepped closer and bent over to rest my hands on either side of her hips. She leaned away from me, but she licked her lips when her eyes briefly fell to my mouth.

"I do," I assured her. "But know this. If you decide to experiment on me, I might not let you go afterward."

Her eyes widened on mine. "What?"

"You heard me."

"You can't possibly think that *I'm* your Chosen?" she blurted.

"I don't know if you are or not, I'm simply letting you know that I may decide to keep you."

She swallowed heavily and, removing my hands from the couch, I stepped away from her. I stared down at her, hoping she'd open her arms to me, but she slid her knife back into its holster and rose to her feet.

"I'll take this watch. You should rest," she said.

I hid my disappointment as I moved further away from her. It would be best if I got as far from Wren as possible when we returned to the others, but I trusted no one to protect her as savagely as I would. Being this close to her, and not having her though, might drive me to do something I would never do under normal circumstances.

I'd never take her without her permission, but I may snap and kill someone else if she tried to be with them. I'd never believed such a thing would be possible, not with me. However, Wren pushed the boundaries of my control more than anyone ever had.

For the first time, I wished Kobal were here instead of at the wall, ruling with River as he should. Kobal would have answers for me, he would know what to do, and he would take me down if it became necessary.

"I'm not tired," I told her, "and I don't require as much rest as you do."

She didn't reply as she walked over to the window. Pulling aside a small corner of the curtain, she peered into the stormy night as the rain beat harder against the glass. A flash of lightning illuminated her lovely features and made her hair appear nearly white. She didn't look at me again when she settled the curtain back into place.

"When you watched humans from Hell, was it because you enjoyed it, or was it simple curiosity?" she asked.

"At first, because I was curious." I perched on the end of the couch and lifted my leg to prop my foot against the side of it. "But then, I came to almost like your species. No matter what, the human race found a way to keep going against some pretty steep odds, but then, I guess demons faced some bad odds while evolving in Hell."

"Hell would be steeper odds than Earth, but you do have that whole immortality and regenerating body parts thing going for you that we mortals lack."

"We do have that," I agreed with a laugh.

A loud screech outside whipped Wren's head toward the window. Her hand fell to her knife as she stepped away from the glass. "What was that?" she whispered.

"Not sure." I lowered my foot to the ground and rose. I strained to hear anything beyond the deluge of rain hitting the windows and pounding off the roof. "Some Hell creature, but not one I'm familiar with. I've had about as much experience with the things locked behind the seals as you."

"The seals of Hell falling means the apocalypse, or at least that's what I was taught."

"Not the apocalypse, not unless we allow it to become that. Remember, humans twisted a lot of what they glimpsed in Hell into different mythologies. Some things they got right, others they got completely wrong, and some they made their own. Demons are not all that is evil; angels are not all that is good. Things are *never* so simple. The falling of the seals left Hell a far different place than it was, but it doesn't mean the end of the world."

"Sometimes, I think the apocalypse happened fourteen years ago and we've all just been waiting for it to get around to ending us."

"I can understand why," I admitted. "And there is a possibility everything we know might still come to an end, but we've worked relentlessly to keep the world going for this long."

"Yeah."

Glass blew inward with a loud crash as something smashed through the window beside her.

CHAPTER TWENTY-FOUR

CORSON

"Wren!" I shouted and lurched toward her as a tentacle lashed through the curtains and wrapped around her arm.

She didn't scream as she stumbled away from the wind whipping the curtains back. Rain pelted through the window, soaking her and the wood floor as whatever held her started drawing her toward the window. Jerking on her arm, Wren tried to wrench it free as she reached across her body for her knife. The Hell creature yanked her back, slamming her against the wall and knocking her blade free from her hold.

The knife clattered to the floor, but Wren still made no sound as she dug her fingers into the blue-gray tentacle in an attempt to pry herself free. Arriving at her side, I unleashed my talons and sliced the tentacle, severing it in one swipe. The detached appendage flopped across the floor, spewing gray blood from it.

I spun toward Wren, my eyes frantically searching her to make sure she was okay. The arm of her shirt was ripped open, and red welts marred her skin. I'd slice this thing to shreds for touching her, never mind leaving marks on her.

Something screeched in the night, and my lips skimmed back. I realized what creature was outside before another tentacle emerged through the window and whipped into the living room. Seizing Wren's arms, I pushed her behind me and released her. When the end of the tentacle brushed over my face, I sliced it off. Before I could stop her, Wren darted away from me and scrambled to retrieve her knife.

"Leave it!" I shouted as the front door burst open and more monstrous arms unraveled until they filled the doorway. They slithered up and down as they stretched into the room.

Wren released a startled cry and threw herself onto the ground. Rolling across the floor, she avoided the tentacle swinging toward her, reclaimed her knife, and bounded to her feet. When another tentacle shot toward her, she sliced off the tip before dashing out of the way of the spewing blood.

She ran toward me as I jumped over another tentacle to land beside her in the center of the room. I stepped forward to block her from the tentacles unraveling through the window. They slashed back and forth, extending further into the room as they searched for us.

"What are these things?" she demanded breathlessly.

"It's a macharah," I told her as I nudged her further behind me.

"It? There's only *one* of them?"

"Yes." I leaned back to avoid taking a tentacle to the face. "We'd be surrounded by them if there was more than one out there."

"I feel surrounded now!"

Shifting her grip on her knife, she swung it sideways to implant it into a tentacle. Her momentum pushed the tentacle into the wall where she embedded it there. The end of it flopped and curled over before Wren yanked her blade free and sliced the tip off.

Snarling, I lifted my hands and swung them back and forth as I used my talons to hack my way through the tentacles and toward the door. The wind whistled as the appendages whipped around my head, seeking to batter me into immobility. I dodged back and forth to avoid having my brains littering the floor. Lifting my hand, I speared a tentacle before it could go over the top of me for Wren.

As I worked my way forward, Wren stayed beside me. She stabbed and sliced her way through the appendages as she dodged the attack with ease. All around me, severed tentacles fell and flopped onto the floor where they melted into a gooey ooze that slid through the floorboards. The macharah pulled away its amputated limbs to allow them to regenerate, but no matter how many tentacles I cut off, more pushed through the door.

When I neared the door and the source of the attack, I turned my shoulder to keep Wren partially behind me and better protected. I caught brief glimpses of the thing attached to the tentacles through the lashing appendages. The macharah had settled itself on the walkway.

"What seal is this thing from?" Wren panted as she sliced off more tentacles.

"The macharah were behind the one hundred-third seal."

The macharah drew some of its tentacles back and placing its arms beneath it, the creature lifted itself off the walkway and plopped down in front of the door. The color leached from Wren's face when the tentacles peeled back to reveal more of the hideous beast.

Thirty-plus, smaller tentacles circled the bottom of the macharah and propelled it forward until it stood in the doorway. The macharah moved fastest through large bodies of water, but it was capable of traveling on land too. The rain probably helped its movements.

Without any eyes or ears, the macharah navigated by scent and touch. Once the tentacles latched onto a victim, they drew their prize into the macharah's mouth, which encompassed the entire top of its nearly four-foot-wide, flat head.

Thousands of teeth lined the inside of that mouth, and I could hear them all clicking together as the teeth swirled about in anticipation of a fresh meal. Looking at the beast, it was easy to tell it had feasted well on Earth. The blue-gray skin covering its torso was stretched so thin that it revealed the bodies of the macharah's recent victims sloshing around its stomach.

Rising on the smaller tentacles beneath it, the macharah's blob-like shape filled the doorway.

"It's hideous," Wren breathed.

I sliced away another tentacle, but one slid past me toward Wren. Before I could blink, it slithered around her arm and yanked her forward. Releasing a bellow of fury, I hacked it off her and raced forward to leap at the macharah.

I dodged the tentacles trying to latch onto me as, on my descent, I plunged my talons into the spongy flesh of the macharah and sliced downward. Blood spilled around me; unrecognizable things tumbled from its stomach to scatter around my feet. I dodged the obstacles the stomach contents created to slash at the macharah again.

Screeching, the macharah reeled backward and battered its tentacles against me. I grunted when a couple of my ribs gave way with a crack before digging my talons deeper into the remains of the macharah's belly. I pulled my hands apart, tearing the creature open from side to side. It gave up trying to beat me off and retreated down the porch steps. Rain lashed my face, flattened my hair to my skin, and poured down me as I followed the macharah into the storm.

It had hurt *Wren*. It would not leave here alive.

A savagery unlike any I'd ever known boiled through my veins as I repeatedly tore at the creature until the macharah faltered and slumped toward the ground. The clicking of its teeth stopped, some of its tentacles rose lazily before flopping down. I found myself kneeling on the macharah's flayed remains as they turned to liquid around me. Swept up in the downpour, the last bits of the macharah were washed away by the rain.

My shoulders heaved as I lifted my head to take in the night. The freezing rain pelting the ground formed puddles and ran in streams down the street. I pushed my dripping hair away from my forehead as I searched for more enemies amid the swaying trees and abandoned homes. Lightning tore across the sky in a zigzagging pattern that caused the air to crackle with electricity.

The wild ferocity of the night matched my mood as waves of thunder punched the air in rapid succession. I took a steadying breath to try calming the need to destroy that continued to race through my veins and rose to my feet.

Already working to repair themselves, my healing ribs snapped into place. I turned back to the house to find Wren standing in the doorway with her knife in hand. I doubted much unsettled Wren, but as I stalked toward her, she edged away from the door, and me.

"Are you okay?" I demanded as I climbed the stairs toward her.

"I'm... I'm fine," she stammered. "What about you? That thing, it—"

"It's dead."

I shoved some of the partially digested remains that had spilled from the macharah, out the door with my foot. Grabbing the door handle, I lifted the door and settled it into place to close it again.

"Do you think there's more of them out there?" she whispered.

"No. They usually hunt solo, and they would have scared off any other demons or seal creatures close by."

"Good."

"We have to go. There may not be any more threats nearby, but this place has been compromised."

"I know somewhere else we can go," she said. "I'll be right back."

She spun away from me and ran into the living room. I watched as she snatched a cushion from the couch, sliced it with her knife and yanked the cover off. Stuffing the cover under her arm, she raced into the kitchen and flung open the cabinet doors.

She shoved the food and water into the cover, blew out the candles, and dumped them in too. She dropped the box of matches into one of her empty jars, recapped it, and shoved it into her makeshift bag.

I took the cushion from her when she returned to the doorway.

When I stepped aside, she slid by me and out the door. The wind whipped her hair around her as she ran over to the terracotta plant, lifted it, and shattered it off the porch. Lifting a piece of broken pot, she slashed lines across the numbers before dropping it. She returned to the broken door and shoved it further open, making it clear that this place was no longer safe.

She didn't protest when I took her hand and led her into the storm. Her eyes scanned the surrounding homes as we raced down the road. Water splashed up around us as we ran, plastering our clothes to us. We were halfway down the street when she tugged on my hand and pointed.

"There!"

I barely heard her shout as the wind and rain stole the word from her, but I saw the small brick house she pointed toward. Lifting her, I held her against my chest as I bolted down the walkway and up the steps of the porch with her. The macharah most likely had chased everything else away from here, but I had to hold her and feel her against me right now. That thing had tried to take her from me, and there were so many other things out here that wanted to do the same.

My feet didn't touch the steps as I leapt onto the porch. Wren's wet hair stuck to my neck and face when she squeezed my shoulders and squirmed in my arms. "It's safe," she said. "You can put me down."

"You don't know that."

She pointed behind me, and I turned to look at the numbers carved into the wooden roof over the stairs. The last date was from two weeks ago. "There are two safe houses in this town," I murmured.

"Yes," she said.

I set her down but kept my arm around her waist. Gripping the doorknob, I turned to study the night once more, but all I saw was the endless rain. The lightning illuminated the night, but it didn't reveal any enemies coming toward us.

When I turned back to the house, another burst of lightning illuminated the number twenty-five on the mailbox hanging next to the door. I twisted the knob, and rested my shoulder against the door to shove it open when the swollen wood stuck for a second. The door gave way and swung open with a squeak of rusted hinges.

The scent of mildew wafted out to me, but I didn't detect the odor of anything else as I stared inside the house. Another flash of lightning pierced the darkness to illuminate our shadows on the floor before me, but little else of the house was revealed. I searched for a predator before the light vanished once more.

Wren's shiver drew my attention to her. Her lips were taking on a bluish tint. Her wet hair straggled around her shoulders and her clothes stuck to her skin. The idea of being inside one of these houses again wasn't one I relished. After the macharah's attack, I was too wound up to be stuck inside again, but there was no other choice, she'd freeze if she stayed out in this storm.

Wren's hands rested on my chest when I lifted her again, stepped inside, and closed the door behind us. With the door shut against the tempest, darkness descended on the house. I stiffened, my nostrils flaring and my ears twitching as I searched for any hint of something approaching us. The storm masked most noise, but my hearing was sensitive enough that I should be able to detect something approaching before it reached us.

"Give me the sack. I'll get the candles out," Wren said through her chattering teeth.

Reluctantly, I set her down and handed her the cover. Her fingers brushed mine as she took it from me and set it on the wooden floor with a small thud. Jars clinked together as Wren dug through it, and then the scratch of a match sounded. A small flame flickered to life before me. Wren extended a shaking hand to the wick and lit a candle.

"Stay here," I told her.

She glanced at me and then froze. I don't know what she saw on my face, but instead of protesting my command, she handed me the candle.

Turning away from her, I prowled into the kitchen, living room, and bedroom in search of anything that could be hiding in the house. Adrenaline continued to pulse through my veins in waves that had me on the verge of shredding the furniture in the rooms I stalked through. I almost hoped something was hiding in here so I could unleash some of my lingering tension on it.

I discovered Wren in the kitchen when I returned. She'd lit more candles and set them on the counter as she unpacked the jars and placed them in the cabinets next to more containers of food and water.

"It's safe down here," I told her. "I'm going upstairs."

So focused on her task, she didn't look at me as she responded, "Okay."

I heard the click of the cabinets closing before I bounded upstairs to search through the bedrooms and bathroom there. Wren had clothes in her hand and was coming from the lower bedroom when I returned to the top of the stairs. She'd wrapped a towel around her and held it against her chest. Beneath the towel, the straps of her bra were visible across her shoulders. She set the clothes on the back of the couch along with another towel. Her boots were turned upside down by the front door.

"I found us some more clothes," she called to me. "We should both get dry before we freeze."

I stood and stared at her as she gazed up at me. The dim light of the candles danced over her pale skin. Her wet hair had curled at the ends and waved around her face. In that instant, I knew only one thing could calm me again—her.

Water dripped from me as I descended the stairs toward her, closing the distance between us in less than a heartbeat. My rapid descent made her gasp and step back, but she didn't try to pull away when my hand slid around her nape and I drew her flush against me.

Her hand tightened on the towel. I waited for her to tell me no, but she stared breathlessly up at me, her chest rising and falling against mine. I stared at her for a second more before crushing her against me and claiming her mouth.

CHAPTER TWENTY-FIVE

WREN

I tried to process what was happening, but then what was there to process? Corson was kissing me, and not just *any* kiss, but one that would consume me. And I wanted to be devoured by him, I decided, as the fiery scent of him mingled with the November rain in an intoxicating combination that ensnared me.

His hand entangled in my hair, and he pulled my head back to deepen the kiss. Dimly, I realized I'd never truly been kissed before, or at least I'd never been kissed as if I were everything to someone. Corson kissed me as if the most important thing to him was having *me*.

My hand loosened its grip on the towel, and before I knew what was happening, it fell with a whisper to pool around my feet. I still wore my bra and underwear, but his clothes pressed against most of my flesh. Instead of his wet body chilling me further, it heated mine more than any fire could have.

He moved me back a step and then another until my back was against the door. The heady evidence of his arousal rested against my belly while he continued to kiss me as if his life depended on it. I eagerly met his tongue as our breaths fell into rhythm with each other.

"If you decide to experiment on me, I might not let you go afterward." His words from earlier drifted across my mind.

Pull away! Yet, I found myself being dragged further and further under by his kiss. I'd never experienced something like this before and I wanted him so badly that my entire body ached for him.

I went to reach for his shoulders, but he seized my wrists. With one swift move, he bound my wrists together with his hand and pinned them over my head. I realized he had me trapped and vulnerable, something I'd vowed never to be with a demon. Being at the mercy of a demon equaled death.

However, I didn't experience any trepidation, and instead of fighting his hold, I arched into him until my breasts flattened against his chest. My mind spun, but it was impossible to grasp any thoughts when Corson had complete control of my body.

He'd let me go if I asked it of him, but I didn't feel dirty, tired, and unattractive with Corson as I so often did. Instead, I felt the complete opposite of those things and alive in a way I never knew I could be. For the past fourteen years, my heart had beat, my lungs inhaled, but I'd only done those things because my body required me to do them.

Now, I did them because I *wanted* to do them.

I hadn't realized I was mostly dead until he made me come alive. This could never go anywhere between us. He'd said he might not let me go, but he would. I wasn't his Chosen. He desired me, there was no doubt about that, but he would find a demon to have demon babies with, and I....

I could be dead tomorrow, and it was time I started living for today.

I could never have a relationship with a demon, and Corson wouldn't want one with me once he found his Chosen, but I would always remember what it had been like to have his touch make me come *alive*.

My breath came in pants as he broke the kiss to gaze down at me. His eyes held mine while he ran his free hand down my side, tracing over my ribcage and down to my hip. The sensation of his bare flesh against mine drove me crazy, and of their own volition, my hips thrust toward his fingers when they trailed from my belly button to the edge of my underwear.

When he pulled his hand away, I almost whimpered, but then one of his talons grazed my flesh. His eyes left mine to rake over my body before he sliced down the front of my underwear. The thin material gave way with a whisper when it slid down my thighs to land on the floor. He must have retracted his talons as I felt only skin when he slid his fingers between my legs, and one of them rubbed my clit.

I mewled before biting my lip to suppress the sound. His eyes remained focused on what he was doing as he spread the wetness growing between my legs in unhurried strokes that caused my legs to tremble.

"You have no idea how badly I want to be inside you," he said as he slipped a finger into me. I was unable to suppress a cry as he bent his head to nibble on my earlobe. Then his lips were against mine once more while he continued speaking. "How badly I want my finger to be my dick you're riding." He moved his palm in such a way that it sent spirals of pleasure through me. "How much I want to hear you screaming my name while I'm buried deep inside you, making you come over and over again."

I didn't have any control over my body as his words and hand did things to me that I didn't know could be done. My hips met the rhythm of the movement his finger created as tension built steadily within me. Then he removed his hand and disappointment crashed through me. My hips pushed demandingly toward him. "Why?" I moaned.

"I have to... I'm so hard it hurts."

I heard a button and then a zipper before I felt his erection touch my stomach. It was so rigid, yet so smooth and hot as it rested against me. His talons emerged a few inches, and he sliced my bra down the middle. Cool air rushed over my bared flesh when my breasts spilled free. Corson's gaze fastened on them and the sound he emitted was one of possession and hunger.

Then, he was dipping his mouth to trail his tongue over my skin. He licked around my hardening nipple before sucking it into his mouth. "Corson!" I cried and he turned his attention to my other breast.

I jerked against his hold on my wrists, needing to feel him, but he refused to let me go. When he released my nipple, and rose over me again, his eyes burned orange fire.

"Tell me to stop, and I will, but I won't take anything less than all of you this time, Wren. Tell. Me. No," he bit out, and I heard the torment in his voice.

I'd watched as he'd torn the macharah apart like it was no more than a piece of paper. He'd moved so fast he'd become a blur, but his destruction had littered the floor behind him. I'd followed his progress by watching the pieces of the octopus-looking creature flop on the ground before turning to ooze and slipping through the floor-boards. The macharah had been a monster straight from Hell, and he'd pulverized it. His desire for me was evident, he could do what-ever he wanted to me and I'd never be able to stop him, yet he'd just given me control. He would do whatever I said.

There were so many reasons to tell him no. *All* those reasons clamored through my head as I stared at him. I opened my mouth to tell him no, that we should stop. I could come to regret this, but I knew I would regret it more if it never happened.

"Yes," I said.

Something crackled through the air and over my skin. I leaned back as I realized it was a wave of Corson's power—a power he'd been keeping somewhat concealed, but it slipped free now. Before I could react, he slid his arm under my ass and lifted me up. Instinctively, I wrapped my legs around his waist. My gaze held his as the movement caused his erection to settle between my thighs and press against my center.

His hand tightened on my wrists, pinning them to the door as the head of his shaft parted my folds. In one swift motion, he plunged deep inside me and froze when I cried out. The sensation of him within me wasn't unpleasant, but it was unfamiliar as he stretched and filled me. I wiggled and then winced as I tried to adjust to the size of him.

"Easy," he murmured, his lips caressing mine as he spoke. "Wait a minute."

I didn't know if he was talking to himself or me, but it didn't matter. Releasing my wrists, he cupped my neck tenderly as his tongue slid into my mouth again. Finally able to touch him, my hands sought the buttons of his shirt, impatiently tugging them free. The last button fell free, and I broke the kiss to shove the shirt off his shoulders. Adjusting his hold on me, he shrugged the rest of the way out of the clothing.

I sighed when my hands fell onto his bare flesh. My legs clenched around him when my gaze followed the rain water trickling from his hair. The beads of water trailing down his chest and abdomen emphasized the ridges and valleys of his stomach as they ran in and out of the dips of his body.

Like all demons, the only hair he had was on his head, eyebrows, and eyelashes, so the water flowed freely down him to where our bodies joined. The sight of him between my legs caused my mouth to go dry, and I gave an experimental rotation of my hips.

"Oh," I breathed and repeated it as my body adjusted more to having him within me.

A muscle twitched in his jaw, and his hand flattened against the wall beside my head as the other remained cupped beneath my ass. His eyes fell to my breasts when my back arched toward him.

"Exquisite," he murmured as he lowered his mouth to run his tongue over one of my puckered nipples.

My fingers curled into the wet, silky length of his hair, drawing him closer. I'd never experienced anything like this before. A quickie in the woods didn't leave much room for touching, kissing, and *feeling*, but now all I could do was feel Corson as he possessed me.

CHAPTER TWENTY-SIX

CORSON

The enticing scent of Wren's arousal slid through the air. Everything about her was softer, warmer, more exquisite than anything I'd ever known before. I continued to savor her as I let her find her way and set her own pace.

She'd been unable to hide her wince when I first entered her. Not a virgin, and unbelievably wet, yet she was still unused to sex. If I wasn't careful, this wouldn't be mechanical for her, but it would be painful.

She's human, be careful. You'll hurt her.

I'd been with many humans, but this was the first time I worried I might injure one of them. With Wren, I knew I could lose complete control, something I'd never allowed to happen before.

The sensation of her muscles gripping my cock became too much for me to take, and I found myself unable to hold back any longer. Drawing back, I thrust into her while I nipped at her breast. Her fingers tightened in my hair as the rapid beat of her heart pulsed in my ears. All other sights, sounds, and smells were drowned out as everything in me became centered on Wren.

Releasing her breast, I lifted my head to watch her as her hips rose and fell and her pert nipples stood proudly in the air. I drank in every detail of her slender body, dusky nipples, rounded hips, and the pale blonde curls between her legs. Drawing back, I watched myself plunge in and out of her.

Her breath came in small pants; her body became more demanding as I pushed her closer and closer to release. When I pulled back before plunging into her again, her back arched, and she moaned as she came apart in my arms. The muscles of her sheath contracting around me nearly wrenched my orgasm from me, but I gritted my teeth and held it back.

She slumped against me, her rapid breaths warming my skin as she nestled closer and kissed my neck. Cradling her against me, I kicked off my boots and strode over to the couch with her. My pants slid further down to hang around my hips as I walked. A mewl of protest came from her when I lifted her off me and set her on the couch.

"I'm far from done with you," I promised as I pulled my pants off and tossed them aside.

Her eyes latched hungrily onto my dick when I stepped closer and bent to rest my hands on her hips. I shifted her so that she lay on the couch with her head on the armrest and her hair flowing out around her flushed face. Lowering myself over top of her, I settled myself between her thighs. Her legs spread further open, her hands fell on my shoulders as I buried myself to the hilt within her once more.

Home.

The realization blazed across my mind as my hand entangled in her hair. Drawing her head back, I kissed her neck while her legs wrapped around me. Her fingers dug into my back, and I drew back before plunging into her again.

I had no more room for any coherent thoughts as something within me fractured, and I became completely lost to her.

∼

WREN

All I could do was cling to Corson as the firestorm of emotions he stoked within me rose higher and higher. The release he'd given me earlier had briefly quenched my yearning for him, but it was back now.

I nearly screamed with the joy the sensation of his smooth flesh moving against mine and his muscles flexing beneath my hands evoked in me. The smell of him, the feel of him, and the sight of his body rising over mine were an intoxicating combination that I craved.

I held him closer, needing to feel more of him. Seeming to sense this, his arm encircled my waist, and he lifted me until his chest was flush against mine. His breath warmed my ear as his tongue traced it. My hips rose and fell faster; my heels dug into his ass as I eagerly responded to the growing urgency I sensed within him.

"*Mine*," he breathed against my ear.

"*Mine!*" This time the word came out more of a snarl, and I dimly realized his voice sounded distorted in a way I'd never heard it before.

I couldn't focus on that though as tendrils of pleasure spiraled out from my core until they became waves that had my head falling back as I cried out in ecstasy.

∼

CORSON

Out of control. Completely out of control. It was all I felt as Wren's body rose and fell beneath mine. Any restraint I'd tried to keep unraveled as I took her with an abandon I'd never experienced before, not even with a demon who I didn't have to worry about possibly harming. Instead of being frightened or pushing me away, Wren's hands and cries urged me on.

An unfamiliar pressure spread up my shaft, building steadily higher. Despite the strangeness of the sensation, there was something pleasurable about it, and I didn't try to stop it. I couldn't stop anything now; I was too far gone in her to try.

"Mine," I told her, finding it was the only word I could get out. "*Mine*."

When I repeated it, I realized something unfamiliar filled my mouth. *What the…?*

My tongue prodded the tip of a canine as it lengthened. Then, I poked at the lengthening canine on the other side of my mouth.

I don't have fangs.

Something tugged at my mind, but as it was tugging, Wren's sheath clenched around me as she came again. The exquisite sensation of her contracting muscles gripping me was too much for me to take. Trusting forward, I gave myself over to her.

I dimly realized that not only was my spine tingling from my orgasm but something more incredible was taking over. My dick jumped within her, the pressure that had been building gave way as, for the first time, I experienced the release of my semen into another. The rush of it enhanced my orgasm in ways I hadn't known possible.

But all of it was buried beneath my need to…

My eyes latched onto Wren's neck as her body bowed beneath me to expose the slender column of her neck. Without thinking, I bent to kiss her shoulder before sinking my newfound fangs into her flesh. Pinning her to the couch, I continued to take her.

Wren cried out; her nails scored my back as she orgasmed again. I released my bite on her shoulder and sank my fangs into one of her breasts. Dimly, I knew what was happening, knew what I'd done and what it meant, but I couldn't stop myself; I'd finally found where I belonged.

CHAPTER TWENTY-SEVEN

Wren

"Wait!" I gasped. "Corson, wait, stop!"

He growled against my breast, the rumbling sensation causing my muscles to quake in response. My traitorous body was more than willing to keep going with him, but my mind refused to shut off again as his bite brought a cold dose of reality with it. Reality, panic, and a surprising heartache that I hadn't been expecting filled me.

I need to think, and I can't do that with him inside me!

I wasn't sure my words reached him, and if they had, I didn't think he would stop as he thrust into me again. But then he released his bite on my breast and lifted his lips to settle them right over the place where he'd bitten my shoulder. His body stilled within mine before he pulled out of me.

I had the overwhelming urge to cry and take him back inside me, while I resisted the impulse to shove him off me. What he'd done couldn't mean what I imagined it might; it *couldn't*!

Corson settled onto the couch beside me while I lay panting and staring at a large, brown water spot on the ceiling. Right now, I didn't know which way was up or down, right or left. I wanted to flee into the night as badly as I wanted to cry.

Corson locked his arm around my waist when I rolled over. He settled behind me, drawing my back flush against his chest as he held me possessively against him. If I allowed it, he would be inside me again, but I couldn't allow it. Not after what had happened.

Mine. The possessive way he'd said the word hammered through my mind. And I'd felt his release inside me. The intensity of his orgasm had triggered another one from me, as had the unexpected pleasure his bite aroused in me. Bites were supposed to be painful, but his had sent me spiraling further out of control.

His *bite!* Corson didn't have fangs, not like some of the other demons I'd seen. I knew there were demons who had permanent fangs, and others who had fangs that extended when necessary, but I'd never witnessed anything like that from Corson. I'd seen him pretty pissed off and excited for a fight before too. No, Corson's teeth had always been perfectly normal or human in appearance.

Bits and pieces of our earlier conversation played through my mind again…

"Demons also only bite another during sex if it is their Chosen," he'd said. *"If for some reason, their bite marks should fade, other demons will always know when another has been claimed and stay away from them."*

"A bite and sex are what decides a Chosen?"

"No, there is far more involved in the bond than that. Male demons don't produce sperm until they find their Chosen and the females don't produce eggs."

I was positive there had been sperm.

"Some of the demons who went to Earth before the angels entered Hell found their Chosen amid humans." He'd also said that at some point too.

My heart raced, and my fingers dug into the fabric of the couch. He couldn't think *I* was his Chosen. I cared for him; I did. I wouldn't have slept with him otherwise. Maybe there hadn't been a whole lot of feeling with Todd, but there was with Corson. There was too *much* feeling with him.

I'd gone into this knowing there could never be a lasting relationship between us. The whole immortal/mortal thing was only one of some fairly large obstacles between us, but I'd thought maybe he cared for me, and not because some screwy demon DNA told him he *had* to to be with me so he could have demon babies.

To my horror, I realized that I wanted him to desire me for me, and not because he could suddenly produce sperm with me!

Not to mention, there was Randy and all the other Wilders to think about. A fling with Corson would have been one thing, but to be claimed by a demon and expected to reproduce with one was something else entirely. I didn't know how they would react to this.

Not much made me feel like crying, but the possibility of losing all of them, and everything I'd ever known, brought a lump to my throat.

I recalled almost laughing over the thought of Corson having to romance anyone into staying with him. There hadn't been much romance involved between us, but this situation was far from amusing.

Behind me, Corson lifted his head. "What's wrong, Wren?"

I hated the trace of hurt in his voice, but I couldn't stop my need to get away from this place and *him*. I had to have time to process all this.

You're getting way ahead of yourself! You've seen bite marks on people after they've had sex before. There was also that ridiculous time Jolie allowed some guy to make a ring of hickeys around her neck. Corson may have been mistaken about that whole biting aspect of a Chosen. He had to have bitten someone else over the numerous years of his extremely active sex life.

Now I could add jealousy to the flight instinct my body had going on as the idea of him with another woman set my teeth on edge. I didn't want to be a demon's Chosen, but I didn't want him biting anyone else either.

I was losing my mind. Somehow, this man—*demon*—had managed to turn me into an irrational mess!

Before he'd sauntered his earring-wearing ass into my life, I'd been nothing but pragmatic and remorseless. I didn't live with guilt or feel bad about possibly hurting someone. I didn't recall the past. Those things would only eat me alive if I allowed them to, yet now I was experiencing all of them and all because of *him*.

"You bit me," I said. I couldn't stop my hand from resting against the marks on my shoulder.

Two punctures, like he was some vampire or something. His bite had shot a fresh jolt of pleasure through me until all I could do was come apart in his hands, and I had come apart, *multiple* times. Still, I couldn't stop the crushing sense of being trapped those marks brought to me, and being trapped equaled death.

"I did." His voice remained casual, but the muscles in his chest became rigid against my back.

"You said…" I swallowed to get some saliva into my parched throat. "You said demons only ever bite their Chosen."

"Wren—"

"You said demons only produce sperm with their Chosen."

"Yes, I said those things."

"Were they lies?"

"No. Do you want them to be?" He didn't breathe as he waited for my answer.

"I don't want to be the Chosen of a demon."

I felt a slight recoil within him though he didn't move.

"Not *a* demon, *my* Chosen," he said in a tone that reminded me of a predator waiting to pounce.

"I'm not… I won't be *anyone's*!" I cried, and my heart twisted at the possibility of hurting him.

Maybe I more than cared for Corson if I worried about hurting him, but I couldn't give myself over to anything more than *sex* between us. Immortal or not, he could die, and I'd lost far too many in my life to endure the loss of another.

I loved my friends and Randy. I would grieve their passing if it came in my lifetime, but I had a feeling Corson's death could tear my heart out and leave me a broken mess afterward. I might not survive it if more developed between us and I lost him. My parent's deaths almost destroyed me, and I'd vowed never to let something like that happen to me again.

"I belong to myself and no one else," I stated.

"You do belong to yourself." He leaned forward to nuzzle my hair with his nose. Before I could stop myself, I melted against him. "But you are also mine."

"No!" I jerked away from him and leapt to my feet before my body betrayed me again. "No!"

Storming around the back of the couch, I snatched up the clothes I'd placed there from where they'd fallen on the ground. I hugged them to my chest as I spun to face him. He remained sprawled on the couch, his long body taking up all of it. His posture was casual, but anger simmered in his eyes, and he didn't bother to hide the erection sticking out from between his legs.

My gaze went to the bead of liquid forming on the head of his cock. Shaking my head to clear it of my impulse to jump him, I started to dress. They would be a small obstacle for him, especially since I no longer had underwear or a bra, but clothes were still a barrier between us.

"Did you suspect?" I demanded as I yanked my pants up one leg. "You said sometimes demons know or at least suspect another is their Chosen before sex, did you?"

He hesitated long enough that I knew his answer before he spoke it. "Yes."

I froze with my foot halfway through my other pants leg. The awkward stop threw me off balance, and I almost toppled over. I caught myself before I hit the ground. I scowled at him as if my clumsiness had been his fault, but awkwardness was another thing I'd never experienced until he entered my life.

Regaining control of myself, I jammed my foot the rest of the way into my pants and pulled them up to button them. They were too big for me, and I had to roll the waistband over twice to get them to stay up.

"I started to suspect earlier tonight, but when I look back, I realize I should have guessed it sooner. You've been in my head for a while. There isn't anything I won't do to protect you. When the ouro and macharah touched you, all I could think about was destroying them. I haven't been with another woman since I first met you—"

"Liar," I said as I tugged the sweater on.

One second he was lying on the couch, the next he stood before me. Gasping, I stumbled back before I could stop myself. I'd never seen *anything* move with that kind of speed. I hadn't known it was possible.

"I am *not* lying." He advanced on me as he spoke, and I edged further away. "If I were going to lie to you, I would have denied that I suspected you were my Chosen before I claimed you, but I didn't deny it."

Refusing to yield any more to him, I stopped backing away and lifted my chin as I stood my ground against him. His orange eyes darkened to a near red hue as he stared at me, his body looming over me and his chest brushing against mine. I had no idea why I didn't fear him, considering what I'd seen him do to that macharah, and he appeared more pissed off now, but I had no worries he would put his hands on me in anger.

"I will take many things from you, Wren, but I will not take being called a liar. I will *never* lie to you. I never have, and I'm not going to start now. The only woman who has entered my mind since meeting you *is* you. And you've been on my mind every night as I've jerked off to imaginings of you. I'm not a human who can't get laid; I'm a demon who can go to any tree nymph or most any other female demon at any time to get off. My hand is *not* something I use. But use it I have, too many times in the past couple of months.

"I should have known what you are to me sooner; I didn't. But I cannot change what happened between us, and despite the fact you drive me insane, I wouldn't change having you as my Chosen. I warned you earlier that I might not let you go. I gave you the chance to tell me no. You didn't."

I gave up trying to hold my ground against him and backed away as his words melted my resistance. He wasn't lying. He hadn't been with anyone else, and he had given me the chance to walk away from him; I hadn't taken it.

He will hurt me. It wasn't a matter of *if* he would hurt me, it was only a matter of *when* it would happen. Human or not, everyone died in the Wilds.

Corson's hands flexed at his sides as he watched me, but he didn't try to stop me from putting some space between us.

"Yes, you did warn me," I murmured.

I should have listened to him more, but I'd been too caught up in the moment, and him, to think it through. Plus, I hadn't believed I could be his Chosen. Things would have been different if I'd known; I would have walked away from him. But even as I thought that, I wondered if it was true. I'd wanted him with an intensity that hadn't left any room for rational thought. I still wanted to give in to him *now*, but terror kept me from doing so.

"We're good together," he murmured.

"The only reason you want me is because you have no choice in the matter," I said and awkwardly tugged on a sock while continuing to move further away from him. His eyes stalked my every move like a hawk circling its prey. "Some biological demon thing has told you that, for some *insane* reason, you can only have offspring with me. If you had a choice, you would prefer someone else."

"No, I wouldn't."

I ignored the cold when I jammed my foot into my soaked boot. "You're only saying that because you just shot your load for the first time!"

Corson lifted a black eyebrow at me; he smiled briefly before suppressing it. What the hell was I saying? I didn't know anymore. I only knew I had to get away from him. I shoved my foot into my other boot and tied the laces with fumbling fingers.

"I will admit that what I experienced with you is beyond anything I've ever experienced before," he said. "I didn't know sex could be *that* good. I've heard what they say about a demon with their Chosen, but I thought they exaggerated. I was wrong. There will never be anyone else for me, only you."

"Because your DNA is telling you to feel that way."

I ran my fingers through my hair in an attempt to detangle it as I edged toward the hallway. I had to keep moving. If I stopped, I would have to acknowledge the sense of loss growing within me.

"I would still care for you if you weren't my Chosen," he said.

"You can't possibly know that, and don't say that!"

"I can know it, and don't say what?"

"That you care for me."

"Wren—"

"The people who care about me die!" I snapped. "The people I care about die. My parents weren't the only losses I've endured over the years. There have been countless others. Maury who had a potbelly and a lopsided grin. He loved Greek mythology and was teaching me about it. He had his head ripped off when a demon crept out of the bushes behind him while he was in the middle of telling me about Hermes."

The sympathy in Corson's eyes didn't make me stop speaking. If anything, it made my words come out in more of a rush.

"Or there was Rebecca, who would watch me when Randy went out to hunt. She'd play games with me and braid my hair. She died while giving birth, and so did the baby. She bit on a stick for hours to keep from screaming, but in the end it was for nothing. I watched as she bled out and the baby never took a breath.

"Over the years there have been so many others who cared for me and died. Do you want to know about them?" I demanded. "Do you want to know their names and stories too? Because I hadn't thought about them or recalled their names in years, but I remember them *all* now."

"Wren—"

"I still have some friends, but I've learned not to get too close to anyone anymore. Randy is the only one who has managed to last these past fourteen years, and even he might be gone now." I hated that my voice choked on those words, but I couldn't stop it.

Corson opened his mouth before closing it again. Before I could stop him, he stepped closer to me and rested his hand against my cheek. "I'm not easy to kill."

I shrugged his hand off and backed further away from him. "You're still killable, and death is the way life works."

"Yes, it is, but I do care for you," he said. "You are *the* most infuriating, stubborn, and hostile woman I've ever met. You're also kind and protective, even when you try to hide it. I admire your ruthlessness and your willingness to kill anyone or anything that endangers someone you care about.

"I've witnessed you placing yourself in front of other Wilders to shield them. I watch you wait until your followers have all eaten before you do, and I see you take less food than they do. You worry about their injuries and speak tenderly to them when you clean and dress those wounds. You show this callous, brash side to the world, but I see through it. You try not to let anyone in, you convince *yourself* that you keep everyone out, but your followers are in your heart, and there is more caring in you than you'll ever acknowledge. You wouldn't have traveled to the wall otherwise."

"What makes you say that?" I asked.

"You've come to like and trust demons and civvies more since going to the wall, but it was your need to make sure your fellow Wilders had a better life that brought you to the wall in the first place. You wouldn't have come for yourself."

"Maybe I was trying to save my own ass by traveling to the wall. I saw what came out of that gateway and knew how much worse the Wilds were about to get."

His small smile melted my heart a little further. "We both know you would have rather died than turn to the demons."

He was right; I couldn't deny it. I didn't care enough about saving my ass to agree to working with the demons, but there were children in the Wilds. When we'd first gone to the wall, we'd kept the children safely hidden from the civvies. As our trust in those at the wall grew, we decided to bring the children there to live with their parents, if they still had parents. The children remained at the wall now.

"Probably," I admitted.

"You may be my Chosen, but that is not why I want you. I want you because you're beautiful. And not just on the outside, you're also beautiful within. You can try to deny these things, but they're all true. I know who you *really* are. I may even know you better than you know yourself, Wren."

My skin prickled at his words. They sounded so arrogant, so sure, but he was *wrong*. He didn't know me as well as he assumed. As my memories had revealed to me recently, *I'd* forgotten who I was, so how could he possibly know me?

"That's where you're wrong, Corson," I said as I braided my hair and knotted it around itself at the end to keep the braid in place. I was exceptionally proud my fingers didn't tremble while I worked.

"And why is that?" he asked.

Tossing the braid over my shoulder, I held his gaze as I replied, "You claim to know me so well, yet you don't even know my real name."

He frowned as he stepped toward me. "What are you talking about?"

"Wren isn't my name, not my real one, not the one my parents gave me."

If I'd reached out, I could have pushed him over with one hand as he stared at me in confusion.

"Get dressed," I said. "I'll be on the porch. We have to leave."

I didn't wait to hear his reply as I turned away from him.

CHAPTER TWENTY-EIGHT

Corson

"There you are!" I didn't glance at the fallen angel, Caim, when the raven landed beside me.

The ebony bird stood at least three feet tall and weighed about a hundred pounds. With a flutter of wings and a ripple of movement, the raven went from ambling beside me to a full-sized man between one step and the next. At six-two, Caim was almost as tall as me and lean in build.

The fallen angel was the last creature I wanted to see right now. No, second to last, I decided. I preferred Caim to Raphael.

Caim the Fallen, or Raphael the Golden, as many whispered of the two very different angels. The two angels had proven their loyalty to Kobal, River, and the rest of us, but my hatred and distrust of angels were ingrained in me from birth.

I especially didn't like the angels who remained in Heaven. They were content to let the rest of us deal with the mess they helped to create when they threw Lucifer and his followers out of Heaven six thousand years ago. Lucifer would have destroyed Heaven if he'd been allowed to stay there. Without Heaven, Earth and Hell would have crumbled too, but the angels should have dealt with their shit instead of dumping it on the rest of us.

I tolerated Caim more than Raphael because he displayed his emotions, whereas Raphael was often as emotive as stone. I also knew that Caim hadn't chosen to follow Lucifer, not really. He'd gotten caught up in the battle the angels waged while in Heaven, and he'd been made to pay for it.

"Here we are," I murmured and glanced at Wren. She continued to walk ahead of me, her shoulders back, and her chin high.

The rainbow colors in Caim's black eyes swirled as he studied her. Those same colors shone within his black hair and onyx wings. The foot-long silver spikes at the top of his wings were visible over his shoulders, while the spikes at the bottom nearly touched the ground as he walked.

Unlike most of the other fallen angels who had regrown bat-like wings after they'd shorn them off, Caim's wings had regrown with feathers. Despite those spikes and their ebony hue, his wings remained more angelic in appearance than the other fallen angels. Caim believed his bond to the raven he could transform into had allowed his wings to regrow as they had.

"We've been searching for you both for two days," Caim said.

"We were gone for two days?" Wren looked back to ask Caim.

"Yes."

She shook her head and focused forward again. When the motion caused her braid to fall off her shoulder, and tumble down her back, Caim's eyes narrowed on the bite I'd left on her neck. My low snarl drew his attention quickly back to me. His mouth pursed to hold back his laughter.

"You're a bigger asshole than Raphael," I told him.

A laugh burst from him, and he did a small skip step away from me as I contemplated wringing his neck.

"Never have I denied it," he replied. "It seems we've been searching in vain; we should have allowed you two to remain alone."

"No, you shouldn't have," Wren retorted. "Where are the others?"

"They're about five miles straight ahead as the raven flies," Caim replied, but he didn't take his eyes off me.

"Is everyone okay?" she inquired.

"We lost Malorick to a barta demon, but everyone else is fine," Caim replied.

Malorick had been the telepathic demon Kobal assigned to work with our group. "I assumed he was dead when he didn't reach out to me to learn where we were."

"Yes, his death was inconvenient timing on his part," Caim stated, and I almost smiled.

"You're all assholes," Wren muttered.

Caim shrugged. "So was Malorick. We were concerned about you two."

"No reason to be," Wren replied.

"I can see that, now, but it's not like the two of you to take off," Caim said and grinned at me. "But some things are always unexpected, and it seems you two might be disappearing a lot more often."

When I took a step toward him, he danced back, chuckling as he moved. "We fell into the trap of the ouroboros," Wren said. "And no, we will not be disappearing more often."

Caim's eyebrows shot up, but this time, he wisely chose not to make a sarcastic reply or appear smug. He actually looked troubled as he gazed between the two of us. "Is the ouroboros dead?" he finally inquired.

"Yes," I replied. "Go back and tell the others we're fine and we'll meet up with them soon."

Caim nodded and unfolded his wings. With a strong flap of his wings, he rose to hover above us. "There is something ahead you might enjoy," he said to me. He was halfway into the sky before he transformed into the raven, released a loud caw, and swooped low over the trees.

"What do you think is ahead?" Wren inquired.

"It could be any number of things," I replied, "but if it was a trap or something waiting to eat us, I doubt he'd give us warning if he wanted us dead."

I kept my attention focused on our surroundings as Wren walked before me. I preferred her back with the others, where she was safer, but once we rejoined them, she would go out of her way to avoid me again. I'd seen and heard the panic in her earlier; I had no idea how to ease it though.

"The people who care about me die. The people I care about die." The anguish in those words had torn at my heart. I didn't want my Wren to know such pain, but I couldn't take it from her. She'd lost too many, witnessed far too much death, and seen too much horror in her life. I could never fix that for her, but I *would* make sure she had a better future.

I suspected Wren believed that by becoming my Chosen she risked opening herself up to a lot more heartbreak, and I couldn't tell her she wouldn't be. I was stronger than many demons, faster, and I'd lived a lot more years than most, but there was a chance I might one day lose a fight and die.

Wren could have convinced herself it was simply sex between us and nothing more, but not after I'd claimed her. Sex was one thing, feelings were another, and Wren's heart had been trampled more times than she'd ever acknowledge. She would do everything she could to protect herself from having that happen again, even if it meant shutting me out and denying herself.

"You claim to know me so well, yet you don't even know my real name."

Her words replayed through my mind. I tried to recall everything she'd said to me and everything I'd learned about her, but not once had Wren said her name was anything different, and no one had ever called her anything other than Wren. I would have remembered if they had.

Was she lying to me about her name, or was it something she

never mentioned to anyone? Did she recall the name she'd been born with?

"Wren—"

"I don't want to talk right now."

I ran a hand through my hair as I watched her walk with a stiffness that was unnatural for her usually fluid body. I'd tried speaking with her a couple of times since leaving the second safe house, and each time she'd replied with the same crisp response. Space was what she required, but I couldn't slip away and let her be until I knew she was safe with the others.

My eyes dropped to the enticing sway of her hips, but I tore my attention away when I realized I was becoming aroused again. I'd been told what a Chosen did to and for a demon, but I hadn't expected this unrelenting desire for her.

Arriving at a boulder, I climbed up behind her as she made her way carefully over the rock. Coming over the top, I caught Wren when she stumbled back, and her mouth dropped. My eyes shot to the forest; my talons lengthened as I prepared for an attack. When I saw what had caused the shocked expression on her face, I retracted my talons before I got us both killed.

CHAPTER TWENTY-NINE

CORSON

"What...?" she breathed, her voice trailing off as her head tipped back to take in the canopy of branches and leaves overhead.

As much as I didn't miss Hell, a smile tugged at my lips as I gazed at the somewhat familiar landscape of my home. The only difference between what was here and the forest I'd once known in Hell was the lack of fires and tree nymphs dancing enticingly through the woods.

"Calamut trees," I told her. "They must have escaped Hell or at least some of their seeds did."

She continued to gawk at the woods before speaking. "How does a tree escape from anything?"

"Calamut trees aren't like Earth trees."

"No kidding," she muttered as her head tipped back again. "There are no trees this size left on Earth; I'm not sure there ever were trees this large. And I've never seen a tree this color before."

"That's not even half of the differences," I assured her. "And these are smaller than normal. They're baby calamuts."

"Holy shit!"

I chuckled as I leaned back on my heels to survey the calamuts. They stood about three hundred feet tall, half of their mature size. Deep grooves etched their black bark and gnarled, twisted limbs. Their hand-sized leaves were smaller than when they were fully grown, but still larger than the leaves on most Earth trees. The leaves were so dark a black they appeared purple in the sunlight filtering through their thick canopy.

"In Hell, the tree nymphs lived in the Forest of Prurience with the calamut trees. Some demons used the fallen leaves of the calamuts to make clothing with. You can see the start of their prury fruit there," I said and pointed to the small, plum-colored balls forming on some of their branches. "When the prury is full-grown, it is the size of your watermelons."

"Can it be eaten?" she inquired.

"River ate some of it without a problem, but the calamuts offered it to her. No one would dare to take the fruit from them without their permission."

"The trees grant permission?" she squeaked.

"These trees can move. I've seen them tear someone in half, spear an ogre straight through, then offer the tree nymphs protection. As I said, they're not your Earth trees. Like everything that evolved in Hell, they're deadly."

Wren gulped. "I see."

"They won't bother us unless we try to hurt one of them or a tree nymph. Then, they'll destroy us."

I grabbed her hand when it fell to her knife. She yanked her hand away from me.

"No weapons, not around these trees," I told her.

"I'm not going to hurt them," she retorted, "but there could be any number of creatures lurking in the shadows of these things."

"The calamuts won't allow a fight in their midst. If we don't bother them, they won't bother us. Come."

I rested my hand on her elbow to nudge her forward before releasing her. Her head tilted back again when we stepped beneath the thick canopy of the trees; her mouth parted as she gazed at them in awe.

"They're beautiful," she whispered after a few minutes.

The leaves rippled over as if a breeze blew through them, though no wind stirred the air. In response to her words, some of the branches dipped lower. Wren gasped and stepped back. I nudged her forward with my shoulder. "It's okay," I assured her. "If they wanted us dead, we would be. Your words pleased them."

"Oh, that's, ah... nice," she stammered.

The leaves crackled when they flowed together once more. "Amazing!" Wren cried.

"Yes," I said, my gaze focused on her, but she didn't notice.

When we stepped from the shadows of the calamuts and back into the woods of Earth, the smile slid from her face as reality returned. Her shoulders slumped, and she gave a longing glance back before focusing ahead once more. I vowed to take her back through the calamuts the next chance I got if only to see her smile like that again.

When a shadow fell over us, I tipped my head back. Against the backdrop of blue sky, I spotted the raven circling overhead. Caim's wings folded against his back, and he dove out of the sky to land beside me once more. Shifting, he fell into step beside me. "A small grove of calamuts," he said.

"Highly observant of you," I replied.

Normally Caim would have smiled at me before coming up with some wise-ass response. Instead, his face remained oddly distant, and no amusement shone in his eyes. "Bale is on her way."

Wren's fingers twitched at her side, and her pace picked up.

"What is it?" I asked Caim when I sensed the strain behind his words.

"Raphael found something while searching for you," he stated.

"What?"

"I don't know all the details yet. I was asked to return to you so the others could follow me and find you easier."

Raphael could have uncovered any number of things while he'd been searching for us. Most of those options weren't pleasant. The snapping of a branch caused Wren to pull her knife from where it hung at her side. I surged forward to stand by her side as I searched for any hint of a possible attack.

I relaxed and smiled when Bale emerged from the forest. Her fire-red hair swayed against her ass as she walked. The reddish hue of her skin resembled that of the humans when they stayed too long in the sun.

"The ouroboros," Bale said as she sauntered toward us. "I hope it's dead."

"Was there any doubt I wouldn't destroy it?" I inquired.

Bale grinned, Wren scowled as she returned her knife to its holster, and Caim chuckled. I glanced at the angel, having no idea what he found so amusing, but he'd forgone his seriousness of only seconds before to smile back at me. He gave a pointed look between Bale and Wren and wiggled his eyebrows.

"There was some doubt," Bale replied, drawing my attention away from the infuriating angel. "After all, you're not as skilled at hunting and killing as me."

"Everyone else would disagree with you," I assured her, "especially the ouro."

Bale studied her nails as if she were bored. "I will give you that it was probably a difficult kill."

"I have to add that I was unable to see when I sliced its head off."

Bale dropped her hand, but amusement shone in her lime-colored eyes when they met mine. "Bragging is unattractive."

"Then you must be the ugliest woman alive!" I retorted, and she laughed.

In truth, Bale rarely bragged about her kills and was one of the most stunning women I'd ever seen. Her smile revealed her teeth, but unlike when she was pissed, her razor-sharp fangs weren't visible. At nine hundred and eighty-six, she was younger than me, but almost every bit as lethal.

Her eyes flicked toward Wren before returning to me. Then, her gaze shot back to Wren and settled on my bite marks. Wren's hand went to the handle of her knife again, but Bale's attention had already returned to me.

Questions swam within Bale's eyes, but I gave a subtle shake of my head. I wouldn't discuss Wren with anyone else. Wren continued to grip her weapon as she focused on the woods. Caim made some strange laughing cough into his hand, before clasping his hands behind his back and assuming an innocent demeanor.

"Where are the others?" Wren asked, unable to keep the concern from her voice as she searched the forest.

"They're coming," Bale answered.

"What did Raphael discover?" I asked Bale.

"He tells me it's nothing good, but he won't reveal anything until we're all together. He's on his way here now."

As soon as she said it, Raphael swooped out of the trees to land five feet away from Caim. Whereas Caim was all that was dark, Raphael was all that was light. His white-blond hair fell to his broad shoulders, and like the rest of the golden angels, his eyes were a violet color. After they were thrown from Heaven, all of the fallen angels' eyes had turned black.

When he'd first come to Earth, Raphael had worn a white robe, but he'd discarded it after a month. Since then, he'd taken to wearing the same clothes as the rest of us. His plate of silver armor still adorned his chest over top of his brown shirt. A broadsword hung at his side; the azure jewel in its hilt reflected the sun across the forest floor and caused a blue light to flash over the rotting leaves. Taller than me, Raphael stood around six-seven.

No emotion showed in Raphael's eyes as he surveyed Wren and then me. "It is good to see you are both well," he said in his clipped way.

When he stretched out his wings to knock the gold dust from them, he revealed the circle of golden feathers inside his right wing. The golden feathers created a pattern that resembled a sun symbol. I had no idea why he had that pattern; perhaps all the Heavenly angels were marked in such a way, but I'd never asked. I didn't care to know any more about the angels than I already did.

Raphael shook off the rest of the dust and closed his wings against his back. No spikes adorned his wings, which were rounded instead of pointed like those of the fallen angels.

"I hear you discovered something while searching for us," I said to him.

"I did," Raphael replied. "Perhaps we should discuss this alone."

Wren glared daggers at him when he looked pointedly to her. Like the rest of the golden angels, Raphael had a connection to life that allowed him to harvest energy from all living things and use it as a weapon. He could kill Wren as easily as she could step on an ant, but that didn't faze her as she held his stare.

"I brought the Wilders to you. I will hear what you have to say," Wren stated.

"It may be best for you and all the humans to return to the wall," Raphael replied.

"I don't run from things."

"She'll hear what you have to say," I interjected.

Raphael's eyes slid to me. He was stronger than I was, but he wasn't more powerful than Kobal, and Kobal had put Bale and me in charge. Because of that, he would do as I commanded. Raphael may not like it, but on this plane, Kobal was his leader.

Raphael nodded briskly, and Wren shot me an irritated look for interfering. I smiled sweetly at her in return. I knew the smile would drive her nuts, but she'd been doing that to me for a couple of months. As I'd suspected it would, her scowl turned into a full-on glare.

"Now that's love," Bale murmured from beside me.

"It's something," I replied. "How long before Magnus, Hawk, and the others arrive?"

"They should be here any minute now," Bale said. "They only

know as much about this as I do. Now that Raphael has a tidbit of information, he's enjoying withholding it from us."

"I bet he is." I looked toward where Raphael stood with his hand on his sword. There were only a few times I'd seen the angel look at all unsettled by something; this was one of them. His eyes traveled continuously over the woods before rising to the sky, where they remained longer than I liked.

"Chatting with your brothers and sisters above?" I asked Raphael. Unlike Caim and the rest of the fallen angels, whose bond to life and the angels in Heaven severed after their fall, Raphael could still communicate with his fellow non-fallen angels.

"No," Raphael replied.

"Good." I wasn't fond of Caim or Raphael, but I *despised* those cowardly pricks above.

Magnus and Hawk slipped from the forest with Erin, Vargas, Shax, and Lix following behind. "Where are the rest of the humans?" Raphael inquired.

"You said you wanted to speak with us privately, so we told them to make camp about a hundred yards that way." Hawk jerked his thumb over his shoulder to point behind him. "You're alive," he greeted as he slapped me on my shoulder.

"It will take far more than an ouroboros to kill me," I assured him. *Or perhaps it will only take one woman,* I thought as my attention returned to where Wren was edging away from the others. She was even trying to avoid Erin and Vargas, who were both as human as her.

Hawk followed the direction of my gaze and his mouth parted in realization when he spotted my mark on Wren's neck. Newly turned from human to demon; Hawk was still learning all he could do, and as a canagh demon, he required nourishment from sexual energy as well as wraiths to survive. He didn't have a problem feeding on the wraiths, but before learning he was a canagh demon and that his kiss could enslave another, he'd accidentally ensnared a human woman when he'd had sex with her.

He held onto enough of his human tendencies that he hadn't forgiven himself for it yet. As punishment, he went far too long without sex. So long that I feared one day the honorable soldier might snap and do something he would regret.

Tall and broad, Hawk was thickly muscled and only a couple inches shorter than me. He ran a hand through his short, dark brown hair as his blue eyes studied Wren. He wasn't looking at her sexually, but I still stepped in front of him to block his view of her.

His eyes flew up to mine, and he stepped back. "I wasn't looking at her like that," he said.

"I know," I replied.

Hawk had spent enough time around Chosen pairs to know not to get between them. However, when she edged further away, I realized the attention Wren was receiving from the demons and angels bothered her, even if she pretended not to notice everyone staring at the marks on her neck.

"Glad you're safe," Vargas said to Wren and squeezed her arm as he walked by her toward me. "You also."

I grasped Vargas's extended hand and squeezed it. There weren't many humans I was fond of; Sergeant Anselmo Vargas was one of them. His eyes, so deep a brown they were nearly black, twinkled with amusement when they held mine. Within those eyes were lighter flecks of golden brown color. His close-cropped black hair emphasized the broad cheekbones and olive complexion of his Peruvian heritage. At five-ten, he was far faster than his stocky build suggested he would be.

"What is it you saw, Raphael?" Caim inquired, drawing my attention back to the angels.

CHAPTER THIRTY

*W*_{REN}

WREN

I hated that my eyes went to where Corson stood ten feet away from me in the small, open section of woods. I tried to get as much distance from him as I could, but I couldn't stop looking at him and Bale at his side.

Had there ever been anything between them? I'd wondered it more than a few times since meeting them. They were deadly when they killed together; I'd never seen anything escape them. Often, they didn't speak to each other as they stalked their prey and they seemed to sense what the other would do before they did it. They read each other better than any couple I'd ever known.

Oh, for fuck's sake, you're starting to annoy me more than Corson! I snapped at myself. *Get it together.* Corson said I was his Chosen, but I had no claim on him, and I didn't want one. He could do whatever or *whoever* he wanted from here on out.

There were ten thousand more important things to worry about right now. Like why Raphael, one of the most powerful beings on this planet, looked like someone had walked over his grave.

Beside me, Erin shifted, drawing my attention to her. She didn't look away fast enough to hide the fact she'd been staring at the bite on my neck. I resisted tugging at the collar of my shirt; it was already up as high as it would go. I never should have put my hair in a braid, but it was my habit to wear it that way, and I hadn't been thinking about the marks when I'd braided it.

It was too late now, and to unbraid it would make it appear like I cared about those marks more than I did. Because I did not care about them at all.

Yeah, and the sky is full of yellow unicorn farts. I glanced at the sky to confirm it was still blue. For all I knew, with everything that had happened, the sky really could be full of some yellow, stinky Hell creature gas. The púca could shapeshift into unicorn-looking beasts after all.

Erin smiled shyly at me, and red color crept into her cheeks. Her almond-shaped, dark ocean-blue eyes radiated warmth. Small and slender, she was as nimble as she was intelligent, and during my time with her, I'd learned Erin Choi was of South Korean and Irish descent.

"What is it you saw, Raphael?"

Caim's question drew my attention back to the two angels as they stared at each other with open animosity. However, no matter how much they acted as if they despised each other, I'd seen Caim and Raphael both protect each other from an attack. They were like the siblings who pummeled each other into the dirt, but if anyone else dared to do the same, the angels turned on them like rabid dogs. I didn't know if they realized their protectiveness toward each other or not, but they didn't hide their bitterness.

Not only were their looks and coloring stark opposites, but so were their personalities. They were both gorgeous though. I assumed that was a given considering God had forged them. The demons and angels may refer to it as the Being, but I'd dutifully donned my little bonnet and dress to attend church every Sunday as a child. The Being would always be God to me.

Raphael focused his attention on the rest of us as he spoke. "The fallen are gathered about three miles from here. They are at the gateway."

A shiver ran down my spine at the mention of the fallen angels. We were here to kill them, but the idea of them so close was more than a little unnerving.

Caim was the only fallen I'd ever had any interaction with, and he wasn't so bad. However, I knew his siblings were a lot different than him. They'd all been thrown from Heaven, terrorized Hell for six thousand years, and helped Lucifer unleash Hell on Earth. They were powerful, cruel, and looking to either destroy or enslave humanity. They'd have to kill me before I allowed myself to be caged by one of them.

"The gateway *did* draw them back," Corson murmured. "We knew it was a possibility."

"We did. I don't like the idea of so many of them so close to us right now, but we expected them to regroup after Lucifer's death. You are all siblings and such, and you tend to stick together," Magnus replied with a dismissive wave of his hand.

I didn't know if Magnus was as bored by this conversation as he acted or if he was trying to irritate Raphael. Lifting a hand, Magnus yawned into the back of it while his silver eyes held Raphael's gaze.

The chiseled planes of Magnus's sculpted face and his ice-blond hair made him appear more angelic than demonic. However, the two six-inch black horns curving back against the sides of his head were entirely demonic. His hair mostly covered those polished horns, but the tips of them were visible. I'd learned from Erin and Vargas that Magnimus, or Magnus as he preferred to be called, was the last demon of illusions and could weave things out of thin air.

"Yes, the fallen all consider *themselves* siblings," Raphael replied, making it clear he didn't consider them such.

Caim rolled his eyes. "Our bond to you and the other angels may have severed when we fell, but we are siblings still. We were *all* created by the same power and from the same Heavenly waters."

Raphael's eyes narrowed on him. "Yes, we were, but those

siblings would happily have my head and yours. They hate you for turning on Lucifer as much as they hate me now. Consider them your brothers and sisters if you will; *I* consider them my enemies as it will help me to kill them when the time comes."

For the first time since I'd met him, Caim didn't seem to know what to say, and it took him a bit to respond. "True," he grudgingly acknowledged.

"We did expect them to regroup, and we were hoping the gateway would draw them in so we would have a better idea of where they are and what they're up to," Raphael continued with a pointed look at Magnus. "We did not expect what I saw."

"And what is that?" Corson inquired.

"There are twenty-eight of the fallen at the gateway. I assume that is all that remains of them," Raphael said.

"I didn't tally up their body count after we battled them the last time, but that sounds about right," Bale said.

"Those twenty-eight are gathering a following," Raphael continued.

"Fucking delightful," Lix said.

Lix pulled the flask hanging from his side free, uncapped it, and took a swig of the beer inside. Though I knew it wouldn't happen, I held my breath as I waited for the liquid to pour out of Lix's skeletal frame. Like always, the liquid remained inside him—somewhere.

Most of the skelleins like Lix stood at about four and a half feet tall, but Lix was a little taller than the rest, and from what I'd gathered, he was their leader. All the skelleins loved games, riddles, drinking, and fighting. One of their favorite things to do was attempt to stump Erin with one of their numerous riddles. I hadn't seen them succeed yet, but they were determined they would.

The skelleins all looked alike with their skull faces and empty eye sockets. I didn't know the names of most of the other skelleins, as they rarely shared them, but they could be told apart by their distinctive accessories or clothing. They all wore swords and flasks, but they often pilfered clothes wherever they could find them. Right now, Lix sported a black bow tie with yellow ducks on it, along with a green belt looped around his hip bones. The skelleins often donned ridiculous apparel, but I liked their jovial, blood-thirsty personalities.

"We expected them to gather as many of Lucifer's followers and seal creatures as they could," Corson said. "Many of those imprisoned behind the seals will resent their time there. They'll be looking for vengeance, and the angels will offer the possibility of that to them."

"Yes," Raphael replied, "there are many craetons there."

"And we will kill them all," Shax said.

Aside from Corson, Shax was the demon I'd spent the most time with. I'd first encountered Shax with Kobal and Bale when I'd tried to kill them before following them to the gateway. Kobal and Bale had been in Hell with Corson, River, and Hawk when I'd arrived at the gateway. Shax had remained on Earth with some of the others. Shax hadn't been thrilled to see me again, but Erin and Vargas convinced him not to kill me outright. He'd continued to distrust me, but I'd gotten to know him better while we were there.

Out of all the demons, Shax was the most human looking. He was six inches taller than me and at least two hundred pounds of solid muscle. His golden blond hair waved around his handsome face. The only thing marking him as something other than human were his sunflower colored eyes.

"There are not enough of us to take on what I saw at the gateway," Raphael replied. "At least not right now."

"How many are there?" Shax asked.

"A few hundred."

Corson's nostrils flared as he looked at me. "There are that many near us now?" he demanded.

"Yes," Raphael replied.

"We have to move out of here," Bale said. "We can't face that many and survive with our numbers, and we can't get in contact with any of the other groups to bring them here now that Malorick is dead."

"That is not the worst of it," Raphael said.

"There's something worse than that?" Magnus asked, no longer looking so bored with the conversation.

"Yes." Raphael's eyes went to the sky again. I followed his gaze to search for black wings overhead.

"What is it?" Caim inquired.

"Astaroth appears to be leading the craetons now," Raphael said.

Caim grimaced before speaking. "Yes, I can see that. Not a wise choice on the part of the fallen, but few could attempt to fill Lucifer's place, and Astaroth is one of the few."

"Who is Astaroth?" Erin asked.

"He is one of the fallen," Caim replied. "He is not as powerful as Lucifer, but he can read minds."

"Oh shit," Hawk muttered.

"He cannot randomly read a mind," Caim said. "He must be focused on an individual to do so."

"I'd prefer not to have my mind read no matter what he has to do. There's not much up here"—Hawk tapped the side of his head as spoke—"but it's mine."

"I agree, there's not much up there," Magnus said.

Hawk gave him the finger.

"Astaroth can also astral project," Caim continued.

"What do you mean by astral project?" Vargas asked.

"He can split himself in two and control the mimicry of himself," Caim explained.

"Ay dios mio." Vargas pulled the cross hanging from his necklace out from under his shirt to kiss it.

"He doesn't do it often," Caim continued. "The mimicry can't be killed, but it can be wounded, and he feels those injuries."

"What if you cut off the mimicry's head?" I asked.

"Then it vanishes, but he doesn't die. Maybe his neck hurts afterward or something; I don't know, I didn't ask. Astaroth was not one I spoke with often."

"Why not?" Bale asked.

"He's an asshole. And I don't mean he's an asshole like Raphael can be an asshole. I mean, whereas Lucifer was insane, vicious, and bent on vengeance for all the wrongs he felt he'd endured, and some were valid." Caim flicked a pointed glance at Raphael as he said this. "I mean, Astaroth was a nasty bastard even when he was in Heaven. The fall didn't improve his already warped personality. Lucifer killed; Astaroth tortures and maims, allows healing, maims again, and so on."

"So he's like the kid who enjoys pulling the legs off spiders," I said.

Caim's eyes swirled with color when they met mine. "He's like the kid who likes to cut the legs off a spider one tiny piece at a time, before feeding the spider to the cat that he later cuts into one small piece at a time and feeds to the dog. Then—"

My stomach lurched sickeningly, and Erin's hand flew to her mouth. "I don't want to hear about the dog," I interrupted and Caim nodded.

I hadn't seen Astaroth, and I already hated him. Most of the dogs in the Wilds were now feral, but some of them would occasionally creep in to get a belly rub and a scratch behind the ears. A few of them moved around with us, offering protection and giving a warning if something approached. Many canines found their own way now, but we all remembered a time when they were our constant companions.

"Lucifer let Astaroth play with demons to keep him appeased and honed for battle, but he also kept him in check," Caim continued. "Astaroth was no match for Lucifer's strength and cunning, and he knew it, but without Lucifer to cage him…"

"He's free to play with everything and everyone he comes in contact with," Corson murmured when Caim's words trailed off.

What would happen if Astaroth got his hands on Corson? What would the malicious angel do to him?

I inhaled a tremulous breath to calm my galloping heart. I couldn't stand to think of anyone torturing Corson, or any of those I cared about in such a way. Life out here had always been brutal and short, but the destruction of the seals and the rise of the fallen angels had upped the ante.

Demons destroyed; angels tortured before decimating.

I gazed at the small group surrounding me. More demons and humans were establishing a camp nearby, but there were only fifty of us in total. And fifty against a few hundred were not odds I was willing to tempt. I fought when necessary, and I hated backing down, but I hadn't survived this long by being stupid and staying somewhere when it wasn't a good idea.

"We have to come up with another plan, get in touch with the other groups and bring them in before we face the angels and craetons," I said.

"That may not be enough," Raphael said, and the tone of his voice made the hair on my neck stand up.

"Why not?" Corson demanded.

"The horsemen have joined with the angels."

CHAPTER THIRTY-ONE

CORSON

"You're shitting me," Hawk said to Raphael.

Raphael blinked at him. "I am an angel; I do not shit."

At any other time, I would have laughed at the look on Raphael's face as he took Hawk's question literally, and the way Hawk's mouth dropped at his response. But when it came to the horsemen, there was no laughing. And to have *Wren* so close to them.

"You should have revealed that detail first!" I snarled at Raphael. "Lix, go back to where you left the others and tell them to pack up *now.*"

Wren didn't edge away from me when I approached her. Standing beside her, my chest nearly brushed her shoulder as I surveyed the forest for any hint of a threat lurking within it. Lix swigged down more of his beer before hurrying away.

"The horsemen? As in *the* four horsemen of the apocalypse?" Erin inquired as she glanced between Raphael and me.

"No," Raphael replied.

Hawk and Erin breathed a sigh of relief.

If only it were that easy, I thought before responding, "As in the *eleven* horsemen."

The humans and Hawk exchanged dumbfounded looks.

"Eleven?" Wren croaked.

"Yes," I said. "Humans mixed up what they saw through the veils about the horsemen. They separated the four horsemen of the apocalypse from the seven deadly sins, but they're all together. They always have been. However, as humans commonly believed, the horsemen weren't originally heralds of the apocalypse."

"But now?" Wren asked.

"Now there's no telling the destruction they could rain down on Earth."

"Lovely," Erin said.

"And they all ride around on horses?" Vargas asked.

"You could consider them horses, I guess," Shax replied.

"I don't like that answer." Erin lowered her head to rub at her temples.

"You and me both. I saw too many monstrosities in Hell for that to be a good thing," Hawk said. "Okay, so there are eleven horsemen. I know some of the deadly sins, and I think I remember two of the horsemen, but not all of them."

"To humans, the four horsemen are Pestilence, War, Famine, and Death. The deadly sins are Pride, Greed, Lust, Envy, Gluttony, Wrath, and Sloth," Magnus explained. "To demons, they are all the horsemen and one woman, and we call them by different names. However, when translated, their demon names pretty much mean the same thing as their human names."

"Why were they locked away?" Vargas inquired.

"Because each of them can influence or create the feelings they're associated with in others," I explained. "War can get two or more demons to fight to the death, Pestilence spreads some pretty nasty things around, and Famine could make a demon or Hell creature waste away from starvation with a banquet of wraiths before them. The demon wouldn't die, but it didn't exactly live either."

Wren shuddered beside me when I revealed this.

"Wrath can make any living creature so incensed they destroy everything in their path," Magnus said. "Lust makes it so sex becomes an obsession. The worst of them all, of course, is Death."

"No explanation needed for that one," Wren said. "What seal were the horsemen locked behind?"

"One hundred fifty-two," I answered. "I knew their seal had fallen, but I'd hoped it hadn't been in time for them to break out of Hell."

"We all had," Bale murmured.

"Are we going to tell Kobal and River?" Erin asked.

"We can't keep it from them," I replied. "They have to be prepared for the possibility the horsemen might head toward the wall."

"I never saw anything resembling a horse exit the gateway," Wren said. "How did they get here?"

"Don't forget that another gateway opened in Hungary at the same time as the one here," I reminded her. "It closed at the same time as this one too, but we don't know what escaped from that side before it closed. All the guards established over there were killed before we could speak with them. The horsemen must have been amongst those escapees, and if the angels wanted them in this area of the world, they could bring the horsemen here."

"Why bring them here when Kobal is here? Why not keep them on the other side of the world?" Hawk demanded.

"Only they could answer that completely, but if you intend to rule the world, then you have to take out its leader," Magnus said. "The angels and horsemen are here to prepare for war. And don't forget Kobal has followers on the other side of the world too. Hell is more dangerous than it's ever been, but Kobal can still take palitons and travel through Hell to fight the craetons over there. The craetons know that. They're as safe here as they would be over there. However, they probably think we're at the wall with Kobal and River, and not traveling through the Wilds in search of them."

"So what do we do now?" Wren asked.

"We prepare to move," I replied. "Before then, I'm going to see them. I'll witness for myself what we're dealing with."

WREN

Corson hadn't been at all happy about my insistence to go with him and the others to the gateway, but he didn't argue too long with me about it. In the end, I thought he knew he would only push me away completely if he tried to dictate what I could and couldn't do.

That didn't mean he didn't stay protectively in front of me or glower at me when I tried to push ahead of him. I glowered back.

Before leaving to see the horsemen, we'd returned to find the camp already packing up and preparing to move on. I'd happily made my way through the Wilders who came forward to see me. I'd shook their hands or embraced them as they greeted me. Malorick may have been lost, but thankfully no Wilders had died while I was away.

When I was done greeting the Wilders, I'd grabbed some bullets for my handgun and a rifle from our supplies. The weight of the rifle on my back and the gun hanging at my side wasn't as reassuring as it had once been, and I would have given anything for my bow.

The horsemen of the apocalypse, all *eleven* of them.

I hated every single thing that had crawled from the cesspool of Hell, but this sounded so much worse than an ouro, and I hadn't imagined anything worse could be possible yesterday.

My gaze fell on Corson's back. Okay, maybe I didn't hate *every*thing from Hell, but I hated a good chunk of it.

I pulled my focus away from Corson as we traveled toward the now closed gateway. Ahead of me, Raphael moved noiselessly through the trees as he led the way. Caim strolled beside him before falling back to walk next to Bale.

"Since Malorick is dead, I will fly to the wall to let Kobal know what is going on," Caim offered.

"Kobal is touring the wall with River to solidify his lead with the humans and to meet with the other palitons; we don't know where he is," she replied.

"Then I will follow the wall until I find him."

She glanced pointedly at his wings. "Any other demon would shoot you down and wear your head as a trophy."

"Then there would actually be a good looking demon in this world."

Bale stared at him before focusing ahead once more, seemingly unwilling to respond. Caim smiled at her before clasping his hands behind his back and doing an unusual little skip step that caused the bottom points of his wings to scrape the ground. I couldn't help but smile over how much he enjoyed annoying everyone he knew.

"We will send some of the skelleins to find Kobal," Corson stated. "Raphael will go with them as the palitons know the only golden angel on Earth is on our side. If the palitons see black wings though, they're going to kill without bothering to ask questions. If Raphael goes with them, the skelleins will have eyes above and an easier time of locating us when they return."

Caim's smile slid away, and a muscle twitched his jaw. Raphael didn't look at all pleased with the decision either, but he didn't protest it.

"They were just ahead," Raphael whispered, and all conversation ended.

Glancing around the trees, I noted the strange rock formation to my left and the thick briar bushes creeping in on my right. Stealing around a large oak, I rested my fingers against the markings carved into the trunk. We were less than half a mile from the gateway.

I took a deep breath to steady my racing heart. Shifting my hold on my gun, I wiped my sweaty palm on my pants before switching the weapon to my other hand and doing the same thing. I'd been in countless tight spots over the years, this was nothing new, yet I felt as if I was heading toward the end of something.

Raphael gestured with his hand, and everyone knelt behind him. I glanced at Lix, Hawk, Erin, Vargas, and Shax as they edged closer to my left side. Raphael inched forward, and we all went with him. Caim, Corson, and Bale were slightly ahead of us and the closest to Raphael. I knew the minute they saw what lay ahead as their shoulders became rigid. Corson's talons extended, and Caim briefly dropped his forehead into his hand before lifting it again.

The burning of my lungs alerted me that I'd stopped breathing. Releasing my breath slowly, I slunk forward to kneel beside Corson. A chill slid over my flesh as I gazed at the scorched land before us. Once, in the center of that burnt earth, there had been a large gateway into Hell.

All that remained of the gateway was this circle of dead land. No grass sprouted around it, no vegetation crept forward to reclaim the acreage it had lost. It was as if the damage the gateway created here would last forever, and I suspected that a hundred years from now, if the Earth still existed, this barren wasteland would remain the same.

Hopefully, the monsters standing in the middle of it wouldn't remain. I gulped as I gazed at those creatures. There were so many of them, each different from the others. The lower-level demons grouped together toward the far side of the clearing. Their more animalistic characteristics made them easy to distinguish from the upper-level demons.

The upper levels stood closer to the angels, their animosity evident in their eyes and postures, but they listened raptly to the angel speaking to them. The remaining fallen angels spread around the angel standing in the center of their loose circle.

If their new leader was Astaroth, then I assumed he was the one standing in the middle. Astaroth held his wings open behind him, and the sun glinted ominously off his blood-red hair. Like the other angels, his face was stunning, but his wings were warped monstrosities. Thick veins twisted through the leathery black flesh of his wings. Those veins pulsed in the sun, revealing what looked like the sludge of rotting corpses pulsing through them instead of blood.

Astaroth used the bottom silver tip of his right wing to point at those gathered around him. Some of the creatures I recognized as manticores, púca, gobalinus, ogres, and rokh. Many of them I didn't know at all, and some of them were so hideous I couldn't look at them.

Then there were the five bear-like creatures standing on their hind legs near the lower-level demons. The smallest one stood over seven feet, and the biggest had to be pushing ten feet tall. They had wolverine claws, pig snouts, red eyes, and thick brown coats. Jagged fangs hung down over their lower jaws.

"What is the thing that looks like a bear screwed a wolverine before mating a pig?" I whispered.

"Barta demon." He spoke so low that I barely heard Corson's reply.

I hoped to never run into one of them at night, or ever. I forced my attention from the barta and back to those gathered before us. The upper-level demons looked half tempted to rip the heads off all the angels, and I didn't understand why they were here. They obviously despised the angels, and I'd thought the upper levels followed Kobal.

Leaning closer to Corson, my lips nearly touched his ear as I spoke my next question. "Why are the upper-level demons here with the angels? Aren't they Kobal's followers?"

He rested his hand over mine, careful not to graze me with his talons. A little shiver went through me at the contact. Then my heart clenched with terror, not for me or because of the things only twenty yards away from us, but for him.

I can't lose him. I swallowed the lump in my throat the realization brought with it. I was further gone than I'd ever realized for this man. That terrified me more than all the demons and Hell creatures put together.

"Remember how I told you there was a time when demons

walked the Earth, but there were laws they had to follow? The one-hundredth seal housed upper-level demons who broke those laws while on Earth. Kobal's ancestors put them there, but many of those demons are still furious with Kobal for keeping them locked away. Since being freed, some have chosen not to fight and to pursue a life of freedom. Others have decided on revenge."

"I see," I whispered.

I searched the group again, but I saw nothing mounted on horse-back. Just as I thought it, the shadows shifted behind the lower-level demons, and red eyes blazed from the forest. I bit my lip to suppress my gasp. Erin twitched beside me, and Vargas grasped his cross. Corson's hand tightened on mine as he shifted closer to me.

A skeletal horse head followed one set of those eyes out of the shadows. The cold hand of death slid over my skin as more of the horse emerged to reveal its rider. Before I saw the rider's head, tucked securely in the crook of its arm and clasped against its side, I knew the pale, bony man was Death.

The headless fucking horseman of death.

My clammy skin cooled as I contemplated slinking into the shadows, curling into a ball, and dying.

CHAPTER THIRTY-TWO

Wren

And Death rides a pale horse.

I couldn't recall exactly where I'd heard that. Probably during one of my Sundays sitting in a church pew while listening to the minister speak. I hadn't been good at sitting still and often fidgeted much to my parents' chagrin. I'd spent most of my church time daydreaming of riding spaceships to Mars rather than paying attention, but something from those sermons, or my Sunday school days, must have sunk in.

The head of Death's horse was nothing but bone with two red orbs glowing from its eye sockets. Pale white flesh covered the rest of the horse's body. Death didn't use a saddle as he sat tall on the horse's back. Broad through the shoulders and torso, the black clothes Death wore hugged his frame. I would have considered the clothes skin tight, but if Death's body was anything like his bony fingers and detached head, there was no skin beneath that clothing.

The skeletal head Death cradled was made up mostly of glistening bone, but its eye sockets weren't empty and because there was no flesh on the skull, those eyes bulged grotesquely. Some white ligaments ran across Death's skull, moving with his jaw and pulling it into a macabre smile as, like an evil pendulum, Death's eyes swung back and forth over the clearing.

Death said something I couldn't hear, but his jawbone moved again. More of the horsemen emerged from the woods. It took all I had not to cower as my shoulders hunched and my head bowed. I clenched my bladder when it threatened to let loose. I hadn't felt this visceral a reaction to something since I'd been huddled beneath the sink, trying not to sob.

I cursed myself as a coward even as the others all slouched a little more. Erin edged back, and Vargas's knuckles turned white from his grip on his cross. Corson tensed as he edged protectively in front of me.

Taking a deep breath, I lifted my head and forced myself to gaze at the eleven horsemen spreading out behind the angels. Some of the things they rode couldn't be considered horses with their double heads, multi-hued eyes, and just plain non-horse-like physiques. Others rode horses that could have only come from Hell.

I recognized Lust as she was gorgeous with her flowing white hair tumbling down her shoulders and spilling over the ass end of the gray horse she rode. The horse was beautiful with its thick neck and its head curved so its chin was tucked against its chest. Lust wore nothing, her voluptuous body on full display to all those nearby.

Some of the demons closest to her stroked themselves through their clothes as they stared at her, while others dipped their hands into their pants and blatantly fondled themselves. The angels all unfurled their wings and drew them forward as if they were trying to ward something off.

My skin prickled, and my heart rate increased as Corson's hand burned into mine. Memories of the way he'd caressed me ran through my mind. *Mine*, he'd breathed in my ear, and I could feel the warmth of his breath against me once more.

Beads of sweat lined Corson's forehead as his eyes held mine and his thumb ran over the back of my hand. I could feel his restraint running through his taut muscles, and I found myself hoping he would let it go. I would welcome him into my arms right now without caring who watched us. Hawk lowered his head into his hands. Bale made a move for him but stopped herself before she could touch him.

Death said something and Lust laughed as she tossed back some of her white hair. Like the fog retreating from the sun, my hunger for Corson eased from my body. It didn't leave completely, but what remained had nothing to do with Lust's spell; I would always crave Corson's touch.

Corson's citrine eyes filled with fury as he stared at the horsemen. Hawk lifted his head and shuddered. Lines etched the corners of his mouth as he gazed across the clearing with hatred in his indigo eyes. The demons closest to Lust stopped pleasuring themselves and backed away from her. We weren't close to the horsemen, yet I felt the lingering effect of whatever it was that bitch had done to me. To all of us.

I wanted out of here, I opened my mouth to say so, but closed it again. I couldn't run and hide from this.

One of the horsemen said something else, and they all nodded. If they could all do something like what Lust had done, we were in for a nasty battle. For the first time, I wasn't sure it was a fight we could win. I suspected Lust had been playing with everyone, giving them only a hint of what she could do. And if War, Wrath, or *Death* unleashed their malevolence, then what?

I studied all of them again. Some were easy to recognize, like Pestilence with the hundreds of flies buzzing around his head. Large, white, blistering sores marred his cheeks. Black rot surrounded where the end of his nose should have been. The tips of his fingers were also covered in black rot as if he had gangrene or some plague. I didn't want to know what the things squirming beneath his putrid flesh were.

Pestilence's horse was the greenish-brown color of bile and also had white sores festering on its flesh. Some of those abscesses ran so deep they revealed the bone beneath. What Pestilence could do to the human race was something I couldn't think about right now.

The horsemen made such a conflicting range of emotions flutter through me that I could barely think. I focused on Astaroth as he continued to point to different demons, Hell creatures, and riders. From the corner of my eye, I noticed hooves shifting as something more was said, and then one of the horses reared back and turned away from the clearing. The scarlet animal disappeared into the trees with a dozen lower-level demons, a handful of upper levels, and some of the Hell creatures. A few angels rose to swoop out behind them.

Lust turned and went in a separate direction with an entourage following her.

"What are they doing?" I whispered.

"Smaller groups," Corson replied. "By spreading out, they can affect more humans and demons."

The other horsemen vanished into the woods until all that remained in the clearing was Astaroth, Death, and a few dozen others. Death lifted his skull and settled it into place on his shoulders. He twisted it to the side, and with a crack of bone, it remained there when he removed his hands.

Astaroth said something more and took to the air. Death stared at him before pulling back on his horse's reigns. Sunlight glinted off its bony front legs when the skeletal horse reared before running into the air. I gawked after him as Death rose higher, its horse's hooves thundering across unseen particles of air as Death followed Astaroth into the sky.

"Death can...?" I didn't know how to describe what I'd witnessed. "Fly?"

"Not fly so much as travel on air," Magnus answered.

"It's the only horseman that can," Corson said. "We have to return to the others."

The crack of a branch sounded from somewhere on our left. Before I could blink, Corson spun toward the sound and planted himself firmly in front of me. The tips of his talons rested on the ground, and his body became that of a predator tensed to spring.

Through the thin tree trunks, I spotted thirteen upper and lower-level demons strolling through the trees. They didn't notice us as they drew closer.

"The horsemen are dangerous," one of the upper levels said.

"They locked us away because we were dangerous too," another one retorted.

"Not like them. And they locked us away because we broke the laws. We didn't belong sealed away, the horsemen did. Astaroth won't be able to control them like he thinks he can."

"So what do you want to do? Slink meekly away and spend the rest of our lives hiding from Kobal or perhaps join his side?"

"*Never would I join him!*" The other one's hatred was evident in those hissed words. "But I think working with the horsemen could result in all our deaths. You saw what Lust did back there, and she wasn't even trying."

"Let the angels and horsemen have their fun. Let them ruin Kobal and the palitons, and then we'll rise to take control of what remains. It's not like the horsemen can level the entire planet in a day or even a year. They aren't that powerful. Besides, the angels and horsemen also need the human race and demons if they're to survive. They won't kill them all."

"They're determined to rule everyone, including *us*. We're the ones they'll turn on after they've accomplished what they wanted to with everyone else."

"I won't be ruled again," one of the uppers stated. "Let them come for us, and we'll tear them apart."

The lower levels all nodded their agreement. Corson looked toward all of us and gave a jerk of his head in the direction of the demons. Bale reached over her back and gripped the handle of her sword. Hawk, Erin, and Vargas pulled their knives free. Shax smiled while Caim rocked on his heels, and Raphael's face remained blank. I recoiled when identical images of us shimmered to life nearby, before realizing that they were all a product of Magnus's ability to weave illusions.

Turning to me, Corson rested his lips against my ear as he spoke, "No guns."

I put my gun away and removed the knife strapped to my side. Following Corson through the woods, we edged closer until we were within feet of the demons. One of them lifted its head; its dog snout wrinkled as it sniffed the air. With the speed and silence of a ghost, Corson rose out of the shadows and plunged his talons straight through the lower-level demon's throat, severing its head from its shoulders before it could shout a warning.

The thud of the head hitting the ground drew the attention of its companions. The blade of Bale's sword glinted in the sunlight when it swung out to sever the head of another one. Hawk and Vargas leapt out to take two lower levels down, while Caim drove one of his spikes through the eye of an upper level, and Raphael hit an upper level with a ball of pure white energy. The energy tore through the demon's chest and took out the one behind it.

Leaping up, Lix hacked the head from another demon. Magnus did some fluid dance around another lower level until he could get behind it and twist its head off with a strange, sucking pop. Shax hit another one so hard its head half tore off before Erin severed it the rest of the way with her knife.

Rising, I jumped onto the back of one turning toward Corson and sliced my knife across the demon's vocal cords before he could make a sound. My hand wrapped around his forehead, drawing his head back as I finished my kill. I jumped off the demon when its body went limp beneath me. Corson spun and sank his talons into the chest of another. Lifting it, he smashed the creature into the ground and sliced its head off with a swipe of his other hand.

I bent to wipe the blood off my blade as Lix killed the last demon. Sitting back on my heels, I studied the trees and shifting shadows while I searched for any hint that something else might be coming.

"We have to go," Corson stated. "The blood will bring more of them."

"If their bodies are discovered the angels and horsemen will know something is hunting them," Lix said.

"I know of a cave nearby," I replied. "We can stash the bodies there."

"We'll take them there," Corson said.

CHAPTER THIRTY-THREE

CORSON

The humans moved through the dwindling line as they gathered their food. The people were unusually reserved tonight, their faces strained and their eyes haunted. Their gazes darted nervously between the man handing out the food and the shadows of the building we'd taken refuge in for the night. Learning of the horsemen had left them unsettled.

After leaving the gateway behind, and disposing of the bodies, Wren had led us to this abandoned school. It was too large for my liking, too difficult to defend, but it was big enough to house every-one. Right now, being outside and exposed wasn't an option, espe-cially with the fallen angels and horsemen having been so close. They could be miles away by now, but I wasn't willing to take the chance they were still nearby, not with Wren's life.

She's mortal, and the horsemen are some of the worst things to ever evolve in Hell.

My hands fisted as I stared at the night pressing against the windows high up on two of the concrete walls. It would be difficult for anything to scamper up the outside of the building and into the small, rectangle openings, but not impossible. However, we should be able to kill anything that tried before it got too far inside. Above the windows, spider webs hung from the metal, dust-coated beams running across the ceiling. The air held the musty odor of mildew, decay, and something I couldn't quite identify.

We'd first entered the school through the large room attached to this one. The numerous, rusted metal doors within that room had kept me close to Wren as I waited for something to spring out of one and attack us.

"It's a locker room," Wren said before I could ask.

"It has too many hiding spots," I'd replied.

She'd stopped at a sink and used some of the water from her bag to scrub the demon blood from her hands, before washing her face and rinsing her hair. I'd cleaned myself too, but my attention remained more focused on her as she scrubbed her flesh until it was raw. Setting my jug of water down, I'd clasped her hands in mine. She'd allowed me to hold her for a moment before she'd removed her hands from mine and walked away without another word.

After entering the gym, we'd chained the door to the locker room shut. Two other doors led out of the gym; four demons guarded each of them, two inside and two outside.

"I have a riddle for you, my dear," Lix said from behind me. I turned to watch as he settled onto the ground beside Erin.

"Let's hear it," she replied as she pulled apart her small piece of bread.

"I am the one true horseman of the apocalypse. I destroy more than war, as I continue without life. I am more patient than famine, as I have eternity to ride. I silence more than death, as all will be still. And I spread farther than pestilence, as I act across the universe. What am I?" Lix inquired.

Erin rolled a piece of bread between her fingers as she contemplated his words. "Entropy," she said and popped the small ball of food into her mouth.

Lix didn't cheer with his usual enthusiasm when she answered one right. Instead, he patted her leg before rising. "Very good, dear. Very good indeed. One of these days, one of us will stump you."

Erin smiled sadly at him. "I look forward to it."

Lix's bony feet clicked against the floor as he walked over to stand beside me. "The fucking horsemen," I muttered and ran a hand through my hair to tug at the ends of it.

"And I bet you thought your biggest problem today was going to be a mortal Chosen who goes out of her way to avoid you," Magnus purred from behind me.

I shot him a quelling look over my shoulder, and Bale's hand tightened on the handle of her sword. I'd happily knock Magnus out, but Bale would take immense joy in severing his head from his shoulders. The two of them hadn't gotten along before Magnus retreated from the war in Hell to work on strengthening his ability to weave illusions, hundreds of years ago. Their animosity had only increased since Magnus rejoined us to fight Lucifer.

Most of the time, I barely noticed their antagonism toward each other. Now, I was not in the mood to deal with their bullshit.

It didn't help that Magnus was right.

I looked at Wren on the other side of the school gymnasium. She sat near the bottom of the wooden stairs that unfolded from the wall. Her damp hair tumbled around her shoulders as she idly tapped her blade against the bottom of her boot while watching the humans moving through the food line. She had to be hungry, yet she waited.

For the first time, I became acutely aware of the passing of time. One more day had passed, which meant there was one less day Wren had to live.

How do humans deal with this constant knowledge of time slipping away? I wanted to stick Wren in a protective bubble where nothing could ever shorten her time further, or better yet, make her an immortal.

While both options were tempting, Wren would hate me for doing either to her. Worse than the knowledge of her death was the possibility of her coming to despise me.

"I don't like this place," I stated as people and demons started placing their blankets on the dirt-streaked, tile floor.

"Try having to attend a place like this on a daily basis," Hawk said from beside me. "I never made it to high school, but middle school sucked, especially with my first name."

Hawk's entire name was Sue Hawkson. From what I'd gathered from Hawk and the other humans, Sue wasn't such a great name for a man to have in the mortal realm, but Hawk's mother had named him after a song. She'd believed the name would make him stronger.

"That really would have sucked." Vargas bit into a piece of jerky and chewed it.

"I'd rather face the horsemen than come to a place like this every day," Shax said.

"So would I," Hawk replied.

"There are too many openings, too many ways in," I said as my gaze ran over the large room once more.

"This is the best place for us in this building. It would be too easy for something to see inside the classrooms. They have more windows and only one door," Hawk said. "The locker rooms—"

"Have too many places to hide," I said.

The horsemen are close to Wren. My fingers tore into the flesh of my palms. The familiar, prodding sensation of my talons looking to break free started beneath my skin. I kept them restrained as my gaze settled on Wren again.

"There are a couple of interior rooms with no windows," Vargas said. "But there aren't enough ways out of them."

"This is the best we're going to get right now," I muttered.

Wren's friend, Jolie, walked over and sat beside her. Jolie drew her legs up and plopped her elbows on her knees as she said something to Wren. Wren turned toward her before focusing on the dwindling line of people receiving their share of the meal.

Jolie said something that drew Wren's gaze sharply back to her. Grabbing her bag, Wren pulled it closer to her and dug into it. All the Wilders had some bag or backpack they carried with them while they traveled. They stashed it somewhere whenever they hunted or fought and as far as I could tell, everything they owned fit into their bag.

This treacherous, sparse existence was all Wren had known for most of her life. She knew the peril she lived in, but I wanted better for her for however many days she had left.

"She's mortal."

"She is," Bale said.

I didn't realize I'd spoken out loud until Bale agreed with me.

"I think that might be the least of your problems when it comes to her," Magnus stated.

I hated to admit it, but Magnus was right. Wren's mortality was a battle for another day. For now, I had to get my Chosen not to want to kick my nuts into my throat most of the time. I'd probably have a better chance of getting a manticore to agree not to eat everything they could skewer with their scorpion tails.

"You claim to know me so well, yet you don't even know my real name."

Her words replayed in my mind, as did everything else she'd revealed to me in the ouroboros's tunnels.

CHAPTER THIRTY-FOUR

WREN

"Did you screw Corson?"

Jolie plopped down on the bleacher beside me, drawing my attention away from the dwindling line of people receiving their food.

"What?" I was proud my voice didn't come out as a squeak. Had I heard what she said correctly? I knew I had, but I didn't want to have this conversation with her. I fisted my hands to keep from fidgeting with my hair. I'd left it down to cover Corson's marks on me, but I should have known Jolie would notice something was off. Maybe, if I played dumb, she would rethink her question or drop the subject.

"Did you... screw... Corson?" This time, she drew the question out like I had trouble hearing.

I hadn't believed she would let it go, but I found myself feeling defensive as I held Jolie's lovely green eyes. Everything about Jolie was different than me, from her petite, five-foot-two stature to her ample breasts, and golden brown hair. Jolie had never found sex to be a mechanical event unworthy of her time. No, she actively sought out new partners, and as she put it, she took each of them for a spin before trading him in for the next one that caught her eye.

We had many differences, but Jolie had become one of my closest friends over the five years since she'd first wandered into our camp. It was impossible not to like her. She could ruthlessly cut the head from a demon one second and give her last shirt to someone in the next second.

I refused to look at Corson as I pulled my backpack closer to me. Jolie had kept it safe for me after Corson and I fell in the ouro's trap. "And if I did?"

"I'm asking if you did."

Her gaze flicked to where my hair fell around my neck. I'd never lied to Jolie; I didn't lie to anyone. It was completely pointless in this world. However, what had passed between me and Corson had been private and I wasn't sure I was ready to share it, or the fact that I had given in to my desire for him.

I should have been strong enough to resist Corson, but I wasn't ashamed of what had passed between us. Jolie wouldn't hate me for sleeping with a demon; some of the other Wilders might turn against me because of it, but Jolie wouldn't.

A sick feeling churned in my stomach at the idea of any of the Wilders turning against me because of Corson. I couldn't stop myself from looking to him, and I wasn't astonished to find his striking citrine eyes on me. Those eyes were magnificent, he was magnificent, and looking at him made me want him all over again. If I were forced to choose between him and the Wilders, it would tear me in two.

"Yes," I said and looked to Jolie again. "I slept with him."

I braced myself for Jolie's response. Her lips compressed and something hardened in her eyes. "Working with them is one thing, Wren, taking them into your bed..." Her voice trailed off, and she shook her head as if she was disappointed with me.

Resentment twisted in my chest. "You have no right to judge who

I do or don't take into my bed. I've never judged *you* for your bedmates."

"I'm not judging you for sleeping with a demon, most people in this room have by now," she replied with a careless wave of her hand. "Including me."

"Wait, what?" I blurted.

Jolie propped her chin in her palm. "What can I say, humans are a curious bunch."

"Why didn't you tell me?"

"Because I didn't know how you would react, and I haven't told you *every*one I've slept with. I'm not sure we'd have enough time left for that!" She laughed.

"I wouldn't have been mad that you had sex with a demon."

"No, you wouldn't have, but you also wouldn't have understood. Now, you do."

"If you and almost every other person here has screwed a demon, then why are you shaking your head at me as if I did something wrong?" I asked.

"Because I knew what it meant when I screwed a demon. I'm in it for the get in and get out with every guy I screw, and it's great that demons are the same way too. No strings, no complications, that's the way I roll. However, you've stayed more detached and warier of the demons than the rest of us have, so pure curiosity and getting off wouldn't be enough for you to bed one of them. If you had sex with Corson, that means there's feelings involved for you, and getting attached to their sexual partners is not the way demons work."

"In case you've forgotten, I didn't have feelings mixed up with Todd," I reminded her. "I was more than happy to walk away from him."

"That's because Todd was a tool who had no idea how to please a woman. His idea of foreplay was sticking it in."

I did a double take at her words. "You slept with Todd?"

"It was after you," Jolie replied. "I ran into him at another camp while you were on a scouting mission."

"You never told me."

"It was *extremely* forgettable. He never should have been your first. No wonder you never pursued another man until now." Jolie glanced at Corson before focusing on me once more. "And with the way that demon's staring at you, I think *he* pursued *you*."

I shrugged. "Mutual curiosity."

"I see," Jolie said. "He watches you in a way none of the demons watch us humans. I think most demons forget who they have and haven't had sex with, but I've done that too. I've never seen any of the demons show so much interest in another, except for the king with his queen."

I fidgeted with the straps of my backpack and glanced toward the dwindling line of people receiving their food. My stomach rumbled, but I remained seated as everyone got their share.

"I watch you wait until your followers have all eaten before you do, and I see you take less food than they do."

Corson's words played through my head. They weren't my followers, not really. I'd been left in charge when Randy left, but he was their true leader. However, Corson had noticed me standing on the sidelines while the others got their food, yet I'd never realized I did it. Randy had always stood back and waited, and every time I'd stood with him while the others received their rations. Then, Randy would send me to get my meal, and he would take whatever remained.

Perhaps Randy had known what he was doing, but for me, waiting had merely been the way things were, and that wouldn't change. I would never be able to eat while one of them stood behind me in line for food.

"I don't want to see you get hurt, Wren," Jolie said, breaking into my reverie.

"I won't," I replied.

She dipped her head to the side in a way that enhanced the prettiness of her elfin features. "Orgasms can do strange things to women. I think it fries some of their brains."

I chuckled. "I assure you my mind is uncooked right now."

"Then maybe you should do some more cooking."

"First, you're telling me you don't want to see me hurt; then you're telling me to go back for seconds."

"I don't remember the last time I heard you chuckle; cooked brain might be worth it. But I'll shove his talons up his ass if he hurts you."

"I'll do that myself."

"Sure, you're the toughest chick I know, physically. Emotionally, you're a stunted teddy bear."

"Jolie—"

"Oh, don't worry, I'm emotionally stunted too. There's no way we can be well-rounded individuals after everything we've seen and endured."

Jolie was at a friend's house when Hell broke open. It had taken her two days to return home where she'd discovered the bodies of her nanny and two younger sisters. She didn't know what had become of her parents. She'd once told me she hoped they were dead.

"But then, this life and the emotionally stunted who rock it are the new normal now," she continued. "There's no going back to those somewhat well-rounded human beings I'm told once existed in this world."

"No, there's not. Are they going to hate me if something develops between Corson and me?" I whispered and waved at the Wilders who were mostly sitting on the floor or sleeping now.

"Some won't like it and I'm not sure how Randy will take it. You're like a daughter to him, but he'll adapt too. Working and living with the demons is the way of things for us now. Most have accepted that. The ones who haven't will die if they decide they'd prefer to be on their own. It might be a little rough in the beginning for you, but what hasn't been?"

"Not much."

"If this is something you want, if this is something you can handle, then go for it."

"I know, I know, life is short, we could all be dead tomorrow," I said what she'd often quoted to me.

The amusement vanished from her face as she stared at me. "If we were guaranteed another thousand years, I'd still tell you to go for it, Wren. There is so much unhappiness in this world that we must take happiness wherever we can find it." She slapped her knees and hopped up. "And don't forget, I'll be here if you need me for anything."

Before I could reply, she stepped off the bleacher and strolled across the gym toward where Chet dispersed the food. He handed pieces of jerky out to her and a chunk of what I knew had to be stale bread.

I pondered her words as I watched her. Most of the people here had also slept with a demon, she'd said. I had no idea how Randy would react if he were still alive and discovered me in some relationship with a demon, but most of those in this room wouldn't hate me. A weight I hadn't realized was bearing down on my shoulders lifted, leaving me feeling lighter than I'd felt in years.

I wouldn't have to choose between Corson and everything I'd known for most of my life.

When Chet turned toward me, I realized everyone else had received their meals, and it was now my turn. Removing my flashlight from the front pocket of my backpack, I tucked my bag under my seat, and rose. I was keenly aware of Corson's eyes following me as I walked across the gym to claim my dinner.

"Hey, Wren," Chet greeted as he handed me two pieces of jerky. "Bread's gone, but I do have a few pea pods."

"No, we'll save them for tomorrow," I replied.

Taking a bite of my jerky, I surveyed the people gathered in the gym. No one had complained about having to sleep on the hard floor with their thin blankets. The forest floor offered softer bedding, but this was nowhere near the worst place any of us had slept.

However, this might be one of the most dangerous places we'd ever slept with its size and multiple entrances and exits, but there was no help for that. There were numerous guards posted, and Caim and Raphael were outside the school keeping watch. They would be able to spot any threats coming toward us. This school was the safest we'd get tonight. Tomorrow, we would come up with a new plan.

Turning away from the people and demons settling on the floor, I made my way to the double doors leading toward the hallway beyond. The two demons in front of them stepped aside to let me pass. I pushed open one of the doors and stepped out. The two demons standing there nodded to me before resuming their guard.

Walking away from them, I strolled down the hall of closed classroom doors. We'd explored the whole building to make sure it was clear of enemies before settling in for the night, yet I wouldn't be able to sleep until I did another walk-through. Two more demons stood guard at the end of the hall, but this was where the guards stopped.

I didn't say anything to them as I stared at the closed, double doors leading out of the school before looking toward the auditorium across from me, and then the stairs on my left. I didn't bother with the auditorium as I turned and ascended to the second floor.

CHAPTER THIRTY-FIVE

WREN

Pulling the flashlight out of my back pocket, I clicked it on and kept its small beam aimed at the floor. Solar powered, and a gift from Randy soon after we'd met, the flashlight had managed to survive with me. I dreaded the day when I clicked the switch on and no beam greeted me.

At the top of the stairs, I stared at the closed classroom doors interspersed with the rusting lockers that lined the hall between them. We'd shut every classroom door after checking them for anything hiding within. They all remained closed now. Most of the locks on the lockers were broken, probably by someone searching for supplies.

Stopping before one of the lockers, I lifted the metal handle and peered into the empty locker. I'd never made it to high school and never had a locker. My elementary school did have cubbies for us to store our things in, or at least I think that's what we'd called them. My memories of the small space with my name in pink lettering over it were fuzzy, but I knew I'd placed my lunch box in something every day to keep it safe.

I'd taken such joy in my metal lunchbox with the Care Bears, or was it Transformers, on it? Maybe I'd had both. Back then, getting a new lunchbox every year had been very important to me. Now, I'd toss that box aside for one bite of the cupcakes or sweet treat my mom always stashed inside. Like my dad, my sweet tooth had been insatiable, and no lunch or dinner was complete without dessert.

The batter for those oatmeal cookies was the last sweet treat I could remember eating. I was certain I'd stumbled across some candy bars or something over the years, but I didn't recall what they'd tasted like. However, I could still taste that batter on my tongue as clearly as the jerky I swallowed.

Now the only treat I had was a six-four demon with an attitude and the ability to make a woman scream in ecstasy.

My pulse quickened at the memory of Corson's body moving over mine. I closed the door on the locker as if that could shut out the way Corson had felt inside me. I gritted my teeth against the memory as I strolled onto the next locker.

Opening the locker, my breath caught when I saw the textbooks stashed within. Chemistry, Calculus, and Sociology were written onto the spines facing me. I ran my finger over the brown Chemistry binding. When the cover broke apart, I realized the book had been bound in paper.

Dust drifted up from the bottom of the locker when I pulled the book out and flipped it open. The scent of mildewing paper wafted up to me. My nose twitched, and I couldn't suppress a sneeze. With watery eyes, I brought the strange equations on the page into focus. In another life, I would have learned what the things in this book meant. Would I have liked chemistry?

I'd enjoyed the science Randy taught me, hadn't been the biggest fan of history, but math was fun. I probably would have enjoyed chemistry. Maybe, I would have been a doctor or a scientist or someone who wore a white lab coat. No one wore white anymore, it drew too much attention, but maybe the Wren in that nonexistent other life would have liked wearing it.

No, I wouldn't have been Wren in that life. I would have been an entirely different woman with a whole different name. Maybe, I would have had a husband and home by now, perhaps a child or two. I could almost see that home, almost hear the love I was certain would have filled it. My parents would have come over to laugh as they watched their grandchildren toddling around.

Now the water in my eyes had nothing to do with dust.

Slamming the book closed, I shoved it into the locker and closed the door on that imaginary life. This was why Wilders stashed away personal items in homes before they established them as safe houses. *No* one wanted to think about the could have beens of their lives and the losses they'd endured.

Resolving not to look into any more lockers, I stalked down the hallway. My eyes roamed over the small glass windows in every classroom door. The footprints of those who had searched this hall earlier were the only things disturbing the dust coating the floor. The spiders had made this high school their home for fourteen years, and they were not thrilled with my interruption. Their eyes followed me as they watched me from the thick webs they'd woven across the ceiling and in the corners of the doorways.

Without the lockers to distract me, my mind wandered to what I'd seen by the closed gateway. *The horsemen, all eleven of them.*

I shuddered at the reminder of what was out there, seeking to destroy us all, just as we sought to destroy them. I recalled Lust's power creeping over me, and icy fingers swept down my spine.

Brushing aside some cobwebs, I found myself inexplicably drawn toward another locker. *Why are you torturing yourself?*

I had no answer for that as I pulled up the handle and the door swung open. This locker was full of decorations and stickers so faded I could barely make out what they said. Beads, necklaces, and other things now dulled by age hung from the hook on the inside of the door.

I wiped away the dust coating one of the necklaces to reveal the shiny blue and green beads beneath. A smile tugged at the corners of my mouth, and I almost pulled the necklace free to slip it on. Instead, I let it go and turned my attention to the rest of the locker's contents.

A small box sat within. When I flipped it open, I found more jewelry stashed inside. I didn't know what compelled me, but I closed the lid and slipped the box into my pocket. Carrying around things I had zero use for was a fool's game, yet I found I liked the weight of the box.

Only one book was in the locker, and when I wiped away the dust on it, I discovered it was a magazine instead of a book. Closing the door, I moved on to the next locker and then the next. I felt consumed by this compulsion to see into the lives of the teenagers who had once roamed these halls.

Their lives would have been so simple, so easy that I imagined they had laughed every day. The ghostly echoes of their laughter floated around me. However, the more I searched, the less I believed laughter had filled these halls.

Some of the lockers lacked anything personal within, and only books marked the person who once made this tiny space their own. Others had angry words scrawled inside like, *I hate it here. I hate my life. Fuck this place. Fuck the world. Mrs. Dooble is a BITCH!!!!*

Well, Mrs. Dooble is probably dead, so there is that, I thought as I closed the locker on the hatred within. I felt inexplicably sad for the teens who had roamed these halls. I stopped envisioning happy, laughing people, and started seeing ones who slunk miserably through these colorless corridors.

What had high school been like for them? How many had survived the opening of the gateway?

They were questions I'd never have answers for. I could ask some of the older Wilders what they'd experienced in high school, but I knew I wouldn't. The past was rarely, if ever, discussed. Some wounds never healed, and tearing them open again to satisfy my curiosity was unfair and cruel.

Sparkles and unicorns decorated the next locker. Inside were smiley face stickers with cute sayings like, *Today is the first day of the rest of your life.*

What does that even mean? The owner of this locker hadn't survived the first day of Hell being open, I decided before moving on. I was opening the door of the next locker when I became acutely aware of non-spider eyes following me.

The uptick of my pulse and the tingles racing over my flesh alerted me to who it was before I spotted Corson leaning against the doorframe at the end of the hall. My mouth went dry, and I opened the next locker to distract myself from his presence.

"Spying on me?" I inquired as I carefully closed the empty locker.

"Making sure you're safe."

"I'm perfectly capable of keeping myself safe. I've made it this far after all."

"You don't have to do that alone anymore," he replied.

I didn't respond as I opened the next locker. I said I was fine with being alone, but had I subconsciously left the gym because I'd hoped he would come after me?

Was it really subconscious? That annoying little inner voice prodded.

CHAPTER THIRTY-SIX

WREN

"What are you doing?" Corson inquired, his voice coming closer as I stared at the plastic doll hanging from a shoelace in the center of the locker. "That's... ah, interesting," he said over my shoulder.

"Not the weirdest thing yet." I shut the door before turning to face him. My mouth went dry; my heart raced faster than a horse as I tilted my head back to take him in. I pressed my fingers against the cool metal locker behind me to keep from touching him.

"Humans are strange," he murmured, his eyes on my mouth. "What are you looking for?"

"I don't know. Supplies would be a lie. If there had been anything useful left behind, it's gone by now, but I can't stop myself from doing something I never do."

"Which is?"

"Wondering what could have been," I admitted. "And I have no idea why I'm telling you that."

"Because I'm so easy to talk to." The smile he flashed had me contemplating how fast I could get my pants off. "Plus, you'll deny it, but you like me. It's impossible not to; I'm good looking and funny."

"Funny looking," I retorted, but I couldn't stop myself from smiling back at him. Funny looking and irresistible.

My breath caught when he rested his hand on the locker next to my head. "Only to some." His eyes met mine before going to the locker behind me. "So what do you think could have been?"

"I don't know. I liked learning when I was a kid, and Randy continued to teach me things as I grew, but he had his limits to what he knew and how much he could teach me. It's not like I could learn chemistry or biology, not when I didn't have the tools and equipment to do so. There was only so far I could go in math and other subjects. He did his best, and I was lucky he was able to do so much with me."

"Why could he do so much?"

His chest brushed against my arm as he moved subtly closer. His masculine scent engulfed me, and those orange eyes became all I could see. "He... ah..." I had to swallow before continuing. "He'd been going to college to be a middle school history teacher when it all happened. He only had a year left to go before graduation. I think it's why he was so determined to save me. He loved kids, and he refused to let me die no matter how badly I wanted to give up in the beginning."

His eyes sharpened on me, and his nostrils flared. "I will not allow you to die."

"Thanks, demon," I teased and patted his chest to soothe any ire my calling him demon might cause him, "but in case you haven't noticed, you can't declare something and have it be true. There's a whole lot of nastiness out there that would like nothing more than to eat us."

He grabbed my hand and flattened it against his chest. "And I will kill anything that tries to eat you. Other than me, of course, and I'm going to enjoy tasting you again, Wren."

His heavy-lidded eyes fell to my mouth once more. Beneath my palm, I felt the increased beat of his heart. Demons may be immortal creatures who feasted on the energy of wraiths, could regrow any body part except their heads, and didn't have the same bodily functions us humans did, but they had heartbeats and breaths, and right now his pulse was faster than mine.

"So sure of yourself," I said and tugged on my hand.

I expected him to continue clinging to me, but he released me and stepped aside. "I am sure I need you."

My lungs had a difficult time drawing air after that revelation, but I finally succeeded in doing so. I forced myself on to the next locker and pulled it open. Someone had scrawled 420 all over the inside of this locker. I had no idea what was so significant about the date or the time, but this person was obsessed.

Someone's birthday maybe. I closed the door.

Now that I'd started, I felt obsessed too. I didn't know if I'd be able to stop myself from looking into *all* of the lockers.

"Corson?"

"Hmm?"

"Was there ever anything between you and Bale?" I didn't know why I'd asked the question. The answer might drive me nuts, but I had to know. I couldn't sit and watch the two of them and wonder all the time.

I thought I saw a flash of satisfaction in his eyes. My hand clenched. If he said one smug thing, I'd knock him on his ass and hog tie him to the nearest desk. If I'd had an apple, I'd shove it in his mouth too, but a sock would do.

"I don't mix business with pleasure," he said.

"What does that mean?"

"Bale and I have worked with Kobal for centuries, but that is *all* we've done. There would have been no jealousies between us afterward, no feelings, but I prefer to keep my sex partners separated from my work ones, and so does Bale."

Relief burst through me, and it took all I had not to clap my hands in delight. "I see."

Corson walked beside me while I continued down the hall and

peered into each locker I opened. "Why does this place smell like that?" he inquired after a few minutes.

I sniffed at the air and sneezed. "It's mildew, dust, and decay," I muttered as I wiped at my nose. The decay wasn't only the wood doors rotting or the lockers rusting, but also the rot of death. I didn't know where it was coming from, but animals and probably some humans had lost their lives in this place. "Everything smells like that now."

Sometimes I wondered if the whole world possessed that musty, dying aroma. The odor hadn't been as prevalent at the section of wall I'd visited, but it had been there too.

"No," Corson said. "It smells like, I don't know, something else."

I scented the air again and smiled when I understood what he meant. "That's the aroma of a school. My elementary school smelled like that too. Every school I've entered has that smell. I'm not sure what it is, or why."

The smell was fading from this school, and perhaps one day, it would be gone for good. Then no one would ever remember the aroma of a school.

"Interesting," Corson murmured.

He stared over my shoulder at the dingy, blue jacket tucked securely within the newest locker. The yellow patch on the jacket's sleeve had a football in the center. Beneath the jacket was a set of white pom-poms. "Would I have been a cheerleader?" I pondered.

For some reason, I couldn't picture myself jumping up and down while cheering. However, I could imagine the happy girl I'd once been, the one who had twirled in her apple dress, leading cheers.

"I'm not sure a cheerleader fits you, Wren," he murmured. "But then, you wouldn't be Wren either."

I winced as I closed the locker. I didn't know why I'd revealed to him that Wren hadn't always been my name. Over the years, anyone who knew my name wasn't Wren had either died or been killed, except for Randy.

"I was thinking the same thing earlier," I admitted. "I'd have been an entirely different person."

"I'm glad you're not."

My eyes widened at the open honesty he radiated with those words.

"What is your real name?" he inquired.

"It doesn't matter," I replied, but for some reason, it did when it came to him. I wanted him to know there had once been a different *me*.

"Does anyone know it?"

"Anyone living you mean, and other than me?"

"Yes."

"No," I said. "Not even Randy knows what my name was, but he did name me Wren." I stopped in front of the next locker. The hinges creaked when I pulled it open to reveal the empty, dusty interior. "I'd forgotten all about my real name. It wasn't until I had the nightmare in the tunnel…" my voice trailed off as I gazed at the emptiness within. "It wasn't until then that I remembered."

"Remembered what?" he asked.

"That at one time there had been a girl who lived for cookie dough batter, twirling in her dresses, trying to get through church every Sunday, and crazy about her lunchbox. Then, one day, that girl's life was overturned, and for her to live, she ceased to exist. As the years passed, I forgot all about her."

Corson rested his hand on my shoulder, drawing my attention to him. Emotion swelled in my chest as I gazed at him.

Don't care about others! I'd repeatedly told myself this over the years, but I realized now I'd failed miserably in my endeavor. I loved Randy and his wife, Nadine. Jolie was my best friend, and I consistently took the last two pieces of jerky without complaint. I cared about others, but to care about a demon…

That was a betrayal of my family, wasn't it? However, Corson and the other palitons were our allies now. Corson hadn't killed my family and countless other humans for pleasure, or at least I didn't think he'd killed humans for fun.

"Have you ever killed a human?" I inquired.

His eyes held mine as he replied, "Yes."

I winced and went to pull away from him, but his hand tightened on my shoulder to keep me in place while he continued speaking. "It was a necessity, plain and simple. I killed them when they tried to kill me. I've never killed when I didn't have to. I don't kill for sport, but I put my life ahead of theirs. I would do so again, especially for you. Have you ever killed a human?"

"I have," I admitted.

"Why?"

"Some to survive, another when he tried to rape me."

His jaw clenched so forcefully that I heard his teeth clamp together and a muscle twitched in his cheek, yet his hold on me remained tender. "Did he hurt you?"

"He tried," I replied flippantly and ducked out of his hold. "He failed, and it cost him his life."

"What happened?"

"I was fifteen, an easy target, or so he assumed. I slit his throat when he became distracted by trying to pull off my pants. Afterward, I was fully prepared to slice off the dick of the next man to try it."

Corson smiled, but rage still simmered in his eyes. "You really can talk sexy."

"You are one twisted demon. Would it grow back if it were cut off?"

"It would, but I'd prefer not to have that experience."

"Understandable."

Stepping away from the locker, I strolled down the hall before stopping and opening another locker. Pictures of a boy and girl who had their arms draped around each other covered every available inch of space. "They look like they were in love," I murmured.

"They do," Corson agreed. "So why did Randy name you Wren?"

"In the beginning, he tried to get me to tell him my name, but I didn't speak for months after what I witnessed with my mom. Then, one day, on a scouting mission we came across a group of people. This was before all Wilders agreed to work together, so everything was fair game back then. While Randy and some others tried to formulate a plan on how to get their supplies without violence, I darted in and stole them without anyone knowing what I'd done.

"I didn't hit my growth spurt until I was thirteen, so I was really small then. When I dropped the supplies at Randy's feet, he'd gawked at them before grinning proudly and hugging me. He'd declared I was like a wren—fast and small, but with a whole lot of attitude. One day he stopped saying I was like a wren and just started calling me Wren, so did all the others."

"And when you started speaking?" Corson prodded.

"By the time I talked again, no one thought to ask if I had a different name, and I didn't offer it to them. There was no point. I was Wren by then, and I didn't want to be anyone else."

"And you said your nightmare made you remember your name?"

"I guess I always remembered it," I replied. "I just hadn't thought of it in years."

He followed me down the hall while I continued to examine the lockers. "Bonnie girl wasn't an endearment from your mom. Your name is Bonnie," he murmured after a few minutes.

I flinched, and my shoulders hunched up as if he'd struck me. "My name is *Wren*," I replied through gritted teeth. I should have known he would figure it out; I had shared all the details of my nightmare with him. "*Her* name was Bonnie, but she died that day. I am *Wren*."

He rested his hand on my shoulder again, and I reluctantly looked at him. I didn't know what I expected him to say as his thumb stroked my cheek. "You can be both," he murmured. "You don't have to be one or the other."

"No one is going to call me Bonnie Wren, and that would be ridiculous. Besides, do I look like a Bonnie to you?"

"I don't know what a Bonnie looks like."

"She looks like a happy girl who eats cookie dough, wears pigtails, is excited about lunch boxes, and loves bear hugs from her dad. She's not a girl who worries about starvation and being eaten by a manticore or corrupted by a horseman."

"She sounds boring."

"Or normal," I retorted.

"So, boring then."

"Yes, boring. Normal is boring."

"And what was your last name?" he inquired as he lifted his other hand to cup my face between his palms.

I frowned as I gazed at his mouth, and much to my horror, it took me a few moments to recall the answer. "Steward!" I blurted when it finally came back to me.

"Bonnie Steward," he murmured.

I flinched again before catching myself. It had been so many years since anyone had spoken my old name out loud. It sounded so wrong, yet so right that my head spun from the dizzying confusion of Bonnie trying to reassert herself into my life. I had the disconcerting notion that Wren was an alien who had invaded her body.

I didn't belong here, but I *did*. This was my body now, my life. *Corson* was mine, not *hers*.

I realized a name was causing my mind to completely unravel when so many other things had failed to do so over the years.

"*Wren*," I whispered.

He bent his head and brushed a kiss across my lips and I knew names didn't matter when I was with him.

He is mine, I realized as his tongue slid over my lips and I opened my mouth to him.

CHAPTER THIRTY-SEVEN

CORSON

Wren leaned against the lockers as I kissed her. I tasted the jerky on her lips, but also something more, something inherently her. Though I didn't eat human food, I could only think of sweet as the way to describe her. So sweet, yet so deadly; so confident about some things, yet so lost about others. She was a contradiction unlike any I'd ever known, and I liked the way she kept me on my toes. I would never be bored with Wren in my life.

Breaking the kiss, she inhaled a shaky breath as she turned her head away. I lowered my forehead to rest it against her temple and inhaled the scent of pine and woods on her. She'd washed, but she'd never rid herself of the scent of the earth ingrained on her flesh.

"Wren," I whispered as I nuzzled her ear.

She turned her head so her lips brushed against my cheek. "I don't know how to do this."

I didn't have to ask what she meant; I knew she didn't know how to handle opening herself up to another as completely as she'd started to open to me. "We'll do it together, one day at a time."

"But I'm mortal, and you're not invincible."

"I can't promise I'll never die, but I can promise I am extremely difficult to kill." Lifting my head, I gazed into her sky-colored eyes with their flecks of green. "I've never felt about another the way I feel for you. There is nothing I won't do for you, including walking away if you tell me to."

"I don't want that."

"What do you want then?"

"You," she breathed. "I want you."

With a growl, I pulled her flush against me and lifted her against the lockers. Bending, I claimed her lips again. I felt half out of control as my tongue delved into her mouth. Her fingers entangled in my hair and gave it a small tug. She mewled as she pressed her body as tight as she could to mine.

Her urgency fueled my own. Stepping away from the lockers, I carried her to the closest classroom, adjusted my hold on her to open the door, and entered the room. She broke the kiss to trail her lips over my jawline before nipping at me. Wren didn't have the instinct to mark me, as I did her, but I found myself craving her bite.

My hands slid under the bottom of her shirt, pushing it up until I could settle my palms on her silken flesh. I kicked the door closed with my heel and carried her to the large, metal desk at the front of the room. She released her hold on my hair and ran her fingers through it until they brushed the tips of my ears. Setting her on the desk, I groaned as I turned into her touch.

"Your ears?" she asked as she brushed her fingers over them again.

"Are extremely sensitive," I told her and stepped closer to rub my erection against the juncture between her thighs to prove what she did to me.

She squirmed closer until I was nestled securely against her center. The fingers stroking my ears and pushing me to the point of near madness slid away when I tugged her shirt up. She lifted her arms for me to pull it off her.

Tossing the shirt aside, my mouth watered as I gazed down at her flat stomach and enticing, handful-sized breasts. I drank in her golden skin and the pert nipples poking against the simple, black bra she wore.

"Mah lahala," I murmured before bending to place my mouth against her nipple and sucking on it through her bra.

She arched her hips up and down against my shaft. Delicious moans whispered from her throat as she used my body to rouse herself to higher heights of passion. "What does that mean?" she panted.

Her husky voice set my blood on fire. I bit at her nipple before releasing it and sliding my hands around to undo the clasp. I'd love nothing more than to shred all her clothes from her and bury myself inside her, but the Wilders had few clothes. Wren would walk around naked if it became necessary, and I would make sure that never happened.

When the bra fell open, I removed it and dropped it to the ground. Cupping one of her breasts, I lifted my head to gaze at her while I ran my thumb over it. Her eyes darkened as she watched me while red color crept through her cheeks. She wasn't embarrassed, I knew, but aroused and growing more so by the second.

"It means 'my love' in demonish," I told her.

Panic flashed across her face, and she stiffened against me.

"Don't," I said, drawing her closer. "Don't pull away from me."

"But I'm not your love."

"Yes, you are." I held her gaze, determined to make her understand. "To me, you are everything, Wren."

The panic didn't leave her eyes, but she softened toward me. Bending my head, I drew her bottom lip into my mouth before sliding my arm around her waist and rocking my shaft against her once more. When I released her lip, her head fell into the hollow of my shoulder.

"I can't get pregnant, Corson," she murmured. "You said humans have had demon children before, but I can't have a baby, not now. It would be a death sentence for our child and me."

"You would be safer at the wall; we could return there if you carried my child."

"I don't want that. Not now."

"I will take care to make sure you don't get pregnant," I assured her.

"The last time we did this—"

"The last time I wasn't expecting what happened. I'll be more careful this time, but know that I would *never* allow any harm to come to you or our child. I'll fight to the death for you both."

A child. It surprised me how much that possibility pleased me. I'd never considered a child before, but now...

My hands tightened on her as I imagined a little girl with Wren's hair and smile and none of the sorrow haunting her blue eyes. I would make sure our child only knew peace and love. Those were the only things I wanted Wren to know, but I couldn't give them to her while our world was so uncertain. It could be years before things settled enough for us to experience peace and Wren might not have years left.

I grappled to control the tumult of emotions the knowledge of Wren's inevitable death brought with it. *My mortal.*

"I know you would protect us," she said and slid her hands inside my shirt. Her fingers ran up my stomach before her short nails raked lightly down it. "I don't think I could handle being a mom with everything I've seen, and we're nowhere near close to the child stage of our relationship, or whatever this is between us."

"This is the beginning of something great."

"Oh is it, demon?" she asked in a teasing, breathy voice.

I found I didn't mind her calling me demon in that tone. "It is."

She tugged my shirt over my head and threw it aside. Her fingers traced the muscles of my abdomen as I brushed her hair aside to reveal my marks on her. The unfamiliar sensation of my canines lengthening into fangs came back when they started to fill my mouth again.

Wren must have detected the outline of them behind my lips as she tilted her head to study me before leaning closer. "Let me see them," she said.

My lips skimmed back to reveal my fangs to her. Her breath caught before she reached up to prod the tip of one with her finger. She snatched her hand back when her prodding caused it to lengthen further.

"Amazing," she breathed. "I never knew you had fangs."

"I never did, until you."

"Did you know that would happen when you found your Chosen?"

"No." My hands fell to the button of her pants, and I slid it free. "I remember seeing my parents' marks on each other, but I never thought about the fact there were always two punctures on them. A Chosen strengthens a demon and brings out things in them they never knew they could do before. You have already brought out some of those changes in me."

I tugged her pants down her legs and bent to untie her boots. Pulling them off, the boots clattered onto the floor when I dropped them before pulling her socks and pants off. She raptly watched me as my hands glided up her shapely calves to her thighs. I pushed her legs further apart to reveal the pale blonde curls between them; curls that were already wet with her want for me. I held her eyes as I knelt to place a kiss against her inner knee before sliding my mouth further up her thigh.

Her breath sucked in when my fangs grazed her flesh before I sank them into her. Her body jerked and bowed toward me; passion darkened her eyes as she watched me. Sliding my hands beneath her legs, I lifted them over my shoulders until her knees were on either side of my head. Releasing my bite, I continued to kiss my way up her thigh until my mouth fell upon her hot center. I slipped my hands under her ass to lift her against me.

"Corson!" She panted when I dipped my tongue inside her. She tasted like she smelled, of the outdoors and something sweeter that brought to mind the honey I'd seen some of the humans eating. Her fingers entangled in my hair, drawing me closer against her as her head fell back and she rode my tongue.

I couldn't get enough of savoring her and greedily took in more and more until I was on the point of coming in my pants. Releasing her ass, my hand fell to shift my erection as it throbbed against my zipper. I slid the button on my pants free, breathing a sigh of relief when I released my shaft from its confines.

When I drew back, I ran my tongue over her clit while sliding one of my fingers into her. I drank in the sight of her body bared before me and my finger deep within her as I pushed her closer and closer to release. Bending back to her, I tongued her clit and spread her further to slip two fingers inside her.

Wren tugged on my hair and cried out as she came in a heated rush. The muscles of her sheath gripped my fingers before I slid them away from her. Rising, I tugged my pants down and kicked off my boots before grabbing her hips and drawing her closer to the edge of the desk.

Her dazed eyes met mine; her lips still glistened from my kiss as a smile played across her swollen mouth. She caressed the tip of one of my ears.

"Fuck," I shuddered as a bead of cum formed on the head of my cock. "Unless you want this over with now, I'd recommend leaving the ears alone."

She grinned mischievously at me before stroking my ear again. Unable to stop myself, I thrust forward, parting her folds and penetrating deep within her. Her muscles gripped me as I stilled and took a minute to savor the feel of us joined together.

Pulling back, I slid slowly into her again before bending to sink my fangs into her breast. Her legs locked around my waist, drawing me deeper. Her blood dripped onto my tongue, but I found no satisfaction in the taste of it, only in the marking of her again.

Releasing my hold on her breast, I rose to gaze down at her flushed face. Her eyes held mine as I pulled back before plunging into her again. She lifted her hands to run her fingers over my cheeks as if she were memorizing every detail of me. Then she leaned forward to nibble on my bottom lip and her hands fell to my shoulders.

I felt my control unraveling, but I was helpless to stop it as the pleasure Wren gave me became all I knew. Cradling her head to my shoulder with one hand, I slid the other beneath her ass to lift her off the desk. I drove into her over and over again, needing to leave my mark on every part of her.

"Corson," she moaned.

Her muscles contracted around me as she orgasmed again. The force of her orgasm caused my semen to rush up my shaft. With a loud cry, I pulled out and came against her stomach before I could stop myself. Clutching her against me, I didn't think my release would ever stop, but finally, it did.

Limp in my arms, Wren nestled closer to me as I cupped the back of her head and a new emotion swelled to life within me. As prickly as akalia vine and as ruthless as any demon, Wren was also one of the most giving and loving people I'd ever encountered.

I may never figure her out completely, but I wouldn't have it any other way as this walking contradiction was *mine*.

Reluctantly, I set her on the desk and released her to retrieve my shirt. With tender care, I used my shirt to clean her while she watched my every move.

"Corson," she whispered when I finished and tossed my shirt aside.

My breath caught when I saw the vulnerability in her eyes and the raw anguish on her face. "Yes?"

"I know you said demons are faithful to their Chosen, but everyone is different. While we're together, don't have sex with another woman."

"I would *never* do that, Wren."

"Good."

I smiled at the decisive tone of her voice. "I'm glad you think so, but the same also goes for you. I won't tolerate you with another man. I would never hurt you, but I will kill him."

"What if this doesn't work out between us and I find another?"

The possibility caused my fangs to throb with the impulse to tear something apart. My talons prodded my skin, but I kept them leashed. She had no idea the jealousy her words evoked in me.

She is human! She doesn't understand or feel the Chosen bond!

Reminding myself of this did nothing to ease the tension knotting my chest. "This *will* work out between us."

"You're so sure?"

"Yes."

"But I am mortal. I will die, and you will find another—"

"No!" I snapped with far more anger than I'd expected. Instead of being wary of me, Wren's eyes narrowed. If I didn't get control of myself, this conversation would spiral into a fight. "No," I said more calmly. "There will *never* be another for me again. The idea of touching another, or having her touch me, turns me on as much as the ouro did. Even if you die, I am yours alone, and I always will be."

"And if I decide to walk away from this?"

I couldn't stop myself from flinching at her words before I instinctively bared my teeth. Her palms flattened against my chest, but she didn't push me away or try to flee. If anything, she'd break my nose again if she believed I might become a risk to her.

"If you decide to walk away, I will let you," I managed to say. It would destroy me, but I couldn't keep her caged; she'd hate me forever if I tried, and I couldn't be the cause of any unhappiness for her. "I would have to get as far from you as possible, but I won't force something on you that you don't want."

"Thank you," she whispered.

"Do you want me to walk away?" I demanded, unsure of how I would react if she said yes.

"No. I just wanted to know what all this meant and what my options are if things go bad. I like the way things are now, and I'm coming to like you more than I'd believed possible, demon," she teased.

"Good," I said gruffly.

She reached down to grip my shaft. "But I had to know I could still have my freedom from you if I asked for it," she said as she stroked me.

"You can."

"I know Hawk changed from human to demon, but I don't want to be a demon." She ran her thumb over the head of my cock before giving it another long stroke.

I didn't argue with her about it. Perhaps, with time, and if she grew to love me, she would change her mind about becoming a demon. However, I was not in a rush to watch her almost die, which is what it would take for me to attempt changing her. Plus, there was a risk the change would kill her. But Wren was strong, if anyone had a chance of surviving the transition from human to demon, it was her.

"I understand," I said, knowing she wouldn't accept any other answer from me. "But know that if you ever change your mind, I would *never* allow another to change you. It will be me."

"My mind is set, but my mortality is something to worry about on another day. I will give you something else to think about now," she said with a mischievous smile.

Before I knew what she intended, Wren slid from the desk and went to her knees before me. She licked her lips before leaning forward to run her tongue from the base of my shaft to the head of it.

Wrapping my hand around the back of her head, I guided her as she took me deep into her mouth.

CHAPTER THIRTY-EIGHT

WREN

Over the next couple of weeks, I found myself growing closer to Corson as we traveled further south and deeper into the Wilds. We'd yet to enter areas I hadn't been through before, but we would soon. All of us had decided to hold off on entering those areas until we were better prepared. This time of year was perilous enough, between the famished animals, the snow and cold; adding in unfamiliar, mountainous terrain could prove lethal if we weren't adequately supplied.

Whenever Corson and I had any time alone, even if it was only a couple of minutes, I welcomed him inside me and rode out the storm of passion he provoked so effortlessly within me. I couldn't deny him, and I didn't try. I'd never believed it was possible to desire someone so much, but I couldn't get enough of him.

Some of the Wilders still gave us curious looks, and a couple of them made snide comments, but most didn't care about what was happening between us. I couldn't say they hadn't noticed as it was impossible for them not to see the relationship between us. I'd tried to hide it in the beginning, not because I was ashamed, but because it was new and part of me feared sharing it with others might somehow ruin it.

Keeping it hidden didn't last long. Wearing my hair down all the time wasn't practical and even if it was, I often found myself touching Corson without realizing I was doing it. He did the same to me. There were times when I'd be sitting, cleaning my clothes, or skinning dinner, and he'd rest his hand on my nape or the small of my back. It would only be the subtlest of touches to let me know he was there, but as the days progressed, I found myself increasingly looking forward to those subtle caresses.

When we weren't alone, he didn't hover or suffocate me by being continuously present. I would have bolted faster than a rabbit if he did. However, I knew he was always nearby. That knowledge made me feel safer than I had in years.

Over time, Corson revealed more about what Hell had been like with the constant fighting between the demons and angels. He told me how he'd fought for over a thousand years to help Kobal claim his throne. Once on Earth, Corson admitted that he grew to hate Hell more and more over the years.

"There is so much light on Earth, different aromas, and colors. There's always something new to see or experience here. There isn't much of that in Hell. There are some things about it I miss, like the heat, but not many. No matter how much I grew to hate Hell, if Kobal had decided to return, I would have followed him," he told me one night while we'd been lying next to each other, our heads together as we stared at the stars.

"Even though you hated it?" I'd asked.

"Yes. He is my king, but more than that, he is my friend."

"What if he asked you to return now?" I couldn't deny the idea had brought a surge of terror with it.

"That wouldn't happen," Corson had murmured before rolling on top of me and pinning my hands above my head. He slid his leg between my thighs as he gazed down at me. "You humans are stuck with us demons from here on out."

"That's not such a bad proposition anymore, demon," I'd teased.

He'd made love to me slowly that night, and with a tenderness I'd never experienced from him before. That tenderness allowed him to dig deeper into my heart. I kept trying to put walls up and keep at least some distance between us, but he kept tearing those walls apart one brick at a time.

One night, I'd gone with him while he fed on the wraiths. When we'd arrived at the cemetery where the wraiths were located, the night had seemed darker and the stars dimmer above the headstones, but I could barely make out the wraiths looping over the gravestones.

Corson informed me the wraiths liked to gather at places where there was a lot of death, and they couldn't tolerate sunlight, so they only came out at night. He'd explained that before the seals fell, I wouldn't have been able to see them at all, but when the seals gave way, something happened to make it so the wraiths could be detected at least a little by humans.

I could see the twisting Hell shadows at noon with more clarity than I could the wraiths, yet being so close to the wraiths had chilled my skin. The malevolence emanating from their souls brought goose bumps to my arms. My heart felt like it shriveled to raisin size in my chest and seemed to have a more difficult time pumping blood.

As I stood there, I realized I wasn't sure if it was the hatred the wraiths exuded or my fears affecting me so badly. I'd killed enough in my lifetime to wonder if this was what I would become after I died. Would I go to Hell and haunt cemeteries while waiting for demons to feed on me?

I hadn't been able to voice the question to Corson. I was too petrified of the answer.

In flashes, I'd watched Corson lift his hand to draw one of those hideous souls toward him. I couldn't quite see the wraith, but I caught glimpses of its long, distorted face and flapping black ends. One second it was fifty feet away from him, the next thirty, and then ten.

My chill intensified when the next flash revealed Corson's hand enveloping the wraith's throat. Then the spirit vanished once more, and it appeared as if Corson was trying to grasp air. I knew he still clasped the wraith when his muscles bulged and the veins in his forearms stood out. The crackle of his power vibrated the air around him as he drew strength from the spirit while inflicting suffering on it.

While Corson fed, a distant sort of screaming sounded in my ears. I was certain it was from the wraith, but though the spirit was only feet away from me, it sounded as if the screams came from miles away.

I'd never wanted to get away from something so fast in my life, but I'd insisted on seeing this part of Corson's life. Now that I had, I didn't plan to ever see it again. It didn't make me love him less, but it unsettled me. When that thought drifted through my mind, I also comprehended that not only did Corson keep tearing down my walls, but somehow I'd fallen in love with him.

The realization jarred me, but once it hit, I couldn't deny it. If he'd been human, I'd have thrown my arms around him and embraced the rest of our lives together. There would always be the concern that I could lose him. However, I would take every one of the seconds we'd have together until the inevitable end. My feelings for him as a mortal still would have terrified me, but our lives would have been straightforward.

Instead, I didn't know where to go from here with him. If I were *really* lucky, I would die from old age, while he remained youthful and immortal. There weren't many bigger obstacles in a relationship.

I'd been adamant that I didn't want to become a demon. However, I found myself watching Hawk for some sign he hated what he'd become; he never gave one. I contemplated asking him how he felt about being a demon, but whenever I opened my mouth to voice the question, it lodged in my throat. What if Hawk said he hated being a demon? What if he said he loved it? Or what if he was plain indifferent?

Until I was completely sure I could handle whatever answer he gave me, I couldn't bring myself to ask—especially when I didn't know what answer I hoped to hear from him. Could I become a demon?

Just weeks ago, that answer would have been a resounding *no*, but I knew more about demons now and understood them better. Yes, demons had slaughtered my family and countless others over the years, but like humans, there was good and bad amongst them. I'd found the good with Corson.

Still, would I be able to feed on wraiths, have giant talons, and endure whatever else came with demonhood to be with Corson?

The idea of the wraiths made my stomach churn. However, a built-in weapon system sounded freaking fantastic, once I got used to having those talons. It would take some time, but guns, knives, and arrows had once been unnerving to me too, and now they were like an extension of me. The talons literally *would be* an extension of me, and I'd witnessed Corson slicing and dicing things with them. They were awesome.

But, I didn't know what I would be like as a demon, if I would survive the transformation to become one, or even what had to be done to become one. Thankfully, I didn't have to figure it out anytime soon. For the time being, I would enjoy this newfound happiness and sense of security I'd found with Corson. I'd worry about possible demonhood later, I decided as I glided through the woods.

While I walked, my eyes scanned the trees in search of a good branch to settle on to hunt from. My head turned at the soft step behind me, and I spotted Corson making his way through the trees toward me. The sight of him caused my heart to lurch with joy, and I couldn't stop myself from smiling.

Lovesick fool. That's exactly what I was, and I was surprisingly okay with it.

Corson smiled back at me as he stepped around a rock. My eyes fell to the black bow he held as he walked toward me. When I left the camp, he'd told me he had to grab something before he could meet me, but I'd never seen the bow before.

Stopping before me, he bent to kiss me. "Hello, lahala."

"Demon," I greeted and nipped at his lower lip before pulling away. If I wasn't careful, I'd drag him to the ground and take him; it was that easy to become caught up in him. "What do you have there?" I waved a hand at the bow.

"Well, what *do* I have here?" His eyes twinkled with amusement as he drew the bow forward to hold it between us. "Why, it's a bow."

I chuckled and shook my head. "You're an ass."

"Yes, I am," he admitted. "What do you think of it?"

When he held the bow out to me, I took it from him and rotated it in my hands. I ran my fingers over the smooth wood as I examined the exquisite craftsmanship of the weapon. Lifting it, I pulled back the string and brought it to my shoulder. Despite its length, the bow was lightweight but surprisingly sturdy. It would take a lot more than the weight of a deer to snap it.

"It's amazing." I lowered the bow and held it out to him but he didn't take it. "Where did you get it?"

"I made it."

"When did you have the time to do that?"

"While you were sleeping, or doing your own thing." He gripped the end of my braid dangling against my breast and gave it a playful tug. "I am a man of many talents, my dear Wren."

"Obviously."

I tried to hand the bow back to him again, but he pushed it back at me. "I made it for you."

The emotion that burst through me left me more shaken than a tree in a tornado. I didn't know how to react or what to say. "For me?" I finally croaked.

Using my braid, he tugged me forward a step. "Yes, for you." His other hand fell on the bow slung over my shoulder. "This bow isn't right for you."

He was right about that. The bow had belonged to a male Wilder who died a few months ago. The weapon was too long and the string too tight. I had a difficult time drawing the string back, but I'd adapted to it. I'd never told him I'd had problems adjusting to the bow though; it was just another one of those things he'd learned by watching me.

"Demon," I breathed as my gaze dropped to the exquisite bow once more. I studied the black wood it had been carved from and frowned. "What tree did you use to make this?"

"Calamut."

My mouth dropped. "You took wood from a calamut tree? They could have killed you!"

"They could have," he said, "but I didn't take it from them. I asked them for a piece of their wood."

"You asked for it, and they gave it to you?"

"They did."

"Why would they do that?"

He removed the bow he'd given me from my limp grasp before pulling the other bow and quiver off my back. I could only stand and gawk at him while he worked. "The calamuts enjoy skewering things, but deep down I think they're just romantics at heart."

"Like you."

He smiled at me as he lifted my shirt up over my head. Corson had taken me many times, in public and not so public places, but never once had I feared something would eat us as I had with Todd. I knew he would keep us both safe.

"Like me," he murmured and bent to kiss me.

I completely forgot about hunting as I wrapped my arms around his neck and went to the forest floor with him. I made sure he knew how much I loved my new bow.

CHAPTER THIRTY-NINE

WREN

Corson's shoulder brushed mine as he leaned forward. When we'd finally disentangled ourselves from each other, I'd been eager to break in my new bow. Now, we sat next to each other on a tree branch, our legs dangling over it. I kicked my feet over the open air, feeling more alive now than I had in fourteen years. Not just because of Corson, but because I also took a moment to appreciate that I *was* alive when so many weren't.

I didn't think I'd ever paused to recognize the fact so many had been lost, yet I was blessed or lucky enough to remain. I acknowledged it then as I inhaled the wintry November air, relished the warmth of Corson's body, and listened to the clicking branches swaying over my head.

I was alive, and it was glorious.

Lifting my face, I basked in the noon sun. When I lowered my head, I focused on Corson as he gazed over the side of the branch and my heart swelled with love for him.

Neither of us had spoken of love, I didn't know if demons talked about it at all, and it had been years since I'd spoken the word out loud to another. I'd never believed I could feel like this for someone, but Corson had me thinking about a future I'd long ago stopped considering.

Surviving a day in the Wilds was a great achievement. It felt like tempting fate to contemplate what tomorrow would be like, never mind a week or two from now. However, yesterday I'd found myself imagining what a child of ours would look like before abruptly shutting the fantasy down.

I could not bring a child into *this* world. I'd been greatly relieved when my period arrived last week, yet I'd experienced a twinge of sadness over it. Our first *oops* might have been my only chance for a baby.

Corson scratched a chunk of bark off the trunk with one of his talons. Once removed, he broke the bark apart, held a piece out, and released it. Leaning forward, I nearly burst out laughing when I spotted Hawk and Vargas standing under us. The bark bounced off Hawk's head, and he rubbed it absently.

Corson dropped another chunk onto Vargas's head, who did the same thing as Hawk. Corson's grin widened when he released another piece on Hawk before dropping two more onto Vargas. When they tilted their heads back to look at us, Corson released the pieces that remained in his hand.

"Asshole," Hawk muttered as he darted to the side to avoid the falling debris. Vargas wasn't as fast and took two bits of bark to the cheek.

Corson laughed as he wiped his hands on his thighs. He'd once told me adhenes were mischievous, but it was rare he exhibited that trait. There were times like this though, when he let down his guard, and his face lit with delight over irritating his friends, that I glimpsed it in him. If things ever became settled, and there were no more craetons to worry about, I suspected Corson would take great joy in pulling pranks on his friends.

"Your heads were too big to resist," Corson called down to them.

"That's what all the women say to me too," Hawk retorted, and Corson laughed while Vargas and I shook our heads.

"Move along now, we're hunting in this area," Corson said with a wave of his hand.

"I'm going to start hunting assholes in trees," Hawk replied, but he and Vargas strolled out from under the tree. They moved deeper into the woods until they disappeared from view.

Resting my head on Corson's shoulder, I inhaled his fiery scent. When his hand slid over mine, my heartbeat picked up with anticipation. One look or touch from him and my body readied to do what he asked of it. His hand slid over my thigh and down to grip my knee. Sex in a tree would be a first, but I had no doubt he could pull it off.

A doe stepped from between the bushes across from him. "Sorry, demon," I murmured. "That will have to wait."

He flashed a smile at me, leaned against the trunk, and propped his hands behind his head. His arousal was apparent in the bulge in his pants, a bulge that only grew when he watched me pull an arrow free and nock it against my bow. I had no doubt I could hit my target with this bow.

Shifting my balance, I lifted the bow and was about to let the arrow fly when the bushes parted, and a manticore swooped into the clearing. I locked my legs around the branch to keep from toppling over backward at the sudden emergence of the monster. With the body of a red lion, a very human-looking head, and green, translucent wings, the manticore was one of the ugliest creatures I'd ever seen. The fact it had a red scorpion tale and an eight-inch horn jutting from the center of its forehead did nothing to improve its hideous looks.

The manticore's stinger speared the doe, injecting its venom into the deer and paralyzing her instantly. Corson leapt to his feet as I released the arrow, catching the manticore in the center of its chest. The creature didn't seem to feel the arrow as it swung its tail up and its mouth opened impossibly wide to reveal its three rows of razor-sharp teeth. Using its tail, the manticore shoved the doe into its mouth and swallowed her whole.

My stomach churned at the disconcerting spectacle of the deer sliding down the manticore's throat before the monster turned its attention to us. With a trumpet-like screech, it rose into the air and dove at us.

"Shit!" Corson snarled.

I swung the bow over my back as his arms wrapped around me and he pulled me backward. I curled inward and didn't make a sound when we plunged out of the tree. Corson's body enveloped mine, and he grunted as his back crashed off a limb. My heart lodged in my throat; my body was jarred, but uninjured from the impact that spun us around and bounced us off another branch.

"Corson!" I tried to reach for him, but he'd pinned my arms against my sides when he grabbed me. He hit another branch, and the sickening crunch of one of his bones sounded. He had to be in pain, but instead of his grip on me easing, he cradled me closer. "Are you okay?"

He didn't respond as he hit another branch before we plummeted into the open air. His breath exploded out of him when we crashed onto the ground. Before I could move, he rolled so his body was on top of mine with his chest to my back.

"Stay down," he commanded in my ear, and his weight was gone in the next instant.

Lifting my head, I turned to watch as the manticore dove at him. Corson dodged to the side and caught the manticore's stinger. With a fierce jerk, he yanked the beast out of the air and drove it into the earth with enough force to leave a ten-foot dent in the dirt. The manticore trumpeted again as Corson sliced his talons up its tail and stomach, gutting it. When the manticore attempted to curl up to protect itself, Corson sank his claws into its throat and sawed its head off.

I launched to my feet at the same time leaves crunched behind me. Judging by the sound, whatever stood behind me was too close for me to use an arrow on it. Spinning, I yanked my knife free. I had only a second to register a gobalinus barreling toward me before it was in front of me.

Swinging down, I plunged my knife straight through the head of the two-foot-tall monster with yellow eyes and warts covering its green, leathery skin. Its piranha-like teeth snapped at the air; its small hands flailed at me while I held it away.

Seizing its shoulder, I ignored the skin flaking off beneath my palm as I yanked my knife free and sliced it across the gobalinus's throat. Slimy green blood spilled over my hand, but the creature came at me again. Propelling the gobalinus back, I fell on top of it and cut the rest of the way through its neck. Its head rolled away and stopped against a tree trunk. Its hands clawed at me once more before the body went limp beneath me.

Lifting my head, I studied the woods it had emerged from to find Corson standing in the center of three more dead gobalinus. Blood dripped from his talons as he stalked toward me. His gaze raked me from head to toe and back again.

"Are you hurt?" he demanded.

"I'm fine. I only had one ankle-biter to deal with."

His eyes continued to scan me before scouring the woods. His touch was tender when he grasped my arm, helped me rise, and pulled me closer to him, but his muscles vibrated with barely contained violence. Clasping my hand, he wiped away the cloying, green blood before turning it over to inspect my palm.

He looked around the woods again. "We have to return to the others."

"Do you sense something more out there?" I inquired as I studied our surroundings.

"No, but we need to get back to check on them and regroup. That was too many craetons together and coming at us for my liking."

He maneuvered me so I stood in front of him, his chest protectively against my back as he kept his hand on my waist. "I don't need you behind me," I said.

"Yes, you do."

I opened my mouth to protest as a twig broke on our right. He drew me abruptly against him and unleashed his talons. When nothing emerged from the woods, Corson eased his grip but didn't let me go. I didn't try to argue with him again. Now was not the time for a fight when more of our enemies could be enclosing on us, but later...

What? I'd tell him he was an idiot for trying to defend me? I could be more than a little bitchy, but that was pushing the limits even for me. If I were going to be in a relationship with this demon, then I had to accept some things would never change about him. He had to accept that about me too.

Corson kept me against him as we continued through the woods to where we'd left the others camped in a safe house at the edge of the forest. When we came around the trunk of a birch tree, I stopped when the house came into view through a grove of oak trees.

Caim lay on the porch roof with his back against the house, his hands propped behind his head, and a pair of sunglasses on. His legs were stretched out and crossed at the ankles. His black wings were spread out behind him as if he were trying to tan them.

Five paliton demons were gathered around something on the porch. One of the demons tugged on it while another one stomped its foot. Having returned to the house already, Hawk and Vargas opened the door and stepped outside onto the porch. Erin exited the house behind them.

Vargas pointed to what the demons held and then at himself. Erin shrugged before shading her eyes to survey the sky. Hawk examined what the demons held before suddenly leaning in and ripping whatever it was from the demon's hands.

The demon launched a punch at Hawk who ducked it. Hawk shouted something at them while Erin stepped forward with her hands raised as if to intervene. One of the demons shoved Erin back, which caused Hawk to lunge at him, but he still didn't release whatever he held.

Vargas caught Erin before she could crash into the porch banister. He set her back on her feet and pulled out his gun to aim it at the demon who had pushed her. If Vargas shot the demon, it could start a fight none of us were prepared to wage; one that might end with all the humans dead.

CHAPTER FORTY

WREN

"No!" I blurted and stepped forward, but I was too far away for any of them to hear me.

Corson put his hand on my shoulder and pulled me back. Another demon tore the gun from Vargas's grip before he could fire. Vargas whirled on him with a fury I'd never seen from the steadfast soldier.

"What's going on?" I breathed as Hawk and the others all started throwing punches at each other. "Why are they fighting?"

The five demons and Hawk tumbled down the steps and into the front yard. Blood flew, tails thumped, and horns were jerked to the side as they beat each other with an enthusiasm that would result in only one survivor.

Corson inspected the forest before turning his attention to me. "Stay here," he said.

"No, I'm coming with you."

"Not while they're doing this. Right now, they don't care who gets in their way. I don't know what started it, but I'll have an easier time straightening it out if I'm not worried about you."

He was right, and while they were busy brawling, someone had to keep an eye out for more enemies lurking in these woods.

"I'll stay and keep watch," I told him and glanced over the barren trees once more.

Bending, he kissed me before straightening. "Stay here until they're done. I don't sense anything nearby, but scream if something comes at you."

I frowned at him. "I don't scream."

"I've heard you scream a time or two," he replied with a wink.

Before I could form a response, he strolled out of the woods and into the clearing. "What is going on here?" he demanded.

No one acknowledged Corson's arrival as he approached the ball of punching, kicking, and... yep, that one was biting another one's leg like it was a chicken wing. The demon being bitten was trying to beat the demon off, but the cannibal wouldn't let go.

I would have laughed over the absurdity of it all if a cold sweat hadn't begun to trickle down my spine. I'd seen the demons fight each other over something as simple as a beer, or their demon brew mjéod before. The Wilders occasionally clashed with each other too. We didn't all live so closely with each other without someone getting irritable and someone else punching them.

However, unlike the occasional fist fights I'd seen the demons wage, they appeared to be in this one to the death, and I'd *never* seen Hawk fight with them before. Ten minutes ago, Hawk was cracking jokes with Corson. Now he was throttling a demon with the apparent intent of popping the demon's head off.

As the demons moved closer to where I stood, I saw that one of them was clutching a black cloth before it was torn away. Vargas and Erin trailed behind the pack of demons, their eyes following that black thing like a dog followed a bone.

I stepped forward when the screen door swung open and crashed off the side of the house. Someone shouted something from within. My heart lurched at the explosion of noise, and my eyes darted over the forest. *Everyone* knew better than to make so much noise. We spent most of our lives making as little sound as possible.

Jolie raced out of the house and flew down the stairs with four backpacks in hand. She careened across the lawn with three Wilders on her heels. Spinning, she bashed two of the backpacks off Dana's face. The blow staggered Dana back, but he quickly recovered and lunged at her.

I understood some of the wrath on Dana's face as he snatched one of the straps. *No* one stole another's bag. If such a thing started happening between the Wilders, it would never end, and the fighting would never cease.

We needed to be able to trust each other, and we especially had to trust each other with the few possessions we owned. We all shared food, bedding, water, and every other necessity we found, but the contents of our bags were *ours*. A person only picked up another's bag to move it if it was necessary, and now Jolie held four of them.

Something was horribly wrong here, but what?

Chet circled behind Jolie and tackled her to the ground. He slammed her forehead off the ground and came up with two of the backpacks. My hand went to the gun at my side with the intent of firing a warning shot, and hopefully stopping this, but I didn't pull the weapon free. If I shot right now, I'd give away my location, and I couldn't do that until I had a better idea why everyone had suddenly gone insane.

Dana punched Chet in the face. A cracking sound echoed across the clearing and blood burst from Chet's nose. His hands flew to his face as from within the house, shouts resonated.

Corson stopped at the edge of the brawling figures. He grabbed two demons by their shirts and heaved them aside. My breath caught when Hawk swung at him. Dodging the punch, a look of disbelief flashed across Corson's face before his eyes darkened with rage. Hawk swung again, but this time Corson caught his hand and threw him back.

Caim uncoiled from his relaxed position on the porch roof. He removed his sunglasses, set them down, and crawled forward. His head tilted to the side as he watched the melee unfolding below him from the edge of the roof.

Our tiny chance of being able to remain hidden here vanished when a gunshot sounded from within the house and someone screamed. Caim took flight and landed on the ground as more humans stumbled out the doorway of the residence, followed by more demons. One of the demons had a hand pressed against the bleeding hole in the center of his forehead. The injured demon lunged at another demon and tore his arm off.

Lix bolted out the door, his sword over his head. Leaping into the air, Lix plunged his blade through the demon's heart just as the demon lifted the arm to beat my friend Darcy with it. Darcy scrambled away. Bale and Shax emerged behind Lix, but they didn't pay any attention to the skellein as they were busy fighting three other demons. Caim hurried forward and pulled one of the demons away, but when the demon kicked at him, Caim became caught up in the brawl too.

Chaos ruled so completely I didn't realize Corson and Hawk were now pummeling each other until Hawk released a startled cry. My hand flew to my mouth when I saw that Corson had driven his talons straight through Hawk's chest.

Never had I thought to see Corson turn on one of his friends in such a way, but he showed no remorse as he placed his foot on Hawk's stomach. When he shoved Hawk back, he ripped his talons free. Lurching to his feet, Hawk glanced at the bloody holes in his chest before his face contorted in fury and he launched at Corson.

What is going on? This was *not* Corson or Hawk or Jolie or *any* of them. Something was making them act like this, and I had the sick feeling I knew what it might be.

Edging backward, I crept away from the house and deeper into the trees. When I'd last seen them, the horsemen had been leaving the gateway with their following of assorted creatures, but I suspected one of them had found their way to us.

I recalled the way Lust had dug her power into me until it became almost impossible for me to breathe. Recalled that I would have taken Corson then and there and not cared who saw us. I'd been on the verge of losing all control, and Lust had only been toying with us.

A horseman determined to annihilate could easily turn friend against friend, and it *had* to be one of the horsemen causing this. But which one was it? Wrath, War, Greed, maybe Envy? For all I knew, it could be all of them working together to destroy my loved ones.

Adrenaline pounded through my veins, but my hand remained steady when I pulled my knife free and switched it into my left hand. I'd spent many days and hours training with weapons over the years. I could wield a knife as well with my left hand as I could with my right.

No matter how much training I put myself through though, my aim with a gun remained better with my right hand. My arrows would be quieter and less likely to draw attention to me, but I would never be able to fire them as quickly as I could a gun, and speed would probably be a necessity.

Pulling my gun free of its holster, I held it at my side as I stole through the woods.

The only way to kill a horseman would be to take its head, like every other demon, but a gunshot would hurt the thing and maybe scare it away.

Not likely.

I didn't think anything scared the horsemen, and if something did, I didn't want to be anywhere near it.

I glanced back at the clearing as Corson yanked the black cloth away from one of the demons and held it triumphantly in the air. Another demon rushed across the yard and tackled him to the ground. I stopped as I was torn between continuing and rushing into the clearing to help him.

No, you can't!

I had to do something to keep them from killing each other, but I didn't dare go any closer to them. Corson had been fine before he entered that clearing, yet he'd turned as raving mad as the rest of them.

If I tried to help, I could become entangled in whatever magic the horsemen weaved to trap their prey. It took everything I had, but I forced my attention away from Corson and back on hunting down whatever was causing this.

Please stay alive until I can stop this, I pleaded, unwilling to think about what it would do to me if I lost him.

Edging around the back of the house, I paused to set my knife down when the direction of the wind changed. Digging into the spongy earth, I scooped up a handful of dirt and rotting debris.

Someone in the clearing screamed a tormented sound that died abruptly. The cry spurred me faster.

I smeared dirt over my face and down the front of my shirt. I didn't know where the horsemen were, if there was only one of them out there or more, but I couldn't take the chance they would smell me. Lifting another handful of dirt, I ran it over my braid while my eyes continuously searched the woods for a predator. Behind me, the shouting and thuds of fists hitting flesh escalated.

Corson. I finished coating myself in dirt before reclaiming my knife and rising to hunt.

CHAPTER FORTY-ONE

CORSON

The demon groaned when I pulled my talons free and threw him off me. Rolling, I scrambled across the ground to reclaim the velvety, black cloak someone had wrenched from me.

A booted foot stomped on my wrist when my hand curled around the cloak. I grunted as bone snapped and looked up to find Hawk leering down at me. Blood continued to seep from the wounds I'd inflicted on him and his eyes burned with rage.

Why did I stab Hawk? My groggy mind tried to figure that out, but the more I searched for the answer, the more it eluded me. After everything we'd been through together, I considered Hawk a friend, yet when he bent to pull the cloth away from me, I knew I'd kill him for it.

It belongs to me! I'd felt its softness against my skin and the rush of pleasure accompanying my possession of it.

Hawk could *not* have it.

Dimly, I recalled something far more important that belonged to me. A stirring of sanity slipped through the mass of *need* twisting like worms in my brain. The scent of a woman and the sensation of pale blonde hair tickling my arm played across my mind.

I stumbled back when images assaulted me. The memory of love rose to the surface. *She* was mine; she made me better. I loved her strength, her stubbornness, and the way she cared for others.

Where was she? *Who* was she?

My head dropped into my hands when the world slanted precariously. I struggled to recall what I'd forgotten as the bones in my broken wrist set back into place with a click and the throbbing in it lessened. Lifting my head, I searched for that hair and smell, but all I saw was blood and fighting.

Then, my gaze fastened on the cloak again.

Have to have it! Have to have it! The words became a mantra in my head.

Fangs sprouted into my mouth. *That's not right; I don't have fangs.*

I do now. Because of her.

Who?

I took a step toward the others to jump into the fight again, but I froze when a face materialized within the tempest rolling through my mind.

Wren!

Once I recalled her, my urgency to possess the cloak lessened. I still wanted it, but I wanted her more. I spun toward where I'd left her in the woods.

How could I have forgotten my Chosen?

Wrong, this is all wrong, I realized as bits and pieces started fitting into place. There's something else I had to recall, and I had to do it now, or we would all die.

A rock hit me in the back of the head with enough force to stagger me forward. Someone launched onto my back, knocking me to the ground. Rolling, I slammed my fist into the chest of the demon perched on me. Lifting him up, I flung him over the top of me and sprang to my feet.

All around me, demons and humans brawled. A few bodies littered the ground; I couldn't tell if they were dead or alive, but if this continued many would die, of that I was certain. Then, the demon holding the black cloak spun around. The end of it brushed over my skin when it swung out, and the compulsion to grab it seized me.

Panting for air, I stumbled away from the fight and toward where I'd left Wren. I searched the forest but didn't see her. That cloak was *nothing* to me; she was *everything,* and I was failing her.

"Where is she?"

Before I could stumble further toward where I'd left Wren, someone kicked my knee out from under me. My leg bent at an odd angle when I hit the ground, and the demons pounced.

∽

*W*REN

I stayed low as I moved around the corner of the house and back into the trees. I caught glimpses of the melee in the clearing, but I didn't look too long. I couldn't be distracted by them right now, and I knew I might plunge in to help if I watched for too long. We'd all be dead then.

After we'd spent the night in the school, Corson sent most of the skelleins to the wall to speak with Kobal, and Raphael had gone with them. It had been the right choice for Raphael to go too, but right now I *really* wished the golden boy with his handy 'suck the energy from things and blast them to kingdom come' power was here.

Creeping around the corner of a large boulder, I spotted something standing amid the trees fifteen feet away from me. Ducking back behind the rock, I studied the forest for manticores, gobalinus, or some other nasty Hell creature coming my way.

I slid my knife back into its holster as a strong gust of wind knocked some of the stubbornly clinging oak leaves from the trees. One of the leaves drifted down to stick to my face. I brushed it off and cringed when it made a small, crinkling noise. Nothing could have detected the sound, but it still made my palms sweat. I took another steadying breath before peeking around the boulder with my gun held before me.

Through the trees, the end of a horse's red tail swept aside the leaves on the ground. I followed that tail up to the vibrant red of the horse's legs, higher to its black body, and toward its front. My breath caught when I spotted the two heads attached to the horse's long, muscular neck. The red stripe down the center of both the heads matched the red of its tail, mane, forelock, and legs. Four strange, fluorescent green eyes watched the clearing from the horse's heads.

The rider on the horse's back sat proudly in the saddle, his shoulders back and his blond hair falling around his shoulders. The pale skin stretched taut over his high cheekbones and pointed chin gave him the appearance of a living skull.

On the rider's right hand, rings covered all his fingers and thumb. I couldn't see his left hand from where I hid, but I recalled seeing him before with the other horsemen and knew his left hand also had rings on it. Each of the golden bands held a different colored jewel. The rings were so large the bands took up the entire bottom half of his long, big-knuckled fingers.

This horseman had also worn a black cloak when I last saw him. I recalled that a jewel, the same fluorescent green as the rider's eyes and those of his horses, had fastened that cloak at his throat. He didn't wear the cloak now.

My heart sank when I realized the others were busy trying to kill each other over that cloak.

The horseman ran his hand over his thigh, causing the jewels in his rings to flash in the sun filtering over his body. A rainbow of light reflected off the trees and ground as his hand moved.

The sudden need to possess those rings almost caused me to burst out from behind the boulder and charge across the clearing at him. I'd bite his fingers off if it meant getting my hands on those rings. Not once had I ever wanted a piece of the jewelry before; if I couldn't eat it, it was of little use to me, but suddenly those rings were *everything* to me.

Mine! I want them! Mine! Mine! Mine!

The words screeched across my mind; my body shuddered as my survival instinct warred with my craving to possess them *all*. I'd wear them, run them over my body, hold them close, and never ever *ever* would anyone else be allowed to touch *my* rings.

You will die if you go for them!

Somehow my survival instinct won the war, but barely. I ducked away again and pressed my back to the rock as my body shook like a jolt of electricity had hit it. My fingers clawed at my palms, tearing away the skin. The pain helped me to focus on something other than the rings as I forced myself to remain where I was.

Somewhat back under control again, I uncurled my fingers and twisted my hands into the dirt to coat the gashes I'd inflicted on myself. Hopefully, the soil would be enough to staunch the flow and smell of my blood until I could make my move.

I was pretty sure I knew which horseman I was dealing with. It had to be Greed sitting over there, proudly creating anarchy between a group that had fought and killed *for* each other until he rode into our midst.

I hated these twisted horsemen as much as the fallen angels. Maybe more so. The angels couldn't manipulate us into killing each other, as far as I knew. However, there was no way to fight a monster who could hide in the trees while he turned people and demons against each other with such ease.

I poked my head out around the boulder again. My teeth grated together when I saw the smile curving the corners of Greed's lips. That smile, and the obvious joy he took in inflicting hurt on those I loved, pushed aside my lingering avarice.

My grip shifted on my gun, and leaning further out, I lifted it. Squeezing the trigger, I fired three rapid shots. One took Greed in the shoulder, the other in his temple and the third in the center of his forehead when he turned to look at me. His head barely moved an inch from the impact of the last bullet.

I gulped when those hideous green eyes fastened on me with a rapacious greed that opened an endless pit within my belly.

Greed can never be satisfied, never be filled. It always wants more and more and more.

This thing wanted *all* of me, and when it was done, it would still seek *more*. My hand shook on my gun as something sinister slithered through my mind. The empty pit of need swelled inside me until it threatened to possess me in a way no one should ever be possessed.

I opened my mouth to beg him to make the awful hollowness stop, but I closed it again. I would *not* beg this thing. No matter how empty I felt, I would not give it the satisfaction of seeing me plead.

Lifting my wobbling hand, I fired another bullet. This one went straight through Greed's throat, spilling more of his black blood. Blinking, I tried to stand, but my knees gave out. All four of the horse's eyes fastened on me when Greed turned his mount. With a kick to his horse, Greed came for me.

CHAPTER FORTY-TWO

WREN

I succeeded in getting my legs underneath me as I turned to face the rider. I had no idea what *I* could do against it, but I refused to go down without a fight. Lifting my gun, I fired again. I was about to squeeze the trigger once more when something burst out of the woods and raced toward Greed.

Corson leapt high, placed his hand on the horse's rump, and propelled himself into the air. He landed behind Greed and plunged his talons through the horseman's neck. Greed's hands flew behind his head; he gripped Corson's wrist to stop him when Corson started to saw Greed's head from his body.

When Greed succeeded in tearing Corson's talons from his neck, I slid my gun into its holster, pulled out my knife, and raced toward them. The horse rose onto its hind legs when I got close to it. Black hooves whistled in the air as they zipped past my head. I reeled away from the horse when it kicked at me again.

The horse's abrupt movement caused Corson to lose his grip on Greed. Before he could topple from the saddle, he plunged his talons into Greed's thigh. A strange, high-pitched hiss filled the air. It reminded me of the ouro, only this one was inherently more sinister.

Corson raked his talons down Greed's thigh, slicing it open to reveal his black muscles and the black bone beneath. When I tried to dash to the side to help Corson, the horse reared again. I lurched back when the tip of a hoof caught my forehead. A burst of pain momentarily blurred my vision as blood trickled down my broken skin and stuck in my eyelashes.

I wiped the blood hastily away and blinked my vision back into focus as Greed rested his hand on Corson's forehead. Misery and rage filled Corson's bellow. My heart lodged in my throat as I realized Greed was making him experience the same emptiness I had earlier.

Swinging up with his other hand, Corson buried his talons in Greed's back and jerked downward. More black blood oozed out of Greed as he strove to stay mounted. The horse twisted to the side in an attempt to throw Corson from it.

Seeing an opening, I lunged forward, but one of the horse's heads swung toward me, and its teeth snapped inches from my face. Its fetid breath blew my hair back as its body spun toward me and it struck out again. This time, its hoof caught my forearm, breaking my skin open to spill more blood.

I refused to be deterred as I dodged to the side to avoid the next hoof the horse aimed at my head. Clutching a handful of the horse's red mane, I jumped up. The horse spun, trying to shake me off as I swung my leg over and hooked it around the beast's neck. I somehow managed to hold on and twist around to straddle its neck.

"Wren, watch out!" Corson shouted, and a hand landed on my back.

I screamed before I realized my mouth opened. Emptiness engulfed me until I was swimming in a bleak pit of melancholy. I fell forward, inhaling the sulfur scent of the horse as I struggled against the overwhelming impulse to drive my knife into my heart and end this torment.

"Shit!" Corson grunted, and that hideous hissing sound filled the air again.

I didn't know where I found the strength, but I somehow managed to turn and swing blindly downward with my knife. The blade plunged into something and I yanked it when I felt the scrape of bone. The hand on my back fell away. I gasped in a breath as the emptiness within me eased a fraction.

Turning, I saw Greed lifting its bloody hand into the air. I slashed out again, slicing more flesh before grabbing his hand and yanking it to the side.

Want! Need! More! More! More! I didn't know what I wanted or needed; I only knew the words hammered ceaselessly through my mind.

Somehow, I managed to work past my insatiable greed as bone broke, sinew snapped, and the last of the muscles holding Greed's hand on gave way. I found myself gazing at the curling fingers of the hand when I pulled it away from the horseman.

Rings! I must have those rings!

With an angry shout, I threw the hand aside before I could pull those rings free and slide them on. I didn't want to think about what would happen if I put them on, but images of becoming one of the horsemen or spontaneously combusting filtered through my imagination. My head lifted, and I found myself gazing into Greed's hate-filled, astonished eyes.

Greed's attention was drawn away from me when Corson climbed onto the saddle behind him once more. With a ferocious shout, Corson buried his talons in the side of Greed's neck and sliced across his flesh. Greed swung out, backhanding me so hard across the face that bells rang in my head and blood burst into my mouth.

My hands clawed at the horse's red mane when it reared again, and I started sliding to the side. Another heavy blow knocked my grip loose. Black hooves filled my vision as I toppled beneath the beast. I didn't have time to roll away before it landed on top of me.

~

CORSON

"No!" I shouted as Wren fell beneath the horse. "Fucker!" I snarled and sliced my way through what remained of the horseman's neck.

The decapitated head bounced off the horse's flank before falling to the ground. I was about to leap off the horse's back when the animal dissolved beneath me. Red and black ash filled the air, sticking to my skin and filling my lungs as I hit the ground.

"Wren!" I shouted as I searched for her amid the cascading debris. "Wren!"

Through the falling ash, I spotted her limp form. "Wren!"

Something twisted and broke within me, rage built toward a breaking point as I scrambled to her. This rage had nothing to do with any of the horsemen and everything to do with the weakening I felt in my bond to her.

"Wren."

Ash coated the blood seeping from the corners of her mouth and oozing out of the gash in her chest. Her breath wheezed out of her. I gathered her in my arms, careful not to jar the broken bones in her concave chest. The horse's weight had crushed her; its hooves had sliced open her shirt and flayed her skin down to the white bone beneath.

I cradled her against my chest as she gazed dazedly up at me. "I should have come sooner. I should have figured out what was happening faster," I whispered as I kissed her forehead.

Her blood-coated fingers curled into my forearm before she lost her grip on me. Her hand fell limply to her side as she inhaled a rattling breath. "Not your fault, demon. It was only... a matter... of time... before my end came."

Her body lurched as a convulsion rocked it. Her blue eyes rolled in her head and more blood spilled from her mouth. Helplessness and anguish rose to replace my fury. I'd just found her, and now I was losing her.

"Listen to me, Wren," I commanded when she became still again. "You're dying and that is one of the steps for the change to occur. If you tell me yes, I can give you my blood for the second step. If you survive the change, you'll live, and you'll be an adhene demon like me."

Her eyes rolled toward me, their whites were bloodshot, and one had a starburst of blood in it. Her skin held the pasty sheen of death I'd seen many times before. Terror spurred me into speaking faster. "You'll feed on wraiths. You may have a difficult time adjusting and controlling yourself in the beginning."

I didn't want to mention any of the bad things that could come with the change, but she had to know everything before she agreed to this. She was dying; she might say yes to life and later grow to hate me for what she'd become if she didn't know it all.

"You could accidentally hurt someone until you adjust to what you are," I told her. "However, if you survive the change, you'll live forever. You'll be stronger, faster, and you'll be with me. No matter what you decide, know I love you, Wren," I whispered as I kissed her forehead and silently begged her to choose life, to choose *me*.

"I love you too, Corson," she said in a blood-choked whisper.

My name and those words on her lips caused me to groan.

"If I die, will I go to Hell? I've killed..." She broke off when a round of coughing wracked her. Agony twisted her features, her fingers twitched on the ground, but she didn't seem to have the strength to lift them as they fell limply beside her once more.

"No, lahala," I whispered, knowing I could be uttering the words that would take her from me forever. "You won't go to Hell. You've killed because you had to in order to survive. You are not selfish or cruel."

A small smile tugged at the corners of her mouth. Tears burned my eyes as I leaned over her. I wasn't ready to lose her, but she was slipping further away from me.

Another rattle emitted from her, and I knew this was the end for her. If she said no to me, I would be holding her corpse. She loved me, but was it enough to chance becoming something she'd hated for most of her short life?

A small smile tugged at the corners of her mouth. "Do it, demon."

I froze, uncertain if I'd heard her right. "You want me to give you my blood?"

"Yes," the word was a whisper on her lips before her breath stopped completely.

Panic filled me as the life faded further from her eyes. The tenuous beat of her heart slowed until I barely detected it. Shifting my hold on her, I sliced a talon down my arm. Blood poured from the deep gash as I held it over the wound in her chest.

My mother threw herself into the fires. I'd witnessed the love my parents had for each other. I'd known what a Chosen bond was, believed I'd understood why my mother had done what she did.

I realized that I'd never truly understood her choice before. I did now.

Wren was so new to me, this bond so fragile, yet the emptiness engulfing me made Greed's touch seem like a gentle caress. My hand clenched on Wren before I released her to reopen my vein. I would pour every ounce of blood I had into her if that was what it took to save her.

CHAPTER FORTY-THREE

W<small>REN</small>

I'd been prepared to die since I was eight, and I'd been fine with dying all these many years. The few who would grieve my passing would continue with their lives afterward. They would probably never speak of me again, and when they were gone, no one would ever remember I'd existed.

Then, one day, my soul would be reincarnated, and if Earth still existed, I would start all over in a brand new life. The new me would have no memory of Wren *or* Bonnie.

I'd been good with dying for a while now, and being taken out while helping to destroy a horseman was not a bad way to go. It might make me a legend who wouldn't be forgotten by everyone. Maybe, one day in the distant future and in a different person, I'd be sitting with humans and listening to the legend of the human, Wren, who had helped to slay Greed.

I might even smile and think how courageous Wren must have been. I might aspire to be like her, and maybe that reincarnation of me would one day go on to do *better* things than this version of me had.

Yep, I was all right with dying; it didn't even hurt so much anymore. When the horse had first come down on my chest, agony had exploded through my entire body as the sickening sounds of my bones crunching filled my ears. Warm blood had burst from my mouth to trickle down my chin.

Then, the pain eased, the blood cooled, and so did the rest of my limbs. I'd watched the horse's hooves kicking in the air and waited for the final blow to come as death crept in to claim me. It didn't even bother me that I'd finally found love and the joy of being alive only to have it ripped cruelly away from me shortly afterward. That was the way life worked, I knew. What I did feel was grateful I'd had the chance to experience those things before I died.

Then the horse had burst into dust above me.

Beautiful. The thought had been crazy, and I didn't know what made the ash so beautiful. Maybe it was the sun filtering through the trees to illuminate the floating dust. Perhaps it was because the ash consisted of the colors of the horse. Or maybe it was because I knew this would be one of the last things I'd ever see.

Whatever it was, the ash had been beautiful as it settled around me in a colorful wave that coated me from head to toe. If I hadn't felt so broken, I might have laughed and thrown up the dust to celebrate Greed's end, but my limbs were too heavy for that.

My eyes drifted closed as Corson's arms enveloped me. His body eased the chill in me, but not enough. He would never be able to stop the ice encasing my limbs, and that was okay. I opened my mouth to tell him everything would be fine, my time had come.

The words stuck in my throat when I saw the sorrow emanating from his eyes and the misery etched onto his features. This would not be fine for him, I realized. My demon wouldn't be okay with this.

There was no reincarnation for him. If he chose to walk his mother's path, that would be the end of Corson. That comprehension was far more excruciating than the horse stomping on me had been. If Corson died, there was no chance future Wren might meet a demon with pointed ears and dancing citrine eyes, who would make her contemplate tearing her hair out at the same time she wanted to throw herself into his arms. There would be no demon for her to love because he wouldn't exist.

I don't feel the Chosen bond as he does. But I felt the stirring of an emotion so raw and primitive that it could only be a long-buried piece of my DNA coming to life.

Was this what soul mates were for humans? Was this why some people claimed they fell in love at first sight? Did some ancient piece of genetic material spark to life in those random few to show them they'd found their human equivalent of a Chosen? Or was I losing too much blood and completely delusional?

Either way, I knew I couldn't tolerate seeing Corson like this. What remained of my life surged forth within me, and I did everything I could to surface enough to comfort him. I loved him, and my death would destroy him.

When he offered to change me, a piece of me recoiled from the idea and the uncertainty of what I would become. But a larger part of me was willing to do anything to take away the devastation in Corson's eyes.

You can't say yes only for him, my mind whispered to me. *You'll regret it if you do and that will only destroy him more.*

Could I live with being a demon?

Yes, I could. I wouldn't be evil, not like some of those I'd encountered over the years. I wouldn't be cruel. I would live forever, with Corson. He warned me it would take some getting used to and I might injure someone in the beginning, but I would stop myself from doing that, somehow. Even if I had to go away and couldn't lead this group of Wilders, I would do whatever it took to stop myself from harming someone else.

I would have an eternity with Corson. How could I refuse that? We were good together. He made me crazier than any man should make a woman, but I loved him more than I could fathom.

So I said yes, and now I had no idea what would become of me, of him, of us, or even if I would survive what was about to unfold. I tried to get my fingers to clutch his shirt, to hold him closer, but they were too weak and clumsy. He sliced open his forearm and poured his blood over my wounds.

No, don't hurt yourself, I moaned in my head when I saw his flayed-open flesh, but I couldn't get the words out as the world slipped further and further away from me. *Did my heart stop?*

My eyes closed as Corson's blood filled me.

∼

CORSON

"What are you doing?" the words were blurted from beside me.

I'd heard them coming, seen them approaching, but my attention remained mostly focused on Wren. A shadow fell over us, and I bared my teeth at the human beside me. Jolie, I dimly recalled her name. The woman gawked at me before focusing on what I was doing with Wren.

The humans knew something had changed with Hawk, but they didn't know how or why. In case people one day got it in their heads to use demons to become immortal too, we'd worked to keep the knowledge of how the change from mortal to immortal occurred from them, but I didn't care if they saw me with Wren now. The humans still wouldn't fully know how the transformation worked, and even if they did, I would do whatever was necessary to save Wren. Let the mortals try to turn on us and use us, it would be the greatest regret of their lives.

Tears shimmered in Jolie's eyes as she focused on Wren. "What are you doing?" she asked again.

Hawk rested his hand on Jolie's arm and pulled her back a step. I sliced my arm open again to pour more blood into Wren's wound.

"Is she dead?" Jolie whispered, her lower lip trembling.

"Dying," I grated through my teeth as Wren's heart gave a little beat and her breath rattled out once more. My blood would ward off her immediate death, but that didn't mean it would keep it at bay.

Hawk's eyes were wary as he studied Wren then me. He'd once told me being a demon was preferable to being dead, but he wouldn't have picked becoming a demon. Fate had chosen his course when Lilitu's canagh blood mixed with his while he was dying. Hawk accepted that course, though there were times he didn't like it.

He would never have agreed to do this. He would never have *offered* it.

"Corson—"

"She agreed," I broke in before he could say more. "I asked her. I told her what it entailed, and she agreed to it. She knows the consequences."

Hawk gave a brisk nod and pulled Jolie further away. Over Hawk's shoulder, I saw the others mulling about the woods. Most of them were bruised and bloodied. I wondered how many were dead, but I'd sort that mess out later.

Bale kicked aside the head of the horseman. Unlike its horse, the rider hadn't turned to dust. "Greed," she sneered. "I should have known."

"We all should have known," Shax said. "We didn't, and that is the point of the horsemen; they work from the shadows, manipulating and playing their games."

"I hate these things," Erin said.

"We all do." Magnus dropped the black cloak onto Greed's body. "Where did the cloak come from?"

"I found it in the woods," Vargas said. "When I was taking a piss. I didn't feel possessive about it in the beginning, but once I brought it back to the house…."

"Your greed increased," Magnus said when Vargas's voice trailed off, and he wrapped his hand around his cross.

"Yes. I set it down, and Hawk and I went to get Erin, but when I discovered others touching it, I found I wanted it more and more."

"So did I," Hawk said.

"From now on, no more picking things up when you don't know where they came from," Caim commanded as he gazed pointedly at everyone gathering around us. "We have no idea how the horsemen work, not entirely."

Lix strolled forward with his sword blade resting against his skeletal shoulder. "Where is Greed's horse?"

"It turned to ash when I lopped off Greed's head," I answered.

Bale stalked toward me and rested the tip of her sword in the dirt beside me. "What will you do if this doesn't work? If she still dies?"

I snarled at her, but she didn't back away from me.

"It is a possibility you must face, Corson," she said.

"Not right now."

Caim knelt by my side. His head turned to the side as he studied Wren. "She is strong."

"That doesn't mean the change will be successful," Bale said as some of the humans crept closer.

"Enough!" I barked at Bale.

Bale took a small step back, and the humans scurried away. One of them kicked the hand Wren had severed from Greed, sending it spinning into the underbrush. Magnus lifted it and walked over to dump it on the body.

"We have to burn him," Magnus said. "And we need to leave here. Our fight won't have gone unnoticed by anything nearby."

"We encountered a manticore and some gobalinus in the woods. They must have been with Greed. We have to leave *now*." I slit my forearm open again and adjusted my hold on Wren. My blood continued to flow into her as I rose from the ground. I swayed on my feet, my blood loss making me lightheaded. Shax stepped toward me, his arms outstretched as if to take Wren from me. "No," I bit out and shifted her away from him.

"You're barely standing," he murmured.

"I'm not letting her go."

I steadied myself and pushed past him to face the others. "Get your things," I commanded. "Set Greed's corpse on fire. We're leaving."

CHAPTER FORTY-FOUR

CORSON

I kept Wren in my arms as I settled into the corner of the small house Jolie and the others had led us to for the night. Jolie placed Wren's bag beside me and scampered away as if I would kill her. With the way I felt right now, the woman had a right to be uneasy around me.

Hawk didn't say a word as he settled on my right, but he stared anxiously at Wren. Caim and Magnus stood nearby. Bale watched my every move as Shax ushered the Wilders out of the room. I could hear the demons shuffling through the house and establishing a guard outside. Shax followed the Wilders out. Lix plopped himself onto the couch, causing it to groan as dust burst into the air around the skellein. Particles of dust filtered down around him as he uncapped his flask, lifted it to his mouth, and took a swallow.

My eyes fastened on Wren as I watched the rise and fall of her chest and studied her pale eyelids with their small blue veins. Her heart still beat, but it hadn't taken Hawk this long to wake. However, it had happened so fast with Hawk, that we hadn't realized he was close enough to death for Lilitu's blood to change him until he'd started exhibiting demonic traits.

"She sustained more damage than you," I said to him.

"Yes, she did," Hawk agreed.

"The horse sliced her open *and* trampled her."

"I was only sliced open," Hawk said.

"And not as badly as her."

"True."

Despite those words, Hawk didn't stop his worried staring, and none of the tension eased in the room. If Wren died, they would try to stop me from going on a rampage if I attempted one. After losing her Chosen, my mother killed herself as soon as she got the chance. I'd seen other demons go berserk and destroy everything in their path until they were taken down. Some demons retained their sanity and became broken shells of their former selves, but they survived for a time. Most of those demons only lived to deliver revenge until they finally found someone to give them the end they'd been seeking all along. I didn't know any who were still alive now.

Long ago, I'd vowed never to make the same choice my mother had. I hadn't realized what I'd been doing at the time, how broken the loss of a Chosen would leave me, but I'd uphold my vow. I would also ruthlessly hunt down and slaughter every horseman and angel who dared to stand against us. I would have them all begging for mercy before I gleefully *bathed* in their blood.

"Even if she wakes. The change takes a while; she could still die a couple of weeks from now," Bale said.

"I know that," I snarled.

"But are you prepared for it?"

Lifting my head, I met her gaze. "I will do what must be done to carry out our mission. I will make them pay."

Bale opened her mouth before closing it again and bowing her head. Turning away from me, she walked over to the fireplace and rested her arm on the mantle. "Raphael and the skelleins should have reached Kobal by now," she said. "Depending on how their trip went, they could return any day now."

"Raphael will not heal her. I don't know if he'd be able to help her through the change, but even if he can, he won't do that either," Caim said. "He will not alter the pathway one is meant to walk."

Bale's eyes narrowed on him. "That's not what I was suggesting."

"Isn't it?" Caim replied.

Bale scowled at him and turned away to focus on the dust-covered, gray stone chimney. Like the other safe houses, this one held no mementos of those who had once lived here, but it seemed this one had gone longer without Wilders in it than the other homes had.

"Wren agreed to let Corson try changing her. As his Chosen, this is the path she was meant to walk," Caim continued, "whether she lives or not."

"Yes." Unfolding his legs, Hawk rose and walked over to pull aside the curtain and peer out the window.

"How many were lost in the fight Greed created?" I asked Shax when he returned to the room.

"One human and one demon," Shax replied.

"Has it made them hostile toward each other?"

"No, I think it's brought them closer," he said. "Greed used and manipulated us all, and it's pissed them off."

"Good," I said and focused on Wren again.

I ran my finger over her pale cheek before tracing her full lips. Her color was returning, her breathing becoming steadier, as her heart thumped solidly in her chest. However, she could live another two weeks and still not survive the numerous differences my blood would create within her body.

At least give me those two weeks. I knew I would only crave more time with her when they were over, but I would give anything for those days with her.

I pulled back the tattered, bloody shreds of her shirt. The skin beneath was still red and swollen, but the bleeding had stopped, and I couldn't see her breastbone anymore. Releasing her shirt, I tenderly pressed my hands against her chest. The bones beneath my palm grated. She stirred, and her eyes moved behind her closed lids. Her bones were still broken, but they were repairing themselves.

Already healing faster than a mortal and making that change toward demon. Would she recognize me as her Chosen when she woke? Two demons always knew when they found their Chosen, but this was different. Even if she didn't accept me as her Chosen, it wouldn't matter as long as she *lived.*

I held her close as the night crept onward. The faintest rays of the sun were creeping around the edges of the heavy curtains when Wren's eyelids fluttered open. She winced and closed them again. Her head turned into my chest, and her fingers gripped my shirt.

The others all held their breaths as they took a step closer to us.

"Wren," I whispered.

"Hmm," she murmured.

"Wren, look at me."

Her eyes opened, they briefly focused on me, and a small smile curved her mouth. "Hello, demon."

The strength of the relief filling me almost caused me to crush her against me, but she was far from healed and I would only hurt her if I did so. I knew this didn't mean she would live, but I hadn't believed I'd ever hear her voice again. My head dropped to hers, and I kissed her ear.

"Hi," I said as floorboards creaked beneath the steps of the others leaving the room. Lifting my head, I gazed down at her. "Do you remember what happened?"

I smoothed my finger over the lines in her forehead when she frowned. "There was a fight…" Her voice trailed off. "And a horse?"

"Yes."

Her hand went to her chest, and her face scrunched up before horror parted her mouth. "I *died.*"

"You came about as close to it as one gets."

"It felt like I died."

"Wren—"

"And then you sliced your arm open and poured your blood into me."

"Yes."

"Am I a demon now? Is that enough to start the change in me?"

"Your almost dying and my blood is enough to start the change, but there is a chance you still might not survive," I replied.

"So I could be like a ticking time bomb, any second, death?"

"Not quite like that. You'll sicken before you die, but it will happen quickly."

She took a deep breath and winced.

"Your wounds haven't completely healed," I told her. "That will take a few days. If you survive the change, you will heal at an even faster rate once you're a demon. The rate will increase as you age and grow stronger. You will also be immortal."

"I see," she murmured.

"Hawk will have a better understanding of the timeline of the change for you, though yours won't be the same as his. I'm an entirely different type of demon than him. The last of my kind."

She smiled at me. "Not if I live."

I did a double take at her words before they sank in. I'd always accepted I would be the last purebred adhene to exist. Now, there was a possibility I would no longer be the last of my kind and that our children would also continue the line.

"Not if you live," I agreed with a smile.

"And I plan to do exactly that," she stated and lifted her chin in her stubborn way.

~

Wren

"I didn't notice any changes, not really," Hawk said the next day when I asked him what he'd experienced during his transition into demonhood.

It had only taken me all of yesterday to feel well enough to walk around and see the others. The rapid healing was almost as surprising to me as the life I still possessed considering I'd experienced my life slipping away from me.

"I mean, I realized I was healing faster," Hawk continued as he leaned against the trunk of a tree and crossed his legs. "That much was obvious from the start, but I blew it off. I knew some of Lilitu's blood had gotten into me, so I assumed that somehow made it possible for me to heal faster. Truthfully, I didn't want to delve too deeply into it either.

"For a while afterward, I didn't *feel* any different or I didn't notice I did anyway. Then the whole thing with Sarah happened..." His voice trailed off; his eyes went to the woods behind me. "Maybe I should have suspected something was different then, but I believed she was nuts, you know?"

"She did go a little off the deep end," Erin agreed as she settled onto a large rock next to where Hawk stood. Drawing her legs up, she planted her feet on the side of the stone. "We all thought she was crazy."

"Yeah," Hawk muttered and ran a hand through his hair. "If I'd known what I was becoming, I wouldn't have slept with her, but I didn't know."

"We suspected something was happening with him," Corson said to me. "But nothing could be confirmed, until Sarah."

"I still regret what happened with her," Hawk said. "I always will."

I couldn't imagine what it must be like for him to live with that guilt. It hadn't been his fault, but what happened with Sarah haunted him, just as it would have haunted me for the rest of my days. Something could still go wrong with me, but at least I had a head's up that my mortal status might be changing to immortal. I'd be able to do something to stop myself from hurting someone before it happened.

"Anyway, it wasn't until we were in Hell that I realized I wasn't normal anymore. All the other humans couldn't make it more than half a mile into Hell without looking like they were going to die. I had no problem continuing with River."

"It was so hot in there," Vargas said as he sat beside Erin. "That's when we began to suspect things were different with Hawk too"— Vargas waved a finger between himself and Erin—"but we were running for our lives, so it wasn't exactly the greatest time to discuss it."

"No, it wasn't," Erin agreed.

"Not only could I tolerate the heat, but while everyone else was thirsty, I wasn't," Hawk said. "When I thought about it, I realized I hadn't been drinking or eating as much as I used to. I also realized I wasn't going to the bathroom as often. When I was in Hell, those bodily functions ceased entirely. I *did* want sex more before entering Hell, but with Sarah lurking everywhere I went, that became an impossibility. And sleeping with her again was *not* an option. The last thing she needed was more encouragement."

Hawk's brow furrowed as he ran a hand through his hair again. "Then, I realized my vision was better; it had been so gradual that I didn't notice it until I saw a lanavour coming at us long before I should have seen it. We'd just entered Hell, the Hell shadows were everywhere, and the lanavour was fifty yards away, yet it was as clear as day to me. I'd been seeing better for a while, but I had that *ah-ha* moment in Hell. I had one about my hearing too."

"What is a lanavour demon?" I asked.

Hawk, Erin, and Vargas all shuddered. "Hideous monsters," Erin said. "They're blue-gray and have no mouths. They can communicate telepathically, and when they touch another, they learn their innermost secrets and fears. They kill by turning those secrets and fears against their victim."

"They sound awful," I muttered.

"They are," Corson said. "They're also mostly dead, and we will make sure to destroy what remains of them."

"How did you know you'd survived the transformation?" I asked Hawk.

"I eventually ceased all human bodily functions," he answered, "and I survive entirely as a canagh demon on wraiths and sex. I assume I also need to find my Chosen to have children."

"I see," I murmured.

"I think that when my human bodily functions stopped is when I completed the transformation, but I don't know for sure. Maybe it happened before then, maybe after, and maybe it's different for everyone who survives the change, but the demons don't know the answer and neither do I. If you progress in the same way, it will be a couple of weeks to a month before you start noticing changes.

"However, you'll be looking for the differences, where I wasn't, so you might notice them sooner than I did. Or it could take longer for you. My bodily functions didn't cease until I was in Hell, entering the place where demons evolved may have sped things up in me."

"That would make sense," I said.

I searched the woods to see if I could detect any changes in my vision, but everything appeared the same, and everything sounded the same.

"It's only been a day," Corson said and clasped my arm.

My skin rippled beneath his touch; my breath caught as a rush of desire seared through me. His eyes widened as he must have sensed what had happened to me. I almost jumped him then and there, but Hawk's cough stopped me from doing so. Hawk stepped away from the tree, jerked his head at the others, and turned to vanish into the forest.

I barely waited for the rest to walk away before I was kissing Corson. Tugging my pants off, I didn't wait for him to get out of his before I wrapped my legs around his waist. I was already wet when his fingers entwined in my hair and I slid onto his cock.

I nearly screamed at the sensation of him stretching and filling me as he sank into me. A few hard thrusts pushed me over the edge, and I came faster and more intensely than I ever had before. I clawed at him, needing more and more as we fell to the forest floor in a tangled heap of limbs.

It wasn't until hours later, when we'd finally separated from each other that I rolled over to stare at the twilight sky.

"Nothing looks different to me, nothing sounds different, but *that* was different," I said.

He rolled over and propped his head on his hand; he smiled down at me as his fingers created small circles on my belly. "I always made you come," he said.

"Oh, no doubt," I agreed with a grin. "But you might have shaken the earth too."

He laughed as he gathered me closer and held me against his chest. I knew he worried I might still die, and so did I, but I was determined to savor every second of the time I had left with him.

CHAPTER FORTY-FIVE

WREN

December brought a cold front with it. We'd moved further south to avoid the worst of the winter, and along the way, we'd encountered another group of demons and Wilders. I knew their leader, Elton, a little, but Randy had more dealings with him than I did. Elton had been leading his group of Wilders for ten years, so he had to be doing something right. Elton's group wasn't supposed to have been in this area, but a rockslide blocked their path and redirected their travel.

We were only a couple hundred miles away from the southernmost section of the wall, but it was still cold enough here to require blankets though fires for heat weren't permitted. Any large fire was a good way to bring death down on us all.

Cooking fires were kept as small as possible and lit deeply in the caves we mostly lived in now. It was easier to hide a fire and the scent of cooking food when we were underground. We often spent days hunting, fishing, and preserving what we could before moving on.

We'd start moving further inland soon, but we'd decided to rest here for at least a week. It had been a tiring journey to this area; we all needed a break. Next week, Elton and his group would continue on their way, and we would go deeper into the Wilds. We were on the border of an area I'd never traversed before. I didn't know how to feel about that.

I was ready to move on, to do more to hunt our enemies down, but I was afraid of what we would find. Elton had said they'd heard some of the strangest sounds when they backtracked away from the rockslide. Some of his followers were standing behind him as he'd revealed this. Pale and trembling, they'd gazed at us with haunted eyes.

I could only imagine what they'd heard. We'd probably encounter it on our journey, but it didn't matter; we had to push on. If Astaroth and the others had gone somewhere in this country to hide, it was deeper inland. The idea of what lay ahead for us made me uneasy, but I would see the end of the horsemen. I also intended to find Randy, or at least discover what had become of him. I had no idea how I would do that, but I'd find a way.

I pulled my blanket over my knees and drew them against my chest as I surveyed the woods. Sitting on a rock outside the cave we'd spent the past few days living in, I caught the faint scent of fire from deep within the cavern . Before Corson's blood entered me, I wouldn't have smelled the burning wood from this distance. It didn't float far past the entrance, but the acrid scent was there.

I'd constantly searched myself for changes from Corson's blood; I'd detected more than a few of them already. The first had been my vision. It had been such a gradual thing that even while looking for differences, I hadn't noticed it until three days ago when I spotted a sparrow perched in a tree a hundred feet away.

No one else had seen the bird, not even Corson until it took flight. He hadn't been able to keep the smile from his face as he'd looked from me to the bird and back again. But I'd also seen the apprehension in his eyes.

The change wasn't complete yet; there was still a chance I would die. That chance lessened every day, but the possibility had the sharp edge of a guillotine hanging over our heads.

A shadow fell over me, and I glanced up to see Raphael soaring low through the trees. The spread of his white wings revealed his golden sunburst of feathers. He'd found us again last week and returned with the skelleins to us. They'd located Kobal on the southern end of the wall, but further east of us, more toward Florida.

Kobal had sent more troops from the wall to join us, and we would be entering the mountains with a force of nearly seventy-five. The king had said he would send more troops, and come himself if Corson and Bale believed it necessary.

Corson had sent a scowling Raphael—who muttered something about not being a carrier pigeon—back to tell Kobal his presence wasn't necessary, they preferred the smaller numbers right now, and Greed was already dead. They would take care of the other horsemen, and Astaroth, but if it became necessary for Kobal and River to become involved, Corson would let them know.

Yesterday, Raphael returned carrying a demon who could telecommunicate. He'd dropped the infuriated demon in front of Corson from fifty feet above. The demon fell on his ass before shooting back to his feet, but he was wise enough not to go after the angel when Raphael landed beside him.

"Kobal says if you must communicate with him in the future, to use this demon, but only if it is necessary," Raphael stated.

"Kobal hates telecommunicating with anyone," Corson told me.

"He also said he would understand if you decided to return to the wall with your Chosen after what occurred with Greed." Raphael hadn't waited for a reply before taking to the sky.

"Guess he doesn't like being the messenger," I said as I'd watched Raphael fly higher.

"But he's so damn good at it," Corson replied with a smile and looked at the demon before him. "Welcome."

"Humph," the demon grunted, straightened his shirt, and walked away.

Corson grinned after him before looking up to Raphael. "I almost kind of like Raphael more for dropping him. It's so very *un*-golden boy of him."

"Maybe Earth is already changing him."

"Let's hope it's for the better."

I'd chuckled as Corson slid his arm through mine and led me into the cave. I'd considered asking Corson again what River was, but decided against it. Because of our relationship now, he would tell me, but I knew it was something he'd prefer to come from Kobal or River. I resolved to speak with one of them the next time I got the chance, and hopefully, they would come to like and trust me enough to tell me themselves. Even if they didn't, I wouldn't put Corson in the position of feeling like he had to reveal it to me.

My attention was drawn back to the day when Raphael landed next to my rock, nodded at me, tucked his wings against his back, and strode into the cave to join the others. I turned away from him and drew my backpack closer to me. Reaching in, I pulled out a piece of venison and bit into it. The chewiness of the meat made me cringe. I swallowed more from habit than any real hunger before returning it to my bag. I'd give it to Jolie later.

Digging through the bag, I removed the meager supply of food I'd stored inside and slid it into the front pocket. I'd give it over to be divided between the others later. My lack of hunger for human food meant I would probably have to start feeding from wraiths soon, but I was surprisingly okay with that, given how much they'd unnerved me before. If Corson was there to show me what to do, I knew I would be able to get through it, and like every other change in my life, I would adapt to it.

I stuck my hand in the backpack to push aside two shirts, an extra pair of pants, and a bra well on its way to falling apart. At the bottom of the bag, I felt something that caused me to pull my hand back. Peering into the bag, I gazed in disbelief at the small box I'd removed from the locker. I'd stuffed it inside my backpack after that night with Corson and forgotten about it. Pulling the box free, I wiped the dust off to reveal a yellow cover with chipped and fading red flowers.

When I opened the lid, the hinges creaked, and a wave of musty air wafted out to tickle my nose. I pushed aside the multicolored plastic bracelets within before uncovering a small ring. I removed the ring and cleaned it on my shirt to reveal the large, dark blue stone set on a thin silver band.

Slipping the ring on, I wiggled my fingers and frowned when the gem shifted from deep blue to a sky color before turning purple and staying there. A distant memory tugged at me and words drifted through my mind.

Here, put this on! It will tell you your mood! A young girl gushed excitedly.

I struggled to recall who had belonged to the excited voice. Some friend of mine from school most likely. Some friend who probably hadn't survived the gateway opening, and if she had, I hadn't run into her again. Perhaps she'd been taken to the wall when the evacuation started; maybe she still lived with her family, and maybe she'd outgrown those buck teeth.

Kristi! I recalled as a face burst into my memory. Despite those teeth and her knobby knees, Kristi had been a pretty girl with a brown ponytail, broad smile, and blue eyes. She'd been my best friend. We'd run and played and giggled over boys who were mostly still gross to us at the time, but some had started to become cute instead of cringeworthy.

Once, we'd each bought one of these rings from a machine at the grocery store. *A mood ring*, I remembered as I brought my hand closer to study the stone more intently.

Now it seemed silly; I knew my mood was normal, not excited, not bored, just here and still kicking. However, the first time I'd slipped one of these rings on, it had been a magical adventure, and I'd believed it could somehow tell me something I didn't already know.

Kristi and I had eagerly consulted the color chart to learn how we were feeling. I couldn't recall what each of the colors represented anymore, but I remembered our heads close together as we giggled and examined our rings like they were the most precious of diamonds.

"What do you have there?" Corson asked as he strolled out of the woods where he'd been on watch with Hawk, Vargas, and Lix. Their shift must have ended, I realized as he walked over to sit beside me.

Lifting my head, my heart swelled with love when my gaze landed on him. I'd loved him when I was a human, deeply, but my love had become more intense, and the possessive feeling I felt for him grew stronger with every passing day. He was *my* demon. Nothing would ever change that, and I'd kill anyone who tried to come between us.

I scratched absently at the back of my hand as the idea of someone knowing him as intimately as I did caused my teeth to grind. I knew there were other women out there that he'd also been with, I accepted that, but he would never be with another and survive it.

"It's a mood ring." I told him about what it did, Kristi, and the rings we'd once purchased together. Slipping the ring off, I slid it onto his finger and watched as it turned black. "I don't know what that means anymore," I admitted.

"Only humans would need something to tell them how they feel," he muttered as he wiggled his fingers. "I do like it though, and if it works, then this ring detects filthy minds."

The suggestive smile he gave me made my mouth water.

"You do like your jewelry," I replied. Jealousy speared like a hot poker through my chest at the reminder of him and his earrings from other women. I turned my head away from him as I struggled to get the volatile sway of my emotions under control. "I thought these rings were great when I was a kid," I forced out. Hoping to keep my unraveling control hidden from him. He worried about me enough without me adding to it by revealing that I was becoming a complete basket case. "But that was a different girl."

"No, it wasn't," Corson said and removed the ring to slide it back onto my finger. "I know you feel that way, but Bonnie and Wren are the same girl. They're just divided by a horrific event."

"I don't know how to be Bonnie," I admitted and chanced a glance at him when I had my emotions under control again. "She was so happy, so innocent."

"You *never* stopped being her," he said and squeezed my hand. "You had to be a tougher version of her to survive."

"I guess."

My eyes focused on a field mouse hopping through the leaves, and I smiled. I never would have seen the small, gray creature with his twitching nose last week. Like I had fourteen years ago, I was changing again, becoming someone else once more, but I welcomed these changes. I'd asked for them.

"She is me, and I am her," I whispered.

I pondered those words as my fingers played with the band of the mood ring. Bonnie was a child, who'd been secure in her knowledge nothing bad could ever happen to her. Wren was a woman who knew something bad could be lurking around every corner. One had been naïve, the other callous, but they had both been me.

Something shifted and clicked into place inside me as I focused on that. I'd been thinking of my life as the past belonged to Bonnie, the present to Wren, and the future to no one. Now I had the possibility of an immortal future with Corson. I'd believed that remembering the past only brought sadness, but now I was smiling at this ring and the memory of a friend who had once been my most trusted companion.

Trying to forget Kristi and my parents was a disservice to them all. They deserved to be remembered and loved, not buried beneath misery and anger. For the first time, I loved Bonnie and all her memories, but...

"I don't plan to try to forget the past anymore, but I've been Wren for more years than Bonnie. That's who I am now."

"Good, I don't want to call you by the wrong name in bed should you decide to change it. I prefer my nuts attached to my body."

A burst of loud laughter escaped me, shaking my stomach, and shocking me more than the ouro had. Corson's eyes widened, and I slapped my hands over my mouth to muffle the sound.

"Don't," he said and tugged at my hands. "I've been trying to get you to laugh, to *really* laugh and not just chuckle, since I met you." He succeeded in pulling my hands away from my mouth. "Your laugh is beautiful, don't hide it."

"It's not that," I whispered, unable to stop tears from filling my eyes. "I have my mom's laugh. I… I didn't realize it. I must have had it as a child too, and I'd forgotten over the years, or maybe it just came as I got older, but I'd stopped laughing by then. It's her laugh though, and I always loved her laugh."

Corson used his thumbs to wipe away the two tears that slid free to track down my cheeks. "Then I will make you use it more often."

"Yes, you will."

I leaned against his side and kissed his cheek. He leaned over to examine the contents of the box. I reached in to pull another piece of jewelry out by its hook. The dangling earring unfolded from between my thumb and index finger to reveal the silver bird twirling at the end of it. Corson wrapped his hand around it to stop it from spinning, and I released it to him.

"It seems that should belong to you," I said.

"My earring-wearing days are over."

"Even if I give it to you and want you to wear it?" I hadn't liked seeing him in the earrings of others, but my mischievous adhene needed them back.

"I would proudly wear your earring every day for the rest of my life," he stated.

"That bird could be a wren, and I'm giving it to you."

He gazed at me before lifting it and pushing the hook through the tip of his right ear. I winced for him, but he didn't react. When he gave his head a small shake, he made the bird fly back and forth.

"Only *mine* though," I said, unable to keep the anger from my voice as a fresh wave of jealousy hit me.

"It will never be another's."

I inhaled through my teeth, but it was difficult getting air into my lungs through the growing constriction in my chest. I knew how much he loved me, knew he would do anything in the world for me, yet jealousy tore at my insides, and I couldn't do anything to stop it.

"Easy," he said as he wrapped his hand around mine.

He didn't need to look at the ring to know my emotions had taken an explosive swing. It had been happening more often over the past week. Maybe I really would have to leave everyone and go somewhere else until I could be sure I wouldn't hurt someone.

"Breathe," Corson coaxed.

I inhaled a tremulous breath and bowed my head as some of my hostility eased.

"Only yours," he whispered as he smoothed a strand of hair back from my forehead before cupping my neck.

"Am I going to be so emotional all the time?"

"No, you will get used to it, and you will handle it better with time. Hawk experienced violent mood swings in the beginning too, but they've leveled out. Part of what you're experiencing might be that you've become demon enough to want to claim me as your Chosen, but you're still too human to do so. Until you can do that, this emotional sway may become more extreme."

"You are *mine*."

"Yes, I am yours," he said, drawing me closer.

I rubbed at the back of my hand again before taking another deep breath. I didn't feel as unstable when he had his arms around me, but walking around with Corson hugging me all the time wasn't exactly the most practical way to go about life, and it wouldn't bode well for our survival.

"I'm okay now," I assured him.

I wasn't, but I had to deal with this, and at least I didn't want to kill something anymore. Digging into the box again, I discovered the other bird earring within. Pulling it free, I let it dangle from my fingers before sticking it through my left earlobe. The prick of pain vanished almost instantly, and I realized that no blood trickled free as my body worked to repair the hole with inhuman speed.

Shaking my head, I laughed at the feel of the bird dangling there. "I see why you like these things."

"I especially like it on you," he replied as his lips nuzzled my temple.

Three women emerged from the woods, and I realized they were part of Elton's group. They stopped when they spotted Corson and me. One of them gave a friendly wave before hurrying toward the cave entrance. The other two stayed where they were, their gazes raking over Corson in a way that sent fury spiraling through me faster than I'd ever believed possible.

I snarled at them before I knew what I'd done. Corson's hand pressed down on my shoulder when I tried to rise. If he hadn't been there to restrain me, I would have torn into them like a dog on fresh meat. The two women took a frightened step back when three-inch-long spikes erupted from the backs of my hands. My rage was briefly forgotten as I gawked at the white spikes suddenly jutting out.

Corson rose and slid his arm around my waist when I lifted my head to the startled women. A haze of red shaded my vision. He lifted me off the ground and held me firmly against him.

"Get inside!" Corson commanded them.

They didn't have to be told twice as they scurried past us and out of view. Their disappearance didn't ease my longing to see them dead.

"Easy, lahala," Corson murmured as he carried me into the woods. "Easy."

"I should have gutted them."

"Spoken like a true demon when someone is messing with their Chosen."

"Hmm," I grumbled, not at all pleased he might be finding this amusing. Then my eyes fell to my hands on his shoulders, and the white talons. "I have spikes in my hands!"

"Baby spikes," he said, and I realized he *did* find this amusing when I heard the laughter in his voice. "But then, mine were once baby spikes too."

"Baby spikes," I muttered and lifted my hands to examine the backs of them. I poked the tip of one spike with my finger and watched a bead of blood form there. "Does this mean I'm done with the transition?"

"You still have some way to go," he said as he set me on my feet and claimed my hands to study them. "But I think it means you'll survive it now. This was one of the bigger changes your body had to endure. My bones are different than other demons, harder. My flesh is different too, at least on my hands. Does this hurt?" he asked as he prodded the skin on the back of my hand.

"No," I said, amazed that I didn't feel any discomfort from the talons poking out of my flesh.

Lifting his head, he peered at me from under the thick fringe of his black lashes. The bird spun in his ear as a breeze flowed through the trees. "My little adhene demon," he murmured.

CHAPTER FORTY-SIX

CORSON

I thought I'd been happy when I'd claimed Wren and made her mine, but now the emotion swelled to near bursting within me as Wren looked from her hands to me again.

"I am no longer the last of my kind," I said to her.

A smile curved her mouth. She reached up as if to run her fingers through my hair, but before she could touch me, she jerked her hands back as if afraid she would injure me. She held her hands helplessly before her.

"I will teach you how to use and control your talons," I assured her. "I'd prefer if you didn't accidentally stab me."

"It might not be an accident," she replied with a smile. "Will they stay this size?"

"Mine grew as I aged, but yours might not. They're still a deadly weapon if they don't grow."

I pushed aside her hair to reveal her ears. Other than the dangling bird, they remained the same, but when I ran my finger over the shell of one, she moaned. Stepping into me, she went to grasp my arms before lowering her hands to her sides again. Frustration flashed over her features.

I took her hands and ran my fingers over her knuckles. Wren gasped when the talons retracted, and then another burst of laughter escaped her. I'd never get enough of hearing that sound.

"Amazing!" she cried.

"Yes," I agreed. Clasping her face in my hands, I lifted it to kiss her.

With a sigh, she melted against me while I undressed her. The cold air brushing over her caused goose bumps to break out on her skin, but her shivers eased when I drew her into my arms. I lowered her pliant body to the forest floor and buried myself inside her.

"Harder," she moaned in my ear as her nails dug into my skin.

The muscles of her sheath clenched around me, and she came with a loud cry. I was about to sink my fangs into her shoulder when her mouth turned into my neck and she bit down. My hands slammed into the ground beside her head; my body went rigid as her two tiny fangs pierced my flesh.

Complete. The knowledge blazed through my mind as I drew her flush against me.

"Mine," she whispered when she released her bite.

"Yes," I agreed as I lost myself to the marvel of Wren.

*W*REN

Being a demon wasn't bad at all. I had that whole immortality thing on my side now, but most importantly I had Corson. His body warmed mine as he locked his leg possessively over my thigh. Leaves crackled beneath us, and the earthy scent of the dirt drifted to me.

The volatile sway of my emotions had eased when my newly discovered fangs sank into his flesh and *I'd* claimed *him*. As a human, I'd loved him enough to change for him; as a demon, I would tear this world apart for him. We were bound together now, for as long as we both lived, and nothing would change that.

My emotions didn't completely calm with the claiming, but whereas before they'd felt like a tornado waiting to touch down and destroy, now they were more like a thunderstorm. It would take time, but Corson would help me gain control and learn more about what I was capable of now.

"I feel it, the Chosen bond. I feel it all the way to the core of my being," I murmured and rested my hand over my heart.

He drew me closer. "It's powerful."

"Yes."

"So that means you understand how there could never be another for me, or for you?" he asked.

"Yes." The idea of being with another man made my stomach turn; the thought of him with another woman made my spikes reemerge. "Dammit. I need to control them before I accidentally stab someone."

He gripped my hands in his. His soothing touch caused the baby spikes to retract once more. "They're small enough that if you're not touching someone, you won't stab them. We'll get through this together."

"I know." I closed my eyes. The scent and feel of him seemed ingrained in me now. His marks on my neck were tender but in a pleasant way. "You're in every part of me."

"Yes," he agreed. "And you're in every part of me, always."

"When this is over, when we kill the horsemen and Astaroth, I want to start a family. I *never* believed I'd want one before, but I do, with you."

He kissed my ear.

"The ears," I groaned.

"Amazing, isn't it?" he said with a chuckle. "And I cannot wait to have a family with you. We can return to the wall. It will be safer there, and if you start your fertile time, we can get to work on that family now. You may even still be on your human reproduction cycle."

"I'd like nothing more than to be somewhere safe with you, but it's not at the wall. Things are far too unstable right now. I also have to find Randy, or at least learn if he's alive or not. We had a mission; there's a chance he's still carrying out his part of it. I can't abandon him."

"We'll find him," Corson promised.

"Besides, I've been in this fight since the beginning; I will see it through to the end, and I know that's what you want too."

"It is," he agreed, "but above all, I want you to be happy."

"I haven't been this happy in years, demon." I rolled over and cupped his face in my hands to draw him down for a kiss.

He grinned at me as he traced my ear, causing me to grow wet again. "And I can say the same to you, *demon.*"

I found I didn't mind being called a demon at all, not as long as I had him as my Chosen. There was still a rough road ahead of us, still many obstacles to overcome, but I knew Corson and I would face them all together. For the first time in years, I looked forward to the future.

THE END.

Look for *Into the Abyss* (Hell on Earth, Book 2) coming in 2018! *Into the Abyss* will focus on Magnus.

If you haven't had the chance to read the series that started it all, then read on for an excerpt from *Good Intentions* (The Road to Hell Series, Book 1) which is available for FREE!

Stay in touch on updates and other new releases from the author, by joining the mailing list.
Mailing list for Brenda K. Davies and Erica Stevens Updates:
http://bit.ly/ESBKDNews

GOOD INTENTIONS

River

It has been thirteen years since the war started, the bombs were dropped, and the central states became a thing of the past. When the war ended, a wall was erected to divide the surviving states from those destroyed. I never expected to go beyond the wall, but unlike all the others who volunteered to go, I wasn't given a choice.

With a dim knowledge of what I could do, the soldiers came for me. They took me beyond the wall where I learned that the truth is far more terrifying than I'd ever dreamed. Alone, with humans and demons seeking to learn what it is I can do, I find myself irresistibly drawn to the one man I should be avoiding most. One who intrigues and infuriates me. One who is not even a man, not really.

Kobal

My entire life, I've had only one mission, reclaim my throne from Lucifer and put right everything that was torn apart when he was cast from Heaven. It's a mission I haven't wavered from, not even when the humans tore open the gates and unleashed Hell on Earth.

Now, I've never been closer to obtaining my goal, yet I find myself risking it all because I cannot stay away from her, a human who may be the key to it all.

*** There are four books in this paranormal romance series which is now complete. Not all things will be resolved in this book. Due to sexual content, violence, and language, this book is recommended for readers 18+ years of age.***

The Road to Hell Series Complete Reading Order:
Good Intentions (Book 1)
Carved (Book 2)
The Road (Book 3)
Into Hell (Book 4)

Good Intentions Excerpt:

Prologue
River
I was nine when the first of the fighter planes flew over thirteen years ago. I remember tilting my head back to stare at them as they moved over us in a V formation. Excitement buzzed through me, but I felt no fear. They had been a more common sight before the military base closed last year; despite that status, they still occasionally flew over our town.

When the planes vanished from view, I turned my attention back to the game of hopscotch I was playing with my friend, Lisa. I was about to beat her, and I wanted to finish before Mother woke from her nap and called me away. Lisa stared at the sky for a minute more before turning her attention back to me. She bent to pick up the rock on the ground as four more planes flew over us in a tight formation. They left white streaks in the sky as their engines roared over us.

The rock Lisa had picked up slid from her fingers and clattered onto the asphalt. Together, we watched as the second wave of them disappeared from view. I don't know why the initial wave hadn't bothered me, but the second wave caused a cold sweat to trickle down my neck.

Following the noise of the planes, the world around us took on an unusual hush for a Saturday afternoon in July. Normally there were shouts from kids playing up and down the street. The rumble of cars driving down the highway, heading toward the beach, was a near constant background noise now that tourist season was in full swing.

Turning my attention back to Lisa, I waited for her to pick her rock up again and continue, but she remained staring at the sky. The planes had unnerved me, but what did I really know? At that point in my young life, my biggest problem was napping in the house a hundred feet away from me. I hoped their noise hadn't woken Mother; grouchy was a permanent state for her, but when she was woken from a nap, she could be a real bear.

I glanced over at my one-year-old brother, Gage. My heart melted at the sight of his disheveled blond hair sticking up in spikes and his warm brown eyes staring at the sky. He lifted a fist and waved at the planes fading from view. His coloring was completely different from my raven hair and violet eyes, due to our different fathers. Mine had taken off before I was born; Gage's father had at least stuck around to see his birth before leaving our mother in the dust.

Turning his attention away from the sky, Gage held his arms toward me before shoving a hand into his mouth. Unable to resist him, I walked over and lifted him off the ground. I cradled his warm body in my arms. I always brought him with me during Mother's naps so he wouldn't wake her, and because I couldn't stand him being alone in the house while she slept. I'd been alone so many times before he'd come along that I refused to let him be too.

Gage wrapped his chubby arms around my neck, pressing his sweaty body against mine. Lisa wiped the sweat from her brow and brushed aside the strands of brown hair sticking to her face. Waves of heat wafted from the cooking asphalt, but I barely felt it. I'd always preferred summer to winter and tolerated the heat better than most others.

Six more planes swept overhead, leaving a loud, reverberating boom in their wake as they sped by. Car alarms up and down the street blared loudly. Horns honking in quick succession, and headlights flashing had all the dogs in the neighborhood barking. The relatively peaceful day had become chaotic in the blink of an eye.

Along the road, doors opened and beeps sounded as people turned off their alarms. Shouts for the dogs to be quiet could be heard over the noise of the vehicles. Some people ran out of their homes and toward the squealing cars to try and turn off the alarms that wouldn't be silenced.

Gage's arm tightened around my neck to the point of near choking. I didn't try to pull him away; instead I held him closer when he began to shake. Then just as rapidly as the rush of noise had erupted on the street, everything went completely still. Even the dogs, sensing something was off, became almost simultaneously silent. The few birds that had been chirping stopped their song; they seemed to be holding their breath with the rest of the world.

I remember Lisa stepping closer to me. Years later, I can still feel her warm arm against mine in a moment of much needed solidarity. "What's going on, River?" she asked me.

"I don't know."

Then, from inside some of the nearby homes, screams and cries erupted, breaking the near silence. Exchanging a look with Lisa, we turned as one and ran toward her house. We clambered up the steps, jostling against each other in our rush to see what was going on. We'd scarcely entered the cool shadows of her screened-in porch when I heard the sobs of her mother.

We both froze, uncertain of what to do. Tears streaked Gage's cheeks and wet my shirt when he buried his face in my neck. He may have only been a baby, but he still sensed something was completely wrong.

Instinctively knowing we would be shut out of whatever was going on if we alerted them to our presence, it had to be grown-up stuff after all, we'd edged carefully over to the windows, looking in on the living room. Peering in the windows, I spotted Lisa's mom on the couch, her head in her hands as she wept openly. Lisa's father stood before the TV, the remote dangling from his fingertips as he gaped at the screen.

My eyes were drawn to the TV; my brow creased in curious wonder at the mushroom cloud I saw rising from the earth. A black cloud of rolling fire and smoke covered the entire horizon on the screen.

Beneath the cloud, words ran across the bottom of the screen. *The U.S. is under attack. Nuclear bomb dropped on Kansas. Possible terrorist attack. Possible attack from China or Russia. Numerous areas of reported violence erupting.*

"It's World War III," Lisa's father said as the remote fell from his hand and her mother sobbed harder.

My heart raced in my chest, and my throat went dry as I struggled to grasp what was going on. I knew something awful had happened, but I still couldn't understand what. How could I? I was a child. My time on this earth had been spent trying to avoid my mother as much as possible. It had also been filled with taking care of my brother, friends, TV, books, school, and the endless days of summer, that until then, I'd been so looking forward to.

I hugged Gage as I vowed to do anything I could to keep him safe from whatever was about to unfold.

Standing there with Lisa, I may not have completely understood what was happening, but I knew nothing would ever be the same again. The only world I'd ever known was now entirely different.

The cries and shouts in the neighborhood increased in intensity when more planes flew overhead with a loud whoosh that rattled the glass in the windows before us and set off some of the alarms again. Turning, I glanced back at the street to find some people running back and forth, hugging each other before running toward another house. Some got in their cars and drove away with a squeal of tires. Much like a chicken with its head cut off, they were unsure of where to go or what to do.

What could anyone possibly do? Were we next for the bombs? The hair on my nape rose.

I turned back to the TV and watched as the cloud continued to rise. More words flashed by on the bottom of the screen, but I barely saw them. I became so focused on the TV, I never heard my mother enter the porch until one of her hands fell on my shoulder.

Tilting my head back to look at her, I realized it must be worse than I ever could have imagined if *she* was touching *me*. It was the first time she'd touched me in a comforting way in years. It would be the last, that wasn't by accident or in anger, for all the years following.

"What is happening?" Lisa inquired in a tremulous whisper.

"The end," Mother replied.

I wouldn't know how right she was until years later.

**_Good Intentions_ is available
everywhere ebooks are sold!**

FIND THE AUTHOR

Erica Stevens/Brenda K. Davies Mailing List:
http://bit.ly/ESBKDNews

Facebook page: http://bit.ly/ESFBpage
Facebook friend: http://bit.ly/EASFrd

Erica Stevens/Brenda K. Davies Book Club:
http://bit.ly/ESBDbc

Instagram: http://bit.ly/ErStInsta
Twitter: http://bit.ly/ErStTw
Website: http://bit.ly/ESWbst
Blog: http://bit.ly/ErStBl

ABOUT THE AUTHOR

Brenda K. Davies is the USA Today Bestselling author of the Vampire Awakening Series, Alliance Series, Road to Hell Series, Hell on Earth Series, and historical romantic fiction. She also writes under the pen name, Erica Stevens. When not out with friends and family, she can be found at home with her husband, dog, and horse.

Made in the USA
Lexington, KY
11 September 2017